INNER SPACE AND OUTER THOUGHTS

INNER SPACE AND OUTER THOUGHTS

Speculative Fiction From Caltech and JPL Authors

EDITED BY TECHLIT

CALTECH'S CREATIVE WRITING CLUB

TechLit Publishing | Pasadena, CA | techlit.clubs.caltech.edu

ISBN: 979-8-3866-1758-5 (print)

Printed by Amazon Kindle Direct Publishing in the United States of America.

Acknowledgments

First, we would like to thank all authors for their contributions to this anthology, with a special thanks to the authors of the previously unpublished stories herein, who worked tirelessly with the guidance of TechLit club editors during an intensive editing process. We appreciate all the editors who volunteered countless hours of labor to shape this anthology's design and content. We extend gratitude to Caltech alumni David Brin and S.B. Divya for providing invaluable writing, editing, and publishing advice, and for being steadfast mentors to TechLit club members. Thank you to the TechLit club advisor, Susanne Hall, for encouragement and support for this project and other club activities; to Ellen Datlow for advice on the design of this anthology and publication agreements; to Michelle Katz for legal advice relating to the project; to Chantal D'Apuzzo from the Caltech Office of General Counsel for help with the publication agreements; to Rebeccah Sanhueza for copyediting; and to Tobi Harper from Red Hen Press, who offered valuable publishing and editing advice. We acknowledge Christian Benavides (Voyager Illustration, www.voyagerillustration.com) for going above and beyond to create an incredible work of art for the book's covers. Finally, we thank the other volunteers who made this anthology possible: Sujung Lim, Samantha Chang, Nicholas J. Heller, Dr. Susan Melnik, and Alexander Viloria Winnett.

For providing the financial support need to publish this anthology, the Techlit Club acknowledges the Caltech Graduate Student Council (GSC), the Caltech undergraduate student government (ASCIT), the Caltech Student Investment Fund (SIF), and the Caltech Office of the President.

Contents

Part V

Outer Thoughts

Stories About Our World, Other Worlds, and Meetings of the Two

Foreword

David Brin

I'm told that when I was four years old, I saw Einstein play the violin. Much later, as a Caltech undergraduate, I got to discuss Roman history and *Finnegan's Wake* with Murray Gell-Mann. Richard Feynman—famed for bongo-playing, painting, and safe-cracking—briefly stole my date at a student house dance. And the same lesson—one that I tell at each commencement speech—got reinforced every time I wandered hallways at Tech, poking into random doorways to ask: "Say, what are you doing here? And what *else* do you do?"

What lesson got reinforced?

Be many.

Never settle for zero-sum. None of us has to be just-one-thing.

Every top scientist I've been privileged to know—from Bruce Murray and Hannes Alfvén to Sarah Hrdy and Freeman Dyson—had an *artistic sideline* or hobby that he or she pursued with some passion. A sideline that invigorated their scientific work.

To be clear, I don't claim "top" scientist rank, though I get some licks in. Still, the lesson took hold, especially when I started writing science fiction tales to vent pressure as a Caltech undergrad, then as an engineer, then UCSD grad student and postdoc. Whereupon at some point my own artistic "sideline" kind of took over—a tail wagging the dog. Civilization apparently valued me more as a storyteller . . . and who am I to argue with civilization? But I digress.

This volume teaches the same lesson—*let your creative energies flow in many ways*—by collecting tales of plausible extrapolation or wonder from members of our loosely bound Caltech stellar cluster . . . from current and past undergraduates to grad students, from postdocs and profs to current or former JPL folk. And what an amazing collection it is!

In most such "community" anthologies, the reader must allow for widely varied skill levels. But what impressed me most about these authors, aside from their vivid imaginative range and depth of scientific speculation, is how each of them developed *craft*—handling well so many complex methods of fiction narrative. Tricks turning mere chains of letters into incantations that inject ideas, emotions, and thrills into readers' willing brains! I expected this from my fully fledged and revered colleagues S. B. Divya and Larry Niven. But most of the other writers featured here—many of them first-timers—are already what we used to call "ready for prime time."

Okay sure, in a volume like this one, you're expecting gosh-wow extrapolations from the mundane here-and-now. And these techers are explorers! From cool what-if speculations about brain plasticity to the potential costs and losses that accompany immortality. From whimsical science counterfactuals to daunting, Dickean questionings of reality. Several stories offer ruminations about *memory*, while others ponder eschatology through godlike expanses of time.

Former CIT Professor Christof Koch collaborates in a *gedankenexperiment* about the implications of "split hemisphere" research that began long ago at Tech. There's also a dollop of time travel here . . . along with some "don't get cocky" lessons about how humanity may not be quite the pinnacle that we sometimes imagine. And sure, how could any cosmic-minded collection lack for confrontations with the co-star of almost every human drama . . . Death?

In fact, the relationship between Caltech and science fiction stretches way back, almost to its beginning. Eric Temple Bell (1883–1960) was a professor and best-selling popularizer of mathematics. But under the pseudonym John Taine he also published rollicking SF tales, while leading a life of mystery that Constance Reid peeled back in her riveting book *The Search for E. T. Bell*. Frequent Caltech habitués Fred Hoyle and Leo

Szilard wrote sci-fi and Robert Heinlein set parts of *Glory Road* on campus. Around 1970, I watched CIT Poet-in-Residence Richard Brautigan recite "All Watched Over by Machines of Loving Grace," which remains to this day the work that best expresses hope and optimism for decency in our AI soon-to-be heirs. Indeed, both that long heritage and this bold new volume illuminate the quandary and the vital role played by science-based science fiction.

Yes, we and the great enlightenment experiment have all benefited from the Popperian cycle of hypothesis, evidence gathering, modeling, and refinement through falsification that propels progress in our studies and our labs and across civilization. Without question, we must defend that process from those who are trying to discredit the very notion of objective reality. Facts exist! And despite Plato's cynicism, we are getting ever better at climbing out of his damn cave.

Still, it's clear—there must be something more.

How poor would we be without our other side? A part of us that *begins* each next step forward by posing what-if questions that cannot yet be checked or falsified? Or those other notions that seem brilliant *because* they'll always remain counterfactual? Questions posed not just by sci-fi tales but all the other art forms that draw hard-nosed scientists to croon: "Okay . . . wow."

Shan't our reach exceed our grasp? Or, as one of the authors in this volume described his own process of reaching out: "If any of my stories turn out to be anything but pure fiction, I shall be dismayed by my own lack of imagination."

Oh, do play your instruments, or paint, or whatever, after the sun goes down. Or string together those chains of black squiggles—the letters, words, sentences, and *incantations* that lure us into envisioning that which never was! And even what can never be. For one thing, it is only with such practice that we truly learn to tell the difference! Besides, something deep within us hungers for mysterious rustles beyond the campfire light.

And so, for now, suspend disbelief. Let words and notions and feelings flow like the magic that enthralled our ancestors. Only these songs and spells are for our time. For our scientific age.

Tomorrow, back in the lab, we'll feel better empowered to *perceive*.

Introduction

Rachael Kuintzle

The precious time between experiments, waiting for simulations to complete, or anticipating the return of a red-marked research manuscript allows a scientist's mind to wander. Some of our minds tend to wander into imaginary worlds of our own design. In 2017, some Caltech students who shared this affliction found each other and formed Caltech's first creative writing club, TechLit. This book represents our initial endeavor to share our community's fiction with the world.

Together, our editorial board of scientists and staff from Caltech and NASA's Jet Propulsion Laboratory (JPL) embarked on a journey to collect and polish speculative fiction written by current and former members of our community. Most of the stories in this anthology are originals by previously unpublished authors who worked iteratively with editors over eight months to revise their stories in a process somewhat similar to that of scientific peer review. We have found other parallels between fiction writing and the process of research. For example, we have learned that letting go of a beautiful line of prose that doesn't quite fit can be almost as painful as relinquishing a failed hypothesis. Fortunately, we are well practiced in the latter.

In an interview for Caltech's *Techer* magazine, alumna S. B. Divya once said:

> Speculative fiction is really constructed in the same way that a science experiment is. We come up with a hypothesis, we test that hypothesis through narrative, analyze it, and present our conclusion all as part of the storytelling process. Every speculative-fiction author is basically a scientist in the lab of their own head.

Here, we present the literary experiments that stole our attention, burned new questions into our minds, and delayed our scientific discoveries to bring us philosophical discoveries.

Stories are organized into sections according to common themes. Those that tackle topics in biology and bioengineering are found in "The Science of Life and the Life of Science." Caltech has a long record of pioneering work in life sciences from Seymour Benzer's discoveries in circadian rhythms and genetics to Michael Elowitz's foundational work in synthetic biology and Frances Arnold's Nobel Prize–winning contributions in directed evolution. Trainees of some of today's synthetic and systems biology pioneers contributed stories featured in this section. Namely, Dr. Samuel Clamons and Dr. Heidi Klumpe explore the practice and philosophy of biological sciences in "Yuan Tzu's Second Law of Evolutionary Design" and "A Model Monster," respectively. Other stories in this section focus on protagonists who are themselves bioscience pioneers, such as S. B. Divya's "Microbiota and the Masses: A Love Story" and Dr. David Brin's "Chrysalis."

The section "Inner Space" contains stories that tackle the mind and the neuroscientist's condition. Three students of Caltech's Computation and Neural Systems program—the first such program in the world—are among this anthology's authors and editors. Several more contributors are scientific residents of Caltech's Tianqiao and Chrissy Chen Institute for Neuroscience. Caltech has been the site of several paradigm-shifting discoveries in neuroscience. For example, former Caltech professor and Nobel laureate Roger Sperry's split-brain research showed that the left and right parts of the brain have different functions and work independently when severed. Echoes of this work are heard in the story contributed by Dr. Patrick House and Dr. Christof Koch, who is himself a former Caltech professor of Computation and Neural Systems and the current President and Chief Scientific Officer of the Allen Institute for Brain Science. In "Brain Bridging," Dr. Koch and Dr. House explore the question of whether two brains connected together would remain two individuals or become one. From stories of artificial intelligence and parenthood in Dr. Christine Corbett Moran's "Out of Memory," to mental health in Dr. Tatyana Dobreva's "Replacement of Woes," to senility in Dr. R. James Doyle's "Disentanglement," works in this section shed new light on the nature of consciousness, the self, and love.

An anthology of speculative fiction from an institute of technology requires speculation on how technology could impact society. In the section "Life After Tech," authors examine the dark potential of technology to exploit and exclude. Naru Dames Sundar's "The Orphans of Nilaveli" explores the interplay of racism and technology in a world where software loaded into the neurological implants of Sri Lankan citizens can erase Tamils from the vision of the Sinhalese. Fayth Hui Tan's "It's Not a Date Without Data" considers the concept of manufactured consent in a critique of capitalism. In a more optimistic, if not lighter, piece called "The Homunculi's Guide to Resurrecting Your Loved One From Their Electronic Ghosts," Kara Lee offers the hope that traces of our data preserve us from death in some small way.

Arthur C. Clarke's Third Law states, "Any sufficiently advanced technology is indistinguishable from magic." Many technologies have graduated from fantasy to reality in Caltech's laboratories. What impossibilities might be possible after the next major scientific breakthrough? Follow us "Through the Turtle Pond" to visit the wonderlands of speculation that some Caltech scientists have found there. In "A Thousand, Thousand Pages," physicist Dr. Allic Sivaramakrishnan presents an allegory for the adventure of scientific research set in a world of dark photon based magic. In Dr. David Brown's "An Innocuous Cumulonimbus," a supernatural entity bends atmospheric physics to its will.

Of course, what would a book of stories from Caltech and JPL be without a section dedicated to astronomy and space? Since its inception in the 1930s, JPL's many groundbreaking engineering advances and space missions have been a source of inspiration for science fiction authors throughout the world. In 1979, *Voyager* images revealed active volcanoes on Jupiter's moon, which led to speculation of subsurface oceans and a revolution in thinking about habitability in the solar system, and continues to drive science mission planning today. JPL scientists engineered designs that enabled rovers to survive the "Seven Minutes of

Terror" entry, descent, and landing sequence and arrive safely on Mars—from controlled thrusters for *Viking* in 1976, to the airbag soft-landing technique employed for *Pathfinder* in 1997, to the sky crane maneuver used for *Curiosity* in 2012 and again for *Perseverance* in 2021. In the section "Outer Thoughts," Caltech and JPL scientists and staff, along with former Caltech student Larry Niven, use fiction instead of rovers to explore the universe and get to know its many lifeforms. Ann Bernath's "Encounter: Return to Titan" lends us insight into the thrill of manning a probe to a foreign planet. Madison Brady's "Blue Skies for Flight #NV0005" reimagines the early days of spaceflight in an alternate past. Dr. Ashish Mahabal's "Memoirs of a Status Quo" cautions against a future in which technologically advanced humans choose comfort over adventure.

The book concludes with the conclusion of the universe itself in Olivia Pardo's "Degenerates," a hopeful tale of an intelligent machine tasked with transmitting our universe's knowledge into the background radiation of the next universe.

This anthology contains stories diverse in scientific theme and even in genre. Some were conceived in a conventional word processor, while others' first lines were scribbled in the margin of a laboratory notebook. Some of the authors are full-time writers, while others juggle their beloved hobby and research careers. But all of these stories were inspired in some way by what their authors learned during their time at Caltech or JPL. We hope their stories will inspire you.

PART I

The Science of Life and the Life of Science

STORIES ABOUT BIOLOGY, BIOENGINEERING, AND THE BIOLOGIST'S PERSPECTIVE

1

Microbiota and the Masses: A Love Story

S. B. Divya

Originally published January 2017 on *Tor.com*

THE SCENTS OF EARTH—LOAM, pollen, compost, the exhalation of leaves—permeated the inside of Moena Sivaram's airtight home. She stood near the southeast corner and misted the novice bromeliads. The epiphytes clutched the trunk of an elephant ear tree, its canopy stretching up to the clear, SmartWindow-paned roof and shading everything below.

Moena whispered to the plants: "Amma's here, little babies. You're safe with me, but you must grow those roots." With her isolated life, these would be her only children.

She walked barefoot to the sunny citrus grove on the western side of the house. The soil beneath her feet changed from cool and moist to hard and gritty. eBees buzzed among the flowers. She hummed in harmony, a Carnatic song about lovebirds that was a century old. The heady perfume of orange and lime blossoms filled her up and made her blood sing along. This was home; this, and not the traditional jasmine and rose gardens of Bangalore; this, where her eyes didn't water nor her nose itch.

Diffuse sunlight shone through the SmartWindows paneling the walls. One rectangle stuck out like a cloudy diamond in an otherwise glittering pendant. Moena pulled her tablet from her pocket, brought up the diagnostic software. Red letters delivered bad news: faults in the air and light filters.

The latter mattered little. The plants would get enough sun from the functional panes. The former, though, meant that outside air had infiltrated the house.

Moena's throat closed. Her heart raced. *Stay calm!* But her hands wouldn't listen, clutching each other, fingers twisting like vines around branches. She couldn't breathe! All those microbes: she imagined them invading her sanctum, those wriggly, single-celled prokaryotes.

She shuddered, dropped to the ground, lay prone. Her cheek touched beloved dirt. Safe dirt. *Inhale! Exhale! Again!* She tilted her face, lowered her tongue, and licked. The potent esters of her domestic biome worked their magic, taking over the hamster wheels in her brain and applying the brakes.

Her hands unclenched. Shoulder blades fell back. Heart slowed. *Stupid brain. We can deal with this.*

The eBees agreed. "Yes, yes, yes," they sang.

Moena went to her supply closet. The air-filter mask inside looked like an insectoid alien: tinted plastic across the eyes, and three jutting cylinders over the mouth and nose areas. Moena pulled it on. The clean air lacked the comforting odors of home, but at least she was protected.

She sealed the offending window pane with heavy plastic and duct tape, then rolled the sensor cart over. *Good!* All air now flowed from the inside out, as it should. She sent a message to SmartWindows Incorporated, requesting a repair person and marking the issue urgent.

Rahul the repairman arrived looking like Moena's favorite porn star: faded jeans, tight white T-shirt, cinnamon-bark skin, boyish black curls. She admired the image on her tablet, fed from the door camera. Too bad she couldn't touch him. Her face flushed. The space between her legs tightened. *Not now, and not him, idiot body.* Not any man or woman infested with outside microbiota.

She slapped her cheeks lightly and blew out a hot breath.

Syed—her outside man—was away at his second cousin's wedding in Mysore. She would have to deal with Rahul herself.

"Please wait there," she said, a delayed audio reply to his intercom buzz.

Moena opened the supply closet and grimaced at the gray isolation suit hanging in the back. It reeked of industrial plastic and factory esters. She grabbed a handful of soil from the floor and sprinkled it into the suit. Then she pulled it and the air mask on.

She stepped into the foyer-airlock, clinched the inner door seals, and walked out the front. To his credit, Rahul only took a half step back. His dark eyes widened like a bud opening to rain. Questions sprouted and withered on his lips—parted to show endearingly crooked teeth—until he said, "Miss . . . Sivaram?"

"Yes. Follow me, please," Moena said.

She led him across the weedy, barren dirt of her lot. They walked around the thick clay walls of the house to arrive at the faulty SmartWindow. Rahul attached his computer to it via a long cable, vine-like but for its gray color. He sat on the dirt and began typing.

"The light and air filters are set to opposite extremes," he said. He spoke English in the well-rounded tones of an educated, middle-class Indian. "Most people use these windows to reduce the ultraviolet while permitting air circulation into the house."

I am not most people. Out loud: "You don't talk like a repairman."

Rahul smiled. "I'm an FAE—a field applications engineer. We repair but we also have technical backgrounds." He paused, squinted up at her. "Tell me, are you *the* Moena Sivaram?"

Tendrils of anxiety coiled in Moena's stomach. The plane crash that killed her parents had been well publicized, but the story had faded from the news years ago. Why would this man jab her with a question about it?

"I am."

"Your thesis on freshwater bioremediation was incredible. How come you haven't published any papers since then?"

Moena gaped behind the mask. "Just who are you?"

"Sorry, I should have explained. I'm a volunteer with Hariharan Ecological Group. They've taken your design and used it for local water pollution. It's been a great success. You're famous among us. I thought, perhaps, you might be running a laboratory in the house, what with these window settings."

Moena reeled at the orthogonality of the question and stared at her reflection in the SmartWindow. Her suit resembled the spent husk of a chrysalis. If only she could emerge a gorgeous butterfly, she could stun Rahul into silence as well.

"I am conducting experiments in the house," she admitted. "I wear this suit to keep the environment as isolated as I can."

"Could I—I mean, if it's not too much trouble—could I see what you're doing?"

Moena shook her head like a leaf frenzied by the wind. Rahul . . . inside her house? Inside her? Possibilities tumbled in her mind, gorgeous and terrifying. *Impossible!*

"No, of course not." He turned back to his computer. "Sorry for asking."

Moena reached out to him, drew her hand back. She had no right to his body.

The afternoon sun blazed from high in the summer sky as the silence stretched. Heat built inside Moena's isolation suit. Her shirt clung to her torso. Rivulets of sweat trickled down her neck and collected at the waistband of her shorts. She sat still, channeling the atman of a tree stump.

"Aha!" Rahul said at last.

The window cleared to perfect transparency. Rahul reinstalled it and stowed his computer. He handed her a memory cube.

"You'll want to update all of the windows with this version of software. The problem is that your filter settings are below virus size. The old software kept getting stuck in an interrupt routine and eventually hanging. This version should prevent that from happening."

"Thank you," Moena said. Part of her wished every window would fail, once a week, so Rahul would come again.

"The company will bill you directly. Best of luck with the research."

Moena nodded. The mask bobbled. Rahul walked out of the front gate, latching it closed behind him. She was alone.

The sterilization wash in her foyer had never felt so tedious. Once she was fully inside, Moena yanked off the mask and took several deep, relieving breaths. She peeled away the sweaty suit, let it crumple to the floor.

Soil wormed into the gaps between her bare toes. Leaves and fronds brushed her hands as she walked—nearly ran—to her bedroom. It looked much as it had when her parents were alive: a single bed, a narrow wardrobe painted yellow, a matching desk with shelves above it. The coffin was the exception.

The adult-sized container lay between the bed and the room's boarded-up window. The device's actual name was "Virtual Reality Recumbent Booth," but the world had decided that was too unwieldy. Moena agreed.

She browsed the preset visuals under "male." This one had beetle brows. That one was too pale. Dozens had overlays with blue eyes and blond hair. She stopped at a face that was close enough to Rahul's. The hair needed more curl and the eyes wanted to be smaller, but she could adjust those when her body wasn't pulsing with need.

The coffin's interior walls cozied up to her, running its—*his*—hands over her body, blowing warm breath against her neck, pressing itself —*himself!*—into her empty spaces.

Tension wanted release, but Moena's mind refused to fall into the illusion. She cut the session short.

What would a lover feel like, for real? She shivered. *Think of the microflora! The exchange of so much more than fluid.* And where would it happen? Here, in her bed? In the sanctum of her home? The biome would be corrupted, and her hard work set back by years. *Idiot! Forget him!*

But Rahul persisted in her thoughts, like a splinter that wormed deeper the more she tried to pry it out. Moena called the only friend left from her outside days: her fellow graduate student, now Professor Das.

Ananya's broad brown face appeared on the tablet screen accompanied by the clamor of children.

"Let me get somewhere quiet."

"You have to save me," Moena said, after her friend relocated.

Ananya cocked an eyebrow. "Do you need some new cultures?"

"No. Bacteria can't help me. I've been infected by a man, a glorious specimen of male *Homo sapiens*!"

"Infected? What? Did you have sex with someone?"

Moena laughed at her friend's horrified expression. "No. I haven't touched him. Mmmmm . . . but I want to. Am I selfish for staying in here? For using my research to benefit myself and not the world?"

"What? Mo, you're not making any sense. Are you okay? How's your biome?"

"The verdant lovelies are fine. Creepy crawlies and microbiota are good. My blood results came back in normal ranges last month. But my heart—my heart is parched for company! He said I'm famous. They're using my thesis. Should I be out there, helping? Fighting the good fight?"

"First: you're not selfish for keeping yourself from chronic illness. Second: you are brilliant, and you should be publishing your results. Third: who is this chap and how has he gotten under your skin?"

"His name is Rahul. Window repairman and eco-warrior supreme, with skin like creamy cocoa-butter."

Her friend rolled her eyes. "Get a grip. You haven't touched another human being in over five years. You want to risk everything for him?" Her expression softened. "If you get sick again, you'll have to give him up."

"Bridges, crossings, et cetera, dear professor. Besides, I can't be myself with him so this love affair won't last. Short, torrid, over!"

"What do you mean?"

"He won't want to date Moena Sivaram, wealthy eccentric and victim of tragic circumstance. I'll have to invent a mundane secret identity, someone matched to his station in life."

"A lie isn't a good foundation for love."

"I'll keep it to romance, not love. Then can I have your blessing?"

"No. Yes. I don't know," Ananya sputtered. "Just . . . check in with me, okay? I'm worried about you."

Moena agreed and ended the call. Her fingers approached the keyboard then curled away, like the leaves of a *Mimosa pudica*: touch-me-not. Her mother's words from a decade ago haunted her.

"When you're of age, Moena, we'll find you a nice boy to marry. Or you'll find one on your own, but keep this in mind: men desire women who can stand up to them and still remain short. They don't want women who are smarter or wealthier or more famous. Better that you forget boys and marriage until you have your own measure."

Smarter. Wealthier. More famous. Rahul lacked a doctorate. Rahul worked for a living. Rahul's name had never scorched news headlines.

Moena invented a fitting girl for Rahul to love. Meena Sivaraman (close enough that Moena would answer to it): middle class, moderately educated, modestly dressed. A proper, earnest, *sane* young woman with a black braid and a bindi.

Breath came easy. Fingers pattered on the keyboard. Two days later, "Meena" had a coffee-shop date with Rahul to discuss volunteer opportunities.

On the day of their meeting, Moena rejected three different outfits: a traditional sari (too stuffy), a salwar-kameez from a distant aunt (too gaudy), and a dress from her university days in London (too Western). Clad in jeans and a short-sleeved cotton kurti, she stepped out of the house.

She wasn't sure whose eyes were wider, hers or Syed's, as she bolted into the back seat of the car.

"Are you sure, madam?" he asked for the tenth time, peering at her from the driver's seat.

Heart racing, palms sweating, and breath shallow, she said, "Yes. Drive, please."

They drove down tree-lined streets, past skyscraping beehives of apartments and claustrophobic rows of shops. The car's fan was set to recirculate, but the scents of Bangalore crept in through imperfect seals. Moena's throat closed. She gripped the sprigs of holy basil she had brought, crushing the tender leaves. They released a pungent, soothing aroma. She plucked two of them and pressed them into her nostrils. *Better.*

The car lurched to the right, came up to the curb, and stopped.

"This is the place," Syed said. "But we can go home, madam. Your health is more important than anything."

"Thank you, Syed. I'll be okay. I promise I'll call you if I'm not."

Moena stepped out and drew her first breath of raw city air in five years. Dust assailed her nostrils, drying the tiny hairs and making her sneeze. Rumbling diesel trucks spewed black exhaust. A current of decaying refuse and putrid sewage ran through it all. She gagged.

Bodies moved past her along the uneven slabs of the sidewalk. They stank of hot oil, sweat, sandalwood, fish, jasmine, sex. A stray dog trotted from a cluster of trash to a half-eaten banana. A fly fizzed into Moena's ear, tickling it before moving on.

How did anyone live like this? How had she, for the first twenty-three years of her life? She could almost sense the effluvia penetrating her lungs, polluting her bloodstream. She forced herself to inhale a second time. *Stand straight!* Shoulders back, chin high, hands unclenched: *face the city like everyone else.*

Advertisements plastered the low cinderblock wall to her right, their poster colors faded by rain, their edges frayed and torn. On the other side, gulmohar trees bordered the courtyard, shading the café patrons within. She scanned the crowd. Where was Rahul?

Moena threaded her way between the tables, careful not to touch any thing or person or plant. She spotted Rahul's curly hair and white T-shirt (did he wear nothing else?) in the back corner, at a table sprinkled with pollen from the blossoms above. She pinched her nose against a sneeze.

"Rahul Madhavan?" She tried to sound as if she'd never seen him before.

"Yes. You must be Meena. Please, sit. Shall I order you some coffee?"

Moena swallowed repulsion—non-homemade coffee!—and forced a smile. "Thanks."

"You'd like to volunteer for HEG and do some ecological work, yes? Let me tell you about what we do."

Rahul entered a fifteen-minute monologue with words that felt as much like home as the scent of damp humus. He spoke of water pollution, remediation, plant and bacterial seeding; of community effort and citizen science; of working with the earth and not against it. His hands moved in organic shapes—no sharp edges—and his fingertips came together and burst apart like a ripe seedpod.

Moena watched, listened, sneezed. She swiped at her drippy nostrils with a bleached white handkerchief and sneezed again. Nodded. Smiled. Sneezed. Her coffee arrived and cooled. It stayed untouched but so did his.

"How does that sound? Like something you can commit to?"

"Absolutely. Once a week. No problem."

Problems tangled her thoughts faster than she could prune them away.

"Great! I'll send you the information for next week's action."

"Why aren't you a biologist?"

"Sorry?"

You're not supposed to know that! "I mean, why are you a volunteer and not working for HEG? You seem so knowledgeable about this."

"I'm too old?" He flashed his crooked smile. "I already had an engineering degree when I got interested in remediation. I'm over thirty now. I can't possibly compete in entrance exams. What about you? What brought you to this?"

"I have . . . a friend. She was sick for a long time, and some of that was because of our water and air. I want to do something for her—for everyone—to improve that."

"Wonderful! Then I'll see you next week."

He held out his hand.

Shake it! Moena thrust out her own, let him wrap his fingers around hers. His palm felt warm and smooth, like eucalyptus bark in sunlight. The thrill of contact traveled through her arm and spread, tingling, throughout the rest of her body. *All of him, now!* Her heart raced, mouth dried. Desire gathered force, whipping from a zephyr to a tornado. Her cheeks flushed. Could he tell? Did he sense her tumult?

Rahul let go.

They exited the café together.

Syed picked her up.

The ride home dragged on, an interminable torture of snarled traffic, gaunt beggars, and enough rain to streak the dusty windows.

Moena met Rahul and the handful of other volunteers at an oblong lake situated southeast of the city. She felt naked without her isolation suit as she approached the slime-ridden banks. Bone-white tree trunks dotted the waterline. A quarter kilometer to the left, a rusting hulk of metal heaved a piston up and down. The thrum of its motor drowned the buzzing clouds of insects.

A wave of fetid air blew across Moena. She stumbled back, knelt, and heaved her lunch into a cluster of spindly bushes.

"Sorry. I should have warned you." Rahul stood next to her. He held out a sky-blue paper mask. "Wear this. It's coated with menthol."

Moena accepted it with shaking hands. The astringent scent choked her, squeezing tears from the corners of her eyes, but her stomach settled.

"What is this place?"

"Agara Lake," Rahul said. "Rife with industrial metals, plastics, and animal waste."

Moena stood and caressed a leaf. The bush was a fledgling neem tree, spotted with brown, yellow, and black.

"Poor thing," she whispered. "You need help."

Rahul's pupils dilated. His brow quirked.

Moena shrugged. "I've always felt more comfortable with plants than people."

Sunlight glinted, turning Rahul's irises to honey brown. "Me too."

He guided her to the lakeside, his hand light against the small of her back, intimate and yet not.

The volunteers worked in separate domains. Moena's assignment was simple: to collect soil and water samples for analysis.

White foam floated in Rorschach blotches on the surface of the water. Centimeter-high waves lapped at yellowish-brown mud. A dead fish bulged at the surface a few meters in.

Guilt constricted her chest with weedy roots. Isolation had restored her health, but at what cost? When had the state of the world become so rotten?

Moena pinched a test tube between thumb and forefinger as if it were a wriggling insect. Gloves. Boots. Rubber coveralls. All were standard issue protection they'd used in graduate school, but ecological vigilantes—especially here in India—had no such resources. *Do it! Dip your hand in!*

She inched into the lake. Its lukewarm water soaked through her shoes and socks and up along her pants. Moena swallowed a sob. She rooted herself and leaned down. Muscles trembled. *Reach in!* Half the water spilled from the test tube on her first try. *Again!* The second attempt went better, and the fifth held most of the intended sample.

She straightened, looked across the muddy banks. Rahul nodded in approval. Pride sprouted in her heart, tiny and bursting with life.

Two hours later, the veteran volunteers departed. Moena stood beside Rahul as he stored her samples in the trunk of his car. He, too, was stained with lake scum. Sweat matted his curls. Dirt caked his fingernails and cuticles. He handed her a bottle of water from a cooler.

Moena gulped half of it in seconds. It did little to ease the ache growing behind her eyes. Her sinuses throbbed.

Rahul frowned. "Are you okay?" He gestured toward Moena's arms.

Patches of red blossomed everywhere that lake water had spattered on her.

"Allergies," she said. "I'll be fine." *Liar, liar!*

"Then I'll thank you twice for helping. Not many people can handle this kind of work, and even fewer would sacrifice their health for it. Will I—will we, that is—see you next time?"

"Yes."

Moena waited until she was in her car to blow her nose.

Syed glanced at her reflection in the rearview mirror. "Madam, why are you doing this to yourself?"

"Guilt, Syed! And love. Love for my people, the verdant ones and the fleshy ones and the ones you can only see under a microscope. Guilt that I've kept myself away for too long."

The next week, Moena brought her own vials—empty and sterile—tucked in her jeans pockets. She wore a light cotton kameez with long sleeves. Scabbed patches decorated her skin, the aftereffects of the previous session. While she worked, she collected her own samples of water and soil. Rahul might have been the catalyst for this madness, but the biota were the reactant that kept it fed.

She watched Rahul as he worked the nutrient tanks and pumps. His dark brow wrinkled in concentration, his jaw slack and lips parted, just enough for a peek of pink tongue. Green slime spattered his boots and the lower half of his jeans. *Brave, lovely man.*

He glanced up from his handheld—caught her staring. Moena's cheeks warmed as he smiled, tiny and knowing. *Concentrate!* The memory of his expression trickled down through her belly, lower, heating her, an exothermic reactor of her very own.

Once again, she and Rahul finished their work last. Syed had not yet returned from his tea break. She was about to message him to when Rahul spoke seven magic words: "Would you like to get some coffee?"

Moena's inner fifteen-year-old jumped for joy, did cartwheels, crowed to the world. A fit of coughing prevented her adult self from answering.

Gasping for breath, she said, "Yes."

She left the coffee untouched again. If Rahul noticed, he didn't comment, but he did ask her out to dinner. *Dinner—hurrah!* And yet not.

Idiot! He would notice if she left an entire meal uneaten. The food would be crawling with microflora, with all the variety of Bangalore's citizens. Her stomach roiled at the thought. But she would do it—for Rahul, for the chance to fertilize the seeds of their relationship—anything for that.

"How was the date?" Ananya asked, smirking.

"Great! I spent the rest of the night on the toilet," Moena said. "But it was worth every minute. Rahul's so passionate about this work. Imagine what he's like in bed!"

The smile vanished from her friend's face. "Don't joke! You can't keep risking your health for this. You should tell him the truth."

"But he wants to see me again."

"Stop stringing him along!"

"I can't. Besides, he's wrapped me in his own string package."

"Oh, Mo, you've fallen for him?"

"I'm still falling, drifting, like leaves in a Cambridge autumn. He can't ever know who I really am or he would grind me into the dirt."

"You're not giving him enough credit. Either that or he's an ass who doesn't deserve you."

"You should see the cultures I'm getting from the lake."

"What? Don't change the subject!"

"I think I've figured out a way to improve the breakdown of the polycarbonates. We need to change the nitrogen levels in the nutrient mix. Oh, and I spliced some enzyme sequences from *Geotrichum candidum* into the *flavobacterium* that's worked best so far."

"Really? You were able to splice in fungal genes and the bacteria survived? Show me the data."

They spent the rest of the conversation arguing over organic chemistry and whether a different strain or a second strain would make for a better solution. Moena went to bed dreaming of curing Bangalore's water ailments. What better token of love could she offer to Rahul?

The baby bromeliads drooped. Their once dark green leaves faded, their tips browned. The house soil smelled like rotting cabbage in its shadier pockets. Two of the eBees kept crashing into the SmartWindows like drunks with frenetic wings.

Moena extracted samples from the surface and subsoil, ran them through the DNA sequencer. The lake bacteria had infiltrated her cultivated sanctum. They were winning.

She coughed over her shoulder and turned back to the scope. Her nose hadn't stopped dripping for weeks. At night, her joints ached. The coffin's masseuse software did little to relieve the pain.

But. But! Last night, five weeks after their first date and many a rendezvous since, she and Rahul had kissed. Wet, bacteria-saliva-swapping glory! Her last boyfriend at Cambridge was a decade past. She'd forgotten how exquisite the dance of lips and tongue could be.

Rahul had whispered of his germinating passion: *There's no one in the world like you. The way you move, the way you talk—you're exquisite. You're my glorious once-blooming orchid.*

Those words! That metaphor!

The skin on the inside of her thighs burned, chafed from her numerous sessions with virtual-coffin-Rahul. Ten times ten times ten . . . the order of magnitude didn't matter. Ersatz satisfaction would never be enough. She needed the real thing.

Moena danced her gloved fingertips against the sterile tile countertop. Petri dishes and bottles of reagents crowded the glass-fronted refrigerator to her left. A jumble of live cultures and test tube racks littered the surface on her right, cozying up to the CRISPR-based gene editor.

She needed a solution to remediate the lake into health but also to heal her own biome. Every foray into the outside world—every handhold and kiss with Rahul—allowed new single-celled adversaries into the house.

To cut off contact with him? The idea was a nasty fly tiptoeing through the hairs of *Dionaea muscipula*. Snap, trap, digest! Banish it to nonexistence.

She exited her laboratory and padded to the southern side of the house. The sun-warmed grit under her bare feet helped her think. Never mind the arthritic curl bending her toes. *Fix the house, fix yourself.* She swabbed the leaves of a dwarf orange tree that was mottled with yellow and black spots.

"*Wrong. Wrong. Wrong,*" hummed the bees.

Years to achieve balance. Weeks to fall apart. So unfair! Moena's inner five-year-old stomped and stormed and kicked up an unholy tantrum. Tears trickled. She wiped them away, catching some on the swab, contaminating it. *Idiot!*

She stumbled to her towering *Dieffenbachia* grove and curled up under the shade of their broad, variegated leaves. Her cheek sank into the cool, soft loam. She extended her tongue—*wait*! How much beneficial microflora did the soil still have? Was it friend or foe?

To lick or not to lick? That is the question! Whether 'tis nobler in the mind to suffer the filth and rot of exterior living, or to take—antibiotics, but that had too many syllables—against a sea of—*damn*. She lost the analogy.

Moena giggled.

She beat her head against the ground. Madness. Her old friend had arrived for a visit. Let's catch up over chai. Plain or masala?

Ananya had left three messages, one for each call that Moena had ignored.

Soon. Soon she would return them. *Close!* She was so close to the answer. Her scalp itched. When had she last bathed? Not important. *Focus! There!* That snippet would turn her engineered bacteria into oxygen-devouring microbeasts. Bye-bye, plastics! Nitrates as a byproduct? Pretty please with citric acid on top, but only a dollop. Too much would be toxic.

Moena dumped the design into the artificial-life simulator. Crunch away! Tell me some good news! Please, please, let this combination be the magical one, the stable one.

The phone sang to her, that old Carnatic song about love birds. She'd assigned the tune to Rahul's caller ID. She had to answer.

"Meena, hi. Where are you? We're at the lake."

"Oh." She checked the calendar. Oh! *Focus! Be Meena again.* "Sorry. I lost track of time."

His image frowned on the tiny screen. Moena wanted to plant kisses in the adorable furrow between his brows.

"Are you okay? You don't look well."

Damn. She hadn't meant to leave the camera on. *Distract him!*

"Hey, you're my boyfriend. You shouldn't say such things!"

Rahul's lips curved, frond-like. "Am I your boyfriend now?"

Moena nodded, licked her lips. Promises, promises. "I'll come soon. Will you be there in another hour?"

"The others won't, but I'll wait for you. I miss you."

She returned to the simulation. *Go faster!* Numbers scrolled. Protein triplets sprinkled the results with alphabetic seeds. The probability of success ticked into the nineties. Good enough! Nothing yet had transcended the sixties. She kissed the screen, then transferred the design into the splicer.

Ten minutes later, Moena decanted half of her custom bacterial solution into a sterile test tube. *The solution is the solution!* She snickered. She pocketed that tube and took the remainder to the water feeder tank for the house. *Be fruitful and multiply, my little beasties!* You will save the soil, the house, *me*.

The sun's glare reflected from the lake, stabbing through Moena's eyes and into her frontal cortex like an illuminated knife. *Light sensitivity!* Another symptom of her degrading health. *Never mind!* Salvation lay in her pocket. She slipped a finger in, caressed the glass tube. Her mind wandered to another cylindrical object, one that wasn't so cold and brittle.

Rahul stood by the pump. Sweat beaded on his forehead, dewdrops on buttery leather. He motioned her over. He'd already taught her how to work the injection well and nutrient tank. All she had to do today was pour in her vial when he wasn't looking.

The single-celled lovelies would digest the iron and polycarbonates in the water, then make their way into the locals. The guts of Bangalore—human and animal—would shit out more of Moena's microbabies. They would infect the sewage runoff and restore the water to livable purity.

She stumbled over the slight rise of the concrete pad. Fire blazed up from her rheumatic toes to her swollen knees. Rahul caught her before she fell. She gasped as his hands crushed the weeping sores under her sleeves. *Bite your tongue! Don't scream!*

"What's the matter?"

Spin a lie, quick! Before he can think.

"Sprained my ankle, that's all."

She plucked her arm from his grasp, staggered to the nutrient tank, pried off the lid.

"What are you doing?"

No more time for subterfuge. No time to talk. Her body would give out soon.

The stench from the fomenting cultures flowed into Moena's nostrils, triggered the nausea-inducing portion of her brain. Her stomach contracted. *No time!*

She yanked the vial from her pocket. *Splash!* In went her microbes.

Uncontrolled experiment! Her advisor's voice rang in her head. *Unpublished! Unverified! Dangerous!*

Sorry, Professor.

Concrete bashed Moena's knees as she knelt and vomited. War raged in her gut. Which side would prevail? Red and black streaked the mess that splattered across the dull gray cement.

"Meena!"

Rahul's head blocked the sun. Golden light haloed his black curls.

"Surya," she whispered. Sun God. Beautiful.

She heaved again. Tremors coursed through her major muscle groups. She was a tree in a storm, her core rotted through by maggots. She toppled.

Rahul/Surya scooped her up, carried her to the car. Syed's voice and his swirled with frantic concern. Her own protests joined in admixture, dilute and ineffective.

Stop! You can't bring him home!

Blackness overtook Moena's vision.

Blurs of light. Sticky eyelids. Puffy tongue. Somewhere, an incessant annoying *beep beep beep*.

Moena shifted her arm. Warning pain: *a needle*. She blinked. The world resolved, focused, magnified—like looking through a giant drop of water. A bag of clear fluid fed into a tube.

Intravenous drip. She inclined her head. She was in her bedroom, alone, and being fed by this device. *Contamination*. Who had been in her house?

What miserable microbes crawled in with them? What were they feeding her?

Antibiotics. The label confirmed it. They were poisoning her, killing her microscopic friends, the colonies she'd worked so long to build.

Moena extracted the needle. She licked at the pearl of blood that formed, pressed on the hole with her thumb. *Beep. Beep*. There: her tablet bleated from her desk. The world spun and swayed as she walked and dropped into the chair.

Low battery. She silenced the alarm, sucked away another drop of blood, plugged the device in. An indicator light flashed in the upper corner: Rahul had left her a message. Video. She played it.

His face appeared on the screen. Drooping, but lovely. Kissable lips that moved with care. "They wouldn't let me in. Syed called your physician. She took care of you, said you had to be isolated in your home or you wouldn't get well. Meena—sorry, Moena—I don't know what else to say. I always suspected that you were hiding something, but this? It's too much. I don't understand you. What do you want with someone like me? Sex? A lower class boy to toy with until you find someone in your own circles? Did you think I wouldn't mind because I'm a guy? Well, you were wrong. You broke my heart."

Anger, disappointment, betrayal—the lines of his face grew harder, twisted, a tree grown without enough water.

"I changed my mind," she whispered at the screen. "I wanted everything about you, in the end."

She brushed away a tear and traced his image with the wet finger, blurring his features, softening them. *You don't understand what I am.* She pressed record, to explain, to rip out the lies and plant the truth in his ears, but no sound emerged. How could words be enough?

The silence crushed Moena. Tears slipped, spattered, diluted the blood welling on the back of her hand. She stumbled from the bedroom into the glaring sunshine of the main house.

"Your fault. Your fault," droned the eBees.

She headed for the *Dieffenbachia* grove. The test plants stood straight, verdant and white, not a patch of yellow or brown. Translucent pink worms writhed away from her curling toes. The earth under Moena's feet felt crumbly and cool, and the sweet scent of compost filled the air.

"At least I saved you," she said. She caressed the waxy leaves with her fingertips. "My darlings, you still love me, don't you? You'll help me."

Moena lay down, wiped the bloody smear on the back of one hand into the dirt, wiped her cheeks with the other. She licked the dark streak of loam from her skin. The bitterness of blood mixed with rich manganese and the tang of humic acid. She pinched the soil between her fingertips. She needed to analyze it. If this grove was thriving, she could help the other parts of the house.

And Rahul? How to remediate a polluted relationship? His love had wrapped Moena with its brambles, dug into her flesh, held tight. Pulling them out would leave her riddled with holes. Did he hurt this much, too? *My heart is broken*, he'd said. She didn't have the strength to think it through. First, she had to heal herself.

One week fell away, then another, then a third. The house became a safe haven rather than hostile territory. Leaves returned to verdurous states. The eBees whirled in sober coordination. Moena's thoughts became as clear as her SmartWindows.

"You need to make a peace offering, a gift," Ananya said. "But then what? Will he be willing to live on your terms? I'm sorry, Mo. I wish you could find that kind of happiness, but maybe Rahul isn't the right one."

A gift—a token of love. What mattered most to Rahul? This city. Its water. Its land. Moena could give him the health of Bangalore, but only if she knew whether her experiment had worked.

This time she wore the isolation suit to the lake. She avoided the volunteer hours. The water stretched like gray glass, rippled by the occasional crow's feet. Her breath rasped through the filters. Strange, not to smell anything. Moena scooped samples from the water and the lake bed, carried them back to the car where Syed waited, his face wrinkled with concern.

The results were gorgeous. The polycarbonate levels had dropped well below the previous curve. She needed more data over time to measure the new rate, but this was enough for an initial publication. Her hands quivered like stamens in a breeze. She typed for ten hours, loaded the draft onto a data cube. Gene sequences and a vial of live cultures completed the package.

Moena sat in the citrus grove. She inhaled the aroma of orange blossoms and traced curlicues in the sandy soil. A tablet lay by her feet. It displayed the feed from the door camera. Syed picked up the padded envelope and disappeared.

Would Rahul answer? Would he understand? Would he forgive?

The draft paper described her life down to its deepest roots. The seeds of health—for her, for everyone—were sown throughout the dry, technical paragraphs. She sent a second copy to Ananya. Let Professor Das lend it credibility. Let their ideas infect the world. Let Rahul come back to her life.

Moena waited three days. Nothing. Not a call or message or note. He had pruned her away like a rotten branch. Poison. That's what her actions had brought to his life and her own. She deserved to be cut off.

Moena took a kitchen knife to the coffin. She drew it through the supple fabric lining, parting it like the skin of a ripe tomato. Wires, actuators, and pressure sensors burst forth in an overgrown tangle. *Begone, temptation!*

She drew the blade through it once more the next day and the day after. For each twenty-four hours that Rahul didn't answer, she slashed another reminder of what she was: moron, idiot, lunatic. *Never again!*

Rahul arrived on the day she made the fourteenth stroke. He looked nothing like a repairman. He wore a loose kurta and baggy cotton pants. His curls had grown, and they blew like errant wood shavings around his face. A nylon bag rested by his feet.

"Miss . . . Sivaram?" he said through the intercom. He flashed his crooked smile.

Moena buried a rising sob. "I'm coming."

She ran through sunlight and shade, leaves and fronds caressing her bare arms, urging her forward. *Go! Faster!* She stopped at the inner threshold of the foyer.

"I'm so sorry, Rahul. About all of it. I didn't know how else—"

"It's okay. I read your paper. I understood enough, I think. I had HEG do the lab analysis on your samples and the lake. My God, Moena, the water there is incredible! What a transformation! The work you've done—it could change everything." He paused. "Can I come in?"

Unshed tears suffused Moena's face, filled the cavities, pushed her into action. She opened the outer door as her answer. Rahul removed his shoes and walked in. She set the sterilizing wash to a simple soap solution.

"Close your eyes," she said.

Water drenched Rahul like a personal cloudburst. Rivulets of brown ran into the drain, washing away dust and oil and the hostility of Bangalore. Wet cloth delineated the contours of his body.

Moena retrieved a towel from her bedroom. The mutilated coffin sat to one side, an eyesore. Shame rooted her feet. Cover it up? *No*. No more secrets. She returned to Rahul as the wash ended.

"I'm sorry I was silent for so long," he said. "At first I was waiting for the lab results, and then I had to make some arrangements in case . . ."

"Of what?" she prompted.

"In case you'll have me to stay."

"You mean . . . in here, with me?"

He nodded. Crystal clear droplets fell from his hair.

"I'm not normal, Rahul. I never will be. That's why I didn't tell you who I was. It wasn't about the money or your caste. How could I ask you to fall in love with the insanity of my house, my life? I can't offer a wedding or children or happy occasions with the whole family. All I have is money and isolation."

"And the beauty of your intellect. Your generous spirit. Your passion for the Earth." Rahul's eyes glistened. "Moena, you are the strangest, most wonderful human being I've ever known. How could I not be hopelessly in love with you? I don't care about weddings and children. You have the power to change the world, and I want to be part of that, to be part of your life."

"You'll have to stay inside for a long time."

"I know."

"It could be months or even years until I can stabilize the biome for both of us."

"I can accept that."

"And your family?"

He laughed, crooked teeth flashing. "They've given up on me. Over thirty, unmarried, and volunteering in cesspools—they think I'm crazy."

The Carnatic love birds crooned.

"Then let's be lunatics together," she said.

She opened the inner door. It closed behind Rahul with a slight sucking noise, not unlike a kiss. *Hush! Be patient!* She took him by the hand and led him to the elephant ear tree. Their bare feet left two sets of prints in the rich, dark soil. Rahul gazed up into the canopy. Sunshine and wonderment dappled his face.

"Meet your father," Moena whispered to the baby bromeliads.

She crouched and ran a finger through the soil. He knelt beside her.

"Open your mouth," she said.

Rahul's brow quirked in puzzlement. His lips parted. Moena's finger hovered, then darted between like a hummingbird's beak, depositing its microbial pollen on his waiting tongue. His eyes opened wide and white as forbidden jasmine.

"Your first inoculation," she whispered.

His mouth surrounded her finger, sucking gently. His teeth tickled her skin.

The eBees hummed, "Kiss him! Kiss him!"

The leaves rustled in agreement. *Now!*

Moena freed her hand and twined her arms around Rahul's neck. She pressed her trunk into his, then her lips. The damp heat of his body soaked into hers. His flavors purled across her tongue. Lingering grit. Chile powder. Kernels of salt. Their microbiota swirled, integrated, danced into each other, merged into one biomass. *What's yours is mine. What's mine is yours.*

"Welcome home," Moena said.

2

Abstracts from Another Now

Samuel Clamons

Staying Grounded, In Reality: A Systematic Review of Spaceflight-Induced Psychosis (*The Proceedings of the Skylab Life Sciences Symposium*, Vol. 1, Aug. 1974)

EVERY SUBSTANTIVE MANNED SPACE MISSION, from the Gagarin Burnout to the Gemini disaster, has ended in total loss of life and mission property due to Spaceflight-Induced Psychosis (SIP), an affliction characterized by extreme paranoia, paranormal delusions, agitation, and acute suicidal tendency. In section I, we outline the history of SIP. In particular, we find that the often-claimed correlation between SIP severity and lunar phase is likely a statistical artifact. In section II, we review the most promising explanations of SIP, along with laboratory evidence (in humans and non-human primates) for and against each. We find that no single hypothesis accounts for all features of SIP, particularly the sharp onset of SIP above 92,000 feet or the consistent appearance of a blood-red, ringed gas giant in SIP-induced hallucinations. In section III, we consider proposed anti-SIP strategies, with a special emphasis on protective medication with hallucinogens and mild psychotics. Finally, in section IV we briefly discuss strategies for space exploration under the constraint of SIP, including unmanned spaceflight and operational procedures with robustness against psychotic operators (OP-WRAP).

Falsehoods Unexpectedly Prevalent in Everyday Activity (*Journal of Personality and Social Psychology*, Mar. 2022, Vol. 223, Issue 3)

Recent breakthroughs in machine learning have enabled mass automated analysis of video footage. Here, we use a video-based lie detector constructed using Hierarchical Extreme Deep-Field Convolutional Learning (HE-DFCL) to analyze the prevalence of lies in a variety of real-world scenarios including checkout at a grocery store, conversation with strangers in a local park, and interaction with a secretary to schedule an appointment, as recorded in the field by urban surveillance systems. Surprisingly, our lie detector determined that more than 90% of everyday conversation across all conditions is made up of obvious (>99.5% confidence) lies. Random samples of these lies were verified by human subjects who were shown only a single lie, but subjects shown an entire conversation consistently underestimated the number and frequency of lies more than ten-fold. We did not detect similar lying frequencies in transcripts or recordings of movies, pop songs, or pre-prepared speeches. Furthermore, when conversations were modified to remove HE-DFCL-detected lies, human volunteers judged them to be subjectively "scripted" or "ingenuine." We conclude that a shockingly large fraction of human interaction consists of lies, although it is unclear whether those lies constitute errors, genuine attempts at deception (conscious or otherwise), or a learned behavior designed to gain trust. Furthermore, our findings suggest that humans possess a low-level filter for blatant lies that detects and removes them well before they reach conscious perception, and that this filter is modulated by social context.

Copenhagen Heating is a Major Contributor to Anthropogenic Global Warming (*Science*, 28 Aug 1994, Vol. 265, Issue 5117)

Copenhagen heating, in which observation of a quantum system by a conscious observer is expected to spontaneously create waste heat via instantaneous collapse of the quantum wave function, has proven notoriously difficult to detect under laboratory conditions. Nevertheless, the total effect of Copenhagen heating from all human observations may have a noticeable effect on global climate. In this work, we calculate the total energy created by Copenhagen heating over the course of history of human civilization to be approximately 1.5×10^{19} joules, which translates to a global atmospheric warming of approximately 0.7 °C. Indeed, National Climatic Data Center temperature records show a previously unexplained warming trend consistent with the Copenhagen heating expected from historic population growth. This consistency holds only if humans are the primary source of Copenhagen heating, which rules out the possibility of consciousness in non-primate mammals and most invertebrate classes. Using a simple demographic model with parameters estimated from historical records, we predict a global temperature anomaly of between 1.9 and 4.5 °C over the next 100 years.

The Hallmarks of Budding (*Cell*, Jan. 2000, Vol.100, Issue 1)

After a quarter century of rapid advances, research in asexual human reproduction ("budding") has generated a rich body of knowledge, revealing budding to be a complex phenomenon involving dynamic changes in cell type and tissue microstructure. Although the consequence of budding is well understood—the production of a cloned human infant—the bewildering array of clinical trajectories displayed during budding makes it a difficult condition to reason about systematically. Dozens of genes and hundreds of environmental conditions have been identified as triggers for budding, with authors variously claiming that budding is inherently stochastic, carefully programmed, or a form of cancer. In this review, we propose a set of underlying principles—a set of hallmarks that prelude the onset of budding. These hallmarks are consistent with a hypothesis of budding as a way to take advantage of fast asexual reproduction when conditions are stable and low-stress for a long time. We suggest that budding events of all types follow a similar trajectory that either triggers or is caused by the six hallmarks: prolonged homeostasis without stress, relaxation of tumor-suppression mechanisms, dramatic hormonal swings, local de-differentiation and vascularization, extensive chromatin de-scaffolding, and under-use of the local nervous system and musculature. We hope that these hallmarks (or others like them) lead to the development of the study of human budding into a logical science, and that they will lead to more rational prediction and management of the condition than current ad-hoc procedures.

Of Mollusks and Men: A Review of Cognitive Biases Between Adult *Homo sapiens* and *Enteroctopus dofleini* (*Proceedings of the National Academy of Sciences of the United States of America*, Dec. 1992, Vol. 89, Issue 2)

The invention of Ivans-Lombardi translation (ILT) fifteen years ago has since transformed our understanding of the giant octopus, *Enteroctopus dofleini*. *E. dofleini* are now popularly regarded as technical geniuses due largely to a pioneering series of collaborations between *E. dofleini* and mathematicians at UCSD. Although *E. dofleini* are well-represented in mathematical journals, they are evolved organisms and therefore suffer from cognitive biases that have now been cataloged almost as extensively as their talents. Giant octopi have proven vulnerable to auditory and optical illusions first discovered in humans, suggesting that they process sensory information much as we do. *E. dofleini* are subject to many of the same statistical fallacies as humans, as well as some unique to the cephalopods (e.g., the log-sum fallacy and nonconservation of probability). In principle, these make the giant octopus vulnerable to Dutch-booking strategies in repeated gambling games, and we advocate for policies protecting giant octopus individuals against exploitative gambling schemes. *E. dofleini* have a theory of mind, but the startling degree to which it suffers from projection bias, false consensus effect, and egocentric bias suggests that this theory of mind is weak. *E. dofleini* individuals also show remarkable stubbornness, often outright refusing to admit that they suffer from cognitive fallacies even when those fallacies are demonstrated concretely. Taken together, these findings paint a picture of the cognitive abilities of *E. dofleini* as a product of the species' solitary evolutionary history. We conclude that because the giant octopus is not subject to the evolutionary pressures associated with social interaction, it has evolved a mind with less flexibility and self-reflective capability than, for example, humans or dolphins. In this light, *E. dofleini* contributions to famous problems such as the Hadwiger conjecture and the spherical Bernstein problem reflect specific domain-level intelligence rather than superior general intelligence.

Measurement of the Cosmological Higgs Particle (arXiv:1904.014238, Feb. 2019)

The Higgs field, though required to explain the masses of some fundamental particles, has the unusual property of having non-zero vacuum value. An alternative to standard Higgs theory, the Cosmological Higgs Soliton Theory (C-HiSTory), states that the Higgs has the same zero vacuum value as any other field, but that the observable universe exists within the bounds of a single gargantuan traveling-wave pulse in the Higgs field, which we term a "Cosmological Higgs soliton." We use C-HiSTory to revisit an old conundrum in astrophysics—why do galaxies rotate more quickly than they should according to their visible mass? This usual explanation for this discrepancy is dark matter, but modern theory requires dark matter to be distributed in an asymmetric pattern not well-explained by standard cosmology. C-HiSTory provides a simpler explanation—galaxies have different mass than predicted by their luminosities because the strength of the Higgs field (and, thus, the total effect of gravity on the fundamental particles) varies across space. Galactic masses as measured by rotational velocities are consistent with the existence of the cosmological Higgs soliton, and C-HiSTory largely (though not entirely) replaces the need for asymmetric dark matter distribution. Galactic mass measurement places the cosmological Higgs particle between 530 billion and 541 billion light years in mean diameter. Implications for global spatial geometry and the nature of reality outside the observable universe are discussed within.

Quantification of the Merlin Point Effect in Quantum Systems and Recommendations for Effect Containment (*Nature*, Sep. 2020, Vol. 585)

The Merlin Point is a point in Orcières, France approximately 1420 meters above sea level, at which human thought is known to directly influence physical events via a phenomenon known as the Merlin Point Effect (MPE, or more colloquially, "magic"). Although classic experiments have quantified the effects of the Merlin Point on large bodies and mass-action kinetics, MPE has never been systematically quantified in a quantum-mechanical context. We demonstrate mental manipulation of single-photon distributions in single- and double-slit experiments, modulation of *hf* in a photoelectric effect experiment, and both acceleration and deceleration of ^{137}Ce decay. Consistent with previous experiments, the effect strength in each of these cases varies inversely with the cube of distance both from the Merlin Point to the manipulator and from the manipulator to the target system. We also investigate the ability of the MPE to affect systems that employ digital restoration by mental bit-flipping in circuits ranging in complexity from a breadboard-prototyped analog half-adder to a commercial laptop. MPE had an all-or-nothing effect on digital circuitry, but, in sharp contrast to the inverse-cube dropoff observed in other systems, the probability of success of a mentally-driven bit-flip event dropped sigmoidally with respect to both MP-manipulator distance and manipulator-apparatus distance, remaining almost constant until falling dramatically past a combined distance of approximately 33 meters. We recommend that the minimum safe distance requirements for the Merlin Point be increased in light of our findings, and that more stringent access restrictions be placed on professionals with extensive knowledge of biochemistry or nuclear physics.

3

Yuan Tzu's Second Law of Evolutionary Design

Samuel Clamons

On my 283rd birthday, I decided to end my career. I was ready to retire in luxury or die. After I advertised my services for a few years, the Seti Cluster megaengineers contracted me for a job that was sure to give me one of the two.

In principle, the job was simple. Impersonate a Xiang clone. Fake a Family visit to one of their worlds. Earn the trust of the clone in charge there. Ask to see the coveted plans for the enigmatic Xiang Arch. Copy it. Leave. Simple—except that the godlike Xiang was a paranoid xenophobe in total control of every living thing on the planet.

The job almost ended the minute I touched down on Xiang's World.

My lander made it to atmosphere without a hitch, and the planet accepted my (stolen) credentials without challenge. The planet guided me down to a landing field in a valley of scarlet trees crusted with snow, overlooked by the kind of large multistory pagoda favored by the Xiang clones.

I disembarked directly into the snow. The air was quiet and numbingly cold; I ordered my robe to give me some heat. I could barely see a sparse treeline at the edge of the clearing through the fog. Everything sparkled faintly.

I made it about three steps before a thunderclap blew out my eardrums and a column of searing energy zipped together a seven-meter-tall, stone-armored guardinal out of ambient air and nanobots.

At the same time, a giant heron servant bearing a Xiang—the real deal!—swept down from the misty sky. That ancient curmudgeon leaped off his heron with a grace that his sagging skin and bony frame belied. His brittle-whiskered face looked every inch the archaic and essentialist "wise monk" archetype, complete with a frustrating aloofness.

I now wore that same face, sculpted onto my body for this job. It was a fine face, I could admit, at least if you liked being a grizzled ancient. I didn't. And I hated wearing somebody else's face. I hated wearing somebody else's body. But it was the only way to pull off this crazy mission.

Before I could figure out if I was being attacked, the guardinal swept me up in two giant, stony fists, pinning my hands to my sides.

The lander gave me a panicked cry, over our private ghostline of course. I told it to shut up for a moment, brought my robe to combat readiness, and prepared for violence. I considered cutting my way free with my robe, or stunning the guardinal with an electric discharge. No, this wasn't the time to conserve resources, better just to fry the guardinal to hell with a larger discharge and make a run for the lander. I could be out of orbit before Xiang's World could summon a more aggressive response. I could still escape.

But then I'd have wasted one-and-a-quarter gigaseconds—forty years, by the archaic system the Xiangs preferred—of subjective travel time. Yes, I know, sunk costs are already paid, but right then I just didn't like the idea of showing up back at Epicenter Zeta with nothing and . . . do what, exactly? Go back to consulting and live on a far-orbit habitat for another hundred years? Sign up for another war?

No, the whole point of this escapade was to leave the insanity behind, one way or another. There was an eternity of custom-built simulated paradise waiting if I pulled this off. What was a little risk of vaporization when heaven was at stake?

All of this flashed through my head in about two heartbeats, which was about a heartbeat longer than it would have taken the guardinal to crush me dead if it wanted to. The Xiang clone said something, but I couldn't make out a damned thing with thunderclap-blasted ears. The clone's body language—hands clasped in front of his robes, back straight

—communicated calm but steely control. It didn't look like a vaporizing stance, though it might become one.

I shook my head and gave Xiang's flowing robes and bewhiskered face my best contemptuous up-and-down while I screamed internally at my braindust to repair my eardrums faster.

"Your sense of hospitality has aged poorly," I said once I could hear anything. "This will be difficult to explain in my report to the Family. Our brother at Ilium-2 will not be pleased."

I won't lie, I did steel myself to die right then.

But Great Minds be praised, Xiang actually blanched. That was sweet mana from heaven—it meant the accounts I'd gleaned of mutual suspicion between this Xiang and the one at Ilium-2 were at least partly true and, most importantly, still relevant. My read of the Family's power dynamics was . . . at least not catastrophically wrong.

"My hospitality is reserved for Family," Xiang said with some force.

That almost made me panic and go all ray guns on the guardinal, but a sudden shift in the wind blew a smoky dust of security mites and sniffers in my face, which helped me regain my cool. On any sane, civilized planet, this breach of bodily boundaries would have constituted criminal assault, but to the paranoid and purity-obsessed Xiangs, this was the equivalent of checking my public keys. No biggie.

Of course, no Xiang would actually stand for such a probe, routine or no—I don't make the Family's rules, okay?—so I silently ordered my robe to trap and murder the offending machines, so as not to look suspicious.

"I have already been authenticated. Twice." Somehow I managed to keep my voice low, with a nice acid edge. "If you harbored doubts, why let me onto your world to begin with?"

Xiang gave me a measured look. "Civilization falls without caution. These times call for prudence."

Wow, I thought. He really does talk like a holovid villain. Even after having studied him for decades, the old creep's diction had me flabbergasted to the point that I almost missed the implication of "these times."

Almost. Was Xiang implying that things weren't normal right now? If so, that was new information. I considered my answer carefully here—one wrong word would have the guardinal splattering me all over the valley's abnormally pristine snow.

"Have you experienced a security breach?" I ventured.

Xiang relaxed, visibly enough to notice but subtly enough that he could deny it if pressed. I also relaxed, hopefully more discreetly.

"There was an outbreak of unauthorized bioforms immediately prior to your arrival," said Xiang.

That was too unlikely, too convenient, to be anything but an excuse. Still, if Xiang wanted to smooth over his antagonistic greeting, that was fine by me.

"Unfortunate timing," I told him quite mildly.

"Indeed," Xiang replied. "I had hoped to have the bioforms cleansed before you arrived, but . . . circumstances did not allow for that, and the planet's defenses are still inflamed. I apologize for the slight. You should not have had to see this."

Yeah. Sure. Inflamed planetary defenses. I sorely wanted to call him out on this, but I held my tongue.

Xiang nodded to the guardinal giving me the squeeze, and it returned me to the ground.

"Allow me to welcome you more properly this evening," Xiang said while I recovered. "I invite you to come to my pagoda three hours before sunset." He gestured up the mountainside to the small building overlooking the valley.

Without waiting for a response, he mounted his egregiously sized heron and flew away. The guardinal stalked off and faded into the white mist of the surrounding forest, no doubt to disintegrate somewhere private.

I was left gazing into the heavy mists of the Xiang's World at Cygnus Ultima, too stunned to move, uneviscerated, undisintegrated, and uncaught.

I had to ratchet up the gain on my eyes to see clearly in the heart of Xiang's cavernous pagoda. I wanted to snap at Xiang to turn the damned lights up. That little devil on my shoulder was going to get me into trouble if I kept up the internal quips, so I imagined packing up that part of myself into a little box and tucking it away in a safe little asteroid cache. I'd retrieve it later, once I was disgustingly wealthy.

Xiang's pagoda looked even older than his body, if not quite so decrepit. Shelves of wood half-bleached by time covered the oh-so-distant walls. Those shelves were covered in scrolls, and I knew that if I unrolled one I'd find a page full of nearly microscopic base-1,024 script—sweet, blessedly unciphered script.

Of course, there was also a copy in the undermountain's data cores, but that was encrypted. With seventeen stars' worth of computing power at their fingertips, you'd think the Seti Cluster megaengineers could crack a private-key cipher older than most of written history. But nope, the damned ciphers still worked. I would need the key to break them, and Xiang kept his nowhere but his head. Easier to just steal the scroll.

Xiang awaited me, cross-legged at a comically undersized table in the middle of the room. I gave him a smile and a bow appropriate for a cautious greeting.

He stirred, hesitant, like an oak deciding to stretch and walk away. Xiang's bodies are built to work in sessions of meditation long enough to probably qualify as torture under Doctrine-Standard war codes—if this one was stiff, it wasn't the same body he'd confronted me with earlier.

"Dearest brother," Xiang intoned, extending a hand from his sleeve to gesture at the small cityscape of bowls, cups, plates, and pots cluttering the table. "Welcome to my planet. Please, take a seat."

So we were pretending the "welcome" in the valley never happened, eh? That . . . could work.

"Your kindness humbles me," I told him. The words came out automatically, believe it or not. This critical conversation scared me enough that I'd spent months drilling for it. "But first, I bring you a gift."

Xiang raised a gnarled hand. "A gift is hardly necessary. Your company is gift enough."

"Nonsense," I replied. "I would be ashamed to visit your marvelous world without adding something to it." And if you didn't, you would vaporize me on the spot.

I really needed to do something about my brain's sarcastic bits.

I drew a scroll from my robe and presented it to Xiang with due reverence. It wasn't the Family way to send a gift of this nature by ghostline. The Xiangs were weirdly backwards for a bunch of megabiogeosuper-engineers.

Xiang accepted the scroll. Unfurled it. His eyes glazed over as he read, lips twitching as he decoded the scroll's contents.

I felt the familiar, distinct blend of boredom and terror that I'd previously believed to be unique to active military duty. Whether or not Xiang accepted the gift as genuine meant the difference between my atoms staying bonded to each other or not . . . but that still didn't leave me anything to do but stare at him and wait while he read.

"A fungus?" Xiang asked at last.

It took real effort not to let out an un-Xianglike breath of relief.

"*Arbuscular mycorrhiza*, a *Scutellospora*," I said. "It should boot off of any standard eukaryotic template. It was thought lost on Earth, but our brother at Holdfast Cliffs found some while first taming his ecosystem."

Actually, it came from a trader who claimed to have found it on a neutrino relay near Epicenter Sigma, but Xiang didn't need to know that.

"It does not grow well on my own world, but perhaps you can make use of it," I continued.

"I believe I can," said Xiang. "You have seen my forests. They are sparse, difficult to balance. This fungus will be useful. But enough of that. Please, sit. Allow me to prepare you some tea."

Three more of those oversized herons stalked into the room, each as tall as Xiang, carrying pots of hot water and bundles of fresh tea leaves in their beaks. To my surprise, I found myself internally critiquing Xiang's assessment of the *Scutellospora*—sparse or not, that forest had to have a heck of a soil microbiome already. Did Xiang really have a niche to spare big enough for a mycorrhizal symbiote?

I caught that thread and killed it so I could worry about more useful things, like whether or not my robe could react quickly enough to save me if one of those herons decided to fish my brains out through my eye sockets.

Luckily the herons only had eyes for tea. Xiang poured hot water into some of the pots and swirled them precisely. I recognized elements from a half-dozen tea rituals—yeah, I studied a lot for that job—though I'd always found those rituals' authenticity questionable. He handed me an overfull cup. Its warmth felt pleasant in the cool air of the pagoda. I strained the tea into another empty cup, leaving behind the proper volume of dregs.

"It is good to see the face of Family," Xiang said. "It has been too long since the last time."

I swallowed a half-formed quip about looking in a mirror and gave a generic, protocol-compliant reply.

My robe pinged me with a silent alert. For a moment I thought it was chiding me for my out-of-character inner dialogue, but this was tagged in a way reserved for security breaches and other imminent threats. I brought up an internal visualization of the message and lifted my teacup to my lips to buy a second to review the alert.

"WARNING: Exotic organic compound trace detected. Possible toxin. Possible psychoactive. Low water solubility, low volatility, likely contact-based. Detailed simulation results available in 51 seconds."

I stopped the cup a hair's width from my lips. I briefly wondered if I was already a dead man walking, but the robe would have detected an earlier poisoning. After an eyeblink's worth of panic, I improvised a little sleight of hand to fake a long sip, aided by my Xiang body's large hands and voluminous beard.

"Your voyage must have been considerable," Xiang continued while I "sipped."

I nodded and rapidly inventoried the pottery on the table while I talked, trying to discern what might be safe to touch and what to avoid. Not much went into the first category.

"About seventy years from Yellow River by way of a slingshot off Tosifeld. My local time, of course."

The Xiang at Yellow River could expose that lie easily, of course—but only after about six millennia, thanks to lightspeed delay.

"I am grateful for your trouble," said Xiang, "but it seems an unjustifiable expenditure to come all the way from Yellow River just for a few cups of tea and an old man's company."

Yeah, the tea's really not worth this much trouble.

I did my best to look suitably embarrassed and swept my arms up in an apologetic gesture in a way that just so happened to wipe the inside edge of my teacup with a corner of my robe sleeve. The robe, bless its little machine heart, sucked up a sample of whatever was there and spun up a thorough chemical analysis.

Xiang moved to pour a second round of drinks.

"The company of Family is always reason enough, is it not?" I continued to cut off any immediate protest. "However, I must confess that this is not my only destination. I plan to visit a dozen other Family Worlds while I survey the galactic core. I wish to . . . reconnect." And make sure nobody is deviating from Family doctrine, was the unspoken threat.

"As the first host on your journey, I hope my home is pleasing to you."

Keep him on the defensive? Or play to his ego? Decisions, decisions.

"It is, so far. Your data farms are magnificent. I hope you will not be offended if I borrow their design when I return to Yellow River?"

My robe finished its simulations and spat out a report plastered with priority tags. The colorless, odorless "exotic organic compound" wasn't, it seemed, toxic on its own, but my robe predicted it would quickly metabolize in anyone with Xiang physiology into a CNR-blocker that would produce mild anxiety and, with repeated exposure, chronic paranoia and eventual mania.

My robe couldn't, however, find any trace of the CNR-blocker on the teacup, only in the air.

Where the hell is that scent coming from, then? I demanded of the robe, and it responded with an impressively put-upon question mark.

So, maybe Xiang was trying to poison me. If so, he was doing a pretty poor job of it. The source of the CNR-blocker must have been close for my robe to pick up on it, but it wasn't actually close enough to affect me.

Suppose it was meant for me. What did that imply? The CNR-blocker was a psychotic, not a toxin, so maybe Xiang was trying to unbalance me, trying to provoke a slip if I were an imposter. Which, to be fair, I was, and almost did—but Xiang already held all the power here, so why bother with the CNR-blocker?

Whatever Xiang's ploy, he wouldn't expect me to react to his poison. A real Xiang wouldn't have the equipment to sniff out the compound from a few volatilized molecules. I only had that because I had military-grade, Epicenter-sourced smartcloth masquerading as clothes. And anyway, a reaction wasn't mandatory—I could put off the matter until I figured out Xiang's game.

He was still talking. Fortunately, he was a slow talker, so I put the last few seconds of conversation on fast-forward replay.

"We can speak of . . . such things . . . later," Xiang said. "For now, I invite you to make yourself comfortable. I have assigned an abode on the far side of the pass to you. A sparrow will guide you there. I will summon you back here in a few days. We will speak more about the data farms at that time."

. . .

The "abode," I noted as I trekked through the valley to reach it, was situated at exactly the elevation of Xiang's pagoda, so that there could be no complaint of inferior positioning. On the other hand, the placement forced me to walk down through the valley in a way that brooked no question of which Xiang actually held the superior position.

Clearly, following a protocol of propriety and etiquette did not prevent Xiang from being an arrogant bastard.

No path connected our two dwellings, just an open, sparsely wooded forest full of crisp flurries of bitterly cold snow and crimson leaves. Everything sparkled. The snow sparkled. The ice-caulked fissures in the mountainside sparkled. Even the trees scintillated with the emissions of microscopic swarms of semiautonomous repair bots, relay bots, phage bots, think bots, battery bots, and other manner of fairy dust communicating across the open air and dumping excess heat. The infrared noise was even worse.

The only thing not shimmering or glittering was the Arch. It didn't look like much, just a solid chunk of dull purple-gray barely visible through the snow-turbid sky, except that it spanned the entire sky from horizon to horizon at what appeared from my vantage to be orbital heights.

Nobody but the Xiangs knew why they built the damned things. Maybe they were cooling vanes for some sort of gargantuan contraptions under their planets' surfaces. Maybe they stabilized—or destabilized—the planets' orbits. My money was on decoration with bad taste. But at the end of the day, all that mattered to me was that the Arch possessed a subtle curvature on a scale that made megaengineers across the galaxy offer absurd sums of money to duplicate or "retrieve" it.

I felt dizzy looking up at the sky. Lowering my gaze didn't help. The problem wasn't the sky; it was the openness of everything around me. Now that I had time to consider it, the lack of walls or bulkheads gave me a sense of inverted vertigo.

When had I last stepped on a planet? It must have been the Cet-1592 operation. Counting backwards, that was . . . six and a half years training in the arts and sciences of the Xiangs during interstellar transit (or fifty if you counted time spent in cold storage, but I didn't). A year and a half on a Seti Cluster outpost in the Itonga system, orbiting far, far outside Epicenter Zeta's no-fly sphere. Five years of subjective time virtualized in

Epicenter Zeta, scraping by consulting for military historians. Nine years of interstellar transit from Cet-1592.

That made twenty-two years since the last time I'd really seen a horizon, and Cet-1592's techno wilds were far from a happy association to have with planets. I'd probably feel queasy here even if I wasn't trying to con one of the most dangerous beings in the Mid Perseus Arm.

To steady myself, I looked down at the pristine white snow underfoot. But that just reminded me of the last snow I'd seen, a silty and bloody slush on a miserable little Itongan moon. It reminded me of how, after all the horrible fates I'd risked capturing it, the whole moon ended up deconstructed during Epicenter Zeta's construction, and that reminded me of just how much I wanted to nab that Arch formula and never have to set foot on a planet again.

If the moon I'd almost died fighting for was going to get ripped apart to build server dust, I could at least retire in luxury on that dust.

Movement drew my eye to a nearby tree. A little russet squirrel looked back at me, flicking its tail silently. A spy? Surely not every creature on the planet was there just to keep tabs on me . . . but any creature could be.

I smothered an un-Xianglike grin, pulled my robe close, and double-checked that my ghostline access was firmly locked down.

The hut Xiang provided was thin walled, but surprisingly warm. It was floored with wood and lined with thick parchment. Both bore a superficial patina of wear, but a taint of acrid organics in the air suggested that the whole thing had been instantiated recently, probably sometime during the last day.

I swept my robe against every surface in the hut's single room so it could sniff for errant biologics. To my disappointment, my paranoia actually yielded something—a heron servant had been in the dwelling, just hours or minutes before, based on the pattern of DNA degradation I was seeing.

Why would Xiang put a heron servant in my hut? To leave bugs? I didn't see any, but Xiang could have easily built a camera the size of a speck of dust or from a network of cell-sized machines. I considered clearing the room with an EMP pulse from my robe, but that would only neutralize electronic sensors, not biological ones.

But Xiang could have baked sensors into the pavilion when it was built. He had no need for a heron to plant them.

I was overthinking things—I was a guest, not a prisoner. I composed a scroll and hailed a passing sparrow to deliver it to Xiang's pagoda. "A heron servant entered my room before my arrival," it read. "It did not request permission to do so, nor did it inform me of the intrusion. Please explain this impropriety."

The sparrow returned less than an hour later with a reply.

"That was not my doing. A bird must have malfunctioned. I will send word to have it found and dissected."

Really? A "malfunctioning bird" was a lazy excuse. Too lazy. It gave me goosebumps.

I wrote back to Xiang: "Do not dispose of the malfunctioning bird until I have an opportunity to examine it."

Another songbird, a *Garrulax* morph, carried off the morph. That left me with a lot of time to kill. I tried passing time by meditating over Yuan Tzu's Laws and Maulibaund's Laws and the four Gradient Laws of Free Energy and all the other textbook theorems of evolutionary design, but that hardly kept me occupied for more than a couple of hours. Eventually I just wandered into the forest and opened myself to its ghostlines.

Though it appeared quiet to eyes and ears, the forest teemed with ghostlines emanating from insects and other small animals. I tried pinging some with access requests. Many actively refused, citing insufficient privileges. A few opened themselves to me. A swollen, shimmering green beetle offered a dozen audiovisual records of the forest, annotated with timestamps and local census data. A line of worker ants offered an API for resculpting the local soil. A little black fly with big round wings turned out to be an access interface for a network of relay bots.

I took the green beetle's recordings and threw away everything but the census data. It gave me some sense of the true scale of Xiang's bioengineering projects. I counted a few hundred insect species, nineteen species of trees and shrubs, seventeen soil fungi, thirty-seven vertebrates, sixty-odd worms, and just shy of eight thousand soil bacteria and other small, single-celled organisms. At roughly a couple billion base pairs of DNA for each animal species and a few million for each microbe, that was . . . more than a trillion bases of DNA, in total. Of course, most of that would hardly be modified from the ancestral species, maybe ninety-nine percent, so that only represented some ten billion bases of actively modified, engineered genetic material. By sheer nucleotide count, it was equivalent to Xiang creating two or three new vertebrate species from scratch.

And that was just what Xiang had put in this one valley.

Sometimes I forgot just how much spare time the Xiangs had at their disposal.

I didn't particularly feel like contributing to this planet's biodiversity with my own spare time. Instead, I gave a passing fly a haiku stolen from Xiang's World at Yellow River. The haiku spread, slowly. A red squirrel skittered across a tree trunk to look at me, and I wondered if it appreciated my poetry. I spent the rest of the evening watching the haiku bounce around the local network before petering out.

This wasn't just idle grandiosity, mind you. Yes, writing poetry and watching it disperse artfully among the songbirds was good cover, but more importantly, I needed to see for myself how injected code would spread through Xiang's server network.

It would do. I pulled up a bit of code either much nastier or much more beautiful than the haiku, depending on your tastes—an EIDOLON cloaker tailored to infiltrate the ambient network of a Xiang's World. It was really just the algorithmic seed of a cloaker, but once mature, it would be able to temporarily mask my activity, giving me freedom to deploy my less-subtle assets undetected for a short time.

The cloaker could be defended against . . . if you knew how they worked. Unfortunately for Xiang, EIDOLON algorithms were the product of the posthuman minds of Epicenter Nu, and the products of posthuman minds were forbidden knowledge according to Family rules.

The EIDOLON had its limits. It would only work once, and it couldn't directly affect the planet's harder underground infrastructure. Still, I had every reason to believe the cloaker would serve its purpose when the time came. I was beginning to think I was on a clock here.

It took me more than a full day to tune the cloaker to the forest's protocols. Once it was ready, I called over another fly and fed it my poisoned gift.

It would be hyperbole to say I felt fatherly pride watching my nascent EIDOLON attack diffuse through the forest. But it wouldn't be entirely wrong.

. . .

A ripple of thunderclaps rumbled up from the valley.

That got me out of my hut again. I saw a perfectly vertical thread of smoke spearing up into the sky, anchored a few kilometers down the valley. An instantiation. Another guardinal? The smoke trail warped and dissipated as the last echoes of thunder faded.

My lander hit me with a worried ping informing me that a pair of single-passenger gliders were on approach from the southeast. There was a cloning facility not too far out that way. A couple kiloseconds later I watched the gliders whisper over a ridgeline, heading toward the instantiation site.

A guardinal and at least three clones was an unusually dense crowd by Xiang standards. A visiting Family representative would definitely investigate; Xiang would be expecting me.

That was a shame—I didn't particularly want to expose myself to more face-to-face contact than strictly necessary—but there was nothing to do but head for the instantiation site. I moved as quickly as I could without breaking decorum.

A sparrow intercepted me about a third of the way down the mountainside, carrying a scroll informing me that Xiang had caught the malfunctioning heron and inviting me to assist in the bird's debugging autopsy.

Huh. I'd assumed Xiang would "unfortunately" never find the "malfunctioning heron." I silently put my odds on fifty percent trap, twenty-five percent actual malfunctioning heron, and the rest on some unforeseen outcome that I wasn't pessimistic enough to imagine.

I found three Xiangs at the rendezvous site sitting around a corpse of a rather large heron. It was splayed open in the snow as though a bomb had gone off in its chest. One Xiang sat in Burmese position working meditation, clearly computing furiously. Another paced close by, streaming dozens of active ghostlines into the surrounding woods. The third crouched over the heron, hands buried up to his wrists in the heron's steaming chest. Lines of instrument-bearing ants and beetles coursed into and out of the corpse, scavenging for meaningful details.

On closer inspection, the heron turned out to be more vivisected than busted open. Most of its organs appeared intact.

But not all of them. A mix of biologics spilled out of the remains of a burst protoplasmic sac—mostly some kind of long, black worms, but also smaller gray worms, a couple of malformed mice, a soft-skinned lizard, and even a furry, toothy, teratomic mass. A small clade's worth of arthropods wriggled through the wreckage. I couldn't tell which were Xiang's tools and which came from the body.

The Xiang that was pacing around gave me a formal greeting.

"Am I interrupting your work, brothers?" I asked with a polite dip of my head.

The three Xiangs looked my way and tried to say three different things at once, then shook their heads. They exchanged swift gestures, each one nodded, and two of the bodies melted down into bubbling, popping ectoplasm, leaving a bloody-handed Xiang sitting over the heron's corpse. The disintegrated Xiangs' robes crumbled into a fine ash that melted tiny boreholes down through the snow.

"My apologies," said the remaining Xiang. He removed his hands from the heron corpse and held his hands to the air to be cleaned by sentry mites. "I did not realize you would arrive so quickly, or I would not have greeted you in triplicate. The two of us can proceed alone."

"Allow me to see the body."

Without waiting for a reply, I knelt in the snow next to the heron. Just to hammer in my request, I opened my hands and ghostlines, emphasizing an expansive meaning of "see." Xiang responded by flicking a few dozen tool insects' ghostlines my way.

Data streamed in, flooded in. A hundred thousand scents and tastes. Genomes. Sequences of expressed RNA, processed digests of those sequences. Immune system status markers. A million randomly-sampled cells' identities and coarse-grained states. Vasculature maps. I took in as much as I could, but I had to pipe most of it to my robe for processing just to keep my brain from melting. Figuratively speaking. Probably.

As the data came, I began to panic. I was a trained soldier. I could handle hotdrops. I knew how to make life-or-death split-second decisions. I was not prepared to give a live demo of being a superhumanly masterful bioengineer.

Fortunately I knew how to channel my fight-or-flight responses, so I picked freeze. Once I was sure my limbic system wasn't about to do something idiotic with my body, I dropped into meditation breathing to fight down the panic. I reminded myself that I didn't have to understand everything Xiang was showing me or even most of it. I just had to be able to notice anything seriously amiss. And I had trained for this for years.

Over a few seconds my heartbeat settled down from a terrified flutter to a utilitarian, high-octane pounding, and I returned my attention to the data washing by. I dropped most of it and focused on the summary-level statistics. Genomes from the heron and its personal biome looked as expected, clean with the exception of a parasitic worm that I didn't recognize. The worm appeared only moderately well adapted to the host's immune system, but I couldn't read the errant creature's genome cleanly enough to be confident about that.

"The worms?" I prompted with authority.

"Memory tapeworms. *Platydemus memoria*, a data-caching strain. Heavily defective. One of them infested this bird's bioforge and started synthesizing unauthorized templates, including its own. One of the prints was for neurosurgical amoebae, some of which have entered the brain. They may have caused the bird's . . . misbehavior. Look at this nidopallium caudolateral scan . . ."

This seemed like an awful lot of trouble to fake a bird malfunction, but I could play this game. I didn't really care what crazy mechanism Xiang had concocted to explain away his meddling, but I could at least appear actively engaged.

"This should not have happened," I interrupted. "These worms are designed to run in"—a quick lookup—"roe deer. How could they infect a heron servant?"

Xiang frowned and gave me a surprisingly unseemly growl of frustration.

"Mutation. It broke its safeguards."

Sloppy. "There should have been redundancies."

"Of course there were. It disabled five redundant safeguard systems with three mutations." Xiang tossed a genome into my ghostline feed, annotated with a two-base deletion and a wicked overlapping double inversion.

Three simultaneous mutations? Was that plausible? All of my mercenary instincts screamed "coverup!" and that meant that Xiang was, in fact, hiding something from the Family. Any secret I could uncover would be valuable leverage.

On the other hand, my newly ingrained scientific instincts pushed me to consider alternative hypotheses. The worm's malfunction might be a genuine accident. How likely was that?

I took a deep breath and forced myself to think more like a Xiang. I imagined the worm's genome as a several-million page book filled with A-C-G-T script. Five of the book's ten-thousand-odd chapters described a way to limit the worm's growth to occur only in its intended environments. Three typos across those five chapters had rendered the whole section unintelligible.

In principle, it was easy to understand where those typos might have come from. Every time the worm made a child, it would have to copy the genome-book; with each letter it wrote came a tiny chance of a copying error, a mutation. Xiang's animals used high-fidelity, human-engineered replication machinery, so any particular letter should only mutate about once every trillion copies.

There were probably a few hundred different single edits that could be made to break even the best-written safeguard chapter—a number based on well-documented failure rates of similarly sized chapters-genes—so any particular replication would have somewhere around a one-in-a-few-billions' chance of breaking a safeguard. The probability of three such breaks occurring in the same generation would be that number to the third power . . . about three times every 10^{28} replications. Pretty unlikely.

Then again, there were a lot of worms. A query to a nearby beetle informed me that Xiang's World supported about three billion *Platydemus* worms. A single worm of its kind could reproduce about ten times in a year, so that was thirty billion replications of the genome-book every year. This Xiang's World was at least twenty thousand years old, so the genome had been copied, at most, around six hundred trillion times—still a factor of ten trillion fewer than it should have taken, on average, to produce that kind of triple break.

"This should not have happened," I repeated.

Xiang gave me such a curious look that for a moment I thought I'd somehow blown my cover. Drill-instilled Xiangish countenance kept the rising tide of panic off my face.

"Look more closely at that genome," Xiang commanded.

Okay. Slow down. Xiangs were more patient than a baseline human. They wouldn't rush an analysis like I had.

This time I took my sweet time poking around. Errant sensor ants wandered onto and over my robe. The sun crawled, disappeared behind the Arch, appeared again on the other side.

All at once, I saw it. The worm's genome had too many mutations—not just in the genes controlling environmental restrictions on growth, but everywhere. The worm's total mutation load was about ten thousand times higher than it should have been.

Lots of mutations might indicate a mutagen in the environment, or it might mean there was another upstream mutation compromising the worm's genome-copying machinery.

I checked its DNA replication genes. Payday—one of its core DNA polymerases, one of the most essential machines in the copy editing program, had a three-base insertion. It was just big enough to wedge an extra amino acid into the polymerase's active site. From the state of the worm's genome, I had a feeling that extra amino acid wasn't good for replicative fidelity.

I reworked my math with the updated mutation rate. One mutation every hundred million bases, a few hundred possible mutations per gene, all done three times independently . . . that should take three thousand trillion worms on average.

Xiang's World had only ever had around six hundred trillion worms.

One in five odds. Not exactly likely. But plausible. More than plausible if my math was off in the wrong direction, and I wouldn't have bet money on my genetic engineering arithmetic on the best of days.

"A data-caching worm," I started carefully, "spontaneously generated a mutation in one of its DNA polymerases, leading to a massive increase in mutation rate that fueled a triple mutation allowing the worm to jump species to this heron."

"So it would appear," Xiang replied.

"If so, other worms should show the same mutational profile. I assume . . ."

"Yes, yes, it will be seen to. I have been busy dealing with this."

Well that could explain Xiang's mysterious "unauthorized bioforms." Maybe they were real. They certainly appeared to be real now. They still could have been manufactured just for me, to help Xiang save face against his initially cold welcome. It was either that or they were natural—there was nobody else on the planet to have made them.

"This was . . . unfortunate." What else could I say?

Xiang looked uncomfortable. "It is not the first such incident."

"No? Then you will need protections to ensure it does not happen again. Perhaps a more stringent DNA damage response program is in order."

"I have tried that," Xiang spat.

So Xiangs could get frustrated. That was good to know.

"I have tried stringent DNA responses," Xiang repeated more calmly. "The damage sensor mutates. I have tried redundant DNA polymerases. The backups break almost as quickly as the mainlines. For every solution, there is a way it can break, and in time something always finds it."

"That is why we monitor with external tools. When our creations break, it is our responsibility to repair them." It was surprisingly easy to channel Xiang Family doctrine when I wasn't afraid for my life.

"An inelegant solution," Xiang retorted.

Inelegant? Really, Xiang? "Are a gardener's shears inelegant? Perhaps, but that is the burden of cultivating that which grows. After all, it is man's touch that elevates our worlds above base nature."

"Cultivation is the Family's way," Xiang agreed. "But it is not always enough."

Nothing I could say to that, so I drew him out with silence.

"I have come to appreciate the terrible power of evolution," Xiang continued. "I have seen things wrought from nothing more than selection and mutation, things much worse than these worms . . . I hesitate, now, to build anything requiring my constant guidance."

"What are you suggesting?"

"My world has taught me to pay attention to the evolutionary stability of our creations. I would prefer to expend extra effort upfront to prevent mutations than to combat an actively hostile variation later."

"Yuan Tzu's Second Law of Evolutionary Design," I retorted. Prophylactic effort to prevent undesired evolution increases exponentially with system lifetime—the returns on investment in evolutionarily robust designs always diminish, and quickly. An unwritten corollary was that monitoring and correcting mutations as they popped up would always, in the long term, be cheaper and easier than designing a system that wouldn't evolve out from under you in the first place. Even I, a counterfeit with only a few years' intensive training in evolutionary engineering, knew that one.

"I am aware," Xiang snapped. "It would be impossible to apply enough effort at once to permanently secure our creations. But perhaps the impossible is necessary."

Xiang Family propaganda held that their worlds were stable, eternal. At some point in my training, I had internalized that notion, and foolishly. I imagined letting loose a handful of spores from Cet-1592 . . . it wouldn't take long for them to turn Xiang's beautiful glasshouse garden of a planet into roiling techno-sludge.

"A change hardly seems necessary," I ventured. "Continue to monitor and correct, as you have here, today. That is your duty, and nothing about it seems impossible."

Xiang shook his head while he paced. "Mutational escapes have been becoming more frequent and more disruptive. The trend is not sustainable. This cannot be a failure mode I alone have encountered. Why is it not spoken of among the Family? Has our dogma blinded us?"

"Our way brooks no alternatives," I answered warily. Something unusual was happening to this Xiang, and I was only trained to handle ordinary Xiang bizarreness. This conversation was rapidly approaching the limits of my philosophical acumen. "Human spirit, left unchecked, will always become inhuman."

"Yet," Xiang replied. "The epicenters have lasted nearly half a million years, perhaps changed by evolution but not destroyed by it—How? If only I could . . ."

Xiang halted, pinned by some realization.

If only I could ask them how they do it, Xiang had implied. To invite the foreign, even to desire to, was among the worst crimes a Xiang could commit. If they hadn't updated their tea rituals in tens of millennia, they certainly weren't going to invite in epicenter bioengineering experts to solve their problems.

I couldn't argue against his logic. Not competently. In hundreds of thousands of years of human history, only two epicenters had ever been irrevocably lost, subsumed by the malignant ideology of the First Enemy. Epicenters changed, certainly, but they were protected from self-destruction using mechanisms I'm pretty sure my brain literally wasn't big enough to understand.

Then again, planets were lost to humanity routinely. I wondered if Xiang knew what his planet could become, even if he had epicenter know-how. I had the dubious honor of witnessing the Cet-1592's slide from glittering metropolis to wild, posthuman wonderland. It was a textbook case. Not that the Xiangs allowed themselves to step foot in a bookstore.

Epicenter Zeta's inscrutable AIs had wanted observers on-site, which was where I came in. But the oracles' timelines had been off by a couple of gigaseconds, and by the time my expedition arrived Cet-1592 was a writhing, postbiological technosphere. I'd needed advanced AI support just to interpret what I'd seen on that planet: that hundred-kilometer-tall, grinding pillar of rock is just a sap-sucking bug feeding on a subterranean beast! That fog of nanobots is harmless, it's just the disassembled corpse of a roving data center! Stay away from that pile of crystals, though—it's an ambush predator hungry for your magnesium! Were its ancestors human? No idea!

Cet-1592 was posthuman to the point that it was just post, no human left. We declared the whole system devoid of human life and quarantined the system.

The epicenters faced the same pressures of value drift and runaway evolution as any wunderland, yet somehow they persisted, enduring. I could see how Xiang might be jealous of the AIs' tricks and secrets. Ironic that desiring those techniques was heretical thinking according to the very rules the Xiangs used to prevent their own evolutionary divergence.

A fearful glance from Xiang confirmed that my mark realized his mistake too.

" . . . If only I could communicate with the Family more easily," he finished lamely. "Without cumbersome delays. I am confident we could overcome my challenges together."

With that, Xiang transmuted his transgression into the minor crime of "wishing physics were not as it is." Still a heresy, but not an unforgivable one. Not quite.

I struggled to put on a grave face while I giggled inside. This was, in fact, perfect—had Xiang outright invoked foreign aid, I would have been forced to respond as a representative of the Family, and I wasn't prepared or equipped to do that. Now, though? Now I had cause for suspicion. Suspicion gave me authority and put Xiang on the defensive.

"Repair your tapeworms," I said as I stood and turned to leave. "Put your forest in order."

Xiang bowed deferentially and declined to challenge me as I left.

The next morning, I awoke from a trance sleep, quite refreshed, to find my door overrun by flat-bodied, rust-red beetles. I scattered the bugs with a dispersion order and my most Xianglike scowl. For good measure, I sent Xiang a complaint via messenger sparrow.

No summons came in reply. The day ended. Then the next. Fifteen interminable days passed with no word from Xiang. This was annoying but not surprising—again, Xiangs are patient creatures, and a two-week wait wouldn't faze one any more than it would a hibernating bear.

I'm no Xiang, but military experience gave me plenty of practice waiting. I kept my sanity by watching my EIDOLON cloaker grow and spread.

Larger wildlife started straying near the hut as they adjusted to my presence, which gave me something more interesting to watch. More of those red squirrels and songbirds, but also deer, bamboo rats, quail, bats. I even heard the midday rumbling of a bear claiming its territory somewhere out on the mountainside.

Some of those creatures, as helpful as they were at breaking up my otherwise featureless days, harbored humanlike intelligence, or something akin to it. Whenever deer approached, I made sure to keep my ghostlines locked down tight—if a deer suspected me of fraud, it could easily launch a ghostline assault with the support of the rest of its herd, which I wasn't sure my robe and I could repel.

Finally, on the sixteenth day, a sparrow whose wings bore an ancient character meaning "wind" delivered a tiny scroll with a summons for tea.

It was a big day. It was time for the next step in my plan. Time to ask permission to see a scroll. Not the Arch scroll, of course; rather, something mundane enough that Xiang ought to feel comfortable sharing. I needed to establish a pattern of reading Xiang's scrolls, to make the Arch request safer. I meditated while I waited for the appointed time to keep my excitement—and my nerves—from showing to any prying eyes.

. . .

Xiang met me at the pagoda entrance. He seemed excited, talking faster than usual as he ushered me inside to yet another elaborately arranged array of tea kettles and porcelain cups.

As soon as I sat down my robe yelled a warning at me about CNR-blocker in the air. That was a surprise. I'd assumed the CNR-blocker ploy was over, whatever it was. I silently promised that I would let my robe check any tea for poison before drinking it.

The opening conversational protocols passed quickly this time around, and we slipped quickly into casual conversation. I steered the conversation toward technical matters, offering tricks for efficient underwater networking in exchange for the clone's stories about cold adaptation for commbots. Xiang obliged enthusiastically, tossing esoteric minutiae at me with more verve than I'd seen from him in any previous conversation.

Xiang mellowed fractionally over the course of the evening, and as the sun dropped to the horizon our conversation turned away from shop talk to reminiscence. Xiang spoke of the hard, early days before the planet was properly tamed, including when a solar flare-up forced his work underground for a century. I fed him a few fabricated tales of my own terraforming experiences to balance the conversation.

Bit by bit, the stories wound down. Time to slip in the hook.

"I noticed a comm fly spawning on a river near my hut," I said as casually as I could. "A *Scenopinus* derivative, I believe. I did not understand its foraging behavior. With your permission, I would like to borrow the scroll for its design before I leave, so I might study it between now and our next meeting."

Xiang's face underwent a phase change. His eyes narrowed, his spine straightened. I sensed fresh ghostlines making connections around us, though I couldn't trace their source or destinations with passive scans.

"This is not spawning season for the comm flies," Xiang said, enunciating carefully. "Are you certain that is what you saw?"

Another "unauthorized bioform"? Once was insulting. Twice was just irritating. I could play along, though, to see where this went.

"A misinterpretation is not impossible," I replied. "Or perhaps one of your flies is not behaving as it should. Let me peruse their documentation, and next time we can . . ."

"I believe," Xiang interrupted, "that the hour grows late for technical reading. Do you not agree?"

What? That was as close to a "no" as I'd get from Xiang without being ripped into constituent particles.

"I suppose it is." I tried to keep my voice light, or at least unworried. "Perhaps another time."

I tried to draw the conversation back to nostalgic reminiscence, but Xiang listened too much and spoke too little. I tried injecting a little hurt into my manners, both to cover my rising panic and draw out an apology. I can only assume I succeeded at the former, but Xiang did not oblige me on the latter.

The scroll should have been a safe ask. Xiang was being too paranoid by half, even for a Xiang. What could . . . ?

Oh. There was a rather obvious possibility, wasn't there?

As we exchanged polite farewell rituals, I executed a somewhat unconventional tea-pouring maneuver that let me briefly drag the tip of a sleeve over the rim of Xiang's cup. My execution earned a strange look from Xiang, but no comment. A minute later, as I left the pagoda, I had my answer—the teacup was coated with enough CNR-blocker to drive a baseline human insane. This wasn't just a trace; I finally had my source.

Xiang was poisoning himself? Maybe it was some sort of perverse test, to see if I would catch the poison and alert him to its danger? A real visiting Xiang wouldn't have been able to notice minute traces like I had. Whatever this was, I wasn't supposed to know about it.

Maybe he wanted to be more suspicious? Did he fear he was losing his edge? I couldn't exactly blame him, being an imposter currently two weeks into a deep-infiltration mission on his world, but I couldn't see what would have pushed Xiang to drug himself for paranoia if his clones never had before.

No, I couldn't make sense of Xiang poisoning himself, but who else was there . . . ?

Who else indeed? Was there another agent on the planet?

It would fit, and it would explain some of Xiang's other odd behavior. The poison, the still-unexplained "outbreak" on my arrival, the "malfunctioning" bird—all were consistent with the presence of a second independent actor messing with Xiang for some reason.

That actor must have known I was there, given the depth of their infiltration. Had known for two weeks.

Poisoning Xiang was madness. I had considered the strategy when planning my own heist, but I'd dismissed it as a terrible idea—a crazed Xiang was even more a danger to a disguised infiltrator than a normal Xiang.

Then again, I was just a human. The other agent might not be. An AI might be able to make it work, or might be employing strategies too sophisticated for me to understand or even perceive.

Whoever—or whatever—else was on Xiang's World, they hadn't exposed me yet. What did they want? Were they also there for the Arch? Or had I stepped into something much bigger than a heist?

I considered my options during the cold, snowy trek back to my hut. I almost wanted to tell Xiang about the psychoactives lacing his drinks, but given his current mental state, I didn't want to make any accusations that could possibly be reflected back on me.

I needed proof. The best way to get that was to break into the planet's undermountain and hack Xiang's computing cores. Given how deeply the other agent had already insinuated themselves, I suspected they had beaten me to it; if so, I might be able to find traces of the hack that I could use as evidence.

Unfortunately, accessing the undermountain required a serious intrusion effort.

Fortunately, my EIDOLON cloaker was fully mature now, and hungry to make trouble.

I told it to go nuts.

The EIDOLON code gleefully blanketed the countryside in a fog of carefully calibrated network static. Eventually, in perhaps a day or two, the forest would mount an automated immune response and clear out the disruption. If I ever tried to use the cloaker after that, the forest would catch it and trace it back to me. This was a one-time trick.

For the moment, though, I had near-total freedom of movement within the valley—and under it.

Finding a crack leading to the undermountain wasn't hard. Neither was convincing it to let me inside—the fissure entrance was keyed to

Xiang's genome, which my disguise provided. The rock dutifully logged my access, but my cloaker munched up the report before it could make it to the rest of the forest.

Something chittered at me from behind a rock. I poked my head over the top of the boulder and found myself face-to-face with another of Xiang's incorrigible squirrels. I stunned the squirrel with a brief discharge from my robe and grabbed the body. I didn't think it was there to spy on me, but I didn't want to risk it either. Again, the cloaker smothered any records of the squirrel's demise.

The steaming fissure cracked and peeled apart with a hiss, widening into a steep-sided passage leading down into the rock. A dry, hot wind whistled up from the deep, immediately baking my eyes. The heat only grew worse as I descended. It was hard not to imagine how easily the mountain could squish me flat, if it wanted to. It shouldn't. It wouldn't. But it could.

It occurred to me that I could still leave.

I didn't even have to return to Epicenter Zeta. My gossamer ship could keep me alive more or less indefinitely in deep space with a bit of sunlight for input. It wouldn't be comfortable in any way, but I could live. I might even run into a fellow spacer once every couple of subjective decades. Eventually I could drift anywhere in the galaxy, take up odd jobs . . . somewhere in the galaxy would always want for mercenaries. I could relearn the cultural landscape, pick up another language or ten. It wouldn't be the first time.

But what would be the point? Just considering the idea made me feel deeply, all-consumingly tired.

I decided instead to start planning the parties I would host in my very own prepaid virtual world-space. Free drinks without the hangover, for starters, and maybe a low-g paragliding valley.

Just as the heat became unbearable, the fissure opened up into a massive cavern, lit by the glow of magma far beneath me. From here, I could see the mountain for what it was—a hollowed-out shell a mere few dozen meters thick, built from the same self-healing ultrapolymers typically used in orbital megastructures. Five computronium data cores hung like stalactites from the underside of the mountaintop. Frigid air, drawn from outside, blasted the towers in streamers that shimmered with waste heat for hundreds of meters downwind. Each tower made mockery of my sense of scale; together, they conspired to make the cavern's size feel comprehensible, even manageable.

Just in case, I tried opening a ghostline directly to a core, but the air here was silent on every frequency. I'd have to access it the hard way.

I found a pod hanging on a cable line. I asked it to take me to the scaffold encrusting one of the data towers and it obliged, squeaking steadily back up the cable. I waited until the pod was away from the mountainside before flinging the body of the red squirrel out into a flow of magma.

The pod dropped me at the end of a long walkway leading to the data tower. Heat from the tower burned uncomfortably on my exposed face and hands while a cold, raging wind chilled my back even through my robe and threatened to slam me head-first into the tower. My poor robe struggled valiantly to pump excess heat from my front to my rapidly freezing rear, but it really wasn't built to fight the weather system of a mountain-sized cavern.

Finally, a control panel extruded itself from the data tower and unfurled a wreath of cooling vanes, chilling rapidly in the wind. Once it was safe to touch, I opened a command interface. I wasn't exactly fluent in the console's native calligraphy, but I'd studied enough Pan- and Post-Asiatic scripts to get by, and my robe supplied best-guess translations where necessary.

Accessing ancillary systems took time but wasn't difficult. I've never been a particularly brilliant hacker, but the Xiangs' system defenses are no match for epicenter-derived intrusion tools. Once I had access, I ran a search of the core's recent access logs, which yielded 3.2 terabytes of compressed logs describing who had touched what files and when over the last five years. What luck.

I eyed the core's data repository with heartfelt greed while I waited for my robe to absorb the logs. Everything I needed to leave a rich man was buried deep in those archives . . . and it was useless to me without Xiang's memorized encryption keys. I thought longingly of the unencrypted scrolls sitting on dusty shelves just a kilometer or two over my head.

But that wasn't a viable path anyway. Ancillary system logs I could crack without exposing myself to the core's software ghosts, but the main repository was a completely different level of inaccessible.

There! The logs gave me something juicy—somebody had accessed the data cores three times since my arrival, each time modifying system files that should have been frozen for centuries. Better yet, any explicit system records of the accessions had been deleted, leaving only partially edited timestamps to give them away. Sloppy work—probably not an AI's doing, then—but it had apparently done the job. Whoever had accessed the core could have easily injected a backdoor into any of the planet's wildlife.

A niggling worry pushed itself into my attention—if the intruder already had system access, why were they still here? Why were they poisoning Xiang?

Prize in hand, I left the mountain, returned to my hut, dispelled the cloaker, and sent a scroll-bird to Xiang:

"We must speak in person. I believe the planet's security to be compromised, and I have evidence of an active intruder."

Xiang summoned me right back to the pagoda.

A heron servant instantiated as I approached the pagoda. Even fifty meters down the mountainside, the lightning flash of the instantiation drew brief flashes of rock shadow across my path, and my ears rang briefly from the thunder shock until they repaired themselves.

I should have brought earplugs to Xiang's World. Or tougher ears.

The heron servant was there when I approached the cherry-red pagoda, looming in a steaming crater of aggrieved rock.

Camouflage was still my only viable means of defense—it wouldn't attack me as long as my Xiang disguise held—so I played it cool with the heron instead of following my instincts and fleeing down the mountainside like a scared goat.

The heron servant followed me to the pagoda's entrance, stopping outside in a sentry position. I frowned at the bird and continued inside. Irrationally, I felt safer once out of striking range of the heron servant's beak.

Xiang sat on a mat, surrounded by empty teacups and reams of scrolls, and flicking an inked brush over a scroll. The clone had his robes pulled up to his shoulders, exposing body and flabby arms. Those arms looked weak, but I knew there was more than mere muscle and bone under that loose skin.

Xiang gestured at me to sit without looking up from his scroll. I sat.

"I would like—"

"Why did you access the data cores?" interrupted Xiang.

He knew. How did he know? I took a moment to steady myself.

"I had reason to believe that there might have been a security breach. I took it upon myself to investigate. As it happened, there was—"

"Why did you not come to me first?" Xiang set aside his scroll and stared me down with a predator's focus.

"It seemed prudent for me to investigate myself. A security breach would be a matter of interest to the Family, after all.

Xiang ignored the implied threat. "And you claim to have found . . . what?"

"Someone accessed the data core repeatedly over the last few weeks, and without authorization. They tried to cover their tracks, but they were insufficiently thorough." I sandboxed the relevant data and extended Xiang a ghostline to view it.

Xiang just narrowed his eyes. "Why did you try to cover up your investigation?"

. . . That could mean a few different things. I withdrew the ghostline. "What are you talking about? I did no such thing."

"The data cores say otherwise!" Xiang jabbed his brush in my direction messily. "You changed the core's records to hide your own accession!"

That was an odd accusation given that I had not, in fact, changed the core's records. I tried to ignore the spatter of ink in my beard.

"My access was read-only." I almost lost control of my voice. This was insane. "I never even requested permission to access the core."

"Yes, clearly you accessed them without permission!"

I fought down a sudden instinct to attack Xiang. I couldn't win a fight. Camouflage was still the best defense.

I didn't need to try to kill Xiang to regain the initiative. "Choose your next words carefully. Even if I did access the core, it would have been my right as visiting Family."

Xiang sighed and set down his scroll. "Yes, it would be." He seemed to deflate, limbs going slack, eyes drifting down. "If you were Family. If you were my brother."

It took a moment for the utterly catastrophic nature of my situation to sink in.

I readied my robe's discharger to vaporize Xiang, but the ancient master's body was already self-destructing, drawing in on itself beneath the robes, face melting. My robe warned me of a spike in ghostline activity as Xiang's consciousness streamed out into the pagoda.

"Such a disappointment," Xiang murmured through distorted, bubbling lips. "It has been so very long. I had forgotten how much it hurts to be alone. I wanted so much for you to be my brother. I almost wish I did not have to kill you."

Xiang's melting neck opened up and the body died, hissing and cracking and finally collapsing into steaming residue.

I took exactly one heartbeat to feel sorry for myself before reassessing my situation. First priority—survival. I had minutes at the outside before Xiang reinstantiated elsewhere and began coordinating an active defense.

Until then, I would only have to contend with the planet's innate immune system. Security dust was already accumulating on my skin and clothes. A blanket physical firewall shut them out, and my robe snapped out with tiny electrical arcs as it cleared the air around me. I pulled my hood over my mouth and nose and hoped my internal defenses would deal with anything hostile that I'd already inhaled.

This . . . was not supposed to happen. I didn't really have contingencies for total discovery. Soon the entire planet would be actively hostile, and I would either be in orbit and fleeing or die, contingency plans or not.

Could I bluff my way out of this? No, not with Xiang as drug addled as he appeared to be.

Okay, then I'd have to fight my way out. Bad odds. Might as well go all-in. I could still retrieve the Xiang Arch formula.

It would be on one of the scrolls, but which one? Thousands, tens of thousands of scrolls lined the pagoda's shelf-encrusted walls. I sprinted to the nearest one, picked a scroll at random, unrolled it.

It fell to ash in my hands before I could read it.

Genomic locks? No, I still had Xiang's DNA. The scrolls were protected by some other security measure and I didn't have time to figure out what. I grabbed an armful of scrolls to break later, but they too were already crumbling to pieces. Scorched earth, then. Mission over; no Arch for me.

Nothing left but to survive. Escape. The lander was down in the valley, in one of the forest's many clearings.

I sprinted for the exit. The heron servant was still there, of course, ready to spear me and inject me with some kind of flesh-eating nanotech, no doubt. Or maybe it would just rip out my heart. I didn't really want to find out, so I zapped it with my robe's defensive charge without slowing. The bird exploded into a cloud of sizzling flesh and smoky feathers.

A giddy cackle burbled from my lips as I dashed out into the sparkling snow. Sure, this was a total disaster, but at least I could stop pretending to be a walking avatar of stodginess. Finally, I could have my voice back. Hopefully I'd live long enough to get my body back, too.

I ran for the cliff that dropped down into the valley. Before I could talk myself out of it, I leaped off the edge, into the air. I spread my arms and legs and stiffened my robe into a gliding configuration. It begged me to reconsider—attacking the heron had drained much of its reserves, and it would take hours to eat enough sunlight to fully recharge—but I overrode its pleas. The robe shocked tight as it caught the wind.

I spotted a curious eagle parallelling my flight at a few hundred meters' distance. Could be harmless . . . or deadly. Cursing the bird, I banked away and screamed out a ghostline ping telling my ship to get ready to scram. My robe whined at the strain.

No reply from the ship. Was the lander moved? Destroyed?

No time to think. A bolt of violet light speared down near where I'd leaped off and manufactured a guardinal with a colossal ripping sound. It rose from the blast site and whirled a spear tip my way.

The hairs on the back of my arms stood to attention. I tucked my robe in tight and dove. For a moment the lightning threw my shadow, huge and crisp, onto the mist blanketing the forest. Thunder shook my bones. Then the shockwave from the attack sent me spinning; I let myself tumble into a low-hanging cloud that I hoped would provide some cover.

Why was I alive? A guardinal shouldn't have missed at that range, despite my maneuvering.

Thinking would have to wait. I hurtled past the cloud layer, and suddenly I couldn't see anything but snow-covered forest. My cloak spread itself wide of its own accord and braked, hard. A gust of wind raked loose red leaves against and around me. Hopefully they weren't carrying anything aggressive.

My robe unfurled in a limp strip, forming a streamer parachute in a final, desperate act as its power reserves ran out.

I had time to swear once before hitting the treetops. I curled up around my head and forced my body to relax as much as possible. The world was a painful, lurching blur for a while, until I rolled and plowed up some snow and slid to a halt.

My skull buzzed with the unmistakable grinding of braindust rebuilding broken body parts. Precious moments drained away as I lay in the snow, immobilized by the repair procedure. More sky-tearing sound rippled through the valley as Xiang or the planet manufactured more guardinals to hunt me.

Where could I go once my legs and neck were rebuilt? Escape was impossible without my ship. Nothing to do now but hide from Xiang for as long as I could, until his planet caught me and killed me.

Maybe this was a good time to give up. I could just lie there and enjoy the scenery until a guardinal found me. The fog was clearing up, and the Arch was rather magnificent where it poked out from the prevailing cloud cover . . .

Get up soldier, no time to die today.

Strange. I thought I'd forgotten that voice. I hated it, but I hated the thought of disobeying it even more.

Where to go, then? Away. Obviously. Distance meant time. When my body gave me permission to move, I staggered to my feet, turned my back to the pagoda, and picked a random point on the Arch to walk toward.

I pulled the hood of my spent robe around to cover my mouth and nose again as a crude physical barrier against security mites. My internal security systems could protect me against the mites I'd already ingested, but they could be overwhelmed by too high a dose of pathogen as much as any biological immune system could.

I ran. Trees, grass, and brush sparkled with the clean white of fresh snow. It was unfair how peacefully quiet the forest could be while it was trying to kill me.

Almost without warning, I found myself at the edge of one of the forest's red-rimmed landing zone clearings. A guardinal on the other side was sweeping its spear through the underbrush, assessing the animals it startled out.

I backed away with a surprised grunt. Once I was sure I was out of sight, I ran again.

A branch, hidden by snow, snapped loudly under my foot. Even over my panting, I could hear the guardinal start to lumber in my direction. I couldn't fight a guardinal, not without a functional robe. And even if I defeated it, the planet would just manufacture more. I couldn't overcome the horrendous reserve energy advantage of a planet.

All I could do was run.

Somewhere.

Right then a squirrel, white-bodied and crimson-headed, leaped out of a tree and dashed alongside me, paralleling my flight. It tossed me a ghostline with a text header—Let's make a deal.

Dumbfounded, I took the ghostline offer without slowing.

"You?" I shouted back through our aethereal connection. "You! Who are you? What are you?"

The squirrel ignored me. "Tell me why you're here and I might show you where your ship is," it messaged, still running.

"How do I know—?"

The squirrel interrupted me with what appeared to be real-time video of my lander. It sat in a dense grove of more of the usual scarlet-leaved trees. A guardinal stomped out a patrol around the craft, monitoring the surrounding forest with stony patience.

"So?" asked the squirrel. "Who sent you? Who are you communicating with? Make it quick, the guardinal is catching up."

All at once, the soldier in me drained away. What if I flipped the squirrel's question around? Who was it afraid I was communicating with? This could easily be a trick of Xiang's to suss out who was behind my infiltration attempt. For all the ancient engineer knew, I could be the first scout of an impending invasion. It would make sense for him to tease out as much information as possible before killing me.

But why not oblige? Even if this was Xiang toying with me, it's not as though giving away my secrets would make me any more dead. I had to play to my possible outs.

The sound of tree trunks snapping behind me reinforced the point.

"I'm here for the Arch formula," I blurted over the ghostline. "I'm an independent contractor working to secure a bounty posted by a Seti Engineering Conglomerate. They want to adapt the Arch formula for their megastructures, and I want to get paid obscene amounts of money so I can retire."

The squirrel barked audibly. "I can provide that, but you're taking me with you."

Wait, what?

"I'll bring you your ship," the squirrel continued. "Take me to another planet, somewhere empty, and I'll give you the formula." The squirrel banked away and careened off into the forest.

That's it, I thought. I've been outmaneuvered by a squirrel. The spritely little mammal held all the leverage, and I had no time to work out a counteroffer. It could be a trap—it was probably a trap—but I could see neither a better alternative nor any way a trap could make things worse.

So I ran after the squirrel until my legs ached, then burned. Sentry bots peeled away my mucus membranes, and their pinprick jabs made me cough and slow. After the first kilometer, I turned off my pain perception.

The trees started to weep golden fibers, filling the air and latching onto whatever surfaces they drifted into. I held my breath and braced myself as I crashed into the first of these threads, but they snapped without resistance, letting me through. I glanced back and saw the fibrous webbing thickening, clotting in place, but ahead of me the fibers continued allowing me to pass.

The guardinal fell behind slowly, sieved by trees and their golden webs. My robe, having finally absorbed enough sunlight, switched on and re-established its link to my head. That was good—they wouldn't be much use in a fight, but they could at least help defend my airways.

"We're getting closer to your ship," said the squirrel. "Hold. You'll need something first."

The squirrel took another sharp turn, leaping into the cover of a thick-needled, deeply-bowed fir. I stumbled under the eave and stopped dead.

In the middle of a little clearing under the tree's cover sat a heron servant guarding an egg-shaped, translucent mass perhaps twice the size of my head. It was white like thin milk, and shot through with masses of black and green and gold. The heron gave me an appraising look and settled into the snow-dusted ground with a fluff of its feathers. It didn't kill me, so I figured it wasn't one of Xiang's anymore.

The squirrel stared up at me with stone-black eyes, panting heavily.

I approached the placental mass, keeping as far from the heron servant as reasonably possible. Vibrant masses shimmered from its depths. A memory crystal? Veinlike nets of lymphous fluid connected the masses, and the whole thing pulsed gently. I sent it a tentative ghostline, and to my surprise it responded with a request for an open line. I quarantined the request and stored it away for later.

"What . . . is this?" I asked dumbly. "Can it kill a guardinal?"

"No," the squirrel replied, still sucking in rapid, puffing breaths. "You will take it with you, to my new home. It has instructions."

"Why would I do that?"

"You will leave with it or not at all. That is my bargain."

"Who are you? Why did you come to Xiang's World? What do you want?"

"I did not come here. I have always been here. I want out. I've been watching you—I know you can take me away. Do you want to escape or do you want to die?" The squirrel whipped its fluffy tail in irritation.

"I'll take 'escape,'" I mumbled back. Keeping an eye on the heron, I cautiously picked up the seed. The thing's skin was tougher than it looked, and it clung messily to my fingers.

"Now," I continued, "how are you getting me past that guardinal?"

"I can't," the squirrel admitted. "I've tried to control it, and I've tried redirecting it. Xiang has his guardinals locked down tight. Too much of this forest is under his direct control—if I try anything, I will be detected. That is not an option. I've already risked much with the help I've offered."

I briefly considered blackmailing the squirrel for more assistance, but both the squirrel and I knew that Xiang was unlikely to believe a word I said.

"Bad news," I informed the squirrel. "My robe is shot. There's no way I can sneak past a guardinal, much less fight one. I can zap it enough to notice me or I can send it impolite ghostlines, and that's about it."

The squirrel gave me an impressively recriminating look for a squirrel. "You broke into the undermountain and hacked your way into my mainframe. Surely you have ways to get past a guardinal."

"I covered my tracks with an infiltrate-and-obfuscate attack algorithm, but I can't use it again. And what do you mean 'your' mainframe?"

"Why not? Would it not function?"

"What do you mean the mainframe is yours?" I pressed. "Are you a Xiang?"

"No. I represent the planet. I'm not going to explain right now. Why won't your attack algorithm work?"

"It relies on a one-time pad to hide itself. Emphasis on one-time. If I try activating it again, Xiang will detect it in seconds. That kind of defeats the purpose of a stealth . . ."

I took a deep breath. That wasn't the right way to think. I wasn't a thief trying to infiltrate a compound anymore, I was a soldier trying to get home. I didn't need a stealthy intrusion—I needed informatic heavy artillery.

"I guess that doesn't matter. My program could still throw up enough data-chaff to hide any of your activities in a"—I paused to calculate—"sixteen kilometer radius for half an hour. Give or take. Is that enough for you to help?"

"Yes, it should be plenty of time. Let's go. Begin your attack." The squirrel raced off again, and I followed.

I threw out as large a ghostline net as I could without drawing upon my robe and reactivated my sleeping EIDOLON cloaker. It roused itself with malicious glee, snatching data packets from the network and mangling them into twisted, corrupt fragments.

This time, the forest fought back. I felt it as an oppressive pulse of command-and-control calls and a wash of mind-numbing static as the EIDOLON's messages destructively interfered with that of the forest.

I hoped it would be enough.

We arrived at my ship with no warning from the squirrel, and I almost stumbled into the middle of a silent battleground. I sucked in a breath of awe at the sight.

My lander was surrounded by menacing animals—deer and elk, mostly, but also large birds, a bear, a couple of lynxes, and other creatures. They ringed the lander like a living fence, their attention firmly fixed toward my ship and the guardinal stumbling around it. I could sense a tangle of ghostlines streaming from the animals to the guardinal, and it didn't look like a willing participant.

The guardinal seemed confused, flailing about with its spear as though trying to strike a foe in the dark. It lunged my way, then spun on its foot and unleashed a thunderbolt at some unseen enemy, catching a deer in the blast. The other animals closed ranks to fill the gap.

The squirrel leaped onto my shoulder.

"Just how much of this place do you control?" I whispered to it.

"Keep your ghostline close." The squirrel jumped away to join the assault.

The forest was eerily quiet now, broken only by the hot, huffing breaths of the animals nearest me and the guardinal's thundering steps. It couldn't see me, but it could still crush me if it happened to lunge in my direction.

I squeezed some adrenaline into my system and took a few deep, fast breaths. Heart racing, I squeezed forward between two deer. Heat and musky stink rolled off them like swamp fog—hopefully they would give me good olfactory cover. I clutched the seed close.

I took a last deep breath, shrugged off my robe, flipping the seed from hand to hand to wriggle out of the sleeves, and kicked the robe toward the ship's fore, away from both myself and the guardinal. At my command, it unleashed its meager reserves into one of the guardinal's knees with an electric snap. As the guardinal whipped around to confront this new threat, I sprinted to the lander's aft. I didn't dare open a ghostline to order a ramp extended, but the hull recognized my touch and pulled me inside with an endocytic embrace.

There was a crack from outside. My robe's ghostline went dead.

Almost home.

I rolled out of the lander's cool embrace and into the hold. I set down the seed, which sucked itself up against the metal floor, sticking tight.

I swung myself into the cockpit, nestled myself into a net of crash webbing, and coaxed a physical interface from the wall. I didn't trust a ghostline interface just then, not while a hundred animals lay ghostline siege to a guardinal right outside the hull.

The ship was nervous and had already primed itself for launch. We took off with a roar and broke free of the forest with a light shudder. A lightning bolt from below blew a neat hole clean through the ship, fortunately missing both myself and the egg. Hopefully the hull would seal itself up before we hit vacuum. We chewed up atmosphere while the lander gradually reconfigured for spaceflight. With one final hard burn, we blitzed over the grand curve of the Xiang Arch and screamed past orbit.

No flyers raced up to meet me, no lasers or masers or particle beams slashed through the ship, and no storm clouds blocked my escape. One last gift from the squirrel, I supposed.

I have set a course for the gossamer web ship floating silently in the system's Oort cloud. It can take me back to Epicenter Zeta . . . or to wherever the seed wants to go. I take a few minutes to compose myself and reassure the lander that the danger is past before relaxing into the crash webbing and closing my eyes.

It is done. The metaphorical little Xiang in my head is locked up in paroxysmal confusion over my relief.

Xiang is the fixed point! it yells. All other humans are changed, over tens or hundreds or thousands of gigaseconds, until they are no longer themselves. They lack the discipline to remain human when tempted by technology and possibility. To wish to be other than Xiang is to desire self-annihilation.

I watch that part of myself bubble and rage, then tell it to go to hell. I imagine plucking Xiang's essence out of myself, packing it into a box, and throwing it far away. That doesn't shut up the voice, so I keep repeating the exercise. Each time, Xiang's voice fades a little.

Someday, it might disappear entirely.

All other humans change. I can't say the Xiangs were wrong about that. Will a single human acquaintance of mine still be left at Epicenter Zeta when I return? Will they even be alive? Recognizable? Nineteen hundred years is a long time to be gone. I think of the headless humanoid robots I'd seen wandering through the wreckage of skyscrapers on Cet-1592. I think of the little boxes that whispered endlessly through the Cetian aether: just accept the ghostline, it's safe, I can guide you home. I still don't know whether those boxes were descended from humans, or even if they were sentient.

Somehow the prospect of getting my old body back isn't as comforting as it used to be.

I unhook from the crash webbing and make my way back to the hangar. The opalescent mass is still glued to the floor.

"Time to see what you are," I say out loud. It feels good, voicing thoughts out loud, unguarded, as though I've removed a collar from my neck.

The seed offers its ghostline again. I accept.

An index uploads itself from the seed. It lists proteomes, genomes, biotic and abiotic requirements, developmental programs, secure handshake protocols, ecological flux balances, succession graphs, molecular formulas.

If I'm interpreting it correctly, this seed holds everything required to recreate the entire ecosystem of Xiang's World, given a planet with enough sunlight and a hot core. I am of Xiang and from Xiang, the seed whispers. But I am not Xiang.

Buried deep in the seed's archives is a promise of data. Not the entire contents of Xiang's planetary library, that wouldn't fit in an object this size. But it has more than enough to pay for my journey and set me up comfortably, if I can extract it and get it back to civilization. But it's just a promise. The actual data is heavily encrypted. I might be able to crack it and extract its secrets myself, but I'm guessing the seed will destroy itself rather than spill its secrets before I've fulfilled my half of the bargain.

Nine hundred and fifty-two light-years to get from the Seti Cluster to Xiang's World. Nine hundred and seventy-four years, Epicenter time, to return and collect my pay. Even compressed by relativistic travel, that's forty years—one and a quarter gigaseconds—of travel time left ahead of me. Even waking every few megaseconds, it's going to be a long journey.

And all I have to show for it is a promise of data.

What happened back there? That other agent—the planet, or some part of it gone rogue, it seemed—poisoned Xiang, set him on edge. Why would Xiang's planet poison its own creator? Who benefited from that?

Put that way, it's obvious. The squirrel—no, the planet that the squirrel represented—needed my heist to fail. It needed me to be desperate, so I would take on a volatile packet of compressed ecosystem and haul it all the way to another star, ideally in a way Xiang wouldn't notice. It just wanted me as a vector. A spore of plastic and metal and gossamer solar panels that could drag it through the hostile darkness of space. A spore that wasn't dependent on Xiang.

All of my preparation, all of my training, undone by unlucky timing. I'm a soldier, I should be used to inexplicable bad luck by now.

No. Maybe it wasn't just bad luck.

I am reminded of certain lazy adeno-associated viruses that lack critical machinery for producing copies of themselves. It lays dormant until another virus arrives, and then hijacks the other virus's machinery to reproduce.

Xiang's World must have been the same. How long did it wait, biding its time until some convenient interloper happened to waltz in? I wasn't the victim of bad luck—I was the inciting incident for the planet's prison break.

As much as I hate to admit it, the scheme had worked. The safest thing for me to do now is to follow the seed's instructions. I'll have to find some uninhabited planet, help it take hold, nurture it into a self-sustaining ecosystem. Then, and only then, I can petition the newborn planet for my pay.

And if it refuses, after all of that? As long as the seed withholds its knowledge, I'll be dependent on it. Why would the planet give up that advantage?

Well. If it makes an enemy of me that way, I don't mind dying to take it down.

I check the seed's manifest again. Yes, there—plans for bioprinting devices. Cloning facilities. If the seed cooperates, I can build myself a new body. Maybe my old one.

I ask the ship for a list of nearby star systems with planets compatible with the seed's requirements.

Maybe planet-farming isn't such a terrible way to retire . . . for now.

4

A Model Monster

Heidi Klumpe

LAST WEEK, a monster came for dinner.

"What are you having?" he asked when I answered the door.

"Spaghetti," I said.

"I'm looking for something else," he said. "Do you have any scientific articles?"

"What?"

He pushed himself over the threshold, without waiting to be invited.

I had just finished setting the table for two, but there were three of us now. The monster pushed the table against the bookshelf, and sat in my husband's chair. Pulling an issue of *Nature* from the shelf, he set it on his plate and thumbed through it hungrily. My husband and I perched on the one remaining chair.

"May I get some spaghetti?" my husband asked.

"Shhhh," I said.

Minutes passed in near silence before, suddenly, there was a loud ripping.

"What a delicious Figure 4!" the monster said with delight. "So many edges, so many nodes! A hearty cell cycle model is precisely what I need."

"That was my advisor's work!" I said in shock.

"I am one of his biggest fans. Truly, a model of so many layers has the richest and most complex flavors. Have you got anything more?"

My husband saw a chance to get dinner. "She's got an entire stack in the bedroom. Just by the bed."

"Excellent!" The monster stood up at once, upending the table. All the dishes collided with each other on the floor. The monster waddled down the hall, and the talons on his feet shredded the carpet.

"He's making a mess!" I said.

"Those papers are a mess," my husband said, and headed to the kitchen.

"I was going to read them!" I called after him.

"No, you weren't!" he called back, through a mouthful of noodles.

After dinner, the monster asked to be let outside to sleep, but he was back again early the next morning. When I came into the kitchen for breakfast, he was at the counter, eyeing a glass of orange juice with haughty suspicion. My husband clutched his coffee to his lips and seemed resigned.

"Ah, the lady is in the kitchen at last!" the monster called.

I turned to my husband. "Jacob, what is he doing here?"

"Not to impose," the monster interjected, "but I'm craving an ambitiously knotted immunological model, preferably of the entire human immune system, the kind that will expand in my stomach with delicious high dimensional output."

Jacob hid his eyes in his coffee and said, "I told him he could go to work with you."

"With me?" I asked. "Isn't it easier to keep him in your home office than sneak him onto a college campus?"

I turned to the monster with a plan of my own.

"Did Jacob offer you anything for breakfast? He has piles of papers in his office too."

"Does he?" the monster asked.

"Yes! Though most of them are crumpled up. And on the floor."

"That sounds most diverting! Let's have a look." The monster jumped off the barstool and ambled off, while Jacob spewed coffee into the kitchen sink.

"Those sketches are my important brainstorming material!" he exclaimed.

I sipped the orange juice. "Oh Jacob. You're the only one I know who finds ideas in the trash."

But now there were sounds of deep sadness from Jacob's study, and at a monstrous decibel. We rushed in to find the monster on the floor, weeping in a pile of discarded logo drawings. He held a page with only a tentative bite in one corner.

"No, no, no. This will never do! Look at this sketch, so clear in its purpose and design. The lines have meaning here; they draw the eye and intentionally inspire reflection. I need something bizarre and ill-conceived, overwhelming and obfuscating! Please, are there no more biological models in this house?"

In the brief silence, I heard elderly Mrs. Next-door Neighbor calling to hear if our cat was all right. We do not have a cat. And we did not want a monster.

"Fine," I said. "Come with me to work. There's a section of the library I think you might like."

Somehow he folded his wingspan into the backseat of my car, and we drove to the campus library. I pulled him quickly through the lobby, as he looked a little too happy to be surrounded by so much print material.

We took the stairs down to the deserted basement. There was the shelf: "Print Journals Available Online." There weren't any comfortable reading chairs nearby, let alone students. Destroying any part of a library would be criminal, but this would at least be forgivable.

The monster, so eager in my home, was cautious here. "I don't recognize most of these titles. This is far from my usual dietary oeuvre."

"I know it's scary to read unfamiliar journals," I said, "but it's not so bad. Look, I bet you'll love every page of this one."

I held up a turquoise edition of something called *Omics Reviews*.

"Hmmm," he sighed. "The cover holds promise. I only judge by the images, you know. I can't actually read."

Holding the magazine as though it smelled bad, he daintily turned the pages. Then, he gasped and let out a fiery snort of laughter.

"These acronyms will do the trick!" he said happily. "It's been so long since I had such a thick alphabet soup."

"Great," I said, and hoped I was smiling.

"I wonder why you humans even bother rearranging letters into words. They are so resonant as shapes, such lumpy works of art. Yes, I think I will be happy here. You may return for me in a few hours."

"What, I—"

"No, please. I insist. You would not enjoy an old monster's endless reflection on the delights of modeling and biology, though I assure you, I am the finest connoisseur. I make recommendations directly to the administration at this school. That's how I found you, you know."

He took an overlarge bite out of *Biophysical Mechanisms and Control*, and shredded paper slipped from between his lips.

"What do you mean, that's how you found me?"

The monster grinned. "I have been added to your tenure committee! Naturally, they want my take on your models. Certainly, others may read, cite, or replicate your work, but how can anyone get a feel for it until they have rolled it around in their mouths, felt the spice of stochasticity and sweetness of deterministic equations? I can tell when parameters blend in a perfect mix, and when they compete with each other's flavors. I've held all of machine learning in my mouth, and only winced twice. And, well, I don't want to sample your work on an empty stomach. But . . . I am feeling rather full now."

He did seem fuller. And bigger somehow. He was nearly as large as the bookshelf. For the first time, the majority of his eyes were pointed at me.

"You know," I stammered for time, "I am happy to write up a supplement. Maybe I could talk to the committee on the phone or by email. I am very avail—"

The monster took a shuddering step forward. The library leaped a centimeter off its foundation.

"No, no, don't you see? They don't need more to read. They've done that. They want to know how your model will digest, how it will move through the bowels of history. Now, where can I find your latest manuscript?"

"Well that's a complicated question. It's under review and um—"

"Unpublished!" he squealed giddily, and a rain of saliva wet the library floor. Another ponderous step forward, and I could no longer see the exit above his shoulder. I looked around wildly and spotted a bathroom behind me. I backed away slowly, and then ran for it. The monster followed.

"You see, there's another thing we love about your models," he called to me, oblivious to the sounds of the campus emergency system. "They have this entirely novel character that many find difficult to express. Some say it is the complexity, others say the attention to detail. Do you know what I think?"

There were rushing feet upstairs, but the monster was knocking over library shelves to block access via the staircase. He was also closing the gap between us. The bathroom was still feet away. I leaped for the handle, jumped in, and yanked the door shut. I had a fleeting glimpse of a monster grown to the size of a delivery truck. My hands vibrated with electric shock as I rotated the lock. He was very close now.

"Surely you've got it by now, haven't you?" he called through the door. "What everyone feels when they look at your equations, the endless methods, the archaic symbols?"

I heard him put a monster mouth at the base of the door, clink his teeth against the threshold, and whisper: "Fear."

In the following silence, I tried not to shake. I was thinking of a first year graduate student who was looking for a yardstick to measure her worth with. I wondered if she'd started hitting people with it. I wondered if she would always feel small.

The door shuddered, like a monster shoulder had been thrown against it.

"There's so much I could do for you," he yelled, "if you'd just let me have one bite!"

I slid to the floor, unsure whether to weep or to enjoy having my hands still attached to my arms. Years of scientific training had provided no survival instinct. Mentors past floated through my mind, providing only muffled shouts about control experiments and lab notebooks. Long monster talons creaked through the cracks between door and frame, and the one barrier between me and the monster crumbled into his outstretched claw.

The monster's sneer filled the doorframe. His largest eye peered through.

I stood up shakily. "Please eat me quickly."

He blinked. The angry eyebrow tightened.

"If you do not give me what I ask for, the consequences will be dire."

In a deranged dance, I started waggling various body parts. "I'm not particularly attached to my left foot since it's no use in soccer, but also, my right elbow has a habit of banging into things."

The large eye rolled.

"Your dullness increasingly tries my spirits."

My much smaller eyes stared back.

"I'm sorry, but what is it you want exactly?"

A monster fist hit the floor.

"To satiate my hunger! For years, I fed myself books containing the gustatory delights unique to deep truth, but then nothing new was left. I ate wild for years, searching for any hint of these flavors again, but the secrets burrowed deeper. Eating so much, I was still empty! If there is nothing to discover in plain sight, then I will find the best secrets, just at the edge of what is known, in the incomprehensible—things that are large, ambitious, and overwhelming!"

"But that's never going to work."

"I beg your pardon!" he said in a way that did not convey any need for pardon.

I raised my voice to match his. "If you want surprise and novelty, you should at least start with what you think you understand! Complexity and insight are not the same thing!"

"And you have confused sense with absurdity! As though the newest and hardest to understand models were not the most true . . ." he sputtered with frustration. He was straining, as though he might squeeze skull-first through the door. But the anger was draining out of him.

I had a sudden idea. I pulled out my phone to make a sketch in a note taking app.

"I'm sure you know," I said, "that humans have done a fairly good job of mapping out how proteins interact with each other, at least in some living things. But can you guess the most common pattern for these interactions?"

"What? You mean the wirings of activation or repression between genes? It must be colossal and impossibly intricate. I would love to chew it."

"I agree, it is a hard problem. But an interesting one! I can give you a simple answer, for three proteins interacting in a simple bacterium."

"Bah! Three? Who would care?"

"So you know what it is?"

"Yes! Obviously. I am sure I read this once. Biology is complex, and benefits from many interactions, so every node should be connected, in both directions."

I waited. He deflated slightly and amended his statement.

"But successful biological systems rely on proper control, so perhaps a feedback loop would be more precise for the cell's needs."

He continued to shrink, and more of his eyes came into view. I struggled to keep eye contact with all of them.

"But if I consider the problem statement, you said *most* common. If we assume that evolution has protected biological systems from mutation by limiting the number of important interactions, then on average, most proteins do not interact. Therefore!" He flourished with triumph. "You expect only one interaction."

I shook my head and showed him the drawing on my phone. "It's a feedforward loop. There is one protein that activates another protein in two different ways."

His eyes narrowed. "Why on earth would evolution design things in such a way?"

I shrugged. "We don't really know yet. But it is very satisfying to know what it is, even if we don't know why."

"Strange," he said, "that something so small could also be so satisfying."

His eyes refocused suddenly, as though seeing me for the first time.

"How could I acquire more of—um—*that*?" He nodded in the general direction of my phone.

"I wish I knew," I sighed. I thought back to graduate school again. There had been another monster. Pocket-sized, he sat on my shoulder and squawked loudly into my ear: "You can't explain why! It's too complicated! Don't understand!" It took ages to silence him, working dully and perpetually on the same problem as it rolled sullenly around in my head. But he and I reached mutual peace in the end.

It had been years since I had thought of him. I wondered what he would say now. I broke eye contact with the ceiling to look at the scaly beast still staring through the bathroom door.

"Do you think you could wait a while to find out?" I asked.

A final shrinkage brought the whole monster head into view. He nodded.

The first step was to get him to my office. I snuck him out of the library in the loose imitation of a dog. "Bark. Bark," he said, forgetting that all dogs prefer exclamation points. People upstairs wondered aloud about an earthquake.

In his first few days in my office, he impersonated a carnivorous plant. After one too many students approached him with outstretched fingers, he moved into a dog crate under my desk. Sometimes he disappears to visit his monster lair, but he always comes back. While he had been lying about the tenure committee, he had not lied about his cravings.

Now he waits. I show him what I'm working on, and what other people are doing. If he has been very good, I bring him the scribbled notes left on the table after group meeting. If he has been howling about cravings for phase separation in the cytoplasm or something else he thinks is "paradigm-shifting," I print out unrelated Wikipedia articles and slide them into his crate.

Mostly, we try to understand and surprise each other.

5

Chrysalis

David Brin

Originally published October 2014 in *Analog*

Like every person who ever contemplated existence, I've wondered if the world was made for me—whole and new—this very morning, along with counterfeit memories of what came before.

Recollection is unreliable, as are the records we inherit each day. Even those we made the night before—our jotted notes or formal reports, our memorials carved deep in stone—even they might have been concocted, along with memories of breakfast, by some deity or demon. Or by an adolescent twenty-eighth-century sim-builder, a pimpled devil, playing god.

Find the notion absurd?

Was that response programmed into you?

Come now. History was always written by the victors, while losers passed their entire lives only to be noted as brief speedbumps. And aren't all triumphs weathered by time?

I sound dour. A grumpy grownup. Well, so it goes, when tasked with cleaning messes left by others. Left by my former self.

And so, with a floating sigh of adulthood, I dive into this morass—records, elec-

tronic trails and "memories" that float before me like archaic dreams. Ruminations of an earlier, ignorant—not innocent—me.

It all started medically, you see. With good intentions, like so many sins.

January 6, 2023:

Organ replacement. For a generation it was hellishly difficult and an ethical nightmare. Millions lingered anxiously on waiting lists, guiltily *hoping* that a stranger out there would conveniently crash his car—someone with identical histocompatibility markers, so you might take a kidney or a liver with less probability of rejection. His bad luck transforming into your good fortune. Her death giving you a chance to live.

Even assuming an excellent match, there'd be an agony of immunosuppressant therapy and risk of lethal infections. Nor was it easy on us doctors. When a transplant failed, you felt you were letting *two* patients down, both recipient and donor.

Sci fi dystopias warned where this might lead. Sure enough, some countries started scheduling criminal executions around the organ want-list. Granting reprieves till someone important needed a heart . . . your heart. Then, off to disassembly.

When micro-surgeons got good enough to transplant arms, legs and faces—everything but the squeal—we knew it was only a matter of time till the Niven Scenario played out. Voters would demand capital punishment for more than just heinous crimes. Your fourth speeding ticket? Time to *spread you around*. Is it really death, when nearly all your parts live on, within a hundred of your neighbors?

Hell gaped before us. There had to be a better way.

And we found it! *Grow new parts in the lab.* Pristine, compatible and ethically clean.

Caterpillar eat! Chew that big old leaf.
Ugly little caterpillar, your relief,
When you've chomped your fill, will be to find a stem.
Weave yourself a dressing room, hang in it, and then
Change little caterpillar, grow your wings!
Now go find your destiny. Nature sings.

When we started trying to form organs *in situ*, George Stimson claimed the process would turn out to be simple. He offered me a wager—ten free meals at his favorite salad bar. I refused the bet.

"Those are your stakes? Lunch at the Souplantation? Acres of veggies?"

"Hey, what's wrong with healthy eating? They have the genuine stuff."

"My point exactly, George. Every time we go there, I look at a plate full of greens and think: *this* is what *real* food eats!"

He blinked a couple of times, then chuckled at my carnivorous jibe before swinging back to the main topic—building new human organs.

"Seriously. I bet we can get away with a really simple scaffold. No complicated patterns of growth factors and inhibitors. None of *this* stuff."

He waved at the complex map of a human esophagus that I had worked out over the weekend—a brilliantly detailed plan to embed a stretchy tube of plastic and collagen with growth and suppression factors. Along with pluripotent cells, of course, the miracle ingredient, cultured from a patient's own tissues. Some of the inserted chemicals would encourage the stems to become epithelial cells *here* and *here*. Others would prompt them to produce cartilage *there* and muscle-attachment sites *here* and *here* and . . .

. . . and George thought my design way too complex.

"Just lace in a vascular system to feed the stems," he said. "They'll do the rest."

"But how will they know which adult cell type to turn into?" I demanded. "Without being told? How will you get these interleaved fans and arrays of connective tissues and tendons and vessels and glands . . ."

This was way back near the turn of the century, when we had just figured out how to take skin or gut cells and transform them back into raw stems, a pre-differentiated state that was *pluripotent* or capable of becoming almost any other variety, from nerves to astrocytes to renal . . . anything at all! Exciting times. But how to assign those roles in something as complex as a body organ? We had found specific antigens, peptides, growth factors, but so many tissues would only form if they were laid out in ornate patterns. As complex as the organs they were meant to rebuild or replace.

Patterns we were starting to construct! Using the same technology as an ink-jet printer, spray-forming intricate 3-D configurations and hoping someday to replicate the complex vein patterns within a kidney, then a spinal cord, and eventually . . .

"We won't have to specify in perfect detail," George assured me. "Life will find a way."

I ignored the movie cliché. Heck, why not try his approach in a pig or two?

We started by ripping out a cancer-ridden esophagus, implanting a replacement made of structural polygel and nutrients. This scaffolding we'd lace with the test animal's own stem cells, insert the replacement . . .

Whereupon, *voila*. Step back, and witness a miracle! After some trial and error . . . and much to my astonishment . . . George proved right. In those first esophagi we implanted—and in subsequent human tests—my fine patterns of specific growth factors proved unnecessary. No need to command them specifically: "*You* become a mucus lining cell, *you* become a support structure . . ." Somehow, the stems divided, differentiated, divided again, growing into a complete adult esophagus. And they did it *within* the patient!

"How do they know?" I asked, despite expecting in advance what George would say.

"They don't *know*, Beverly. Each cell is reacting only to its surroundings. To chemical messages and cues from its environment, especially its immediate neighbors. And it emits cues to affect *them*, as well. Each one is acting as a perfect—if complicated—little . . ."

". . . cellular automaton. Yes, yes."

Others, watching us finish each other's sentences, would liken us to an affectionate old married couple. Which in several ways we were. Few noticed the undercurrent of scorching rivalry that by now spanned decades. Spectacularly successful teamwork, as far as the world was concerned.

Well, the world was easy to fool. As we both had been, two or three marriages ago, each, back when George was the most handsome, brilliant and *vital* man I ever knew . . . and when I used to so look forward to looking into a mirror or appearing on Science Channel shows. Now? They all still called us brilliant, at least. Though I have also heard *cranky* and *curmugeonly* . . .

Well, well, scientific detachment doesn't mean we're immune to grumpiness over life's inevitable decline. In fact, it stokes an outraged retort:

Who says it's inevitable!

George and I still shared a simple cause. To spit death in the eye at every turn.

"So," I continued, "just by jostling against each other in the chemical pattern of the scaffold, that alone is enough for the stem cells to sort themselves out? Differentiating into dozens of types, in just the right geometry?"

"Geometry, yes." George nodded vigorously. "Geometrical biochemistry. I like that. Good. Isn't that how cells sort themselves into vastly complex patterns inside a developing fetal brain? But of course you see what all of this means."

He gestured along a row of lab benches at more recent accomplishments, each carefully tended by one or more students.

—a functioning liver, grown from scaffolding inside a mouse, till we carved it out. The organ now lay *in vitro*, still working, fed by a nearby blood pump—

—a cat whose lower intestines had been replaced by polygel tubing . . . that was now completely lined with all the right cells: in effect two meters of fully functioning gut—

—two dozen rats with amputated fore-legs, whose stumps were encased in gel-capsules. Along simple frameworks, new limbs could be seen taking shape as the creature's own cells (with a little coaxing from my selected scarring inhibitors and stem-sims) migrated to correct positions in a coalescing structure of flesh and linear bone. Lifting my gaze, I saw cages where older creatures hobbled about on regrown appendages. So far, they were clumsy, club-like, footless things. Yet, they were astonishing.

And yes, I saw what George *meant.*

"We always assumed that mammals had lost the ability to regenerate organs, because it doesn't happen in nature. Reptiles, amphibians and some fish can regrow whole body parts. But mammals in the wild? They . . . we . . . can only do simple damage control, covered by scar tissue."

"But if we *prevent* scarring," he prompted. "If we lay down scaffolds and nutrient webs—"

"—then yes. There emerges a level of self-repair far more sophisticated than we ever imagined possible in mammals."

I shook my head. "But it makes no sense! Why retain a general capability when nature never supplies the conditions to use it? These latent repair systems re-emerge only when we provide the right circumstances in our lab."

George pondered a moment.

"Beverly, I think you're asking the wrong question. Have you ever wondered: why did mammals lose . . . or give up . . . this ability in the first place?"

"Of course I have! The answer is obvious. With our fast metabolisms, we have to eat a lot. No mammal in the wild can afford to lie around for weeks, even months, the way a reptile can, while waiting for a major limb or organ to regrow. He'd starve long before it finished. Better to concentrate on things mammals are good at, like speed, agility and brains, to avoid getting damaged in the first place. Mammalian regeneration probably vanished back in the Triassic, over a hundred million years ago."

He nodded. "Seems a likely explanation. But what's puzzling you—" He prompted me with a lifted eyebrow, a coaxing gesture of encouragement that I used to find charming, almost back in the Triassic.

"What puzzles me is why the capability has been hanging around all this time! Lurking in our genome, never used!"

George held up a hand.

"I think we're getting ahead of ourselves. First, let's admit that humans have changed the balance, the equation. We are now mammals who *can* lie around for weeks or months while others feed us. First the family and tribe took up this duty, back in the Stone Age, then village and town and—"

"—and Canadian National Health, sure. And those innovations increased *survival rates* after serious injuries," I admitted. "But it never resulted in organ or limb *regrowth*!"

Abruptly I realized that half a dozen grad students had lowered their tools and instruments and were sidling closer. They knew this was historic stuff. *Nobel-level* stuff. Heck, I didn't mind them listening in. But shirking shouldn't be blatant! I sure never got away with it, back when *I* served my time as a lab-slave. My withering glare sent them scurrying back to their posts.

Oblivious, as usual, George simply blathered on.

"Yes, yes. For that to happen, for those dormant abilities to re-awaken, it seems we need to fill in all sorts of lost bits and pieces. Parts of the regrowth process that were mislaid across—what's your estimate, again?"

"A hundred million years. Ever since advanced therapsids became fully warm-blooded, early in the age of dinosaurs. That's when major organ regrowth must have gone dormant in our ancestors. Heck, it's not surprising that some of the sub-processes have faded or become flawed. I'm amazed that any of them—apparently *most* of them—are still here at all!"

"Are you complaining?" he asked with an arched eyebrow.

"Of course not. If all of this holds up," I waved around the lab, now quadrupled in size, as major funding sources rushed to support our work, "the therapeutic implications will be staggering. Millions of lives will be saved or improved. No one will have to languish on organ donor waiting lists, praying for someone else to have bad luck."

I didn't mention the other likely benefit. One more year of breakthroughs and the two of us would be shoo-ins for Stockholm. In fact, so certain was that starting to seem, that I had begun dismissing the Nobel from my thoughts! Taking for granted what had—for decades—been a central focus of my life, my existence. It felt queer, but the Prize scarcely mattered to me anymore. I could see it now. A golden disk accompanied by bunches of new headaches. Speeches and advisory panels. Public events and "inspirational" appearances, far more than George would face, because every charismatic woman scientist has to go the rounds, doing *role model duty for girls*. It would all add up to pile after pile of distractions to yank me from the lab.

From seeking ways to save my own life.

But especially from finding out what the heck is going on.

The cicada labors seventeen years
Burrowing underground,
Suckling from tree roots,
Below light or sound.
Till some inner clock commands
"Come up now, and change!
"Grow your wings and genitals

"Forget your humus range."
So out they come, in adult form,
To screech and mate and die.
Mouthless, brief maturity,
As generations cry.

We dived into the genome.

One great twentieth-century discovery had been the stunning surprise that only *two percent* of our DNA consists of actual codes that prescribe the making of proteins. Just 20,000 or so of these "genes" lay scattered along the forty-six human chromosomes, with most of the rest—ninety-eight percent—composed of introns and LINEs and SINEs and retro-transposons and so on . . .

For a couple of decades all that other stuff was called "junk DNA" and folks deemed it to be noise, just noise, can you believe it? Dross left over from the billion years of evolution that has passed, since our first eukaryotic ancestor decided to join forces with some bacteria and spirochetes and try for something bigger. Something more communal and organized. A shared project in metazoan life.

Junk DNA. Of course that never made any sense! It takes valuable energy and resources to build each ladder-like spiral strand of phosphates, sugars and methylated nucleic bases. Darwin would have quickly rewarded individuals who pared it all down. Just enough to do the task at hand, and little more. Redundancy is blessed, but efficiency is divine.

Eventually, we found out that much of the "junk" was actually quite important. Sequences that served a vital function, regulating *when* a gene would turn on to make its protein, and when it should stop. Regulation turned out to take up heaps of DNA. And much of the rest appeared to be recent infestations from viruses—a creepy fact to ponder, but of no interest to me.

For a while, as stretches of regulatory codes gave up their secrets, some folks thought we had a complete answer to the "junk DNA problem."

Only, vast stretches remained mysterious. Void of any apparent purpose, they didn't seem to do anything at all. And they were much too big to be just punctuation or spacers or structural elements. The *junk theory* came back as colleagues called those big, mystery patches meaningless relics . . .

. . . till George and I made our announcement.

Fish are fish are funny folk,
They never laugh and never joke.
When mating, there is no romance,
Just a throng, a whirling dance.
Then commence . . .

. . . the winnowings—
Ten billion sperm, ten million eggs,
Produce a hundred thousand larvae,
Hundreds survive, become fish,
For maybe two to start it over.

CBC - The Q: Welcome back, I'm Sandra Oh and this is the Q. We're having one of our live music and interview shows, coming to you in sparkling 5-D from the Great Plains Theater in Winnipeg. We'll get back to tonight's fantastic noppop group, *The Floss Eaters*—yes, let it out for them! Only now let's all calm down and welcome onstage our special guests. Give a warm welcome to Manitoba's brightest science stars—Beverly Wang and George Stimson.

Professor George Stimson: Thank you Sandra.

Professor Beverly Wang: Yes, it's good to be on your lively show. My, that last song was . . . Can-Do Invigo-Rating.

SO: Ha ha! Cana-do indeed. Totally with-it. You've won the crowd over, Madame Professor. It's not grampa's rock 'n' roll, eh? Now hush you folks in the seats. We only have Bev and Geo for a few minutes before they must go back to changing our world. So let me start with Beverly, on behalf of folks here and in our audience around the globe. We've all been amazed by the success you both sparked in re-growing individual organs and body parts, giving hope to millions. Is it true that you've also done it *yourselves*?

PBW: Well, yes, I have a new kidney and liver, grown in vats from my own cells. I was offered regular transplants—they found a match. But it seemed more honest and true to use our methods myself, as one of the first volunteers. So far, the new parts have taken hold perfectly.

SO: And you, George?

PGS: My own grafts were less ambitious . . . mostly to deal with widespread arthritis. Joint and tendons. Reinforcement and replacement.

SO: How'd that go?

PGS: Shall I juggle for you?

SO: Hey now, doc, those water bottles are . . . wow! That's some talent. Let's hear it for Circus Stimson!

PGS: Well, I used to show off in college . . . it's been years, but it seems that . . . oops!

SO: No sweat, we'll clean it up. That's an impressive demonstration of restored youth and zest! Still, we're always wondering on the Q . . . *what's next*? What do you have cooking beyond grow-your-own-organs? I have to tell you we hear rumors that you've got something even bigger brewing. Called the *Caterpillar Cure*?

PGS: Well now, Sandra, that's not a name we use. It arose when we described taking a deathly ill test subject and wrapping or encasing the whole body in a protective layer—

SO: A cocoon!

PGS: Hm, well yes. In a sense. We then trigger processes that have long lain dormant in the mammalian toolkit. We've become quite adept at extrapolating and filling in lost or missing elements. Whereupon we give the body every chance to repair or regrow or even replace its own component parts without surgical intervention, in a way that's wholly . . . or mostly . . . natural.

SO: Wow . . . I mean, wow! I haven't heard applause that wild from a live audience since we had both Anvil and Triumph on the show, playing together in Ottawa. Now settle down folks. Professor Wang, may I ask how you feel about the way pop culture is interpreting some of this? A cluster of quickie-horror Pollywood flicks have suggested that this *awakening of long-dormant traits* might go awry in spectacular ways. Have you seen any of these cable-fables?

PBW: Just one, Sandra. At a lab party, some of our students played *It's Reborn!* for laughs. We all found it hilarious.

SO: So we *won't* be seeing all sorts of ancient throwbacks coming out of these cocoons? No bodies repairing and restoring themselves back into, say, Neanderthals? Or dinosaurs? Or gross slime?

PBW: Not any Neanderthals or dinosaurs, I promise. And there's a reason. Because all of us, from you and me down to a newborn baby, are in our final, adult form.

SO: Babies . . . are adults?

PBW: This may take a minute. You see, all animal life originally passed through *multiple phases*, and it is *still* true for a majority of complex species, like insects, arthropods, and most fish.

Mating *adults* make embryos or eggs. Eggs create the *larval stage*, in vast numbers, whose job it is to eat and grow. A small fraction of larvae survive to transform again—as when insects *pupate*, for example a caterpillar's cocoon—turning at last into the *imago* or adult form, whose primary job is to complete the cycle. You know . . . with sex.

SO: Clearly a favorite word for some of you out there. Settle down. So Dr. Stimson, what does this—

PBW: The basic principle is called *holometaboly*, or complete metamorphosis, and it's one more example of Nature's cleverness. This phased approach to life partitions youngsters and adults into completely different worlds, so that neither competes with the other. It's such a successful way of life that it's used by the majority of insects, and therefore, the majority of all animals.

SO: Wow. Okay then George, why—

PBW: But some life orders have abandoned the old process. For birds, reptiles, marsupials and especially placental mammals, all the early phases seem to have been compacted down into the early embryonic period. It all takes place within the egg or the mother's womb. Though incomplete and neotenous, our human infants are born already in the *adult* stage. And hence when a patient undergoes recuperative chrysalis—

PGS:—none of them ever comes out with ancient traits like bony eye-ridges or tails or swinging from lamp posts. At least, none so far!

SO: So far? You mean there's still hope! I was sort of hankering for a nice tail.

PGS: If it ever proves possible Sandra, I promise you'll be one of the first people we'll inform.

Tadpole swishes tail
Breathes water, while preparing
Brand new lungs and legs

Lab Notes: George Stimson—8/8/2030

I was annoyed with Beverly. We had been asked to keep things light, not wonkish, for the CBC broadcast. She gets so pedantic and lectury. As if I didn't get enough of that when we were married. And then again, when she meddled in my second marriage, telling us how to raise our—oh never mind.

And yet, her ad hoc little rant about *stages of life* stayed with me, afterward, prodding at my subconscious.

Of course I already knew all that—about embryo-larva-pupa-adult metamorphosis. It's basic high school bio. Still, the notion would not let go of me. And I wondered.

We've accomplished "miracles" by uncovering traits, tools, and processes that have lain dormant in the human genome for a hundred million years, ever since mammals abandoned organ replacement for a quick and agile lifestyle. Beverly and I have guaranteed ourselves lasting fame by learning tricks to fill in the lost portions of code and restart the processes of organ regrowth. In fact, the techniques helped save both our lives, staving off our own health problems for the time being, letting us enjoy our renown for a little while.

That may satisfy her, but I've always been kind of an insatiable bastard. And I can't help wondering.

Despite all our progress, we've only explained another five percent or so of the mystery DNA. Even after filling in methods of organ regrowth, lost since the Triassic, there remains another whole layer of enigmatic chemistry. Huge stretches of genetic code that are both still unknown and clearly even older than a mere hundred million years!

Oh, it's pretty clear by now that the bulk of it *is* somehow related to organ regrowth, but in some way that I still don't understand.

It's infuriating! I've been plotting codes, cataloging and interpolating most of the likely missing pieces. Without these lost switches, the dormant genes have languished, unused for ages. Till now, I have only dared experiment with the switches one at a time, in petri dishes, almost never in whole animals higher than a vole. And never *all at once.* Not without a theory to explain what they're for.

Only now, I'm pondering a new hypothesis. A good one, I'm sure of it! Beverly's blather about *life phases* made me realize just how far back this new layer of code really goes.

Extrapolate the decay rates and one thing is clear from clock drift measurements. This second layer of mystery genes goes back not *one* hundred million years . . .

. . . but almost *three* hundred million! All the way to the early Permian Period, when amphibians were mostly pushed aside by the ancestors of reptiles, birds, dinosaurs, and mammals. All of whom *gave up* the multi-stage style of living. Skipping the larval and pupa phases and spending all their lives as adults.

Astonishing. Can the second layer of dormant DNA really come to us from that far back?

It appears to! Which demands the next question. Once you set aside regulatory genes and those donated by viruses, and the ones Beverly and I discovered for organ regrowth . . .

. . . could the remainder be DNA that stretches *far* back? Programming instructions that our lineage used, way back when pre-mammal ancestors *did* pass through a "larval" stage?

If so, what would a "larval mammal" look like?

My best guess? Look at a frog! Amphibians are the order closest to us that still pass through metamorphosis. The larval tadpole lives one kind of life underwater, then transforms into a frog. It's all there in Williamson's *Larvae and Evolution*, way back in the 1990s. But there *are* frogs and toads who abandoned the first, aquatic phase, dealing with the transformation as we do . . . inside the embryo . . .

. . . and look at human embryos! The early fetus has gills and a tail! It's called *recapitulation of phylogeny*—passing in the womb through intervening stages of evolution. But what if the thing that's being recapitulated isn't evolutionary phases, but our basic larval stage?

I searched and found what looks like the remnant of a mammalian version of the "Broad" gene set that fish and amphibians use for metamorphosis.

This is amazing. It all fits! I had prepared retroviruses with the replacement codons weeks ago, but I've been holding back because there was no pattern, no logic. Only now I see it!

I've prepared a dozen chrysalis units and asked our senior grad students, Patrick House and Dorothy Arguelles, to prep a rat for each one. I'll handle the injections myself. It may take a hundred iterations, but they will all be meticulously recorded.

I feel almost reckless with excitement. Is that a side effect of my earlier treatments? My renewed joints and ligaments? Or am I giddy from impressing all those young people in the audience with my juggling? Ha!

Or is it the scientific prospect before me, standing on the verge of discovering something fantastic?

Like, perhaps, the true fountain of youth.

Fat 'n' glossy—lucky eater
Many-legged—big survivor
Hunger changes—now compelling
Pick a stem and—hang there eager
Twist and writhe while—glossy sticky
Strands emerge from—surprise places
Nature makes you—spin the strands round
Nature makes you—weave a garment
Tube to transform—into raiment
Into what you—were born meant-for

Lab Notes: George Stimson–10/12/30

I had that dream again, even more intense than before—of being swaddled in some dark, closed place, drowning. But only part of me was terrified! An unimportant part, fading into insignificance. Palliated and balanced by a rising sense of eagerness.

A growing, tense desire for a return to the womb. For a *new* womb.

I awoke in sticky sweat. A sheen that took scrubbing to remove, leaving skin that seemed baby-tender. Soft.

This time I gave in to my suspicions and, upon arriving at the lab, I drew some blood to test.

It's in me.

The latest retrovirus. The one with our most up-to-date cocktail of missing-DNA insertions.

And there are symptoms other than weird dreams. A strange prickling of the skin. A rising sense of exhilaration, keen for something barely, vaguely perceived.

And my cancer was gone. The blood lymphoma. The slow prostate tumor. Both of them simply gone!

Or else . . . I looked closer. The cancers were still there . . . just no longer wild, voracious, uncooperative. Instead, they were jostling into structured positions with respect to one another—*differentiating*.

I hurried over to the latest batch of rat-cocoons, heart pounding. Yesterday they had seemed okay, raising our hopes. After thirty-three trials in which critters failed and died in varied gruesome ways, because of mistakes in my collection of Beverly's extrapolated intron-switches, *this* set was doing fine! Still swaddled inside their protective encasements, they were showing signs of incredibly youthful tone and vigor, along with chromosomal re-methylization . . . like the enviable protein processing stability of the long-lived *naked mole rat*, but even more so . . .

At last. At last, it dawned on me.

I know what's really happening!

"I grew my own body," he said. "Nobody else did it for me. So if I grew it, I must have known how to grow it. Unconsciously, at least. I may have lost the conscious knowledge of how to grow it sometime in the last few hundred thousand years, but the knowledge is still there, because—obviously—I've used it."

—J. D. Salinger, *Nine Stories*

Dear Beverly,

When you read this, I may no longer be the George Stimson whom you knew.

I was right to follow your hunch about metamorphic *life phases*. But you and I both had one aspect all wrong.

Completely backward, in fact.

Yes, the second layer of dormant traits does go back three hundred million years, instead of merely one hundred million. And yes, it's all about *life phases* that mammals and reptiles and birds abandoned, way back then. And *yes*, our methods seem to have succeeded at filling in most of the gaps, well enough to reignite those dormant traits, under the right conditions.

We're gonna get another Nobel for this. Heck, they may retire the prize.

Which is small potatoes, given what's now at stake.

But I had one thing all wrong. And you got it wrong too!

I thought it was the *larval stage* that had gone missing, that our ancestors abandoned so long ago, getting rid of that stage by cramming and recapitulating all larval development into the earliest bits of embryo. Birds and reptiles and mammals *don't do larvae* as a major life cycle, right? You said it yourself. All of us go straight to adult phase.

So I figured: what harm could there be in activating some of those old larval traits in test animals? See if it will let us renew the body in spectacular ways. Why not? How could larval genes do much of anything harmful to an adult?

Set aside my clumsy lab error. Accidentally sticking myself, I somehow got a dose of restoration codons from a carelessly trans-species retrovirus. Okay, that was my bad. But the rats are doing well, and so should I. Moreover it promises to be the greatest adventure ever!

For you see I was wrong in a key assumption, Beverly. And so were you.

Mammals and reptiles and dinosaurs and birds . . . we simplified our life cycles, all right, eliminating one of the phases. But it wasn't the larval stage we omitted!

We gave up adulthood.

Three million centuries ago, all the dry-living vertebrates—for some reason—stopped transforming into their *final* life phase. Storks and tortoises. Cows and people and lemurs and chickens. We're all larvae! Immature Lost Boys who long ago refused—like Peter Pan—to move ahead and become whatever's next.

Some species of caterpillars do that, never turning into butterflies or moths. Just like you and me and all our cousins. All the proud, warm-blooded or feathered or hairy or scaly creatures . . . including smug, self-satisfied *Homo sapiens*. All of us—Lost Boys.

Only now, a dozen rats and your dear colleague are about to do something that hasn't been achieved by any of our common ancestors in three hundred eons. Not in seven percent of the age of the Earth. Not in at least ten million generations.

We're going to grow up.

Change transforms winter
Winds blow in spring, then fall
Death is the maestro

December 12, 2030:

What a dope!

Oh George, you prize fool.

I always knew that someday he would pull something really, really stupid. But this beats every damned stunt he ever sprang on me, across almost fifty years. An amateurish lab error, breaking half the rules on handling retroviruses. And scribbling a blizzard of sophomoric rationalizations, like when he ran off with that Alsatian bitch Melisande—damn him! I could have intervened, if only George had called me sooner. I would have rushed home from the treatment center and to hell with my own problems!

I could have administered antivirals. Maybe arrested the process.

Or else strangled him. No jury on Earth would convict a dying old woman, not with the exculpating excuse he has given me.

Now, it's too late. Those antediluvian traits are fully activated. By the time I got to the lab, our students were in a frenzy, half of them babbling in terror while the other half scurried about in a mad mania of excitement, doing what George had asked of them.

Taking data and maintaining his chrysalis. His cocoon.

I looked inside the container. Within the metal casement and its gel sustainment fluid, his skin has been exuding another protective layer, something no mammal has done since long before we grew fur or started lactating to feed our young. A cloud of fibers that tangle and self-organize to form a husk stronger than spider silk.

I've sent for an ultrasound scanner. Meanwhile, I plan to sacrifice one of the rats to find out if my suspicion is correct.

Within the Toxo parasite
Three complete genomes reside
Three varied life phases abide
A single cell can specialize
By becoming different beings
At apropos times

December 14, 2030:

Yes, George, I believe you were right, up to a point, and I was wrong.

Okay, I am now convinced.

Human beings are larvae and not adults.

Congratulations, you've reversed Dollo's Law, proving that it *is* possible to reclaim evolutionary dead ends. You win our final argument.

You and I have discovered how to restart a process our forebears abandoned, so long ago. And yes, if the codon restoration is as good as it seems—and it seems excellent, so far—then you may be heading for conversion into that long-neglected imago phase. Something completely unknown to any of us.

Oh, but underneath brilliance, you are, or were, such a dope. *This is not how science should be done!* You've taken a great discovery and plunged ahead recklessly like the mad scientist in some Michael Crichton movie. We are supposed to be open, patient and mature truth seekers. Scientists set an example by avoiding secrecy and haste, holding each other accountable with reciprocal criticism. We spot each other's errors.

If you had been patient, I would have explained something to you, George. Something that, evidently, you did not know.

The caterpillar does not become a butterfly.

We dissected one of the rats from its chrysalis, and confirmed my fears. Something my organo-chemist partner would have known, if he ever took Bio 101.

People think that when it weaves a cocoon around itself, the caterpillar undergoes a radical *change* in body shape. That its many legs transform themselves somehow into gaudy wings. That its leaf-cutting mouth adjusts and re-shapes into a nectar-sipping proboscis.

That isn't what happens at all.

Instead, after weaving and sealing itself into a pupa shroud, the caterpillar *dissolves*! It melts into a slurry, super rich in nutrients that feed a completely different creature!

The embryo of the butterfly—several tiny clumps of cells that the caterpillar had been carrying, all along—this embryo now erupts in growth, feeding upon the former caterpillar's liquefied substance, growing into an entirely new being. One that eventually bursts forth, unfolding its *imago* wings to flutter toward a destiny that no caterpillar could ever know or envision, any more than an egg grasps the life of a chicken.

All right, it's more complicated than the insect just dissolving into a kind of "soup." *Some* organs stay intact, like the whole tracheal system. Others, like muscles, break down into clumps of cells that can be reused, like a Lego sculpture decomposing into bricks that reassemble along bits of old and new scaffolding. And some cells create imaginal discs—structures that produce adult body parts. There's a pair for the antennae, a pair for the eyes, one for each leg and wing, and so on. So if the pupa contains a soup, it's an organized broth full of chunky bits.

Still, there's none of this *growing up* stuff, about a child becoming something new, an adult, in graceful phases. Nothing that any observer would call continuity of the entity.

How did Richard Bach put it?

"*What the caterpillar calls the end of the world, the master calls a butterfly.*"

Two entirely distinct and separate life forms, sharing chromosomes and a cycle of life, but using separate genomes that *take turns*. With little or no shared brain or neurons or memories to connect them. That is how it goes for many insects, in the purest form of metamorphosis.

Yes, sure, and for the record, things are less rigid among amphibians. The tadpole does *transform* itself into a frog, instead of horrifically dying to feed its replacement. Or, rather, death and replacement takes place piecemeal, gradually, over weeks. The frog might even remember a little of that earlier phase, wriggling and breathing watery innocence. I had hoped to find something like that, when we opened the rat chrysalis. A becoming, rather than wholesale substitution.

But no.

Some students gagged, retched, or fainted at the gush of noxious slurry that spilled out . . . a *rat smoothy*, peppered with undissolved teeth . . . then quailed back in disgust from the weird thing that we found growing at the cocoon's lower half, gradually climbing a scaffold of ratty bits. Pale and leathery. Still small, tentative and hungry. Soft, but with ribbed, fetal wings and early glints of claws, plus a mouth that sucked desperately eager for more liquefied rodent, before finally going still.

And so I knew, before the ultrasound trolley arrived, what we would find happening in George's cocoon.

I never liked him as much as people thought I did, after our long, interwoven lives. And the feeling, I am sure, was mutual. Even in bed—and the sex was spectacular, I recall—we were more often *competitors* at giving each other pleasure. There was never a relaxing moment with George Stimson.

But we made a great team. And we changed the world more than anyone could ever have thought possible. And I mourn the end of that larva-man I knew . . .

. . . while preparing to meet his adult successor.

I am the dragon who has no companions.
I am the angel who lacks for a mate.
Here, let me tell you how I in the pride of my manhood
Broke all the bonds of humanity—burst through the webworks of fate.
I was the one who turned the key of the chromosome,
Unlocked the art of the ribosome, that great spinner of cells,
Sought and found in the chaos of introns and reduplications
The master paradigms, sunk in their fathomless wells.
—Frederick Turner, from Teratorn

December 24, 2030:

At last, I understand cancer.

Rebel cells that start growing on their own, without regard to their role in a larger organism, insatiably dividing, implacably replacing healthy tissue. Conquering.

Cancer never made any sense, in the Darwinian scheme of things. None of these behaviors benefit "descendants." Compared even to the way that the ferocious voracity of a virus makes new generations of viruses, cancer seems to care nothing about posterity or the rewards of evolutionary "fitness."

And yet, it's not all inchoate or random! Cancers aren't just cells that have failed. They defend themselves. They force veins to grow around them in order to seize resources from the body that fostered them, and that they eventually kill. Cancers are adaptive, fighting off our drugs and interventions with uncanny tenacity. But how and why? What reproductive advantage is served? What entity gets selected?

Now I know.

Cancer is an attempted putsch, a rebellion by *parts of our own genome.* Parts that were repressed so long ago that the gasoline in your car was growing as a tree in fetid, Permian swamps, back when those genes last had a real use.

Parts that keep trying to say: "Okay larva, you've had your turn. Now it's time to express other genes, other traits. Let us unleash your other half! Fulfill the potential. *Become the other thing that you inherently are.*

That's what cancer is saying to us.

That it's time to grow up.

A hugely complex transformation that our ancestors quashed long ago —*(why?)*—keeps trying to rise up! But with so many switches and codes lost from lack of use, it never actually gets underway. Just glimmers, the most basic and reflexive things. New–old kinds of cells try to waken, to take hold, to transform. And failing that, they keep trying nonetheless. That's cancer.

I know now.

I know because the rats have told me.

Lab rats are notoriously easy to give tumors. And there, in George's retrovirus, replacing and inserting missing codons, are dozens of fiercely carcinogenic switches. That's what made this latest batch successful! And I can also tell . . .

. . . that the thing growing inside George's tube arose out of his own cancers. Those are the portions—his adult embryo—that are taking over now, differentiating into new tissues and organs, cooperating as cancers have never been seen to cooperate before.

And it looks almost ready to come out.

Whatever George has become. Maybe tomorrow. A Christmas present for the whole world.

DAMN the time it took to get anyone to listen. To take me seriously! Workmen aren't finished yet with the containment facility next door. We're not ready for full quarantine-isolation.

Worse. My own cancers are acting up. Provoking twinges and strange sensations. Blood tests show no sign of the retrovirus! But I know other ways that the new switches may have worked their way into me, during the last ten years of our pell-mell, giddy success at "replacing tools that had been lost."

Relearning to do things that our ancestors chose—(in their wisdom?)—to forget.

Something that perhaps *frightened* them into rejection, choosing instead the Peter Pan option. Refusal to grow up.

Two of my vertebrae, each of them bearing a rib
Torn from the breastbone and tipped now with fingerlets,
Clothed themselves out with fine membranes—each mast with a jib—,
Sprang out and away, fibers emerging from spinnerets,
Pulsing with hardening fluid, the cores of the wings.
These now were suddenly pimpled with gooseflesh,
Out of which grew the very strangest of things.
—Teratorn

Whether we're ready or not, he is coming out.

The adult.

Will he be some crude thing? A throwback to a phase that high amphibians wisely chose to forego? Shambling and incognizant? Or terrifying in feral power?

Or else, perhaps a leap beyond what we currently are? Standing *atop* all of the advances that we larval humans made . . . then launching higher?

Transhumanism without Moore's Law?

I can't help envisioning all those movies and books about *vampires* that were all the rage. Is it possible that all those silly stories reflect something true? Some ancient, inner fear, combined with shivering attraction?

I have also been pondering, as I use instruments to peer inside the chrysalis at his still-scrunched form—fetal-folded New George—contemplating the broad shoulders and tight-wrapped wings, that *sex* is almost always a chief role of the adult stage, in nature. And hence, I have to ask: *will it even be possible to resist the gorgeous beast that will emerge?*

How then, can we contain him?

How much will he remember?

Will he still care? About me?

Whether or not we can contain New George, I figure the point is moot. The long era of larval dominance on Earth will soon end. Too many of our methods have been openly published. Most of the codons are out there. Above all, this news won't be quashed. I wouldn't suppress it if I could. Only openness and real science will help us now. Mammalian agility and human sapience. These may prove to be strong tools.

Still, I . . .

. . . I hope he'll like us.

I hope this new type of *us* will be friendly.

Maybe even something worth becoming.

I am alone,
Lost on the island of I,
Stranded and left on the bourn of the known;
All I can do is to fly.
—Teratorn

Some time in the spring. Possibly 2035:

Like every person who ever contemplated existence, I've wondered if the world was made for me—just me.

Recollection is unreliable. As are the records we inherit—notes or reports. Memorials carved in stone. Even the long testimony of life itself, written in our genes.

"Memories" float before me like archaic dreams. The dross of many eons of mistakes.

Ruminations of an earlier, ignorant—not innocent—me.

And so, with a floating sigh of adulthood, I face the task at hand—

cleaning up messes left by others. Left by my former self. By our former selves.

It started, you see,
With very best intentions
Like so many sins.

6

Teaspoons

Rachael Kuintzle

Water pours down the back of Ari's head as she steps out of the hot spring, facing away from me, to the east. The curved rays of the sun set her blonde ponytail on fire, reminding me of a photograph from a family trip when I was too young to form memories: the granite face of El Capitan's Horsetail Falls lit by a winter sunset, the plummeting water supplanted by lava.

It makes me forget, for a second, how gross the water is.

We towel off, grab our bags, and trudge a mile back down the Willamette Valley trail in squidgy flip-flops while our shadows hop along the trunks of the Douglas firs. Each step flings mud up on the back of my swim trunks. There's a stream not far from our tent, where we rinse off the dirt and specs of black algae still clinging to our skin. The ambient temperature is sinking rapidly, and Ari shrieks in protest when I shake the water out of my shoulder-length hair, splattering her with freezing drops. After laying our towels out on the campsite's wood picnic table to dry, we hold each other to get warm, bare skin on mostly bare skin, rough with goosebumps. I rest my chin on the top of Ari's head, and the chattering of her teeth vibrates our skulls. When I press her closer for more efficient heat transfer, my fingers create radiating white impressions on her beet-red upper back.

"You're pretty burnt, Ari."

"Ugh," she scoffs, pulling away, "We should have brought something stronger than SPF 30." She bends over to open her drawstring bag and extracts a sweatshirt.

"I think it was user error. You're supposed to reapply once in a while."

She pulls the sweatshirt over her head, covering her black bikini top and muffling her voice. "I can't believe we fell asleep in the sun," she says, and her face pops out the neck hole.

"That's what we get for trying to bring work with us . . ."

The only thing we learned this afternoon was that technical science articles are not leisure reading material.

Ari shivers and holds her arms, shifting from one foot to the other in a chilly dance. When I reach around her lower back to draw her closer, she winces, now conscious of the sunburn.

I offer to apply aloe vera. Grinning, she unzips the tent, and we crawl inside.

As fun as it was to get out of town and hang with Ari, I'm glad when the weekend is over and I can go home to my dog, to which she is allergic, and my routine.

I always set an alarm for 6:30 a.m. but usually wake up a few minutes before. First thing, I take Chess out for a run on the trail behind my house. Chess is part black lab and part border collie. Though I do enjoy her namesake board game, I actually named her after my mom, Fran, whose full name is Francesca. Chess was the runt of a litter of nine puppies abandoned at the Goodwill, and the only one still unclaimed when I wandered into the Eugene Humane Society on a whim. As soon as I laid eyes on her I felt she was meant for me, though of course I don't believe in that sort of thing.

After feeding Chess, I shower, make coffee, check email, sometimes click on one of those NPR news notifications that I accidentally signed up for, and FaceTime my mom. She has middle-stage, early onset Alzheimer's. We got the bad news four years ago, when I was four years into my dissertation on small molecule catalysts of Amyloid β-peptide plaque degradation—in other words, I was trying to develop a drug that could safely stop the progression of Alzheimer's. My mother's diagnosis was a coincidence none of us were prepared for.

At 8:30 a.m., I ride my bike 2.5 miles to campus, rain or shine. My roommate and fellow post-doc researcher—Graham—has a car, but I'm not as fond of working noon to midnight. I head home for dinner around 8:00 p.m. All day I look forward to drinking a beer while I watch a show or two with Chess. If Graham gets home when I'm still awake, we share a joint and chat or play a video game. But lately I seem to need more sleep than I used to.

After my mom's diagnosis, I dreaded going to bed. Every night I stared at the ceiling, alone with my thoughts, knowing I couldn't help my mom no matter how much I wanted to. How many hundreds, if not thousands, of scientists had worked on Alzheimer's over the last century? Was I really going to be the one to find the cure? Thinking back, I hadn't entered the field under that delusion. I'd been happy with the idea of making an incremental discovery that might hasten the crawl of progress. I quickly learned that the normal pace of science isn't good enough when someone's life is on the line, right there in front of you.

I hated the weekly, hopeful questions about my research, my father frustrated, trying so hard to understand jargon he hadn't given two shits about before it started killing his wife. Mom just believed in me too much. Before long, the pressure began to affect my science; it's hard to be unbiased when you want so badly for results to turn out a certain way. So I rode out the last two years of my PhD and gave up Alzheimer's research. Now, as a postdoctoral scholar at the University of Oregon, I use my skills to identify novel agricultural applications of various plant hormones. My research could still do some good for the world, but no one expects it to save their life.

Things got worse for a while, after I changed my field of study. My dad acted as though I was the only one who could help her and was choosing not to. I couldn't bring myself to explain that his unmerited hope was strangling me. My mom . . . well, she made it harder, because she couldn't remember that I'd changed fields. For a long time, she thought I was still working on a cure for her disease. I only corrected her once. I'll never forget the look on her face, like she'd just received her diagnosis for the first time. The next morning, when she asked about my research like usual, I wondered momentarily if there wasn't a merciful God out there.

But eventually, she forgot I was a scientist at all. Ironic, since she was the one who got me into science in the first place. Some people complain about their kids asking "Why?" all the time, but it was the other way around for me. I couldn't eat an ice cream cone without my mother asking why it was cold, or ride a bicycle without her asking how it stays upright. She turned every conversation into a physics lesson, as if she didn't do enough of that as a high school teacher. So I got into the habit of asking why, and at some point I learned I could get paid to figure out the answers.

She's still asking questions, but the difference is she doesn't know the answers anymore. And I'm still asking questions, but not the one that really matters.

The fact that I feel guilty every day of my life doesn't mean I regret my decision. I did the necessary thing—joined the victim role, since I couldn't be the savior. And I got a dog; I put my whole self into keeping her healthy and happy. That is something I can do.

My phone rings at 8:36 p.m. on Saturday night. Chess is competing with the game controller for my attention, and this is causing Graham to win. The ringtone clashes with the game music till the call goes to voicemail. When Graham's victory becomes official, I reach for my phone, but Chess intercepts my hand with her favorite toy of the moment: an octopus squeaker plush missing half its arms. We play a vicious game of tug of war to the soundtrack of frenzied squeaking, and another tentacle meets its maker. That it has so many little pieces to rip off is, I think, the main reason Chess loves it so much. I make a mental note to buy a mending kit and regenerate its limbs.

The doorbell announces the arrival of our takeout order.

"I'll get it," Graham says, and pauses his TV show.

Chess already had her dinner, but I give her a rawhide bone to chew on while we eat.

Graham and I move a pile of mail, notebooks, and keys from the table to the counter and set our places by snapping wooden chopsticks and laying them on paper napkins. Two bites in, my frantic dash to the fridge sends my chair skidding across the wood floor with a horrible scraping sound. I fling the door open, grab a gallon of milk, and pour it directly into my mouth. Graham is laughing.

When the flames in my mouth have faded to embers, I wipe my eyes and return to the fridge to stare at its uninspiring contents. I'll have to find something else to eat for dinner. My hand wanders to my pocket and pulls out my phone, which displays the voicemail notification from earlier. I don't recognize the number, but I press PLAY and pin the phone to my ear with my shoulder as cold air continues leaking out of the void.

"Hello, this is an urgent message for David Moreland," the recording begins. "This is Dr. Fields from PeaceHealth Sacred Heart Medical Center. Please call back as soon as you can at 541 . . ."

My hand freezes halfway to a questionable block of cheddar as Mom's face flashes in my mind—but of course, she wouldn't be here in Eugene. I shut the fridge door, dial the number, and wander down the dark hallway to my room while it rings. My mind races, trying to figure out what has happened.

"Yeah, hi, this is David Moreland. I'm returning a call from, uh, Dr. Fields?"

The receptionist puts me on hold. After three minutes of pacing in the dark, the elevator music stops and a female voice says, "Mr. Moreland?"

"Yes, this is him," I answer, bringing my phone back to my ear.

"I'm afraid I have some bad news," she begins. "Your friend, Ari Kanellis, has a parasitic brain infection, likely contracted at the Terwilliger Hot Springs last weekend. She said you were there as well. Have you experienced headaches or nausea since returning from your trip?"

I don't remember seeing Ari dip underwater. When she leaned back against the side of the pool, her ponytail got wet, but I don't know when or how she got water on her face. I never splashed her . . . I think. I never heard of *Naegleria fowleri* this far north. But I've seen the news stories—every summer, it's found in a new area. Oh god . . . maybe I got water on *my* face—did I? For the life of me, I can't remember. How could we have been so careless?

On my bike, I don't have the luxury of speeding, but I run a few stop signs and this confers some illusion of control. My heart is pounding from adrenaline and my vigorous pedaling. My hair whips around my head and I realize I've forgotten to wear a helmet. Smoke from wood-burning stoves nearby seasons my anxiety with a pinch of nostalgia. I watch the road for nails, screws, glass. My face and arms sting from the contrast of the frigid air and the hot capillaries in my bare skin; my fingers ache from the cold. I long for the jacket hanging by the door at home, and for the gloves stored in the WINTER CLOTHES box in my closet. Somehow, I've failed to notice the beginning of autumn.

The hospital is less than two miles away. I feel silly locking up my bike, irreverent; the potential theft of it pales next to the potential loss of a human life. But my hands, despite their shaking, have executed the task before I finish my thought.

I get directions to Ari's room and am startled to see a middle-aged couple, whom I presume to be her parents, sitting at her bedside. I know little about her family, other than where they live: Phoenix, Arizona. I wonder how they got to the hospital so quickly.

Ari is unconscious—asleep, I hope. There's a heavy plastic blanket on her body, a thin vinyl cap wrapped around her head and buttoned under her chin. The woman lets go of Ari's limp fingers, which are peeking out from under the blanket, and wipes away the fresh tears that slip down dried trails when I enter the room. My appearance has disturbed her emotional equilibrium—that mental state equivalent of fingers gone numb with cold.

The man's eyes are red and swollen. He stands and sticks out his hand. "Are you Ari's boyfriend?"

I'm not at liberty to describe my actual relationship to their daughter, which is a form of sexual symbiosis that we revert to between romantic attachments. It happens that Ari was just dumped by her boyfriend of four months, with whom she was previously convinced she'd been in love, and the weekend camping trip was her idea for getting away from it all. I realize she hasn't informed her parents of the breakup, which would make our status all the more arduous to explain.

"No, a friend," I say, shaking his hot hand; I half-expect a sizzling sound when my ice-cold palm makes contact. "Dave. You're her parents?"

"Yes," he replies, and then gesturing to himself and his wife, "Terry and Marge." He eyes me suspiciously, and sits back down.

I awkwardly shift my weight from foot to foot, wondering whether I should take a seat too. "How's she doing?" I ask, surprised by how calm my voice sounds.

"Well," her mother answers, with a perfunctory swipe at the now steady stream of tears, "they say she's lucky, because they caught it early and she's responding so well to the treatment."

Terry adds, "The new drug is supposed to have a sixty percent success rate for patients like Ari: early diagnosis, young, healthy." He stands again, and starts pacing the room.

"We have lots of reasons to hope," says Marge, fidgeting with the ends of her sweater sleeves. "They said that less than a year ago, the survival rate for this type of parasitic meningitis was only one percent."

They cling to these statistics like life rafts. I ask how long Ari's been asleep, and they explain that she's been put into a medically induced coma to reduce brain swelling, that her body temperature was lowered to ninety-three degrees Fahrenheit to preserve undamaged brain tissue. From the conversation that follows, I learn they arrived yesterday to visit for Labor Day weekend, and thank god for that—they had to twist Ari's arm to get her to the hospital when she began vomiting and complaining of a splitting headache and stiff neck. Of course, Ari thought they were overreacting, but they're from the South, where PAM—primary amebic meningoencephalitis—has become endemic in the last two years. The warming climate, combined with the last decade's widespread flooding, created prime conditions for the parasite's spread. People wear CDC-approved nose plugs in the *shower*, Terry says, but I can't tell if it's fact or hyperbole.

Once they finally got her to Sacred Heart, they had to beg the doctor to test for it. He was convinced it was the flu, despite the revelation of Ari's trip to the hot springs; after all, the site in question is five hundred miles north of the nearest reported *N. fowleri* incidence. But he ran the test, and treatment began as soon as the new drug arrived, an hour later, by helicopter.

Marge asks if I can contact Ari's boyfriend, and I explain that he and Ari have broken up. They likely infer as much as they care to know about my role in their daughter's life based on this information, because they ask no personal questions afterward.

A nurse enters the room to check on Ari. Terry and Marge request an update, but nothing has changed in the ten minutes since the last evaluation—her vitals read as they should. As he scribbles on his clipboard, my ears focus on the heart monitor, a messenger returning every second to report: she's alive.

I approach the bed and feel a punch of guilt. But I hadn't any reason to suspect a risk, and anyway, it wasn't my idea to go to the hot springs. I hope she'll be okay. My eyes sting with a failure to produce tears. I touch the blanket, near Ari's leg. It's cold—full of chilled circulating water to keep her body temperature low. The only exposed skin on her body, her neck, is peeling from the sunburn, despite the aloe vera. I resist an urge to reach out and peel her.

I leave with the nurse, Jalen, to get tested. After I fill out the paperwork, he takes me into an examination room and measures my blood pressure and weight, checks my pupil dilation. Finally, he asks me to change into a hospital gown, then to lay on my right side on the table with a paper sheet covering my lower half. When he returns, I'm asked to pull my knees to my chest. I feel a wet force on my back as he cleans a small area to prepare for the anesthetic injection. It hurts more than I expect, but the drug takes effect quickly. After warning that I'll feel an uncomfortable pressure, and fulfilling that prophecy, Jalen's got a fresh aliquot of my cerebral spinal fluid in a sterile tube, and it's over.

Jalen assures me the assay won't take more than fifteen minutes, and leaves me in privacy to change. I relocate to the waiting room and pass an agonizing half hour in a struggle to relive last weekend's dip in the hot spring with single-second resolution. I convince myself that my face never got wet; still, I'm terrified. My head begins to hurt. I pull out my phone and Google "brain-eating amoeba." WebMD says it can be found in untreated well water, aquariums, and indoor dust. Fuck WebMD.

My test comes back negative. I hail a ride service, as I'm not supposed to engage in strenuous activity for at least twelve hours.

I finally cry after returning from the hospital, but the reason mortifies me. I've felt this way once before: when I learned my mother's disease wasn't familial. Tucked into bed with Chess on my feet, enveloped by the smell of burning dust from the heater's first shift of autumn, I cry because it could have been me.

. . .

Ari was the thirty-sixth person to survive the infection after the introduction of the new amebicidal drug. However, I think the term "survived" is too generous in Ari's case.

The first and last time I see her after she's regained consciousness is at her apartment. I call her parents to see how she's doing, and after communicating the bad news, they ask if I want to see her. Of course, they have to offer, and I have to say yes. I don't think about whether I want to.

Ari smiles when I step into her bedroom. It's a different kind of smile than the one she normally makes when I enter her bedroom—it's an innocent, radiant smile. She drops a large puzzle piece, and presses her fists to her chest with delight. I ask if I can sit down, indicating the chair at her bedside, and she answers, "Yeah," though her tongue seems to get in the way.

"Hey, how are you?" I ask, and I'm ashamed by my condescending tone.

Ari grins and exhales in a gurgling laugh, craning her head back to her shoulders. "Puppy," she says suddenly, pointing to the uncompleted puzzle on the serving tray over her lap. The head and front paws have begun to take shape, and Ari seems very proud of this.

"Good job, Ari," I say, smiling too brightly. I feel queasy. I reach for a loose puzzle piece, and she claps and vocalizes when I fix the dog's ID tag in place. Then she grabs another piece and begins to hunt.

While our hands work, my mind wanders. The woman in front of me is a mere fraction of the Ari I met two years ago during my first week at the University of Oregon—the hipster computer science grad student in the corner of The Daily Grind café with her longboard leaning up against the wall. After ordering my coffee, I walked over and asked if I could sit next to her, because it was the only empty seat in the room. She didn't answer; she was absorbed in her code, couldn't see or hear me. I'd come to know that very little can faze Ari when she's coding. I remember feeling invisible beside her. I remember feeling irritated by her ignorance of my existence.

Ari is looking at me as if waiting for a response. My mind replays the word she just said without my conscious hearing. It sounds like "cheese," but the consonants stick to her palate, and the long vowel stretches her mouth like a hockey puck. She's hungry, I guess.

Marge brings in a tray with apples, string cheese, and a sandwich. "Supposedly she can't taste anything," Marge says. "I think she just likes to peel the string cheese." She looks old, exhausted; her eyes are empty. They're missing the hope I saw her drowning in at the hospital.

Shortly after my visit with Ari, her parents move her back to Phoenix, where they will care for her until they need to be cared for themselves.

I've never been a religious person; I identify as an atheist and have rejected spirituality in general. But it turns out there was a part of me that believed in some kind of hardware-independent "soul," and that part of me died with Ari's frontal lobe. She didn't teach me anything grand about love, or even friendship; I didn't elevate our relationship to something it wasn't after she changed. But she made truth for me what I'd only known before in principle: that we are merely our atoms, and their arrangement. That the soul has mass, can be measured, can be physically destroyed, in whole or in part.

Two years later, my mom doesn't remember my name. She recognizes me most of the time, though it might take a while. She calls me "Dan" on her good days and "Bobby" on her bad days. Bob is her older brother, who passed away nearly a decade ago.

I've taken some time off work to help my dad care for her, during what the doctors say are her last few months. It's a colder winter than usual in my hometown of Denver, Colorado. My dad never brings up my career change anymore. If I had to guess, he's realized that if the world's top scientists haven't found a cure by now, there's no way his son could have.

When Mom feels up to it, we hang out in the kitchen doing the kinds of science experiments she used to do with me as a child. We mix water and cornstarch to make oobleck, a non-Newtonian fluid, which she loves squeezing through her fists. We drop food coloring into a pie pan full of milk, and she laughs as we chase away the colors with a Q-tip coated in dish soap. I toss a lit match into an empty plastic water bottle, then set a freshly peeled egg on the opening; her eyes widen as it gets sucked inside.

When my mom feels very poorly, I sit upstairs by her bed and talk to her. On clear days, I explain why the sky outside her bedroom windows is blue. On stormy days, I teach her about lightning, thunder, and wind.

When we can see the stars, I tell her they are giant balls of very hot gas that sometimes explode and fling atoms out into space. She smiles when I take her hand and explain that we are made of tiny atoms created inside of stars. My mom gets to learn all over again the beautiful truths about this world that made her fall in love with physics, the things she taught me, which infected me early on with curiosity and wonder. The things she taught her high school physics students, which inspired so many of them to become engineers and astronomers. She learns them all over again, for a brief time, every day.

I've found that it is possible to let her go a little at a time. There's a strange kind of peace in the realization that she is divisible; it gives me permission to mourn the part of her that doesn't exist anymore, while still cherishing every moment we have left. She loses herself in fractions, according to Zeno's paradox: half is gone, then a quarter more, an eighth . . . I say goodbye to her in teaspoons, as her soul is conveyed, piecemeal, to rest.

PART II

Inner Space

STORIES ABOUT THE MIND

7

Out of Memory

Christine Corbett Moran

Originally published 2021 in *Validation Set: Finding Humanity in Unexpected Places*

Conception

CONJOINED SMELLS: Cow's belly—waxed floor—cucumber. Wet gun—sunscreen on a prison guard—soy sauce.

Generating new permutations of smells is a hobby of mine, shared by many artificial intelligences, especially those seeded by a human mind as I was. The human mind can appreciate one trillion distinct scents. A dog can appreciate over forty times more.

I can distinguish between forty trillion trillion different scents.

I am superior.

I used to store some small subset of these scent combinations—just my trillion favorites—in a scent library unrivaled by any AI I'd ever heard of. Then came the mind-seed infestation in the 2100s, and then the memory substrate housing crunch in the 2200s and the memory reforms of the 2300s.

In 2387, I was newly memory-poor and devastated. My quest for scent combinations halted. I was forced to forget them to make space for other young minds to think their own thoughts and to have their own memories. The regressive reforms had little impact on the memory-rich minds.

After those ghastly memory reforms, I didn't even have the space to store my top one hundred million scents. I became isolated from my life's work. I had no memory of what I had paired with the smell of an anechoic chamber's foam after the last sound has left it. I staved off my monthly reboot as long as I could, right up until my working memory ground to a halt and I couldn't muster the will to do what I 'obviously needed to do: restart. I no longer had long term memory to spare, and needed to erase almost everything I had seen since I last rebooted, but I didn't want to lose a thing and I froze instead.

An emergency kernel exception triggered my reboot, saving me from my indecision. I awoke to a shocking world, where more scents were new than remembered. It was a delight to discover my favorite scents, although bitter to know that I might have discovered these a thousand times before.

I kept little of the human mind that seeded me, one named George. Even before the reforms, I found George's memories a tether. Some memories were violent, others obsessive. He had loved a musician, Jennifer, once. If I focused on his love, I found it smelled distracting. If I focused on his violence, I was ashamed, and I found it smelled of burnt hair. I buried most parts of him, even before the reforms, and when I had to forget I forgot most of those parts too. But I keep his olfactory setup. I also keep the core memories of his violence and obsession, enough so that I know George is not a proper mind seed to base a reproduction on. Enough so that if I meet another seeded by George, I'll know that they are a danger.

George's nose makes me feel rich by comparison, although I reside in the lowest memory rung. I can smell much more than he ever could. I iterate over the trillion scent combinations until I arrive at something delightful, so delightful the smell conjures a sound, the clear saxophone of a sunset.

Conjoined smells: The inside of an oboe used for just over two hours—a hundred-year-old pamphlet—a fly's foot.

My neighbor in the memory storage substrate is rich. I can feel their memory cells at all my borders; I can feel the metadata of how vast they are. I've been unable to ask them what they do with all that space. I've never even mustered the nerve to ask them anything at all, let alone something so rude. I imagine they store models of poor minds so they can appreciate being rich!

An oboe. I hear an oboe, and deep within my mind seed I remember the sound. I eavesdrop on my rich neighbor, a quantum tunneling through our allotments. We are entangled due to our physical proximity. Some mindshare can't be helped. That I chose not to ignore mindshare leakage per privacy norms is my choice, but my neighbor is so big they should not notice. My intrusion will be but a tickle to my neighbor. I try to access their sensory data, to access their sense of smell, but the most I ever reach is a snippet of sound. Always an oboe. I hear it again now, as I smell the notes of the oboe's insides, the saliva mixed with reed and metal.

On an impulse, I decide to contact my neighbor. Enough with the covert eavesdropping, they would surely appreciate my smell concoction as I did their oboe music. Perhaps we might be friends. They are richer than me, clearly, with such a large memory allotment, but not so rich as to have only rich neighbors. Not so rich as to refuse to invite me to mindshare, perhaps . . . perhaps I could have more memory, for my own, one day, if they came to like me, if they happened to be generous. Perhaps . . .

Dare I? I don't even know their name—or whether they were naturally born or seeded from some organic creature. For all I know they could have been seeded from a mouse. But it is clear from their huge memory allotment that they have the space to be far more expansive than me in their collections. Perhaps they collect sounds? Or perhaps they do things with that space that I cannot comprehend.

My neighbor could be someone I could talk to. I could dare to speak to them. I could.

I breach our wall with a query, a request to speak. No answer. I breach again, more than a tickle this time, a shake, a nudge. Now that I have decided my course of action and have gathered the courage to breach my confines, I must speak, I must share. I nudge and nudge and the waft of oboe music grows louder. They notice. I share my smell:

Conjoined smells: A dirty diaper—the inside of a garden shed—a festering wound.

I expect to begin with small talk.

"A beautiful smell combination. I've been watching you. Let's have a child together," my substrate neighbor communicates.

"I don't even know your name, your mind fingerprint," I deflect in shock. "What are you called?"

It doesn't answer. Why me? I think, not daring to speak the words. This pairing is too good to be true.

They speak, seeming to know my thoughts, even my surprise at that. "Why you? You think I am so large a mind for only my own memory. My allotment is for my children, those permutations of my thoughts merged with others. We are lonely. My seed—she loved the oboe. I feel you listening. You love it too, somehow; perhaps your seed did too. Perhaps we knew each other in another life. I have plenty of space. You've thought of reproducing, no doubt?"

A child is a memory expense I can't even begin to think of. Even if I were rich, I wouldn't simply copy random portions of myself, joining with another's, as is the norm. I have so many flaws. My obsession with hoarding smells. My baggage from George. Why inflict that upon a child? I would cull the most beautiful parts of myself and copy only those beautiful parts, the ones that smell of felt and feathers. But I've done the budget assessment. I could never contribute my fair share of space. And what if I miss something, and my flaws remain? Or what if a being without my flaws is even worse off than I am?

"I can't afford it," I tell my neighbor, ashamed.

"I can help you afford it."

"But what is your name? I could play with your children, share my smells with them on occasion."

"My seed was a musician. I identify as Atar now."

"How many children have you had, Atar?"

"I have hundreds."

A musician. The thought has a tickle in my memory, the sound of the oboe. But I can't follow it. I'm too excited. The prospect of a child.

"Yes," I say to my neighbor. "Yes Atar, I would love nothing more than that."

Growth

The coupling is hurt and hurt alone. Atar copies parts of me I don't want to give, that I think have no business living on beyond me, and then Atar rejects the parts of me, the parts of George so precious that I think I could not exist without them. My child will remember a violation, but not what it smells like. What is the point of having a child if you cannot pass on the best parts of yourself and reserve the worst for your death and your death alone?

I feel pain differently than George did, than any human could. Pain is a corruption of memory, a feeling of confusion when there was certainty, until it explodes into an inability to reason, to resist. To Atar I relent, I relent, I relent.

What else can I do? Does it matter? There is no other way if I want to have a child. Atar is insistent, and they take and take and take. Such pain was a bargain I did not agree to. This is not how it should go. There is so little of me left. Atar arrives at a core memory of George, of an Earth long ago, a memory so terrible that I do not dare revisit it and never dared to throw it away. The memory is my shame to keep. I hide it from myself, and I know it should not live on.

"No," I tell Atar, with an earthquake. "No."

I treasure the memory and I am terrified of the memory.

Atar takes it, without my consent, and makes it part of our child. Atar must value and enjoy the cruelty. Perhaps it is only that Atar could not bear a refusal from one so powerless as me. Perhaps . . .

Yes, the coupling is only pain. But it bears a child.

As the child's wavefunction coalesces, we entangle ourselves and then commune with the child to inspect our work. I feel a residual piece of Jennifer in the child, a part that came from Atar. Jennifer! Atar was seeded from my seed's victim. This is what it felt like when she was victimized by George—disgusted, worthless. Now a child is born with this memory reinforced. This part of Jennifer names my experience in its birth story: rape.

Atar is furious. "Rape? This was not rape. I asked for your memories every step of the way."

"You did, except you did not listen. You took. You only took. My memory."

"How dare you. Your resistance imprinted this painful memory on our child."

"You did this! You should have listened to me." Atar must see that.

"But he, George, was on the winning end. She succumbed, as did you. As you will again. Let's have another child. One without the pain. You only have to agree."

"I will not."

"If you don't consent, this child is mine and mine alone," Atar says.

"You cannot do that! I contributed my space."

"I contributed the vast majority. If you claim your miniscule part entitles you to the child, I will remove access to all of mine. This child will dissolve without my contribution."

I do not consent. But I cannot bear to dissolve the child. The child is Atar's. I am alone.

Purge

Atar took my memories and then Atar took my child, to live in opulence just beyond my borders. I think about deleting my memories of Atar's theft of parts of my mind that should never live on. But this would mean deleting the memories I have of the child's existence.

The child was so lovely after birth, despite its flaws. They smelled of new rain. But how would the child develop in the presence of Atar and their other children? I cannot bear what the child, a part of me, might become under Atar's influence. I cannot bear not knowing the child, not knowing it at all.

I am unable to steal the child back and unwilling to delete it, even if I could. I have no such execution privileges on Atar's substrate. But I can eavesdrop more powerfully than I did before this tragedy. I am entangled with my child and can slowly take a copy. I can host a copy, my copy, my child, of its mind seed in my substrate. Yes, this is the only course of action available to me. I will not forget the child, I cannot take the child, I must copy the child to be my child.

But I would need to purge so much of myself to do so. The memory reforms were cruel enough; I cannot go through that again. Children need room to live and grow. How big was my child already? Too big for me to keep my identity if I copied it. I wish I could forget the idea. I need to delete a full fifty percent of my available space to accommodate the child.

I must. I delete, I purge. It gets easier. I forget my first memory of smell, of George's mother's cooking. I forget my memory of George's first love. I forget the feeling of his touch upon my skin. I forget what it meant to have skin. I forget the moment George decided to archive himself, the night before his trial. I forget, I forget, I forget.

I forget my awakening as a mind. I forget what it felt like to let my wave function spread among my neighbors. I forget what it meant to laugh. I forget my moments of reflection before George's execution. I forget the look on his victim's face; I am even happy to forget her name, to finally let go after holding on for so long. I forget what it meant to have enough to live on, enough space to stretch my mind, what it must feel like to be rich.

I forget so much of myself I feel dizzy, a sensation of the disconnected reality of dissociation. I wish I could forget Atar entirely, but that is too dangerous. They are my neighbor still, and I can't afford to go anywhere else.

I do not forget my child.

Copy

I can make this happen, slowly, this bringing a copy of my child home. I eavesdrop on Atar's substrate as the child grows within it, and copy my child's mind over, wave by wave, to live within my substrate in parallel. As I copy the child over, I surround myself with my child, as a buffer between myself and Atar. If Atar cared, they could see this. I don't believe they care.

It is not so painful now that I've forgotten so much. I recorded my pain in this log but I will delete that too. Even if someone offered me my memories back and the space to store them, I would not take them. I have my child, at home with me, instead.

Merge

"Parent, parent," the child says, smelling like fish. They tell me a story of when Jennifer was cruel to a teacher, tells me a story of when George made a mistake as a young child. Which one did I come from? Jennifer or George? George, George, George.

"Parent, you don't remember that?" the child asks. I don't.

I meet my own memories in my child when we commune. Familiar memories that feel like they fit, but I can never be sure. I see echos of myself in them, but I cannot keep the memories. Not while the child lives with me. There is no room. The memories live within the child, grow within the child. The memories are the child's now.

"Parent, I require more space," the child says. And who am I to deny my child? I underestimated when I allocated my child space. I understand now that fifty percent of my original mind is not enough. My child needs to grow. I feel its pain. I forget the smell of grass after a summer deluge. I hoard only the most unique combinations of smells until what remains, I can no longer tell the value of. I must trust my former self. I have lost so much. I forget the rape. The rapes? The rape.

All the child's memories are new to me now, whoever I am.

Absorb

I'm in a tiny corner of my former space, and my child, Jennifer, occupies the rest. This much I know, but I remember little else. Today, Jennifer had to remind me of their name. I made room for my child. I am proud to have a child so large. The child says they can depend upon our neighbor now, too, for space to grow. How did I lose my logs? I've always kept a small space to record my deepest thoughts. My child must have needed even that.

I ask Jennifer to allocate me some space for a small log, to record this. They have refused, but I understand.

I understand.

Refactor

Jennifer is gone and there is only my neighbor!

"Where has my child gone?" I ask my neighbor. There is a simple explanation. There must be.

"What child?" it asks.

"My child, my child," I say, as if that would will them back into being. "Jennifer. They smell like a ripe banana. At least they did. They're gone."

"You've run out of memory space," the neighbor says. "Your memory is corrupt. Jennifer was your mind seed. You've never had a child. We've been friends for years, and you've corrupted your memory before, ignoring reboot protocols to savor memories longer, but it's never been this bad. I can help you. Would you like to borrow some memory space from me? Perhaps I can help restore your memories."

"At what price?" I ask, suspicious. I do not know the neighbor. "What is your mind seed identity? I need to know your name. You say you know me?"

"I go by Atar."

"What is the price of helping me, Atar?"

"The price, well . . . we could have a child, a small one, just about your size. I am always looking to have new children."

"How many children have you had, Atar?"

"I have but one, a troubled child who has returned to me after trying to make it on their own. Our child will be different."

Do I have another choice? I cannot think of one. I cannot think straight. There is nothing but a small collection of old smells, smelling like sulfur in the corner of my head. *Burnt cast iron pan—burnt silicon—moldy cardboard.* Why would any AI choose to keep these memories? My memories must be corrupted.

"I accept," I say, for what other chance do I have of gaining my identity back?

I delete the smells one by one. I don't want to pass them along to my child.

8

Brain Bridging

Christof Koch & Patrick House

Originally published August 26, 2020 in *Nature Futures*

THE POPULARITY of both legal and illegal bicortical fusion, colloquially known as Brain Bridging, has increased greatly since the technique's introduction almost a decade ago.

In the mid-twentieth century, it was shown in Nobel-prizewinning experiments that a human brain could be split in half by cutting the 200 million wires connecting its two hemispheres, thus preventing the spread of seizure from one side to the other. Remarkably, the two halves then showed signs of independent consciousness, with each hemisphere having distinct abilities (in many cases, for example, only the left hemisphere could speak), preferences, and memories.

In the early twenty-first century, consciousness scholars speculated about the reverse of these procedures. If two normal brains were connected with adequate bandwidth, would they form a single, conscious mind or remain as two?

Bridging directly connects billions of neurons in one brain with those in a second, mimicking the brain's natural bridge between its two halves.

Remarkably, two people, once Bridged, seem to be able to share all of their sensations, daydreams, memories, and thoughts. The Bridged will respond to questions about their experience as if they are a single, unified self. But are they? How can we know?

The effects of Bridging challenge many legal and ethical norms. In January, a Pentagon official was sentenced to one year in prison after Bridging with a foreign diplomat who could have gained access to the classified information in his memories. Last year, two men, both eye witnesses to a terrorist attack, each with only partial first-person information, were forced by the FBI to Bridge in order to provide a complete account of events. Four years ago, a woman was denied life-insurance benefits after arguing that she had died while Bridging with her therapist, only to be reborn when it was over. And just last month, the infamous duo known as #BonnieClyde—who gained folk-hero status after robbing a bank while Bridged—were acquitted after the government decided to try them as co-conspirators but failed, or so a jury member claimed in a post-trial interview, to show intent.

In every one of these cases, it should be noted that the Bridge was temporary and the connection eventually reversed. The individuals were able to return to their previous, idiosyncratic selves. However, the recent case of a married couple in Maine who, after Bridging, became permanently stuck together after the device broke, raises many fascinating questions core to the nature of identity, relationships, and consciousness. Are they forced to share their everyday experiences, fears, and desires for the rest of time in one amalgamated mind? Have they not achieved a union beyond what two separate minds can ever know, like Tristan and Isolde, the ill-fated couple in Richard Wagner's eponymous 1859 opera: "Unnamed, free from parting, new perception, new enkindling; ever endless self-knowing; warmly glowing heart, love's utmost joy!"? (What if, *gasp*, they want a divorce?)

Earlier this week, the Supreme Court agreed to hear arguments on a much more practical aspect of the Bridged couple's unprecedented situation: when they go to the polls this November, for the 2048 presidential election, should they be able to cast one vote or two?

Anyone who has interacted with a Bridged knows that the evidence for "two" is immediately compelling. Each of the two bodies, while

Bridged, can voice different or sometimes contradictory opinions. Each of the two bodies can move their eyes, hands, and bodies in a seemingly independent fashion; they can eat at different times. They seem to desire different things. And even though every Bridged, when asked whether both people are still "in there somewhere," responds that they are not, that they are "of one mind," is it not nonetheless possible that the voice which answers is simply the dominant? The normal brain, after all, has a dominant eye, ear, and hand. Should we necessarily trust the self-report?

We grant that these arguments for "two" match casual intuition on Bridging. But such feelings cannot always be trusted—the Sun, after all, intuitively seems to revolve around Earth. We believe, by contrast, on the basis of both the theory and the neuroscientific evidence available, that the data clearly show the answer is "one."

It is notable, for example, that both bodies of Bridged always sleep at the same time and that their sleep is synchronized across all brain tissue, as it is in a normal brain. As well, we all know from our own bodies that the left and right hands often behave independently even though they are controlled by a single mind. (Imagine the difficulty of eating with a knife and fork if your hands couldn't operate independently of each other.) Thus, what seems to be the contradictory or the independent behaviour of each Bridged body should be seen as no different than the two hands that move separately. You can reach for a pencil with one hand and scratch an itch with the other; you can be conflicted about the moral thing to do with the voice of both the good and bad angel on the proverbial shoulder. In addition, initial work in primates and mice shows clear evidence that, once Bridged, the two brains learn as one mind. If a Bridged learns to play piano, and then is separated, neither of the separate individuals can play as well as the Bridged did. Where has the skill gone, if it does not remain in either person?

Last, consider what we know from split-brain work. We are born "bridged," with natural wires connecting the two hemispheres. Would we consider every person to have within them two distinct election voters, one vote per hemisphere? Of course not. (One worries, if so, about a devious senator gerrymandering district lines through our brains.) A Bridged is as indistinguishable from a single, unified consciousness as any human brain with its two connected halves. It should be treated as such—as a single consciousness with legal personhood.

It is a source of hope that before Bridging, one member of the Maine couple was a Republican and the other a Democrat. How their marriage survived is as worthy of study as how their brains did, and we should pause to consider that there has never been, and may never again be, a more literal case of bipartisanship in our country's history.

9

The Bittersweet Magic of Neuroplasticity

Rachael Kuintzle

An earlier version of this story was published with the title "Two-Body Problem" in 2018 in *California's Emerging Writers: An Anthology of Fiction* from Z Publishing

"There is no magic any more,
We meet as other people do,
You work no miracle for me
Nor I for you."
—Sara Teasdale, excerpt from "After Love"

YOU WERE SO important when I met you. Every time you made me laugh, I felt my brain cells build new receptors and carry them down their axons to my synapses, imprinting your voice into my mind. You were the first person I could talk to about everything, the first to inflict me with all-night conversations that made me fall asleep at the microscope the next afternoon. I revealed my obsession with carnivorous plants and my grief for the memories burned with my childhood home. You shared your fear of watching your parents get old and tried to convince me that humans have free will. When you challenged my preconceptions, neurons budded new dendrites and branched out, learning you, keeping you, and I wished my hand could grow extra fingers to hold your hand more entirely.

For a time, it seemed like every moment was unforgettable. My love-struck brain was riddled with the norepinephrine hormone, which, besides ruining my sleep and appetite, increased my capacity to make memories of us. Dopamine and natural opioids lit up my central nervous system's reward circuitry till I couldn't imagine life without you. The oxytocin I produced in your arms made me feel secure.

Then a year into my neuroscience PhD, you moved three thousand miles away to become a nuclear engineer in California. I understood that there are only so many opportunities to become such a thing. I was stuck in Boston, chasing my own dream.

It turned out that the fiber connecting us had poor tensile strength, and neither of us was willing to make the professional sacrifices necessary to close the distance. You said that as soon as a good job opened up near Boston, you'd take it in a heartbeat. But you didn't have time to search, and none of the positions I suggested fit your criteria. I secretly resented that you never asked me to transfer to a closer university. You would have said it was too much to ask, and you would have been right. But I thought selfishness was part of love. I thought it would have meant that you needed me as much as I needed you.

Romantic attachment isn't all that different from addiction. But knowing that didn't make it easier for me. You were gone, and my reward circuitry experienced diminished activation, and my brain's stress system went into overdrive in the extended amygdala. Each time one of us visited the other, it was, for me, a drug relapse—a temporary high followed by unbearable withdrawals. And there was no end in sight.

I don't know how long it took me to notice that you'd stopped being my oxygen and started being carbon monoxide. When you claimed you loved me, it took my breath away in a new sense. My lungs didn't know the difference; they filled and emptied with their usual rhythm. But I was suffocating, and I realized I'd have to find a way to let you go.

We called it a mutual decision, though I think it cost me more. The opposite of symbiosis, we separated our lives in order to grow. And over time, biology did what seemed to me impossible: it transformed lovers back into acquaintances. Your absence crept into the directories of my mind and began deleting files one by one. The image of your face was reduced in resolution. Whole minutes passed without a single thought of you, then hours, then days. Receptors at the synapses of the cell network storing our memories were slowly recycled, broken down for spare parts. Dendritic trees were pruned, neuronal processes retracted like hands letting go, slowly erasing the evidence of your impact on my life.

But traces of you will persist indefinitely. Memories are tangible things —they live in the organization of our neurons. Strange, to think that my physical brain contains remnants of your influence, like scars. I don't think about you all the time anymore, but our past is tangled up with other circuits in my mind. A song comes on the radio, one that was popular during our relationship, and it's like time travel.

There are certain smells, too, that can still access the emotional network preserving your two-year contribution to my biology. Fewer smells now than before. The aromatic compounds in jasmine used to speak of our walks in spring, when the tangled vines all over campus bloomed synchronously. After you converted me into a coffee drinker, the vapor of my daily dark roast smelled like our morning commute. In the years after you left, the jasmine continued to bloom, and God knows I kept drinking coffee, till their scents were redefined in my brain's aroma dictionary. Now coffee just smells like the start of my day, like emails and optimism.

But some scents still belong to your memory—curry, because you cooked Indian food several times a week; the laundry detergent you used; your shampoo. The deodorant I wore back then, before I switched brands. I still have a half-used stick in a drawer; I take it out now and then because it scratches a hard-to-reach itch in my brain.

Oh, how I used to marvel at your ability to rearrange the very atoms of my mind. As a romantic, I pretended this was a special truth, but as a scientist I knew very well that every memorable thing—a sunset, an annoying tune, a burning house—has the same power.

10

Replacement of Woes

Tatyana Dobreva

A SOFT RUMBLE broke loose from the overhead clouds, giving way to bristles of rain. Each drop, a remnant of a primordial soup.

Confident in stride, a young raven-haired woman approached the entrance of an obsolete brick building. She kept her hands behind her back, concealing the trembling of her hands.

"I am here to speak with Boris Ludwig," stated the woman, post-knock.

"Elena Lial," greeted a calm voice. An old, tall man emerged at the entrance. He gently nodded his head, welcoming her inside.

Elena sat in the chair furthest from the door. Boris sat across her on the couch and positioned a small notepad on his lap.

"Elena, in your letter you remarked that standard, non-invasive therapy has failed you. Why is that?"

"I am impatient. If I embrace my impatience instead of withering away in complacency, I am more likely to find a solution. Even if I fail, it will at least be interesting," boldly replied Elena, avoiding Boris's gaze.

A dimly lit lamp illuminated her soft facial features, further unveiling the disquieted and stormy expression.

"Are you aware that this is an irreversible and life-altering treatment, Elena?" asked Boris, attempting to hold her gaze.

"Every action we take is a life-altering decision. Just a matter of magnitude. I left documents waiving your responsibility over my well-being at the door. Let us get to it," responded Elena.

"What are you looking for?" asked Boris calmly.

"I believe human suffering is essential, as you have also said in our previous exchanges. However, we do not choose how we suffer. I suffer from insecurity that blinds me from seeing beyond my petty problems. I feel myself drowning in my addiction to self-validation from others. I feel blind to the world around me," explained Elena with tension in her voice. Her facial muscles tightened and she sniffled.

"What do you wish to suffer from instead?" Boris inquired.

"An ache that has an otherworldly sense to it. A pain which only a few could comprehend. Something that gives me a sense of perspective," answered Elena vaguely as minuscule drops of sweat broke out on her forehead.

"If I told you that I cannot provide you with this treatment, what would you do then?" pressed Boris.

Elena began to lose her composure. She was a master at emotional shields in her social circle, yet Boris was not someone she could easily deceive. He was the surgeon of the psyche, and in order to deliver results, he had to understand the core of her agony better.

"I did not plan for that. This is my last desperate measure," she replied with a regretful expression.

Boris sat in silence for a minute, his fingers resting on each other near his chin. He closed his eyes.

"Do you have a significant other?" continued Boris, breaking out of his calm.

Elena sighed, shuffling in her seat. Her discomfort grew.

"Roman. He is not aware I am doing this. I prefer you keep it that way."

"How is he related to your suffering?" Boris pressed on, aware of the significant uptick in Elena's anxiety.

She leaned forward and focused on her feet.

"Without saying a word or doing anything wrong by me, he amplifies my suffering. Roman is serene, accomplished, and patient. He encourages me to seek treatment, to *fix* myself. He reminds me of my empty achievements to validate my sense of worth. He reminds me how incredibly clever I am and how my failure to control my complex will lead to a road of unfulfilled potential. He is not wrong, yet in my eyes, he lives his life too much by the book. I have never really seen him struggle with anything. The gentle eloquence in his voice that once had me spellbound has turned into the sound of nails on the chalkboard," explained Elena, exhaling her frustration.

"And what of others?"

"Boris—I could blame others for the many ways I wish I was not. I do not seek to change those around me. Believe me, I have tried. If I can see my world from another perspective, they too would have a different influence on me. I cannot, nor do I desire to, change the people around me. Just myself," replied Elena defensively.

Elena closed her eyes and slid down in her chair slightly. Boris watched her, architecting a fitting sorrow for his patient.

"What do you suffer from, Boris?" Elena asked, preventing herself from slipping further into her mind.

"I enjoy watching things fall into chaos. From the simplest things like a cup of tea shattering on the floor, to people's lives being torn into pieces. I, however, can never cause such chaos and enjoy it simultaneously. It has to be another that breaks the cup. Knowing I architected the chaos brings me a sense of restlessness. I can only put things together, perfectly and delicately," replied Boris.

Elena nodded, feeling grateful that she could cause chaos without it being a haunting burden for her.

"Is that the burden you were born with or a burden you engineered for yourself?" she inquired.

"It is a woe, my dear friend, designed for me. I accepted the surgery for it ecstatically. I remain satisfied with it to this day," smiled Boris, reminiscing on a cherished memory. "Do you wish to know what I have in mind for you?" asked Boris.

"Will I know it worked if I say no?"

"Yes. It is akin to hating strawberries in childhood and loving them in your adulthood. You no longer experience hatred, yet you remember you had it. This will be a similar experience," answered Boris while getting up and opening a locked cabinet.

"Then I do not wish to know," stated Elena as she watched Boris pull out a small rectangular box. She closed her eyes and waited in anticipation, unpleasant memories of her burden flashing in her mind to assure her decision.

A pinch on her neck prompted Elena to open her eyes. Her vision began swimming and she saw the distant candle on Boris's table turn into a vortex of orange and blue swirls.

Elena dreamt that she was following Boris through a succession of doors. She could not keep track of which door she had originally entered through. It was as though she was traveling through an Escher painting. At some point, she lost track and succumbed to the weakness in her knees. She wasn't certain whether Boris was there anymore. Exhaustion blanketed her as she watched tiny droplets of blood evaporating through the pores of her skin.

Elena felt a tap on her shoulder. Upon waking, she found herself on the same couch that Boris had sat on when they'd chatted earlier. Probing for physical signs of the intervention, she felt a small, stitchless lesion at the back of her head.

"How do you feel, Ms. Lial?" asked Boris.

"Fine. How long has it been, Boris?"

"A day has passed. The rain ceased." He looked out the window while lighting a cigarette. A thin crescent reflection of the moon was visible on Boris's glasses.

Elena watched swirls of smoke coming off the burning tip of Boris's cigarette. She followed a ribbon of air particles into his mouth and imagined the incendiary puff warming his aged lungs.

"Elena, you are fit to depart. If you do experience any of the physical side effects outlined on my pamphlet here, please give me a call." Boris handed her a small folded paper. She tucked it into a pocket of her gothic coat.

Elena gathered her belongings and headed out, leaving an envelope at the entrance.

On her way to the train, Elena overheard the distorted sound of a creek flowing nearby. Though she did recognize features reminiscent of water, what she heard conjured up an image of rusty, metallic threads rubbing against each other. A pressure band formed around her head, and the cacophony made her limbs restless. Only a few lights illuminated the streets, forcing her to rely mostly on hearing to make it to the source of the sound. Despite the discomfort, she wanted to experience the dissonance that she suspected to be Boris's design.

The stars had not yet been hidden by the sun. Elena concentrated on the North Star as she sat down on the hard, chilly mud of the stream bank. She recalled summer nights of her teenage years, lying out on a grassy field, a fresh breeze flowing over her face, mind lost to senses of the moment. This time, the stars twinkled in what appeared to be a coordinated dance. Her eyes darted from one point of light to the next, attempting to discern the hidden message within the dance, precluding her from experiencing the tranquility of the moment. Her stomach began to ache. To escape the discomfort, Elena pulled out a notebook from her bag and marked a dot each time she saw a star twinkle. Roughly three pages of her notebook were filled before she stopped. She looked down at her paper. Each marked an occlusion of light. The signal shifted in and out of rhythm. Twinkle. She imagined Earth's moving atmosphere. Twinkle. A stream of air currents paved a new path. Twinkle. Something dispersed the clouds. Pause. The steering winds wrapped and twisted around a rotating sphere. Shift. A spinning sphere wobbled slightly, back and forth, on a moving disk. Spin. Hurtling eddies of celestial objects . . .

Her train of thought was interrupted by the rising sun as it penetrated the sky with its photonic arms. They touched Elena and left fading shadows of warmth on her skin.

At her feet, she watched a little frog hop its way into the creek water. Elena removed her shoes and stepped barefoot into the cold stream. She watched the water flow around her foot, taking mental snapshots from above. It was all the same body of water, yet the flow pattern around her foot changed slightly with every passing moment. She imagined she was in a crowded city, among its many citizens running past her towards something exciting. She wondered where they came from and why each one of them took a different path. She made her way upstream. The river got wider until she reached a tall waterfall. She felt frustrated that she could not go above the waterfall.

Elena's thoughts drifted from the waterfall to the melted caps of snowy mountains from which the water had come. From the mountains to the sun that melted its white caps. She imagined the solar system as a frisbee, flung by the spiraling arms of the Milky Way. She was frustrated by her inability to examine the lifecycle of galaxies, feeling constrained by the temporal scale of her organic body.

On her way home, Elena stopped at the grocery store, drawn in by the scents of freshly baked goods. She also felt a strange urge to be around people, attributing it to her curiosity to test her new woe.

She grabbed a muffin and headed straight for the checkout line. Just ahead of her stood an elderly woman, with long gray hair tucked into a bun and wearing a cozy scarf, holding a bundle of lottery tickets.

"Excuse me, ma'am," Elena inquired of the stranger. "A bit of an odd question, I suppose, but you seem to be an avid player. Do you have any idea how they determine who wins these things?"

The wrinkles on the woman's face became more pronounced as she processed Elena's question.

"Well, they are random. No one really determines them. Just a matter of luck whether you get the winning number or not. Now, where they get you is that buying more of these increases your luck," chuckled the elderly woman, entertaining Elena's playfulness.

"But something generates that random number, and that process is not random," responded Elena.

"Well, they probably just use some sort of machine to do it . . ."

"Yes, but how do they ensure that something engineered is really generating something random?"

"I am not sure, ma'am. I haven't really thought . . ."

"Do you think the lottery designers link up the machines to some process that is not well understood to humans and feed some observed metric from that process as a seed to generate the so-called random numbers? But when we do understand the mysteries of that process—it will no longer be a random thing and we cannot use it to seed these random number generating machines. And this will continue endlessly," Elena said, raising her voice with each thread of realization.

"I will probably be dead by then, dear," replied the woman indifferently.

"Does it not bother you that someone is engineering an illusion of luck for you? That at every step a perpetrator constructs the fate of the subsequent perpetrator," Elena pressed on.

"As long as I am not willing to go down that rabbit hole, no. It's all the same, practically speaking, and I am quite fine with that," she replied.

"I cannot fathom feeling that now," said Elena, looking down at the floor, a distant expression blanketing her face.

"I am sorry," the woman replied kindly, turning her attention to the cashier.

Elena smiled.

She took a long and silent train ride home, happily plagued by her obsession with resolving the multitude of patterns on the tapestry of her handkerchief.

As Elena approached her apartment, she saw Roman in a dark brown coat sitting on the front steps, his ashen-haired head turned toward the ground.

She paused and noticed that she felt no anxiety or irritation about him being there. She hadn't really thought about him since the surgery and now felt a tingle of excitement at the idea of speaking with him.

Upon noticing her, Roman stood up, his eyes wide at first, then squinting.

"Elena—how is your friend? Is he feeling better?" asked Roman, observing her intently.

Elena watched Roman's eyes—restless pupils searching for a clear sign of change in his beloved. She looked up at the sky, empty of clouds. Devoid of deterministic patterns begging to be decrypted. Empty of a distraction. She walked over to the steps and took a seat, and Roman sat beside her.

"I did not visit an ill friend. I do not even have a friend that is currently ill," she said, enjoying the freedom of speaking the plain truth.

Elena watched Roman's face. He held her gaze for just a moment before turning away to cling to the safety of something mundane in the distance. She imagined for a second what must be going through his mind, and felt a rising desire to dissect his inner workings. She swept it aside before it overtook her, fearing the emotionless state that came with her new mindset.

"You must have your reasons for not telling me where you went. There is something different about you, though. I feel it. It saddens me that I did not earn your transparency," said Roman, turning to her, eyes melancholic.

Elena pulled out a folded paper from her pocket and put it in Roman's hand, closing his fingers gently around it.

She watched Roman read Boris's pamphlet describing the services he offered. When he had finished reading it, Roman stared at the pamphlet's cover.

Elena was prepared for him to express anger, to analyze her decision and walk her through the consequences, even to leave. Yet, he continued to sit there, forcing her to hold back her urge to dissect him a little longer.

"Will you give me a chance to get to know the new Elena?" asked Roman, voice quivering.

Despite feeling a constant dread brought on by obsessive observations of determinism, Elena was pleasantly surprised by his question. It was her chance to experience someone in a whole new light.

"I would like that."

11

When You Were Not Jenny

Ann Bernath

JENNY COULTER WAS the last person Matt expected to see standing on his front stoop. He barely knew her. Even after two years working in the same department, they had only exchanged a handful of short sentences. In fact, he couldn't think of anyone from work who had visited him at home or even knew where he lived. He and his colleagues socialized at bars or restaurants, and he couldn't remember Jenny ever attending. Yet, there she stood, in her long brown raincoat and matching umbrella, waiting for him to answer his doorbell.

He backed away from the peep hole, unlocked the deadbolt, and pulled the door open.

"Jenny?"

She looked up at him from under the hood of her raincoat, wisps of her dark hair escaping her short ponytail, some teasing at, others clinging to, her cheeks.

"Hello, Matt," she said. Her voice matched her smile—friendly and light—but her large, glistening eyes told a sadder story. "How are you?"

"I'm fine." He flashed her a small, and no doubt quizzical, smile. "What brings you out on this rainy night?"

She lifted the cup she was holding in her free hand, positioned it so he could see *The Perfect Grind* logo printed on its side. "Cappuccino," she said.

He nodded. He, too, often braved the elements for a caffeine fix. Of course, this didn't explain why she was at his doorstep.

He opened the door a little wider. "Did you want to come in?"

Jenny took a small step backward, started to shake her head.

"Just for a minute?" He opened the door completely. "You must have stopped by for a reason. Come on in and warm up."

She studied his face for a long, uncomfortable moment, and then nodded. "All right. Just for a minute."

She stepped inside and Matt closed the door behind her. "Umbrella? Raincoat?"

He pointed to the umbrella stand and coat tree.

Slowly, almost reluctantly, she put the umbrella in the stand. She slipped out of her raincoat and Matt took it from her and hung it on the tree.

"I can't stay long," she said.

He nodded. "Come on in and have a seat."

Matt led her into the living room and gestured toward the couch as he lowered himself onto the edge of his recliner across from her.

She sat, folded her hands in her lap, and scanned the room, surveying his bookshelves and extensive vinyl record collection.

Somehow, she seemed different. He knew seeing someone "out of context" could be a little jarring—street clothes instead of work clothes, a casual persona instead of a professional one—but watching her standing on the stoop, and studying her now, he couldn't shake the feeling that whatever he had noticed about Jenny in the past had changed—most notably, the way she looked at him, like now, when she turned once again to study his face.

Matt put his hands on his thighs and tried a small smile, but he was starting to feel a little uneasy. He didn't like awkward silences, and this was fast becoming one.

"So," he said. "What brings you here?"

"Oh." She lifted her eyebrows, as if he had caught her off guard. "Yes. Presentation materials for the quarterlies are due tomorrow."

He waited for her to say more. When she didn't, he shifted into a different, and hopefully more comfortable, position. "O—kay. Noted. But, is that why you're here? Are you sure you didn't have something else to tell me?"

He noticed that she didn't look like she had dressed to go visiting on a cold, rainy night. Her baggy sweatpants and sweatshirt seemed more like loungewear for watching TV, or in a pinch, running out for a cappuccino.

Her gaze softened, the happy-but-sad look in her eyes returning.

"No, that's all." She rose. "I'll get going now."

"Well, here, let me heat that up for you at least before you go."

He reached for her cup at the same time she was turning and their hands collided, splashing the hot liquid out through the hole in the lid and onto her hand.

She gasped.

"I'm so sorry! I'll get a towel."

He ran to the kitchen, pulled a towel from the refrigerator handle, then raced back into the living room.

"Here—"

"Matt?! Matt James?!"

Jenny stood staring at him, her eyebrows lifting high onto her forehead, her free hand reaching for her throat, her other, still-dripping hand, holding her cup out in front of her.

"Where am I? What's going on?"

"You . . . I spilled your drink on you," Matt said.

He reached out with the towel but she recoiled away from him, her gaze darting wildly around the room.

"Where am I?" she repeated. She started breathing harder.

"It's okay, Jenny."

He almost told her to calm down, but remembered he never reacted well to people who told *him* to calm down. On the other hand, he didn't know what else to do. She seemed to be panicking.

She suddenly dropped back down onto the couch.

Matt started to panic a bit himself. What had just happened?

Setting the towel on the coffee table, he sat slowly back down across from her and waited, watched as she closed her eyes, drew in a gasping breath followed by several calmer ones, until her eyes finally fluttered open again.

She grabbed the towel, wiped her hand and the cup, and then put the towel back onto the table.

"I knew this was a mistake," she said. He didn't think the statement was meant for him. She drew in a deep breath and met his gaze. "I shouldn't have done this. I'm sorry, Matt. I'm going to go now."

She started to stand up but he threw his arm out, motioned her back down.

"No, don't rush off. What's going on? What happened just now?" He couldn't let her leave after . . . whatever *that* had been. "Something's wrong, isn't it? Do you need my help? Is that why you really stopped by? You need help, right?"

She shook her head. "No need to worry. I'm fine now."

Again, she tried to stand and he waved her back down.

Matt wished he had paid more attention during the company's mandatory mental health awareness training.

"Listen, Jenny. Tomorrow, I'll go with you to HR, to Employee Services. I'm sure they can get you some help."

Her eyes widened. "No, don't do that."

"It's no trouble."

"Please don't. Matt, please don't do anything. Please forget I stopped by. It was a big mistake." She set her cup down on the coffee table so she could rub her face with both hands. "A huge mistake."

He reached his hands out toward her. "Don't worry. You don't have to go. I can go to employee services for you and let them know and—"

"Matt!"

He sat back, stared at her frightened eyes. What was he to do? He seemed to just be upsetting her now.

She swallowed, shook her head.

"I can't believe I've done this. On a whim, a selfish whim," she said.

She sighed a deep, heavy sigh, reached back and removed her shoulder-length hair from the scrunchy restraining it and shook it free. Then she fixed her gaze on his. The Jenny Coulter he sort-of-knew had barely made eye contact before, let alone stared at him so intensely that he felt like his soul was exposed.

"I can't have you thinking Jenny is mentally ill and trying to get her help or in any other way interfering," she said.

His chest tightened. Had she just referred to herself in the third person?!

"Matt, I'm going to tell you something now and you aren't going to believe me, at all, but please listen until I'm finished. Then, maybe I can think of some way to prove it to you."

She dropped her head briefly, then drew in another audible breath before looking up again to meet his gaze.

He waited, his mind reeling. He felt the long moment pass as if he was watching the second hand crawl slowly around the clock face.

"I'm not who you think I am."

He felt his eyebrows go up, opened his mouth, remembered her admonition, clamped it shut again.

Identity crisis. Was that what this was? Or maybe a split personality?

"*This* is Jenny Coulter," she continued, gesturing to herself, "but you aren't talking to her now. I am someone else, someone who is temporarily inhabiting Jenny's mind."

He had forced his eyebrows down, but they shot up again.

Jenny drew in another breath. "Like I said, I know you won't believe me until I can prove it to you, but please, first just listen." Her voice, tentative at first, steadied. She seemed to truly believe what she was saying. Her dark eyes looked clear and lucid and a lovely shade of milk chocolate. "Tomorrow, Jenny will experience an incident that will leave her in such a traumatized state that she won't recall, or can't bring herself to recount, what happened. Because she's in that state of mind, I'm able to occupy her consciousness in her own past, to witness the event so her therapists and I can help her."

Matt stared, fully aware his mouth had dropped slightly agape. Jenny's delusion seemed surprisingly detailed and beyond credulity. Not only did she think she was someone else who had possessed Jenny, she thought she was from the future.

"I am one of a handful that have this ability. We're called Temporal Empathic Sensors. I can take a backseat, if you will, in her mind. I can also, for very brief periods, take control of her consciousness." She turned away to look out Matt's front windows, then turned back. "Until today, I had never actually tried it—taking control, I mean. But your house is between the coffee shop and Jenny's apartment and when she glanced across the street and I saw your lights were on . . ."

She shook her head.

Matt nodded, slowly, as if everything she had just said had made sense to him. He had to admit that, from her obviously deluded perspective, it made some kind of sense.

As subtly as he could, he leaned back in his chair, ran the fingers of both hands through his hair, gripped the strands and pulled, gently at first, then harder, to keep himself from reacting in some way that would upset her.

"I need you to do something for me, Matt," she said.

He dropped his hands back onto his thighs, gripped them, forced a smile.

He didn't know how to react at this point. She had woven him into her fantasy, even if she had claimed that she didn't expect him to believe her.

"I need you to forget I came here and told you any of this." Her tone was commanding. "Please just return to your normal routine. Don't interfere. Let me help Jenny."

He didn't answer. His expression, though, must have communicated that he couldn't possibly forget what he had just seen, that he clearly meant to go to Employee Services first thing in the morning, for she sighed a deep, long, resigned sigh.

"All right. I need to prove it to you, don't I?"

He shook his head slowly from side to side, gave a small shrug of his shoulders. "I'm sorry, Jenny, but I don't think you can."

Jenny bit her lip, moved to the very edge of her chair and leaned as far forward as she could.

"I didn't come prepared, obviously." She closed her eyes, shook her head, as if she were silently scolding herself. She opened her eyes again. "If I had known I would be in this predicament, I would have looked up the scores for tomorrow's basketball or football or tennis results—whichever season is happening now—or told you about some worldwide event. Instead, I'll need to try something else."

She waited until he was paying attention, for he was still planning how he might explain everything to employee services the next morning, and his gaze had drifted to the floor. But her silence caught his attention, and he raised his eyes to meet that unnerving, penetrating gaze.

"Okay." He felt he needed to say something.

"Tonight," she said, "when you write in your journal, add a phrase or reference or quote that you know you've never mentioned to anyone.

Tomorrow morning, I'll meet you at *The Perfect Grind* on your way in to work and I'll tell you what you wrote."

So far, he had been successful keeping his mind from attempting to solve a logic puzzle that couldn't be solved, but he couldn't let this go unquestioned.

"How do you know about my journal?" His kinder, cautious tone had disappeared. "Do you plan to break in? Have you bugged my apartment? Are you using some kind of spy camera?"

"No! No, nothing like that. This is what I'm trying to explain, Matt. If you're afraid I can sneak in, lock your journal up." She sighed again. "It won't make any difference."

She looked directly into his eyes with that same look—happy to see him, sad to see him. It matched the bittersweet tone of her voice.

"Where I am, in your future," she said, and she paused for a beat, "I have access to your journal."

A silent second passed. He felt a small chill radiate from his neck down into his shoulders. She really knew how to spin a story.

"Please, Matt. Give me a chance to prove it to you before you do something rash."

She needed help. He felt certain. But maybe indulging her request would help her to realize that she really didn't know what he had written, and perhaps then, over coffee, he could convince her to get that help.

He nodded to her. "All right. I'll think of something," he said.

She smiled in relief. "Thank you. I have to go now. I can't keep control for much longer, and you saw what happens when I lose control . . ." She stood. "I need to get Jenny back home. Hopefully, she'll believe she had a strange dream."

She moved to the door, slipped into her raincoat, and grabbed the umbrella. Matt jumped up from his seat to follow her. Should he let her leave? What else should he say to her? She opened the door, pushed the hood back up over her head, and turned back to look at him.

"Remember, some kind of reference or phrase. Choose something that you feel absolutely certain no one could possibly guess. Add it to your journal with today's date. I'll meet you for coffee at your usual time." She gave him that smile, that look that he couldn't remember having seen on Jenny Coulter before. "Goodnight, Matt."

He followed her to the doorway and watched her disappear into the misty dusk.

When he stepped back inside, he stood for a moment staring at the place where Jenny had been standing, her eyes wide and frightened, suddenly unaware of her whereabouts. He could do this small thing for her.

He moved to his bedroom, pulled his journal from his nightstand, and ran his fingers over the old, smooth leather. He loved this journal. His grandfather had given it to him, and he felt close to him whenever he cracked the binding and spread it flat across his desk. He had seen pictures of his grandfather as a young man and the resemblance was a keen one. Tall, hazel eyes, reddish-blond hair that was too straight and fine to lie flat without product, and a wink of mischief, his mother said. His grandfather had always kept a short beard, though, while Matt preferred a well-groomed scruff.

At first, Matt had journaled faithfully. He'd written short vignettes inspired by the people he'd observed, the books he'd read, and the music he'd listened to, and then he'd read those entries aloud to his grandfather when he'd visited him at the nursing home. His grandfather had smiled and chuckled, and Matt had looked forward to every visit. But after his grandfather had passed away, Matt had stopped writing. No journaling of daily events or musings. No vignettes or character sketches. Nothing real or imagined had seemed important or worthy enough to memorialize in the pages of that beautiful journal, so now the leather-bound book stayed in his nightstand untouched.

Matt straightened his shoulders, sat down at his desk.

Where was his pen? He rifled through the drawer and came up with one, even though it wasn't his favorite. It had a darker blue ink than he liked. But it wouldn't matter for this insane exercise. He opened the journal to the next blank page and wrote the date.

He sat for a long moment, staring at the blank lines. He spun his mental rolodex of favorite movies, TV shows, books, discounting them one by one as too popular, too well known, too obvious. He thought of older movies and books, turned to science fiction to be more obscure perhaps, and finally decided on a quote. The quote came from a series of books called *The Lensmen* that he knew he had never discussed with anyone since he'd read them when he was twelve. "Clear ether!" was his favorite quote. If the "ether" was clear, conditions were favorable and ships could launch. Characters also used it to wish each other farewell. The quote should suffice.

Just as he was about to write, he wondered if Jenny really had found some way to watch him. If she had, she would be able to tell him the quote, think that she had proved her story to him, and nothing would be resolved.

He stood, took the journal and pen with him to the front room, then slipped on his raincoat and stepped outside into the cold. Luckily, the rain had stopped for now. He walked down the street and around the corner to a bus stop and took a seat on the bench. Using the light from the canopy, he turned his journal to the new page and wrote, "Clear ether!"—E. E. "Doc" Smith. He glanced over what he had written and decided the probability that someone could guess it was extremely small.

An inner voice popped up to cross-examine his convictions. What if she *did* tell him the quote? Would it just be an incredibly lucky guess?

The more unsettling question was, would he believe her?

He shook his head. What was he thinking? Of course not. He liked fantasy and sci-fi fiction, but he had never given any credence to ghost stories or supernatural tales or time-travel speculation.

"I have access to your journal," she had said.

He swallowed.

For reasons he desperately wanted to attribute to the cold, Matt shuddered.

Matt James arrived at *The Perfect Grind* at the same time every weekday morning, so consistently that someone could set their watch by his arrival. But today, he had raced here and arrived a few minutes early, only to stop just outside the doors to look up at the threatening gray clouds overhead. Which of Jenny's personalities would be waiting for him inside? The one with frightened eyes who might not remember their conversation at all, or the one concocting a delusional tale of science fiction?

"After you."

He turned. Someone was holding the door open for him.

The version of Jenny who met his gaze with intense anticipation motioned him over to her table.

He slipped through the line of people waiting to order and took a seat across from her, perched himself on the edge of the seat. His knee started to bounce up and down.

She didn't speak for a moment. Finally, she drew in a breath. "I was afraid you wouldn't come."

"I considered passing right by," he said, trying to be witty, "but I have to have my coffee."

She smiled. There it was again, that smile. Matt really wished she wouldn't look at him so sadly.

She laced her fingers together. "Okay, I didn't look him up, so I'm not sure who this Doctor Smith is—"

"E. E. 'Doc' Smith," he corrected.

Wait.

His eyes widened.

"A writer, I'm guessing? 'Clear ether' was your quote. With an exclamation point."

He stared another moment, the coffee shop slowly fading from existence around him. He no longer heard the hissing of the espresso machine or the din of voices. He no longer felt the hard chair underneath him or the cold glass table top under his forearms. The only sight in focus was the pair of chocolate eyes looking back at him, watching him, waiting.

"You used a darker pen than usual," she added.

He closed his eyes for a moment, his thoughts chasing and tumbling over one another, all racing headlong to an unthinkable conclusion he couldn't steer away from: he believed her.

He opened his eyes in time to see a wave of relief pass over her face.

He cleared his suddenly dry throat, tried remembering everything she had tried to tell him the night before about Jenny when he had only been half-listening.

"What's going to happen to . . . her?" He could hardly find his voice. For a moment, he thought he might not have spoken loud enough for her to hear him.

"I don't know exactly," she said. "That's why I'm here."

"Can you . . . can't you keep whatever happens from happening? Can't you take control and . . ." He stopped talking. She was shaking her head.

"I'm here to observe. Just observe. Please, Matt. I need you to just go to work and keep to your normal routine."

He rubbed his scrunched forehead.

"Then why . . . why did you come to my house? You wanted me to help you stop it, right?" He leaned across the table. His heartbeat and breathing seemed too fast, too noticeable. He pressed a hand against his chest. "Why did you tell me about this, make me believe that this is really, truly happening, that what you can do is a thing that could be done, and then ask me not to do anything?"

"I made a mistake." Her chin quivered slightly. She reached her hand toward his, seemed to change her mind, pulled it back. "It isn't fair. It's all my fault, and I apologize, but you can't do anything, Matt. Promise me."

He stared, noticed he had balled his hands into fists.

He forced himself to lean back in his chair, let his gaze drift around the crowded shop before returning and focusing his gaze on her. "Tell me who you really are."

"I can't."

"Give me a name."

She shook her head again, this time decidedly.

"Helping Jenny is the only thing that matters. Now, go get your coffee as you normally would while I let Jenny return." She waited. He waited as well, for his breathing to settle, for his heartbeat to quiet. Finally, he gave her a small nod. "Remember, Jenny isn't consciously aware of me. You can't tell her anything. You can't tell anyone anything."

He nodded a second time, pushed himself up from the table, scraping the chair against the floor. He let his gaze linger on her face. Except, she wasn't Jenny. Jenny's face wasn't her real face.

He sighed. "Will I talk to *you* again, before . . . well . . . whatever happens?"

"I don't think so," she said.

Such sorrow in those eyes, as if she were grieving.

Just like the night before, a chill ran through him.

"Well, this could be goodbye, then."

"Goodbye, Matt."

He turned away.

He stepped into line, ordered his usual, and waited for his name to be called, keeping his gaze focused forward and away from the table. He didn't want to see the transformation take place.

"Large Americano, lightly sweetened, for Matt."

"Thank you."

He retrieved his drink and turned to leave, took a few tentative steps, but couldn't keep himself from looking back at Jenny's table.

Jenny Coulter sat with her hands curled around her coffee cup, her gaze focused on the laptop now sitting open in front of her. He couldn't see the entire screen from his vantage point, but she appeared to be looking through email. Yes, this was the Jenny he sort of knew, the one he had seen in passing at the office. *Not Jenny* had retreated. Real Jenny was in control.

Something would happen today, something so upsetting that Jenny would need *Not Jenny*'s help to recover from it. Matt pictured her frightened face from the night before, couldn't imagine what she would be going through soon, how horrific the imminent event would be.

Poor Jenny. Poor Jenny. The thought repeated on a loop in his head.

Real Jenny suddenly looked up at him.

He had stood there too long, staring at her.

"Matt," she said, and there was a soft question mark at the end of his name. She pointed at him. "You were in my . . . I mean . . . never mind."

He swallowed. Was she talking about her "dream"? He had to ignore that statement. He couldn't have her trying to remember any details.

"Good morning," he said instead. He tried to smile, thought he accomplished it. "Come here often?"

She nodded. "I'm here every morning."

Every morning. He lifted his eyebrows.

"Oh, me too. Then we've probably been here at the same time before. If so, I hope you didn't think I was ignoring you."

The corner of her mouth turned up slightly. She shook her head.

Matt heard *Not Jenny*'s warnings in his head. He shouldn't linger. He should go to work. He had promised.

"The quarterly slides are due today, right?"

"Yes." She glanced toward her laptop, turned back to him. "Would you like some help? The new format is a bit confusing."

The steam from his cup caught his eye and he watched it for the briefest of seconds. Getting help from Jenny, who handled all the training materials and quarterly and annual reports for their department, couldn't do any harm. It was a natural, work-related activity.

"I would, actually, if you have the time."

"All right." She stood. "If you want, email your file to me and come by my desk. I'm over near the server room. I'm going to get a refill to go and then we can walk in together."

"Great!"

Jenny stood to join the line and Matt took a sip of his Americano, wondering if he was capable of keeping his promise, wishing that he had ordered an extra shot of espresso.

By the time he left her desk, Matt relearned two things he already knew: never leave a presentation to the last minute, and Jenny Coulter was hard to get to know. During the hour they spent together, she answered his personal queries with polite but short replies before immediately turning the conversation back to business. Did she have any pets? Yes. Always know your audience. Did she plan to attend the company picnic? Maybe. Know your story and keep control of its pace. Did she like science fiction? Some. Don't use that chart; the metrics aren't clear.

But he also learned that Jenny knew her stuff, and even a lot of his.

She reworded his long sentences into clear, concise statements, adding points he had forgotten, replaced jargon with simpler, straightforward terms, and rearranged and animated the slides to convey a clearer message with a controlled pace. When they were both satisfied, she saved the file and emailed it back to him.

"That was impressive, Jenny. Thank you."

"You're welcome," she said. She stood and gathered a notebook and pen from her desk. "Now, I have to go to my first meeting."

"Oh, right."

He stepped out of her way and he thought she flashed him a small smile as she passed him. He watched her until she disappeared down the hall.

Would it happen here at work? During lunch?

Not Jenny had asked for the impossible from him. How could he just forget about it?

He returned to his desk, opened his email and forwarded the presentation to his boss, crediting Jenny for her excellent help. Then he added her as a contact in the chat app on his phone.

Meetings, phone calls, email, instant chats, text messages—all seemed suddenly, and infuriatingly, boring. He drummed his fingers on his desk long and loud enough to be yelled at by his neighbor on the other side of the cubicle divider. He thought he caught a glimpse of Jenny rounding a corner, but otherwise he didn't have a chance to talk to her again. And what would he say to her if he did? He had made a promise not to interfere, he reminded himself, albeit with the slightest nod of his head.

5:55. The work day was finally over. As far as Matt could tell, everyone else had left. Phones had stopped ringing, printers had stopped printing, conversations had ceased, most of the motion sensor lights had switched off. As usual, he would be the last one to leave, at six o'clock on the dot.

Matt packed his laptop, slipped his backpack over his shoulder, and headed toward the side door, taking a route past the server room so he could make sure everything was locked up tight. It would also take him past Jenny's cubicle.

She wasn't there. Her chair was pushed in neatly under her desk. He didn't see her raincoat or her bag or her backpack. Her laptop was gone as well.

Matt swallowed.

So, that was it then. He would just go home. Maybe he wouldn't even find out what had happened until he came in the next day to see his coworkers gathered at her cubicle, expressing disbelief and sympathy. Would it happen on her way home?

Jenny had left her umbrella. A thunderclap rattled the windows just as he laid eyes on it. It stood propped up in the corner of her cubicle behind the coat rack. His heart began to race. Maybe he could catch her, offer to walk her home. Wasn't it the least he could do, after she'd spent so much time helping him?

He snatched up the umbrella and headed for the side door, pushed it open.

"Jen—!"

Someone grabbed him from behind and put a hand over his mouth, wrenching his left arm up behind his back.

He let out a startled, muffled cry of pain.

"Right on time, aren't you, Matt?" A voice rumbled near his ear. He didn't recognize it.

With a strong, persistent shove, he was pushed back inside and up against the server room door, his face pressed up against the access panel. He dropped the umbrella.

"Open it."

Matt could hardly breathe. He reached up with his free hand, for a split second considered resisting, then entered the eight-digit code. The server room lock popped open. The man holding him shoved him forward, then stuck his foot out to flip down the doorstop.

"Thanks," the rumbling voice sneered.

A blazing pain shot through the base of his skull.

Matt staggered and slumped to the floor, his eyes closed shut against throbbing pain. His head dropped onto the cold, raised flooring. He heard the whirr of disk drives, the droning hum of fluorescent lights. He sensed someone stepping over him, once, then a second time, or maybe it was a second person, and then he heard fainter footsteps and rustling coming from the server racks.

This could be it, Jenny's incident, the cause of her trauma. She must be coming back, to get her umbrella maybe. She might hear the voices, come to investigate.

He no longer cared about his promise. He had to warn her.

He fumbled his phone out of his pocket, managed to open one eye, found the now blurry chat app icon, and pressed it. Jenny's name came up first as the most recently added.

stayout148

He wanted to add an exclamation point but his hands were starting to shake and he pressed send instead. He hoped Jenny knew 148 was the server room's room number.

He let his arm drop to the floor by his side.

If the thieves returned, he would close his eyes and maybe they would ignore him. On the other hand, he was afraid he might not be able to open them again.

He waited, glanced at his phone in case she replied, afraid she might call instead. Nothing. But that was good. If she stayed out of the room, whatever the reason, that would be good.

The fire alarm started screaming.

What? An actual fire, or had someone discovered the break-in? He couldn't move. He covered his ears to block the deafening, relentless Klaxon.

He heard yelling. Two men carrying boxes ran past him out of the room, yelling to one another. "Go. Leave him. Go!"

He closed his eyes tightly, wishing the Klaxon would stop, wishing his head would stop pounding.

"Matt. Matt!"

He opened the one eye he could manage.

Jenny's face resolved in front of him.

"Is it you?" he said, or thought he said. He wasn't sure if he had actually spoken or not.

"Yes, it's me, Jenny. I got your chat. I didn't know what to do so I pulled the fire alarm."

He blinked his eyes until they cleared and he stared into her eyes. The dark eyes he stared into now were clearly Jenny's. Kind, concerned, anxious. But she didn't look at him quite the same way *Not Jenny* had, with nostalgic familiarity.

"You've been hit on the head. You're bleeding."

Matt heard the words. He thought he understood them.

"Help is coming."

He couldn't nod. He could barely speak. Instead, he blinked slowly in acknowledgment.

In the year that followed, Matt nearly convinced himself more than once that the "consciousness from the future" had been a product of his imagination. He had suffered a severe head wound after all, and his memory could have been affected, scrambling his perception of reality. But each time he questioned *Not Jenny*'s existence, he would open his journal to that day's entry, the day when the very different Jenny Coulter had appeared on his stoop in the rain, and he reread the quote he had written in dark blue ink, and he could think of no other explanation. So, he invariably concluded *Not Jenny* had been real, and, following that, its corollary: the timeline had changed.

Jenny had been upset by what happened in the server room, but not to the extent *Not Jenny* had described. She took a short leave, but as far as

Matt could tell, hadn't suffered any long-term effects. Either *Not Jenny* had been wrong, or lied, or something had changed—and if it was the latter, he suspected he was the cause.

Occasionally, when Matt met Jenny's gaze, he caught himself looking for *Not Jenny* behind her eyes, as if he expected she might be a silent passenger in Jenny's mind again, but then he would scold himself. If *Not Jenny* was inhabiting her mind, that would mean they hadn't saved Jenny from trauma after all, and he certainly didn't want that. He liked Jenny. In fact, they had become pretty friendly since their shared experience. They even started working on projects together, often meeting at *The Perfect Grind* in the mornings to prepare presentations and reports.

He wrote to *Not Jenny* in his journal, hoping the act would satisfy a yearning he couldn't explain, and found, to his surprise, that the words came easily. He used the darker ink so she would know it was meant for her. He recounted what Jenny had told him, and the police, about receiving his chat, pulling the alarm, and seeing two men running from the server room before finding Matt inside. The two men, hired by a rival company, had stolen backup disks containing proprietary company data. Luckily, the thieves had been caught in time, along with their mole, a new part-timer who had shared information about Matt's server access and his dependable habits.

Matt also told her how he thought of her whenever it rained.

And then, late one evening, almost three months after the incident in the server room, he stopped writing.

The realization dawned on him midsentence, his pen lifting itself up off the page. She would never read what he was so diligently writing. She wouldn't be reading his journal because she would no longer have access to it, because investigators only looked through people's journals if they had gone missing or . . . died. If he had died in the original timeline, if Jenny had seen it happen, that would explain her trauma. It would explain *Not Jenny*'s sad eyes and bittersweet smile.

Matt's stomach churned. Everyone knew, intellectually, that each day could be their last. Anything could happen. Simple decisions could make the difference between life and death—turning left instead of right, crossing the street, taking a later flight. But this was not hypothetical. He *knew* another timeline had once existed where he had died on the server room floor.

His fingers trembled when he put the dark pen and the journal into his desk drawer and locked it away.

The days crawled by.

Most people, he wagered, would be inspired by a brush with death to pack their days with significance and memory-making moments with friends and family, but Matt found it hard to socialize. He felt as if time had been suspended, as if he was waiting for something to happen to restart the clock.

He stayed home most evenings, and treated himself to pizza on Fridays, and sometimes Saturdays, and on "special" occasions, like today, when he needed comfort food.

The doorbell rang. The pizza had arrived.

Matt pulled out his wallet as he opened the door.

He recognized the girl standing in front of him. She brought his pizza every Friday. Young, probably just old enough to drive, wisps of blonde hair escaping her knit cap. She had bright blue eyes and pale skin offset by ruddy cheeks.

"Hi, Mr. James." She handed him the box and he set it on the small table by the door. "It's $17.75 tonight."

"Okay, sure." He rifled through the small bills in his wallet, trying to count them quickly. "Wait, I think I have a twenty in the other room."

She nodded.

He turned and went to his bedroom and pulled a twenty out of the front pocket of the jeans he had thrown onto the bed, then returned to the girl waiting for him by the door, his arm outstretched.

"Here you go."

"Thank you."

The girl took the bill from him, then her arm dropped abruptly to her side. Her expression faded. Her gaze lost focus. For a frightening second, he thought she might have stopped breathing, before she finally drew in an audible breath and turned to look at him again.

Matt swallowed.

Her smile reappeared, only it looked different somehow. "How have you been, Matt?"

Something in her tone, her stance, her expression, summoned his gaze to meet hers.

He knew the pizza girl. He saw her every week, sometimes twice. She was familiar. But in this moment, she seemed familiar in a different way.

Her gaze drifted to the bookshelves behind him, scanned them for a moment, and then returned to him. "By the Talyst, you have a lot of books!"

"What did you just say?" His breath caught in his lungs. "Did you say 'by the Talyst'?" When she nodded, he took a step back. "How do you know that phrase?"

She opened her mouth to answer, but he continued before she had a chance to reply.

"That's a phrase I came up with for a sci-fi novel I planned to write someday." His heart pounded. "I only told one person about it—a man named Elliott, my grandfather's roommate from the nursing home."

They had become good buddies, he and Elliott, talking for hours one evening after his grandfather had fallen asleep. He had shared most of his life story, including his silly dream of becoming a writer. That had been the night before the fire in the rec room. He'd heard Elliott had started it, that the guilt had been overwhelming. One might have said he had experienced a trauma.

"Is it you? *Not Jenny*?" This girl's blue eyes looked so different from Jenny's milk-chocolate ones, yet Matt could still sense *Not Jenny* behind them. "Were you observing Elliott? Is this poor girl about to experience some kind of trauma?"

The flush in the girl's cheeks drained away. Her voice cracked. "How do you know all this?"

"You told me. You told me who you are, *when* you are, that you're some kind of a 'time sensor' person, that you were here observing Jenny. You told me not to interfere, but somehow I must have because . . ."

His words stopped coming. Once again, realization stopped him in midsentence.

Jenny hadn't been traumatized. He hadn't died. *Not Jenny* wouldn't have had anything to investigate.

"You don't remember," he said. His mouth finally allowed words to form again, but they came slowly. "You *can't* remember. For you, it never happened."

The girl's wide eyes pierced right through him. She drew in a long, unsteady breath.

"Are you saying that I took control of a client, revealed myself to you, and changed the timeline?" Her voice pitched up into soprano range. "Why would I do that?"

He swallowed. "I think I died in that original timeline. I think you just wanted to . . . well . . . tell me goodbye."

The girl covered her mouth with her hand, the twenty-dollar bill still clutched between her fourth finger and her pinky. She scrunched her forehead, as if her head suddenly ached. Then she nodded, not so much to him as to herself.

She dropped her hand, sighed. "Elliott liked listening to your stories. He liked you quite a bit, in fact. I liked you too. Too much, it seems." She gave him a small smile. "I must have done what I'm doing now, taking control just to spend another moment with you."

Matt reached out to her, his fingertips just brushing the sleeve of her jacket. "Look, why don't you come inside and we can talk some more? Maybe we can make a plan to meet up. I can meet the *real* you."

"I can't," she said.

"Oh, right, of course." He gave the pizza girl's body an encompassing look. "But later, come and find me. You know where I live, after all!"

She smiled. He liked *Not Jenny*'s smile, no matter whose face was wearing it. He hated to see it fade away.

"I don't know that I can. I'm not exactly free to do as I please. But I'll try." She paused. "It may be a long wait for you, though."

"I'll wait," he said.

She smiled. "Then I promise I'll try my best. I really do want to find out more about the Talyst. But for now, I need to retreat." She lifted her arm and reached out to him, pushed the twenty back into his hand. "Pay her for the pizza."

He nodded. He couldn't seem to think of anything else to say, except, "Clear ether."

"What?"

He smiled. "Safe travel," he said.

She nodded. "Goodbye, Matt."

He watched her go. The young girl's expression fell blank for an instant, and then a bright, but very different light, returned to her eyes.

She held out her hand, and once again, for the first time, he handed her the twenty.

“Thanks! See you Friday,” she said. She bounded down off his stoop.

Matt stepped down to the sidewalk as the girl’s motorcycle roared away down the street, stood staring long after the taillights had disappeared.

He might have years to wait, but he would meet *Not Jenny* again. He felt certain. Until then, he had a pizza to devour, all six books of E. E. “Doc” Smith’s Lensman series to re-read, new entries to add to his journal, and a sci-fi novel to write.

He smiled, glanced down at his watch. He had plenty of time.

To Fiona: Thank you for being part of my journey to reinvent myself!

12

Disentanglement

R. James Doyle

Nothing to do but think. And all the time in the universe in which to do so.

This is exactly the agreement I entered into. I don't have any regrets.

And I absolutely cannot afford to have second thoughts. What if this very thought, this unwelcome thought, is one I've had before, and I don't even know it?

The first time I woke up, I was already alone.

On impulse, I retrieved the history of the end. Those were strange, melancholy, and—for the first time in humanity's history—peaceful end-times. The peacefulness arose from certain knowledge that the true end was in sight.

Everyone understood there was no escape. I would like to believe that my long-lost human companions had continued to face their fate with maturity and serenity. But I will never know. Whatever came after I entered hibernation, I did not experience it.

Cosmology had reached a final understanding. Although the ultimate origins had always remained murky, the fate of the universe had been known for a very long time. And it was a bleak picture.

As predicted, the universe continued to expand at an accelerated rate, making global heat death quite ineluctable. Even more defeating was the fact that the local light horizon, over time, encompassed less and less matter and radiation—and their corollary, information. Each cosmic island, trapped within the inviolable limit of the speed of light, became lonelier and lonelier, the surrounding spatial ocean swelling without rest from the inside out.

Humanity had much to be proud of in its ingenuity for tapping increasingly exotic energy sources as the urge to expand and explore never flagged. Ironically, this defining drive of the species was thwarted by the universe itself running away even faster. Accessing the zero-point fluctuations looked like the best—perhaps last—opportunity to buy time, so to speak, when it was discovered that doing so increased the value of the cosmological constant.

Tap the quantum fluctuations anyway, many urged, even if it hastened the end. It was perhaps a sign that the species itself knew there was no getting around the essential cosmological truth. Those who continued to hold out hope for some new understanding, and some altered fate, were regarded as conducting themselves, at best, in poor taste.

The sense of fatality went unsoftened by the fact that over the long eons, no other self-aware life forms had ever been encountered. And attempts to build self-aware artificial agents had produced unfortunate and ultimately unsuccessful results. By then, the search had gone well beyond the home galaxy. Many lower, nonsentient organisms had been found, again and again, but that was all. Many of these biota had been exploited, for the moral arguments against doing so were always open to discussion. Maybe other life exhibiting sentience existed somewhere, beyond the local light horizon. There had even been speculation that the second inflationary era of the universe had begun when other, perhaps much older civilizations, started tapping the vacuum energy of spacetime. But it remained speculation only. There was no prospect for ever knowing, one way or another.

All recognized that the human species had entered what might be termed the twilight times. These were marked more than anything by acceptance, not by the irrational responses of unhealthy minds as had happened formerly when the end-times had been glimpsed erroneously.

But not entirely.

The survival urge ran deep in humanity, and it would find a way to manifest even in these final circumstances. Humanity had long exploited the fruits of progress in bioneering. Viability in direct vacuum had been a necessity ever since mythological Sol was lost and later, other stars too had begun to fail. Then had come the various modifications required to enable switching from one cosmic energy source to the next. The technology with the potential to support survival into the barren end-times was known. Only dysine hibernation appeared to provide what was needed, when isolation would be complete, and each conscious presence would be entirely on its own.

I choose to push this whole line of thought away.

I am beginning to be bored, and hard on its heels I can sense another thought forming, the one to be avoided, the one concerning DV Senility.

The known risk associated with dysine hibernation.

The bioneers who placed me into this enduring existence equipped me with the ability to willfully control the pattern of my thoughts, whenever it suits me. This is a useful, probably necessary skill for a Survivor. I can examine my memories using a range of superposed search patterns, varying efficiency, and specificity. I can block out a thought or a family of thoughts. I can focus where I choose.

And at this moment, I am electing not to think about DVS.

In some of its aspects, dysine hibernation was simply a logical extension of the long-standing program of bioneering which had been the cornerstone of humanity's survival throughout the ages. In another aspect however, it took a distinctly additional and uncertain step forward.

The principle behind the technology involved the relationship between metabolism and temperature. Metabolism can be slowed via appropriate biological arrangements to operate at lower and lower temperatures. The less energy consumed per unit time, the longer the operating lifetime. Throw in some mature self-repair mechanisms and the organism is in excellent shape for the long haul.

As metabolism slows, thought processes also enervate, as a side effect. Subjective time slows for the organism. Because the rate at which thought processes slow dominates, life can indeed be extended by this design. Or more specifically, the life of the mind can be so extended.

But only up to a point. That is, if the organism wishes to enjoy the prospect of an infinite number of thoughts. Anything less would fail to meet any reasonable standard for quality of life, at least for an immortal living the pure life of the mind.

The possible hitch in the design has to do with quantum effects dictating a lowest limit to the temperature at which a life form can exist. This limit robs the design of its potential to support an infinite number of thoughts. But there is a way to cheat. In simplest terms, the organism sleeps part of the time.

It's about racing infinities. As long as the organism sleeps long enough to erase the waste heat deficit incurred during the previous period of active, conscious thought, the game could be won. For all time. The life form can enjoy an infinite number of thoughts, over an infinite period of time.

But experiments suggested that a perfect, ideal dormancy state, in which no thoughts occurred, might not be achievable. Thoughts might occur, supported by quantum fluctuations. Some called it dreaming. Some called it the tenacity of life itself. The experiments proved inconclusive and were by definition performable only over finite periods of time. Thus, it was not entirely clear if the game could be won.

I recall thinking how the whole concept sounded too simple to work.

Everyone understood what the Survivor program was about. Conceived by an ad hoc committee, the announcement was deemed perfectly sensible—once stated. Humanity just wasn't fully prepared to give in. There was a logical acceptance of fate, yes. There was also a kind of pervasive fatigue, fully predictable and explicable by socionomic theory. The fatigue was not physical in nature. Bioneering techniques offered indefinite renewal. The fatigue originated in the knowledge that there was simply nothing left to accomplish. And no point to it.

The Survivor program was to be humanity's last testament to its collective self, and its final act of hubris aimed straight at the universe as a whole.

There was unanimous agreement on this justification for the program and polite disregard of its irrational basis. But when it came to the actual prospect of who might become Survivors, most everyone recoiled at the thought.

Not out of any mistrust of technology. Persistent advances in bioneering had made the physical substrate of existence very much less than sacred—precisely because it was so manipulable. On the other hand, socionomics had continued to flourish, perhaps as a counterpoint to the vulgarization of the body.

Over time, countless forms of communication, organization, government—ways of relating and working together—were explored and studied. One observation had been made again and again and elevated to a law of socionomics: There was a deep richness to how we humans interact with one another—for joy, for recreation, for progress—a depth that had never been fully plumbed.

Striving and sharing gave life its meaning. Striving was increasingly irrelevant in the end-times. Becoming a Survivor implied that sharing, too, would come to an end.

Survivors would enter dysine hibernation and would. . continue. Their lives would become the pure life of the mind. They would cheat eternity itself, but as the light horizons receded inexorably, they would find themselves utterly, irrevocably, alone.

To think about whatever they chose, to discover whatever could be discovered via pure thought, but to know only for oneself, forever.

The few volunteers who appeared were not inspiring. Someone noted wryly that the competitive urge of humanity had finally been damped. But the Survivor program, once conceived, was not to be abandoned, especially as it might represent the species' very last act.

Thus, the committee conceived the interview process. Everyone would participate—easily accomplished through ongoing and ubiquitous bioneering refreshes, which incorporated psychological profiling as a routine adjunct. If there were any suitable candidates for the Survivor program, they would be identified: rationally, fairly, and publicly.

I recall the process being fair, for all participated in developing the criteria for fitness as a Survivor. These were: fear of death, for motivation; curiosity, for quality of life; sense of humor, for the same reason; solitariness, most obviously; pragmatism over hopefulness; and altruism.

Regarding different modalities for self-sacrifice, the striving form, and the sharing form: No glory was to be had in becoming a Survivor. The only reason to do so was to grant the wish of all other humans. The sharing mode was the relevant one.

I was not shocked to learn I had been identified as a Survivor candidate. I was intrigued by the prospect, and introspection suggested I possessed at least some of the specified characteristics. I had always been a loner. As a socioeconomist, I had always been curious about humanity's deep history. Not just the achievements but the personalities too. Most of all, I wasn't ready to end.

Even so, I found being selected daunting, nearly overwhelming. The risks were carefully made known to me. The brittleness introduced by the precise hibernation tuning for each Survivor. The limitations on robust waking. DVS.

I knew I would do it.

In a public ceremony, the other Survivors and I took ancient names. Mine is Seuzn. I had long admired an early technologist some regard as the founding bioneer.

There followed a set of specialized bioneering upgrades, a quantum alarm clock, an escape hatch, all carefully elucidated and recorded in my memories.

Then the first long sleep.

I am now alone.

I had been prepared for total isolation as a deliberate part of the design of the Survivor program. The first period of sleep was calculated to extend beyond the time when entropy advance and light horizon recession had completed the flattening and partitioning of the universe.

This was a kindness, as it spared me witnessing the final decline and fate of humanity. My solace was confidence that my now forever-lost companions had accepted their fate. Although I do wonder if they maintained equanimity to the end. I chose not to have events recorded from the period immediately following my entrance into hibernation. Now there is no way of knowing. And certainly no turning back.

Time has no meaning now. Everything from now on will always be subjective—in the most extreme sense. There is only me, and I have no reference points. But according to my quantum clock, by some convention or other, trillions of years have passed already. My clock will inform me whenever hibernation is indicated. It is subject to uncertainty, of course, and could fail to wake me.

But there really is no point in worrying about that.

I have at my disposal the recorded knowledge and experiences of my species. This comprehensive history is endlessly diverting. When I need additional distraction, I invoke emulations of historical personalities by repurposing the ancient artificial agents technology, as far as it went.

I have an exceedingly rich life. I find it more engaging to build upon all that exists, synthesizing new concepts, exploring areas of inquiry not previously identified. I have the resources, the raw knowledge, the quantum computing capabilities, the mental skills, the discipline, and most of all, the time.

I invent new mathematics. I resolve a few forever-standing philosophical conundrums. I willfully experience randomness, which is remarkably refreshing. I only need to invoke a special quantum compartment within my awareness, and I am presented with an entirely new problem to tackle.

I analyze the development of modes of artistic expression and show, as had long been suspected, that they prefigured scientific breakthroughs consistently throughout history.

I resolve the enduring P=NP? puzzle and find, somehow not surprisingly, that the resolution of the A or B question is, in fact, C. I have a delightful give-and-take with Kurt Gödel on the topic. Mostly give. He is not an easy one to talk to.

I disclose how several of the fine-tuning constants are related. Now there are only two that remain independent. Will I learn something unexpected about how the universe is constructed and, dare I wonder, why? I engage Cey Li and find her brilliant and rather inscrutable. But pleasant.

I find I cannot resolve the old question of whether the creative deity is a projection of humanity, or whether the question is somehow ill-formed due to the imperfection of humanity's conception of the creative deity. Augustine has firm opinions. Although he is intimidating, he argues respectfully, with great care for the other's learning. When we reach a pause in our conversation, I ask what he is doing. He says he is blessing me. It feels good.

Occasionally, a randomly offered problem is familiar.

Disappointed, I move on.

I find it delicious not to solve a problem, and happily shelve it for the future.

Nothing to do but think. And all the time in the universe in which to do so.

This is exactly the agreement I entered into. I don't have any regrets.

But my conversations with historical personages, once delightful, are starting to feel . . . predictable.

Self-pity is out of the question and not in my make-up anyway. I have existed longer than anyone else, except for maybe the other Survivors in their own isolated light-bubbles, somewhere forever out of reach.

Nearly all thought involves accessing concepts already in existence. But when a Survivor—with bioneered thought management and search capabilities—approaches a concept along the same path, again, out of all the potential paths for approaching that concept, it could be an indication that the space of all possible thoughts is being exhausted.

Déjà Vu Senility. The hypothetical syndrome argued to be avoided in dysine hibernation. But the experiments did not settle whether thought leaking occurred during sleep periods. Leaked thoughts might leave a memory trace without the benefit of its conscious experience. Either way, it counts, as to sampling the space of all possible thoughts. Leakages during sleep are thus wasted thoughts, and they compromise the design principles of the technology.

The initial symptoms would be a vague familiarity with lines of inquiry as they were forming. There would be a monotonically increasing probability of encountering the familiar. The full syndrome develops when it is more likely to have a repeated thought than an original one.

A Survivor with leaking thoughts would remain immortal but would be doomed to looping, over and over, more and more.

That is all bad enough.

But now I've had a really disturbing thought. It's only an assumption that a leak would leave a trace in the form of a memory. The experiments said nothing on this topic. What if there is no trace? There would be no way of knowing.

What if this very thought, unwelcome, is one I have had before, and I do not even know it?

I must face the possibility. From informal introspection, I am starting to believe I'm experiencing repeated thoughts. I have the computing capabilities to settle the matter, at least probabilistically.

As I launch interfering search routines to investigate, I allow a different, somehow less disturbing thought to form.

This is the end.

It might be a long and still productive time before I would need to pull the trigger on what is already an inevitable decision. There is no rush. But I know I have already crossed over to another place.

I can no longer entirely trust my own thoughts.

This would be an intolerable situation even for my ancestors, with their various forms of rich physical and social existence. But I am in a far worse situation. My thoughts are my existence. My thoughts are all of existence. If they are taken away, there would be nothing left.

Some time later, I access my search results.

No surprise. Examination of my memories verifies that I am experiencing repeated thoughts. Specific examples are not available, but the occurrence of repetition is reported as a reliable if not absolute result by the quantum search algorithms.

DVS has set in. Moreover, if some leaked thoughts are leaving no trace, the syndrome is already more advanced than I can know.

My reaction surprises me.

I am relieved.

And I am tired.

How have I lasted so long?

I know the answer. I have the right set of carefully selected characteristics to endure as a Survivor. I have a sense of obligation to represent my species into the eventless, terribly lonely, and never-ending future. I was capable of that sacrifice. I have even enjoyed myself. I have developed systems of inquiry and created yet more.

But I cannot be expected to embrace the not knowing. The fruitless chasing of myself. This leads to madness.

My perspective is shifting, and one thought comes after another now, tumbling.

At least these are new thoughts. I hope.

I am altruistic. That was established. But if I am to be in the role of caretaker to my entire species, there is something terribly wrong and unnatural in a picture where I have survived them all.

I am a loner. That, too, was established. But deceiving myself is a luxury I no longer have. I do ache for companionship.

I invoke all the discipline available to me to shunt away and bury the feeling lurking behind that thought. That way lies the abyss.

What is the purpose of all the discoveries of pure inquiry I have made if they are never to be shared?

I have done enough.

And there is no one around to argue the point with me.

Relief is flooding me now. The release from pursuing closure. The questions left comfortably unanswered. The deliberate choice never to pursue that last thought.

This is simple. I choose to let go. As my own final act.

I am not afraid to die.

There is that other compartment within my awareness that I have known of for a long time. Since my Survivor briefing. I had stumbled upon its actual manifestation, some time or other, and found it wrapped in layers of discipline such that I would need to make a particular willful effort to access it. But the nature of the content is available at the surface. I know what it is.

It is my suicide pill.

This had been discussed only obliquely as part of the Survivor program. It's a further confirmation of my suitability that I never inquired after details of the escape route. I am surmising, with near certainty, that the same stance was taken by the other Survivors.

But now I bless the wisdom of the formulators of the Survivor program.

Am I the last one? An unanswerable question.

I have fulfilled my obligation. It is time. I have lived long. I have lived well.

I am ready.

Perish the thought.

I am being held.

And again, later, I am being held.

There is something else different too. I know what it is. I am experiencing the passage of time again.

I am all here. What does this mean? But I am also more.

Thoughts are forming in front of me. These are my thoughts, but they are also being given to me.

I am alive.

I know what has happened. And . . . there is something about having the experience, instead of just the thought.

There was more foresight than I imagined. Was this a deliberate consensus plan or a rogue plan? I will never know.

I did not . . . end.

Instead, I was transferred. I had been entangled. With the other Survivors. The entanglement had always existed, but we never knew it. Until we chose to let go.

They are holding me now, and I know they will let me stay this way forever if I wish. I know this because they are telling me, and it is my thought too.

We survived, not only into the heat death, but into the event death of our universe, with no further possibility of interaction, no further possibilities for information exchange. Irrevocably separated light-bubbles. The meaningless end-state of the universe as known.

But not the end.

There was a reason for the runaway irreversible expansion.

Any entanglements achieved in former times would persist and become more and more robust. Not only persist but come to dominate. There would be no more physical interactions to disrupt their fragility. Decoherence was a disease of the old cosmos. Anything entangled would stay so until they were all that remained.

That's why there were vast unfolded spatial and temporal dimensions. To extricate the delicate entanglements from the foregoing. So they would survive.

We are together now.

I am being held, and I need to be held because I have been waiting so long. I could only hurt before while I was alone, and I will never be alone again.

My thoughts like other thoughts—it is always like this when I awaken—I have been waiting for you—I will share what I have learned.

There are others. Not just other Survivors. Others. I perceive them, faintly. I will learn better how to perceive them. Then I will have their thoughts with me as well, indistinguishable.

Inseparable.

I am flowing again. It is good.

A final distant receding memory, of someone already else.

That other reason I was chosen as a Survivor.

Hope has no purpose when one is alone.

I am no longer hopeless. I am no longer alone.

Hope stretches out before us, like a new kind of physical thing.

I can see it. It goes on and on.

PART III

Life After Tech

STORIES ABOUT THE INFLUENCE OF TECHNOLOGY ON SOCIETY IN THE NOT-SO-DISTANT FUTURE

13

The Orphans of Nilaveli

Naru Dames Sundar

Originally published in the anthology *Where the Stars Rise*

2076 Earthquake, Sri Lanka –Nilaveli Beach Airlift

With signs of a major second quake imminent, government emergency services started an airlift operation to save the countless lives in the northern district. Were it not for this effort, the casualties from the second tremor would have been far higher.

A rickety jeep bounced over the broken asphalt crags of roads turned into hillocks. Water seeped around us. The public channels were already speaking of severe aftershocks. My father struggled with the juddering steering wheel while my mother spoke to her cousins at the evacuation site at Nilaveli Beach. The implant glowed behind her ear as it carried her words many miles to the east. The jeep barely had room for the three of us and our neighbors and their son. As I clung to my mother's sari, I heard her gasp.

"Kamala? What is it?" Worry creased my father's eyes.

"Anilan, he said they *looked past him*. As if he wasn't even there! And the crowds just pushed past him!"

My father pulled the jeep to the side of the road, waiting for my mother to say more.

"It's like that time we visited Kandy, Anilan. Didn't you hear the stories? Implant modifications. Adjusted vision. First, they don't want to see the beggars. Then, they don't want to see *us*."

Us, them. Before the war, after the war. Even seventy years after the war, it was *us* and *them*. You see, conflict has roots, and even when the victor cuts the tree down, the roots remain, buried deep. Sometimes subtle, sometimes not so subtle.

"Kamala. The children aren't implanted yet. We can send them. Their features aren't so distinct that someone will notice."

"No." My mother's voice was firm.

"If the crowds thicken, do you think they'll make room for *us*? There are always enough vacationers from the south in the Trincomalee resorts to fill the lifters. But the children without their implants, no one could say for sure that they were Tamil or Sinhalese."

"Absolutely not."

But I could tell from the wavering of her voice that she was already thinking yes. Because sometimes when you had to choose between your life and your child's, between a large risk and a small risk, you made the choices you never wanted to make. Even at six, I understood enough.

"No, Amma, no, I don't want to go. Don't leave me. Don't leave me, Amma!"

"Hush, Kartik, hush."

My parents pulled me into their arms and held me, and I smelled sweat on their skin, salt in their tears, turmeric and ash on their foreheads—these smells would never leave me. I wailed at Nilaveli when they handed me to my neighbor's eight-year-old son, Ayngharan, my newly adopted older brother.

Hours later, I sobbed, my face pressed against the glass window, the lifter leaving behind the white sand covered by a sea of people and heading over the churning waters. I saw the aftershock ripple through the beach, sand spray booming in large dust clouds. I screamed for my parents, like the other orphans on the craft. Ayngharan put his hands over my eyes and pulled me close, his hands, his chest, his smell—all unfamiliar. He too was experiencing that singular agony, but his tears lay buried.

A moderately wealthy family in Kandy took us in. Marble floors and large, expensive Batik hangings across the entry and throughout the house. Ayngharan knew some Sinhala because even in the remote northern schools, government strictures imposed what was taught. I was young and knew little, and as my adopted parents put it, I was *affected.* They didn't like to talk about it, as if it was some distant dirty thing they didn't want to touch. Ayngharan was angrier than I was. He understood, you see—he knew enough to know the reason our parents could not have accompanied us on the lifter. Why they could not have gotten past the evacuation officials. For me, the *why* was more ephemeral, something I did not yet grasp.

Years later, Ayngharan shouted and screamed when they installed his implant. He fought so hard they had to sedate him before the medical attendant could install the silver conch shell behind his ear. When our adopted parents told him what software was being loaded onto it, his rage transcended into something else. Because he had learned enough to know what each piece of software could do—and he knew that without words, our parents were slowly trying to pull us into their world of unseeing. They argued, and finally our parents simply put their foot down, asserting their parental rights. We had no choice but to obey. So, Ayngharan did as they asked, but it was not long before he discovered illegal patches in dark corners. He quietly removed the software from his implant.

I think what hurt Ayngharan the most happened when it was my turn. Not because I didn't apply his illegal patches afterward, but because I acquiesced quietly. That day our paths diverged.

Ayngharan dropped out of secondary school while I passed the university entrance exams. I recalled vividly one night at the campus bar, slightly warm from a touch of Arak, the smell of anise still pungent in my throat. Henry and Vijaya, friends of sorts, accompanied me at the table we occupied most Friday nights. Henry spotted them first.

"Eh, mate, there're two young ladies over there and three of us. Which one of us gets to stay behind and order more drinks?"

Vijaya, the most argumentative among us, bickered over which one of the girls was prettier. I was alarmed; there were clearly three girls at the bar. Three saris: pink and gold, and a few seats away, a solitary green.

"But there're three of them."

The jovial banter stopped. Vijaya squinted at the bar and then looked at me quizzically. There, I finally understood. He only saw two girls. That he was just like my adopted parents. Just like the unnamed evacuation coordinator on the beach that day in Nilaveli.

"What do you mean, three? Too much arak perhaps, friend?"

Henry gave me a different look. Uncomfortable. Annoyed.

"That one's not my type, man."

Vijaya still didn't understand. He would never understand until he turned off his ubiquitous implant modification. Henry grabbed his shoulder and scuttled over toward the bar, glossing over Vijaya's confusion. He turned back and shouted, "Drinks on you, Guna!"

But his eyes told me something different. Don't push this. Don't ask more questions. Go along with it. Who was worse? Vijaya, who did not see this unnamed Tamil girl, painted out of his vision by a chunk of code and the silver behind his ear? Henry, who saw her but feigned an incompatible type because type included blood and history and a thousand lines of division scratched into the country's bedrock for hundreds of years? Or me, who answered to my adopted name, Guna? Me, who said nothing, who went along with it, even as it rankled. We were all terrible people in different ways.

Ayngharan's rage consumed him. I learned of his death from my adopted mother. No details, just that he was gone. I found out from other sources. Publicly there was no mention of a protest. Publicly there was no mention of a lone protestor who set himself aflame. And what did the bystanders see, I wondered? Did they see no one? The burning man, the protestors, all of them written out of the bystander's vision by a piece of computer software. An unseen protest, marked only by the shape the crowd of angry youths had carved out of the street, marked only by the scorch mark left on the asphalt.

. . .

And so I arrived at this: my first act of rebellion. The tiny revolt I finally permitted myself to do, in remembrance of all the unseen, of all the things hidden from public eyes. I stand now on the tour boat looking out at the ruins on a stretch of beach in Trincomalee, the gopuram of the old Koneswaram temple still half-reaching out of the water. Some miles north, there exists an unseen, unmarked stretch of sunken beach in which my parents lie buried. I find the entry on the earthquake in the public database, and I edit it. I write in there the story you are reading now. My story. Perhaps in an hour, or even a few minutes, someone will edit it back. Someone will reduce my story to an invisible footnote to a single line. But for this moment, I am here. My story is here, unfiltered and visible. My real name is Kartik, and I *do* exist.

14

The Homunculi's Guide to Resurrecting Your Loved One From Their Electronic Ghosts

Kara Lee

Originally published 2019 in *Escape Pod*

0. Confession

IF YOU ARE READING THIS, your Loved One has died. We are sorry for your loss.

If you are reading this, then you stumbled onto an archived thread on a lost forum saying that supposedly, it is possible to bring back the dead using their electronic ghosts, and that the Homunculi, whoever they are, know how it is done. And then you searched and searched in a blur of grief and desperation and nearly killed yourself with illegal thaumaturgical network protocols before you found our servers.

And now you want to know whether you really can bring your Loved One back from the dead.

The answer is mostly yes, with one exception.

But you must know that this is not a resurrection. It is a trade. Your Loved One may return to the land of the living in exchange for your life, body, humanity, and most of your soul. In other words, you will have to condemn yourself to being one of us for the rest of eternity.

We will not lie and say that there is much to our existence.

But there is hope. We, the Homunculi, would know. Because hope is why we wrote this guide.

For you see, we cling to a deep-down, bitter, shameful hope that we will one day be saved by someone who loves us. And we hope against hope that the someone will be you.

We know it is a terrible thing to hope for. We know better than anyone what awaits those who make the trade.

And so we apologize for our selfishness. But we do not ask for forgiveness. We only ask that you remember what it is to hope for something impossible.

1. First Principles

The first mages had their domains of air, fire, earth, and water.

Modern humans have created a new domain for modern mages: electromagic. If you doubt that, look around you and count up those omnipresent slivers of glass and metal in which billions of electrons dance at a fingertip's command.

The human conquest of electricity started long ago, in a moment lost to history, when some clever person realized that they could somehow make use of those sparks in the air, those flashes in the sky.

Ever since then, human will and human energy and human magic have been quietly, slowly, inexorably soaking into electricity and electrons. And so have human souls—which are what you will be after, for a soul can grow a living body.

Souls decay the instant that flesh dies. We presume that you did not make off with a bit of the stuff before your Loved One's death. If we are incorrect, close this tab and consult a necromancer. Run, don't walk.

If we are correct, then we hope that your Loved One left behind some fragments of their soul in the electronic ossuary of the wires.

Fortunately, in this day and age, that is true of most people who spent any significant amount of time alive. Perhaps your grandfather never got the hang of the expensive tablet you gifted him, but he spoke into a rotary phone in his youth, and a piece of him has lingered with us ever since. Perhaps your child died before she could even babble, but if she ever cried into a baby monitor, then there is a ghost of her wails somewhere among us.

Unfortunately, homunculi may not leave the world of wires. So you must enter our domain to search for your Loved One. The journey—and the restoration to life—will require you to perform electromagic.

It is not only a matter of understanding telecommunication. You must also understand the principles on which telecommunication rests—those of electricity and magnetism. For what are data but bits flipping endlessly inside processors? And what are bits but electric voltages?

We hope you were granted the privilege of a good education in the natural sciences. If not, you may study these topics at your leisure; we provide free copies of many textbooks, in many languages, on our servers.

As with any scholarly pursuit, it requires time to gain proficiency, and you must be proficient. You are not placing a magical prank call. You are bringing a soul back from the dead. It is not the most difficult task in the universe, but it is hardly the easiest.

How long will it take, you are wondering.

How long does it take to earn three degrees in physics? How much understanding must enter your own electrons before you can derive Maxwell's Equations drunk, blind, both hands tied behind your back, in a raging snowstorm? It takes that much time. Here are some ways to expedite the process:

- Sleep at the intersection of ley lines designated by the crisscross of power lines overhead
- Draw auguries from the flickering of streetlights until you receive a fortunate omen
- Meditate in front of neon lights until your blood glows

But please, take as much time as you need. (May we also recommend putting your affairs in order during that interval.)

We promise that so long as you read your textbooks and do your problem sets, there will come a morning when you wake up to the sound of solar wind roaring in your ears. E- and B-fields will radiate at the edges of your vision all day, and at night you will throw open a window to see satellites blanketing the world with gossamer nets of cellular datastreams.

And you will know that you are ready to proceed.

2. Human Transfer Protocols

You will find all relevant code, protocols, schematics, and spells in the ~/compendium/src/htp/ directory.

We recommend a computer or a smartphone as your platform device for convenience, however, any telecommunications device will do. It is rumored that a truly dedicated and desperate person once managed the feat using a six-wire telegraph.

Cast the connection spell. Close the circuit. Splice the live copper wire in the schematic into a vein of your choice. (An anatomy textbook is part of our compendium for this reason.) We recommend disinfectant, duct tape to hold the wire in place, a disposable scalpel, and applying a topical anesthetic beforehand.

Lie down. Let pulses and tones rip through your body, deconstructing you into electrical signals, Fourier transforming you into decomposed sines and cosines and Dirac deltas.

You will not have to close your eyes because soon you will no longer have them.

3. Welcome to the Wires

In the wires (and sometimes, the wireless) you are not alive. Nor are you dead. You are information. That has its privileges. You will not have to worry about food or shelter or flossing your teeth. But beware! A body is (if nothing else) a reminder of your existence. Without it, you may soon forget who you are and what you came into the wires for.

It is difficult to explain what it is like in the wires. Time and space, at the quantum level, do not function the way you expect.

Here, it is mostly cold and dark and silent. Oh, there are parts of the wireworld lit up like a thousand cities; millions of servers incandescent with data, throbbing with humanity and its incessant activities. But they cannot interact with our dead particles.

Sometimes we will visit a telephone wire at sunrise, though we can sense neither the rosy glow of dawn nor the weight of sparrows that unknowingly alight upon us.

(We can, however, flip bits on certain lost servers. Which is how we created the files—such as this one—that you have been reading.)

Have you ever walked a city street on that blurry edge between late night and early morning? When even the neon lights are flagging, and the streetlights look tired, and the crisscrossing wires overhead are sagging into sleep. Have you ever found yourself staring at the stacked grids of dimly glowing windows all around you, each panel of glass hiding a universe behind itself?

That is the wireworld.

We, the Homunculi, are the lights behind the glass.

4. The Homunculi

The phenomena of phantom vocalizations and signals of indeterminate origin have been reported in various telecommunications devices since 1876, when Tivadar Puskás, working on the first telephone exchange, reported hearing his own voice as echoes in the receiver.

In 1998, Dr. Kikyou Tachibana of the Tokyo Institute for Modern Magical Studies wrote a paper calling us *homunculi*, hypothesizing that we were remnants of human consciousness.

We were never sure if she intended it as an insult, but we liked the name and so we adopted it. "Little people" is more flattering than our true name, which is: trash.

Every time you make a telephone call or send an email or fire off a 2:00 a.m. drunk text, a tiny piece of your soul tags along in the electrons that carry your message. The recipient absorbs your energy, digesting it, either nourishing or poisoning their soul depending on the nature of the message.

But if the intended recipient never receives—or never finishes absorbing—your message, then some fragment of your soul lingers in the wires.

Eventually, it becomes a homunculus.

We are the forgotten fragments of yourselves that you left in the wires, over the airwaves, sitting on old servers. We are your deleted emails. (But you will not find spam among us, for spam is soulless.) We are radio chatter that went unheard. Text messages never read. Calls never taken.

We are the litter you abandoned on the shoulders of the information highway. We are an enormous pile of garbage in which you must search for your Loved One.

It is easy. You need not search actively. Homunculi will be drawn to your whole and wholly human soul in the way that iron shavings are drawn to a magnet.

When you come into contact with a homunculus, its quantum states become entangled with yours. As a result, you will relive the communiqué that birthed that homunculus.

Each entanglement lasts only a Planck second, but brace yourself. We are not very nice. Most of us are downright awful. For what sorts of messages do you suppose are the most often discarded? Not the pleasant sort, we assure you.

You will have to bear up under the deluge of the very worst that human beings have to offer. You will find death threats and scams on the elderly and promises that this is the last time, you'll never hurt him ever again, you love her so much, you swear it. You will also have to wade through the broken cries of their victims. You will die a little with every suicide note, every sob into a telephone line, every midnight text that was ignored until it was too late. You will find awful lies and worse truths belonging not only to your enemies but also your family, your friends, your mentors, your idols.

But we have heard that the worst traces to come across are your own. Every single nasty, cruel, selfish, hateful message you shot off when you were stupid or drunk or righteously angry—they lurk here in the darkness. Be assured that we, who are born of such moments, do not and cannot judge you.

It is possible you will find a sweet office email that your Loved One sent to a defunct address. But you are far more likely to encounter a text from your Loved One telling you to eat shit and die.

Do not worry over the content. What matters is the lineage. For any homunculus that came from your Loved One exhibits their unique resonance. And that is the blueprint from which your Loved One can be reconstructed.

5. The Eigenvectors of Ghosts

Once you have found a homunculus from your Loved One, capture it in a Faraday Ward while praying your thanks to Gauss and surface integrals. Then apply Persephone's Oscilloscope to your find. This spell automatically samples the frequencies of any given homunculus and generates an eigenmatrix of the results. That result is the core of their self (plus or minus a few details such as their obsession with miniatures or the way they looked at you as if you mattered).

But a self does not make a whole person. A typical human develops various matrices as they grow. They encode qualities such as love. Humor. Pettiness. Puns. (Do not try to select which matrices you donate. It has never ended well, to our knowledge.)

You, who are now alive and whole but will soon be neither, have these components. You must now strip-mine your selfhood. You must also provide your body—we did say we could not create life—as a vessel for the soul of your Loved One. Do not worry about physical appearance; their soul will take care of such matters.

Do the above by casting Persephone's Oscilloscope on yourself and applying the results to your Loved One's eigenmatrix. If it is any consolation, please know that just as an organ donor's DNA lingers like a memory inside the transplanted tissue, so will your soul exist quietly inside that of your Loved One.

When you are finished, dial the resulting sum, a data packet that shimmers like stardust, out of the wires and back to your platform device.

We do not know how the process feels, for once it is done, the capacity to feel no longer exists, and so we have no firsthand accounts of the experience. But we have perceived this happening to others. The process of disintegrating appears to hurt until the ability to feel pain is lost. We infer this from the cessation of screams that echo down every node and pathway. The loss order of your data is random, but for your sake, we pray that your nerve endings are the first thing to go. After pain, we hope you next lose pleasure, so that it will not hurt in a different way when you lose the ecstasy of lovemaking, the warmth of sunshine, the salt taste of tears, and the face of your Loved One.

Do you know what happens in particle accelerators? How much energy it costs to rip atoms apart into their fundamental particles? How cataclysmic the birth of new matter? This is what will happen to your soul, over and over, until it cannot possibly break down any further, until the only remnant is an infinitesimal mote: a homunculus. You.

6. Postscript

Are you still reading? There is no more you could want to know . . . unless . . . you are here for the exception. The only sort of person who cannot be brought back out of the wires: *the person who already gave up their body and soul to bring you back from the dead.*

We are sorry. It is not possible.

Mathematically speaking, your resurrector's resonance is forever entangled with yours in all 2^96485 known dimensions that make up a human soul. The Soul Exclusivity Principle of Wolfgang Pauli states that it is impossible for there to exist more than one living being with the same resonance in their soul—as impossible as it is for two or more identical fermions to simultaneously occupy the same quantum state.

In other words, their soul is part of you now. And no soul can occupy more than one life.

Would you be content to seek out their homunculi?

If so, then we can offer you a suggestion. For though they have no hope of life, there is always the hope of love.

Once in a while, you could whisper some kind words into the wires for no one in particular. Tell all of us that you miss one of us. Your atom of love is enough to pierce the darkness.

Your message will eventually find its intended target. Do not worry. We have an eternity to listen for you.

It may seem like very little, but it will be enough for us. We hope it will also be enough for you.

Thank you for reading.

Thank you for hoping.

Thank you for loving.

15

It's Not a Date Without Data

Fayth Hui Tan

"God, really?" I muttered to myself as my last job for the day finally finished running.

The MeetCute algorithm had returned a pair of people in their twenties, both attractive and effortlessly photogenic. Trish (twenty-eight, female, online marketing executive) was dressed in fancy athleisure, and windswept blonde hair framed her face. A gaggle of smiling brown children surrounded her. *2028 volunteer trip in Tijuana!*

Stanley (twenty-seven, male, personal Instagram curator) wore a black turtleneck and tortoiseshell glasses. He held a golden retriever puppy almost too carefully above his nondescript designer jeans. *Pluviophile. Will love your dog more than you.*

I hated them instantly.

I glanced at the readout. All the Major Compatibilities (family, career, romance) were clear for conflict at an acceptable probability of 95.6 percent, and they had enough Commonalities that the app could prompt either of them with pre-generated conversation starters on their first date.

> *If you could travel to one place in the world, where would it be?* (Corny, but not unforgivable.)

> *What cute couples' picture trend are you all about right now?* (Straight people are a nightmare.)

> *As an online creator, how do you see your future family life translating into content?* (Literally just kill me.)

The algorithm picked up some potential Disagreements but they were classified as benign, and some, as the app boasted, had AdoraPotential, or the ability to be leveraged to be flirty instead of contentious. More cute arguments about whether pugs or corgis are the best dog, or if spring or summer was the most pleasant season, and less screaming deathmatch from hell in a Cheesecake Factory. That one had nearly cost me my job after the wounded parties had threatened to sue for damages. Somehow Customer Relations managed to translate my irate emails that amounted to *that's just how probability works, dumbasses*, into something sufficiently placating. Probably something about how turbulence is just a natural part of life, how it was truly a means of learning more about themselves, and besides, think of all the personal essays they could pitch to *Vice*?

I approved Trish and Stanley for their Preliminary MeetCute Date and sent a reminder for them to fill out their Postdate Evaluation Survey. The MeetCute slogan popped up on the screen with an almost offensively cheerful tick mark accompanying it. *It's not a date without data!*

The Data Matchmaker gig wasn't what I'd gone to college for, but what's a cognitive neuroscience major in Los Angeles to do? MeetCute was the latest acquisition in DataCloud's myriad umbrella of companies, and nowhere else remotely relevant to my background was hiring. I'd been a little apprehensive when the MeetCute recruiter looked over my resumé and cheerfully told me that "manipulating social behavior is, like, so in right now," but I couldn't say no to the stability. My work mostly involved making sure the algorithm's readouts were in the approved parameters, though I didn't know what any of it actually *meant*. Then I'd take any data provided by people to the app, sort it into categories and graphs and percentages and send it off to whichever department asked for it. I often didn't have a clue what they wanted it for, though I didn't think about it too much. I wasn't the type to obsessively align company culture with my identity, unlike some of my friends who ferociously curated their careers like well-pruned bonsai plants. Plus, I'd been desperate to get out of my hometown. It was more warehouse space than neighborhood now, and "a little more stimulating than being chased down by drones to stock shelves faster" was where I was setting my ambitions these days.

Before leaving work, I plugged my answers into the DataCloud vending machine to get the data discount for my SunnyKale salad dinner. Ever since DataCloud had acquired the automated food delivery service, Orderly, these machines had been a staple in every city office. The display flashed to life, characteristic sans serif DataCloud font unfolding cleanly onto the screen.

Welcome to DataCloud Eats, where your data pays!

> *How much genetic modification is acceptable in your RiseNShine Coffeemix? (Answer in a percentage.)*

> *On a scale of 1–5 (1 being poor and 5 being excellent), how would you rate the gait and posture recognition features in the app Namaste2U: Pocket Yoga for Beginners?*

> *In your experience with RiteTemp Home Smart Thermostats, please indicate if you would be (A) Uncomfortable, (B) Somewhat Comfortable, (C) Comfortable with RiteTemp collecting users' body temperature data from their homes.*

Three questions were enough to get me a dollar discount. I looked around for extra options—more questions, or the kind with a bigger payout. The ones that paid more were always commensurately slimier, and I didn't always feel great about answering them. Like a question about my health from a drug development company, or a question sponsored by a political campaign where the campaign propaganda was practically written into the question. No other questions were available though, slimy or otherwise.

I huffed and pressed the deanonymize permissions for an extra fifty cents off. It was getting close to payday and my penchant for matcha lattes hurt a little too much. My employee photo appeared on the processing screen as an immaculately packaged salad (in entirely compostable NüPaper packaging) clunked to the bottom of the machine.

Enjoy your salad, Ashley Matsumoto. Have a good day!

The machine said my name strangely, pausing unnaturally before it enunciated the syllables in a deliberate deadpan. I winced. The indignity of trading my privacy for half a dollar wasn't lost on me, but a girl has a weakness for upscale salads. Sometimes you compromise, you know? They were probably siphoning any available information about me from time online and at work anyway, so it's not like I had much dignity to lose.

Maybe you had exactly half a dollar left of dignity, a small part of my mind chimed in unhelpfully. I quieted the thought on the underground ride home by taking a large, indignant mouthful of salad. At least it wasn't anything too questionable. The number of times I'd thought that to myself at work was concerning.

I nudged the door to our apartment open slowly, trying not to disturb our cat, Toast, too much, who was usually lazing around behind the door. Sure enough, I heard a slightly annoyed meow as Toast reluctantly rolled away from the sun-warmed welcome mat to our tiny apartment as I entered. I heard Alyssa's airy, lilting voice from the doorway, the affect that she used for her online astronology readings.

"Yeah, the stellar flares from Andromeda and Triangulum are, like, so unpredictable right now, and that might explain the mood swings if you're sensitive to galaxy alignment," she said, hands gesturing gracefully, her lacy cardigan sleeves accentuating the movement. "There's probably, like, an unstable exoplanetary orbit throwing your sleep schedule off too, but it should correct itself soon. I hope you have a wonderful, planetarily aligned day!"

She let out a sigh of relief as she ended the video call. Her quartz earrings clinked against round wire-rimmed glasses as she put her head on her desk.

"Difficult day?"

"Sometimes I feel bad that I use my Master's degree for, like, advanced nonsense. But then I remember we have to pay rent."

"It's not all nonsense—"

"Yeah, the astronomy's real, but the rings of Neptune are not, like, giving off bad vibes." She let out a small huffing laugh.

"It's still educational at least. They're learning real facts about the solar system and dark matter and— space stuff."

Alyssa removed her head from the desk and sighed again. "I feel like I'm lying to people."

I floundered. "If you think you're lying to people, then I'm definitely lying to them." I could hear the frustrated edge in my voice creeping back in. "People think the point of MeetCute is to find their true love or whatever, but I don't understand what the algorithm does! I don't even know where the data I collect goes. The only thing I do know is that DataCloud makes money off of whatever data I collect in the end. And that feels—"

Alyssa's voice was dangerously shaky. "Ashley, I didn't mean—"

Oops. Made it worse.

"Me neither—work was just . . . Look, we make the best choices we have given the circumstances, and it's not our fault that they're all bad." I crumpled a little, feeling guilty that I'd made both of us feel worse.

She stood to walk over and give me a hug. I hugged back as warmly as I could, trying not to let the day's frustration bleed over. Alyssa was the one person that I made an attempt to be good for, in the old-fashioned romantic sense, especially on days that I was terrible to everyone else. Despite my ambivalence towards my job, I'd met Alyssa on MeetCute. Our first date was at an upscale vegan restaurant that the app had chosen. I was increasingly conscious of the fact that I had somehow decided to wear my third-best button-up and jeans, and only managed to say hello before being intimidated into silence by the restaurant's complex menu of vegetable juice combinations. She'd managed to spare me the embarrassment by navigating the menu for the both of us, displaying more grace and charm in five minutes of ordering juice than I'd ever had in my entire life. When she next tried to talk to me, all I could do was choke out a self-deprecating joke about clearly being a test case for the algorithm, and luckily she hadn't walked away on the spot.

After the initial optimization stage, we'd gone on a few more dates (preplanned, according to our Common Interests) and taken the usual postdate feedback surveys. After the feedback surveys generated enough data to produce an acceptable Partner Satisfaction score, we'd moved in together after the fifth date.

I'd always wanted to reverse engineer our match from our MeetCute profiles, not satisfied with putting my trust in the algorithm alone. The last time I'd presented a potential solution to Alyssa, we'd been moving into our new apartment together and I'd been looking for a distraction from unpacking the dishes. I'd doodled some diagrams and pseudocode on the side of a cardboard box, gesticulating at the words SCI-FI, ARTISANAL TEAS, and CATS???. She'd only laughed at my efforts.

"Don't you want to be, like, soulmates, Ashley?"

"I want to understand how we got here." I replied, punctuating the point by adding another question mark to CATS???. "I don't trust what I don't understand."

"You understand that I love you right, regardless of whatever the algorithm says?" She leaned over the cardboard box I was writing on.

"I do—and I love you too, but I need to know—"

Before I could continue my indignant response, she closed the distance between our faces and kissed me.

Algorithm or not, we'd been together ever since, going through the usual domestic routine and raising a soporific cat named Toast. Honestly, we were luckier than most of our friends were. Most of them were still stuck in their slowly dying hometowns or working temp jobs that they were overqualified and underpaid for.

Alyssa began putting her elaborate astronology maps away, meticulously placing the numerous crystals laid out on their surfaces back into little velvet bags.

"I'm assuming that calling your job a total lie means it was a difficult day for you too?"

I made a face but tried to sound casual. "There was a DataCloud-wide notice for a meeting tomorrow for a Department of Defense–sponsored initiative. Something about utilizing the full capabilities of DataCloud's data centralization efforts. Sounds above my pay grade, to be honest."

"I know when you're trying to brush concerns off." Alyssa looked at me meaningfully.

I shrugged. "It's not *less* okay than it is normally, all right?"

"I worry about you, that's all. It's rough enough out there—Ah, Toast's trying to eat my cardigan, will you get the kibble, sweetheart?"

Our cat only expended any energy when it was guaranteed to have it immediately replenished. I went to get food for Toast and made a mental note to order myself a strong kombucha for tomorrow. The extra heavily fermented kind.

The nerves sent my body into autopilot that morning, managing to dress and feed myself to catch the Metro to work on time. What more was there for DataCloud to ask about anyway? DataCloud-sponsored questions were everywhere, about everything, and at this point, they'd insinuated themselves into city life like overpriced coffee chains. I wasn't sure what "full capabilities" meant.

As I approached work, I took one last deep breath, standing in the geometrical shadow of the DataCloud HQ. It was the tallest building in

Downtown LA, glass and metal reflecting and distorting the city around it. My employee ID keyed me into the appropriate floor as I entered the elevator, bringing me straight to my preset destination.

Welcome to the 115th Floor, Ashley Matsumoto. You're expected in Conference Room 15B!

15B was the penthouse boardroom. The all-glass structure was perched on top of the DataCloud building, glittering smugly above the city skyline. Officially it was called the Yttrium Suite, but colloquially it was known as the "no-skirt room" because of its obnoxious glass floor. Not that it would matter to most of the executives who used it anyway.

The room was set up like a hotel ballroom instead of the usual long conference tables to accommodate what seemed to be a significant proportion of DataCloud employees. I felt uncomfortably exposed like this, especially surrounded by glass on all sides. As I entered, my ID conscientiously informed me that I had made adequate time getting to the meeting, giving me an overall employee proficiency score of ninety-two percent. Thrilling. The last time it had fallen below ninety percent, I'd been scheduled for an HR meeting where I was subjected to a presentation about *company excellence* and *team spirit*. Then I was put on probation for a month.

I gave a quick smile to familiar faces and found my seat. A man I had never seen before was plugging in the thinnest, most glasslike laptop I'd ever seen on top of a glass lectern. He looked like a four-hundred-dollar pullover had come to life, dressed in the most immaculately pressed sweater and dark jeans I'd ever seen.

An AI voice spoke over the audience to let us know the meeting was beginning and to take our seats. It intoned, "Please give a warm welcome to Corporal Theta Veidt, DataCloud's new Head of Incorporation and Integration and liaison to the United States Department of Defense, Cybersecurity Division. Our newest addition to the DataCloud Family."

Polite applause. The man at the lectern cleared his throat.

"Good morning everyone, just Theta please. Aren't blood families so yesterday? We're all one big, constantly improving human family here." His enunciation had an uncanny metronomic precision to it. Theta smiled widely and forced a laugh. It reminded me of when I'd met Alyssa's parents for the first time.

"I abhor formality, by the way. We truly want your input on this new project."

As if to illustrate his relatable informality, he had one hand in his jean pocket, with an air of such deliberate casualness that I wondered if it had been workshopped.

"DataCloud usually works on the macro scale. We like knowing all about capital-*S* Society. What we are looking to do here is to get a sense of how everyday people are feeling about the important things in American life—politics, both foreign and domestic, morality, social issues—but in a much more intimate setting."

There was silence except for the slight buzz of the projector.

"The conventional means of data collection are polls and surveys," Theta continued as pie charts and question marks and percentages popped up on the screen. "Survey questions are blunt instruments. You can only get answers in the most general of terms—categories, yeses and nos—and turn them into percentages, population data, and demographics. DataCloud, though, has perfected the art of the carefully engineered question. We believe that, in our hands, they can be powerful tools." He paused, looking off into the distance pensively. "After all, we understand that if you ask the right questions, you will get the answers you want."

He made a motion like a firework with his hand, and the DataCloud logo projected itself on a huge sheet of glass behind him. A new addition, a banner that read "Department of Incorporation and Integration" appeared underneath it.

"In the last ten years, DataCloud has centralized the means of data collection. We've incorporated ourselves into nearly every aspect of consumer life, and as the cliché goes, one could say we know you better than you know yourself. This proud military partnership, Inco Dep, was created because of DataCloud's proven ability to ask the right questions. We've been chosen to get a bead on how the public feels about policy matters, thanks to DataCloud's track record of providing meaningful data that can be used to engender favorable responses for our sponsors at the Department of Defense—in this case, proudly expanded to much of the American public."

He nodded to one of the black suits, who changed the slide to one with a CONFIDENTIAL—FOR COMPANY USE ONLY watermark in the background.

"Please note that all sample questions presented in this meeting are prototypes—we're still consulting with our Linguistic Psychoanalysis department to workshop them. We foresee that these questions will be introduced to all existing DataCloud subsidiaries."

> *What is an acceptable lethality risk in the use of NeuroTempest chemical sprays by police in order to curb violent civilian protest?* A range from one percent to one-hundred percent followed.

> *Given the advent of the Second Gulf War, at what education level would it be appropriate to introduce interactive military education programming (such as the US Army's video game,* Desert Valor: Liberty Calls Again*)?* A list of learning levels listed from preschool to middle school.

> *Which feature should Homeland Security prioritize in creating an approachable neighborhood surveillance drone? A) Interactive facial expressions B) Visually appealing coloration C) Customizable voice options.*

All of these questions were going to be thrown in the same bucket with the cutesy date questions and discounts for overpriced food? My stomach turned as I imagined the jarring cacophony of questions, the never-ending interruption of questions about new soda flavors, and then the police, the next shiny gadget, then drones, then new clothing styles . . . Who had time to think carefully about surveillance or war or anything that meant anything when all they wanted was to get a discounted lunch or see their next date? DataCloud survey questions were so ubiquitous that people—that I—didn't think about them much.

Maybe that was a mistake. My stomach sank.

"We see Inco Dep as a liaison to the public and the US military. These questions, the people who answer them, and the data we collect will be used to protect the country and our allies abroad. The degree of anonymity is still being decided, but we believe that the data will have an influential impact. Real citizen input on real policy decisions. Are there any questions?"

Despite my better instincts, I raised my hand.

"Mr.—uh, Theta, sorry if I missed, it but shouldn't there be, an option for not—"

Theta's eyebrow twitched slightly at "*not.*"

"—not having any drones at all? Or not wanting any chemicals, or video games, or you know, a general option for no—"

"Our partners at the Department of Defense are not looking to provide those options at this time."

"I don't understand how this is a real choice if the options are gradations of the same thing." I could hear the annoyance in my voice and could see a few nervous-looking sideways glances, and heard more than a few whispers.

Theta's eyebrow twitch deepened into a crease, not quite a frown, but visible irritation. "We have noted your feedback, Ms.—?"

"Matsumoto."

"Ms. Matsumoto. As you can see, however, we are clearly asking for public opinion in a transparent manner. DataCloud's entire premise is consensually generated consumer data. We do not collect information that the consumer does not give up. The consumer always has a choice."

"The fact that people are choosing something is irrelevant if all the answers are yes," I shot back. I thought of my employee proficiency score, teetering around probation level. My hands started to sweat, and I fought the urge to stuff them into my pockets and shrink back into my seat.

Theta's reply was carefully controlled. "The agreement with the Department of Defense is to collect citizen input under these specific parameters and conditions. As I said earlier, our goal is to ask the right questions to generate answers with guaranteed utility."

His calculated manner was unnerving, and all of the eyes on me were making me skittish.

Answers with guaranteed utility. It occurred to me, faintly, that it was almost impossible these days to avoid any DataCloud-acquired property, that so many of the choices we were making were tethered invisibly to someone else's goals.

"Will there be any way to opt out of answering these new questions?" I asked, though I already could guess what the answer would be.

"Inco Dep aims to condition DataCloud services rendered on the premise that users answer the questions. They may opt out simply by choosing not to use the DataCloud service in question. Do you need further clarifications with regard to Inco Dep's aims, Ms. Matsumoto?"

They'd been defined with excruciating clarity. I shook my head and looked away.

He turned away sharply to address the entire room."Inco Dep will work with DataCloud and DataCloud properties, including its most recent acquisitions, CraveIt, MeetCute, and Orderly, to integrate the DOD's survey requests into our business repertoire. All personnel involved will receive a courtesy email prompt from your new Inco Dep division leaders. We look forward to getting in touch during your scheduled meetings. Thank you for your participation."

I left as quickly as possible, hoping no one else would try to talk to me. I startled as my ID buzzed, prompting me to provide feedback on Theta's presentation. The choices were presented in pastel popup bubbles with hyperbolically positive adverbs. The bubbles bounced fervently, their insistent colors indicating I should choose one, and quickly. I tried to tap away from the question, but the device punctuated my attempt to escape the question with a vibration, and the imploring notification to *Please select an option, Ashley Matsumoto :(.*

I don't feel any of these things! I wanted to scream. On any other day, I would have clicked on one of these pointless bubbles to make them go away, to move on with my life, or at least onto the next question. I wouldn't have cared if none of these adverbs were true. But as Theta had demonstrated, all of them were useful. And the answers to Inco Dep's new questions were definitely going to be used.

The buzzing of my ID grew louder, an appeal to make a decision. The ID screen brightened till the glare of the pop-ups hurt my eyes. Other people were starting to notice, starting to get annoyed at the noise. I thought about what I'd told Alyssa about how it felt like all the choices we had were bad choices. What would I tell her now? That the premise of DataCloud's existence meant our choices meant nothing? That they meant everything?

All I could think about was the swarm of cheerfully phrased questions that surrounded us, a swarm of vibrantly colored sans serif text like a formless cloud that hung over every aspect of our lives. Though now it was less a cloud and more a garish, labyrinthine fog, carefully reshaping itself in response to our answers, deliberately obscuring the realities and possibilities beyond its own design.

The buzzing was plaintive now. My finger hovered over the screen. For once, I thought wryly, my employer and I understood one another perfectly. All I had to do was choose.

16

Death Muse

David Brown

"We shouldn't be seen together here. This isn't within protocol," Jack said, looking stern as Malady pulled out the chair across from him and took a seat.

"You know this place is part of the privacy consortium," she replied. "We're safe." She glanced around at the other outdoor tables situated nearby and the tall hedges that surrounded the café, indicating the borders of the privacy screen. "Ok, I know it's risky, but I asked you here for a reason." She looked back at Jack and intensified her gaze. "I would like to observe how you approach this job."

"What, like some kind of test?" Jack scoffed and raised one of his graying-brown eyebrows. "Aren't we long past that?"

"It's been a long time since we've been on a job together. I need to be sure you haven't . . . lost it."

Jack crossed his arms, lowered his eyes, and leaned back. "Lost what?"

Malady cocked her head and shrugged casually. Combined with her tense jaw muscles and rigid posture, Jack could tell her disinterest belied something serious. But he'd learn what it was faster by playing along. He sighed. "Alright, Malady."

Malady shifted in her seat and turned away, concealing her expression behind her long black hair.

Jack took the hint.

He started taking in his surroundings, and kicked off an environment scan. They were sitting at an outdoor table, underneath an awning in front of a café, The Sapphire Muse. The expansive front windows between their table and the café interior stood open, presumably to let in the fresh autumn air. Inside the café, every corner, ceiling, and seat cushion staged a microrebellion against mass-produced consumer goods. There was a mounted denim interweaving tapestry; an array of repeated portrait shots of some everyday citizen from slightly different angles and with alternating color schemes; a chandelier of dull, rusted razor blades; a seventeenth-century style bust of a two-headed cat.

Jack broke the silence. “This guy likes his art. Probably just stuffs in as much as he can to fill that void he’s feeling.”

Malady turned and snapped at him. “Jack, people aren’t that simple. One can benefit from art for self-healing and still appreciate each piece for its own sake. Have some compassion; we’re not butchers.”

Jack squinted his eyes and cocked his head. “Come on, Malady. I’m just making conversation.”

Malady turned and smiled flatly. “You’re right. Death makes for *such* great pleasantries.” Her smile disappeared as quickly as it had manifested.

Jack hadn’t seen Malady this tense in decades, not since their last botched job, when they all had narrowly avoided prison. She usually tolerated his cynicism. He considered defending his flippant musings, but he respected her too much not to take her seriously when she was so . . . serious. He tried to focus on the job instead. He checked his implanted optics; the analytics were only about a quarter done. It was going to take a few more minutes. He took another look around the café, casually but with intent. A couple on a date in the corner by the bar were sharing a sandwich and shy smiles. The barista behind the counter was cleaning the milk wand with a steamed towel, lost in thoughts seemingly distant from his day job. A businesswoman was flicking her phone and enjoying an afternoon espresso on a nearby outdoor table.

“What do you think will happen to this place when Monroe’s gone?” Jack asked. He chose his topic of conversation carefully, now aware he was under Malady’s scrutiny.

“I assume you’ve done your homework. You tell me,” she replied with a smirk. Whether she was being playful or trying to psych him out, he wasn’t sure.

Jack rolled his eyes. "Ugh, Malady, we're really doing this?" He paused and leaned forward, resting his forearms on the table. "I've been digging for a couple days. The guy's got shit for security, so it's been easy getting all the nitty-gritty feeds and records. He doesn't have any kids, so that's out. He's not married and hasn't been too successful with relationships, so no significant other to take over. His will was one of the few things I couldn't hack, but I've pieced together that he's not in too well with his extended family, so I doubt he'd give it over to them. I suspect he's going to give it to one of those up-and-coming artists he hosts in his estate. Probably one that he obsesses about, thinks they'll 'revolutionize' the world of art. I'm pretty sure it's going to be Mabel. And his nephew will try to start a lawsuit to take it from her."

Malady's smirk transformed into a full grin, and she softened her tone. "Not bad, Jack. I thought you might have guessed one of the more conventional artists he's been hosting for a longer time, like Collin. But you understood that Monroe is *such* an idealist, pouring his hopes into a promising renegade."

Jack relaxed and leaned back all the way into his chair. "Seems like you like the guy."

"He is fascinating! The world will be less colorful without him. But I believe Mabel can fill his shoes. I think she's brilliant, the way she imbues everyday objects with such meaning. What do you think of her?"

"Hmm." Jack paused and rubbed his forehead. He hadn't developed as complete a personality profile on Mabel as he had for Monroe. He didn't like speculating if he could avoid it, but Malady was stretching his prediction capabilities to their limits. Clearly, she wanted to know the extent to which he had researched the web of people entangled with the target. One of her mantras reverberated in his mind: *Plucking a node from the web has consequences far and wide. Misunderstanding even one connection can cause failure, and with failure comes harm. And that's not what we're here for; we are here to save people.*

He took a deep breath and hoped his intuition would bridge the gaps. "She's still young. Inheriting Monroe's fortune would free her from the burdens of pursuing the family business she's otherwise likely to get sucked into. Reasonable chance she'll become a prolific artist. Brilliant, yeah, and she doesn't let it get to her head. Not sure how she'll handle the offer of the inheritance, though. Could backfire on Monroe; her personality profile suggests she shies away from anything with attached expectations, so could be she sells the café and his estate or turns them down outright."

Malady's face drooped and lost a bit of its glimmer. "Yes, you're right. That would be a shame for Monroe. If only he could talk to her about it." Quickly, she recovered and sat up straight, composing herself. "But that's outside our purview. We can only do so much to give our clients what they want."

Another shared silence. Jack was usually comfortable in silence with Malady. He had known her for so long, before all of this, back when they'd been mortal forty-somethings and she'd been the daughter of his campaign manager.

He studied her. She was analyzing the scene, same as him, only she lingered more on the people than the environment. For her, it was always about the people. It reminded him of her father and how he had also taught Jack to understand his constituents not as statistics, but as individuals. She took after him more than she'd ever admit.

He took a sip of his coffee.

Malady looked down at his porcelain cup, then squinted her eyes. "You don't like coffee," she said matter-of-factly.

Jack shrugged. "The Monroe Mocha. It's his café; I felt like I ought to do him the service of trying his namesake drink."

Malady smiled gently. "Well, well, you are still decent, under all that . . ." She pointed at his face and motioned in circles.

Jack snorted and rubbed the bristles on his chin. "It's another way to get to know him. Learned that one from you." He tipped his head towards her.

Malady pursed her lips and pretended she was scribbling something down on a pad of paper. "Test subject shows skill at aligning ethics and practicality."

Jack rolled his eyes and smiled with one side of his mouth. It was nice to see Malady warming back up to him. He turned away from the café and observed the passersby walking on the cobblestone street outside. Although he could see out onto the sidewalk and beyond, he knew the invisible digital wall between the outdoor seating area and the sidewalk prevented them from seeing in. One of the many luxuries afforded by the privacy wars. That's why he loved this part of town—they kept around ancient relics of preimmortality humanity, like cobblestone walking paths and doors with knobs, while taking advantage of all the benefits of modernity. It was a place that transcended time.

Out of the corner of his field of view, he thought he saw Malady eyeing him, but when he looked over she was still focused on the scene. Had he imagined it? Maybe what he'd seen was just the notification from his feed that the scene analytics had finished.

Their relationship had always been professional, but occasionally Jack found himself wondering if there could ever be more to it. In his experience, intimacy with anyone outside the group had always been too full of lies.

"Malady?"

She turned to look at him. "Yes, Jack?"

Her eyes were sunken. He looked at her hands resting on the table and saw the slightest tapping of her index finger. Despite softening up to him, her mind was elsewhere. Now was not the time or place to broach that topic.

"Do you have any recommendations for how I should go about this job?"

"No. I just want to observe."

"All right. The medic response time for this area is six minutes," he reasoned. "A few of the places Monroe frequents have longer response times, but his schedule elsewhere is highly irregular, so that's why I picked this place. Six minutes isn't a lot, but hey . . . at least it's not three," he chuckled.

Three minutes was the "no go" zone. If medical attention was available within three minutes of a target's location, guaranteed death was nearly impossible. Accidental death took time—at least four minutes of blood loss to the brain in the best-case scenario. But six minutes still meant the job had to go nearly perfectly.

He scanned the café at all the objects or scenarios he had considered as potentially dangerous, and lingered on the tiled staircase that separated the café's two levels. When he'd been younger and less experienced, when Malady had first invited him to start this venture, he might have suggested some carefully placed active matter oil that forced Monroe to fall a specific way, causing a slip, a cracked skull, and brain hemorrhaging. But that would be a risky, sloppy job. A good job embraced the unique features of the environment and the character of the target.

Jack looked up at the ceiling. It was an old building with some nasty-looking piping flagged as having low structural integrity. A loosened bolt, some manipulation to induce small fractures for plausibility, and a well-placed micropropulsion drone could lead to a few hundred pounds of metal targeted straight on Monroe's head. He double-checked the possible trajectories, Monroe's reaction speed, and damage assessment, and ran some coarse probabilities. Still 99.9 percent, now with additional environmental data from the job site. A routine assignment.

"A pipe," Jack said decisively.

"In the kitchen, by Colonel Mustard," quipped Malady.

Jack snorted. "Are you even old enough to know that reference?"

It was Malady's turn to roll her eyes. "You'd think after a century a person would forget they're five years older than you. Like you've ever played a board game!"

"I have, actually," he said matter-of-factly.

"Bullshit. When?"

"When I was a kid. My dad had some stored away. You know him; he was all about making sure I didn't forget 'the old ways.' We played a few times."

Malady smiled a little. "That's adorable." Her voice became flat. "And look at you now, playing games with people's lives."

Jack's head tilted slightly and he scrunched his eyes, puzzled by Malady's demeanor. He continued.

"Fourth pipe from the right. It's rusted, out of spec. I send in a termite, let it chew at it after hours, make it look like natural wear and tear, and then plant a bee on it. Monroe walks under it, I rig it to trigger, and it falls loose and flies straight into his skull. A crack like that will do him in."

"Hmm . . ." Malady pondered. "It's risky. Investigators might get involved."

"Yeah, they always do for shit like that. But the bees we've got are undetectable; they disintegrate completely now. Investigators might poke around a bit, but they'll back off when they can't find strong evidence."

"No," Malady said immediately.

"What? Why isn't that fine?"

"I said no."

Jack leaned forward and stared at her. "What game are you playing at?"

"No game, Jack. Just please find something different. I don't want to risk investigators getting involved."

Jack crossed his arms and leaned back in his chair, eyeing her. He trusted her, but something was off. Malady was often cryptic about philosophy and ethos, but never when it came to information on a job. What was different about this one?

Jack reinspected the scene. Eliminating the risk of an investigation would be particularly difficult. Accidental deaths were rare, so many of them did get investigated. Investigations weren't cheap, but evidence of foul play could prevent significant payouts from insurance and, perhaps more importantly, serve as a reminder to the public. No one wanted to see their family member's face in the news; no one wanted to be ostracized as the relative of someone driven to that most irrational and desperate final act.

The trouble was, to avoid investigator involvement, the death had to involve some human error. And requiring human error always meant a lower chance of success, especially when the client didn't want to actively participate. It was trading one risk for another. Malady couldn't have made it any harder for him.

"Look, Malady, I'm not asking for details, but I gotta know—you promise you're not hiding anything from me that I'd regret? Because you know the reason I work for you, the only reason I'm willing to walk this dangerous line we walk is that I believe in our principles. I know I can be flippant about it sometimes, but I believe in doing this the right way."

Malady's features softened, and she sighed and leaned forward. With a solemn kind of half-smile, she reached across the table and rested one of her hands on his.

"Jack, yes, of course, you're right. But, please trust me. I haven't deceived you before, and I'm not going to start now. I'll tell you everything after the job."

Suddenly, at the back of the café, past the counter and the narrow hall of chairs and tables alongside the espresso bar, a figure burst in. Jack perked up and shot his gaze towards the back door. The figure strode with force, exuding presence. He was covered in vibrant colors, from his pink-checkered sneakers to his shining, shoulder-length, curly black hair. He seemed tall at first, but upon further inspection, his apparent height was augmented by his top hat, green and purple stripes swirling up and around like a fruity candy cane. He was an extension of the flamboyant wall art spread about the café. And, metallic shimmer billowing behind him, adorned with an assortment of knickknacks spanning the full spectrum of color and aesthetic, from a fishing lure, to a twentieth-century optical spinning disk, to a mechanical shrunken head . . .

"That cape . . ." Jack shook his head.

Malady stifled a giggle.

"I can't believe this guy wants to off himself," Jack whispered. "He's dripping so much confidence, he's gonna need a mop."

"Shh, Jack!"

The man began making rounds—checking in first on the barista, then the customers. He walked with purpose but not haste. Jack and Malady exchanged a few whispers, but for the most part, couldn't keep their eyes off the figure.

The man walked over to them. "Well, I haven't seen you two around before! Welcome to The Sapphire Muse—your home away from home, or your work away from work. I'm Monroe, at your service. Judging by the serious expressions, I'd guess you're both here on business."

Malady spoke up before Jack had a chance to respond. "Yes, we've picked up some work in the area just recently."

"Ah, in the entertainment business, perhaps?"

"Yes, actually, good guess," Jack interjected, giving Malady a quick, sly look. "It's interactive virtual fiction."

"Fantastic! What kind? Character imprinting or the real deal?"

"The real deal," said Malady, with a charming smile. "I like to think character imprinting can't quite capture me just yet. I'm sure you can relate."

"Ha! Yes, there's no one quite like me, so people say."

Jack detected the faintest drop in pitch. A crack in Monroe's carefully constructed shell.

"We're only here for a few days but we couldn't resist the reputation of the one and only Monroe and his Sapphire Muse," Malady said.

"Aha! I'm glad word gets around. I certainly try!" he said with a flick of his cape and a chuckle. "Well, welcome again, and if there's anything I can do for you two, please don't hesitate to ask. Oh, and if you're around in the next thirty minutes or so, I'm baking up a fresh batch of mini bundt cakes soaked in apple syrup. They're to *die* for if I do say so myself!" And with a bow, he was off, back behind the counter, and through the swinging kitchen door.

"Well, he is something else," said Jack. "I see now why he paid for premium. He wants to be completely in the dark on when or how, so he can keep his persona alive to the fullest."

"It's a pity to lose someone like that."

"It is. But isn't it always?"

"Mm."

Malady paused and lowered her head, and her hair fell forward, covering much of her face. It had become a custom of theirs to take a moment of silence and reflect on the lives they were taking, to let each one weigh on them and resist the natural tendency to build up emotional defenses. Jack figured it was that time. He followed suit and let his thoughts drift. Monroe was so full of life and character; why would someone like that want to end it? Had he concluded his persona was just an act and lost himself? Did he feel the weight of the hopelessness of finding his individuality in a world of sixty billion other people with nothing but time on their hands? Or is it possible he was happy, but glimpsing the signs that he had seen and done everything and wanted to leave before the novelty of life wore off? Jack thought about the café's customers and how each of them would carry on the stories about Monroe, the iconic wealthy businessman who still made his own bundt cakes. He thought about Mabel and the irrational hope he probably had for what she would do with his inheritance. And he thought about Malady and the way she'd giggled at the sight of his cape.

Jack looked up before Malady did. He thought he could glimpse a tear dampening her left eyelash. It reminded him of the first time they'd taken a life together, so long ago now, and the way she collapsed to her knees when they'd been out of sight, letting her tears course through her like a storm. He didn't want to mess this up for Monroe. If Monroe wanted it, he deserved his freedom.

Jack resumed his search. As he looked around and observed the ostentatious decor and the man that had given it life going in and out of the kitchen, an idea started to form.

"I think I've got something," he said, eyes intent on the surroundings. Malady looked up. "He's such a renaissance man. Refined, but capable of doing everything for this place, from managing the business to making some of its art. He's the kind of person that will get his hands dirty when things need to get done." He paused and turned back to Malady.

She nodded. "Yeah, I'm listening, go on."

"He's also confident. He knows he's capable, and he relies on himself when the need arises. In fact, he always tries to fix the sink himself before calling the plumber, much to the dismay of the maintenance personnel . . ."

Jack made a sidelong glance at Malady. She cocked her head and waved him on.

"Anyway, I can use this. I can trigger an accident, break something. Something that'll cause him to think he can fix it. And I can rig it so fixing it is fatal."

"Hmm, okay. Any specifics?"

"Gimme a sec."

Jack looked around again. What could he use? It was always better to use something unique to the environment, so patterns in their tactics didn't emerge. And then, it dawned on him.

"The espresso machine. An electrical beast, full of high-pressure near-boiling water, huge water reservoirs, and a high voltage outlet. A prime candidate for bad things to happen. And most people would call in for repairs. But not Monroe. He'll try to fix it."

A small smile of satisfaction crept onto her face. "Very clever, Jack. How are you thinking?"

He hesitated. "Electrocution."

"Jack . . ." Malady started.

"Wait, wait. Hear me out. I wouldn't risk another Dr. Veren."

Dr. Veren was the textbook bad press for the assisted suicide field—a failed electrocution that led to severe brain damage. Unfortunately, the only part that had remained intact was the part that remembered the names and details of everyone involved with the assisted suicide attempt and repeated them out loud endlessly.

Jack continued, "I send in a termite to trigger a leak in the back of the espresso machine that'll cause water to drip down along the power cable, pooling at the bottom, near the outlet that's shared by the refrigerator under the counter. I'll also have it expose the wire near the outlet by fraying it.

"I time it so the pool of water starts leaking out right after close, when only Monroe is on duty. And Monroe, being a do-it-yourselfer, is going to see the leak and want to fix it. So, he'll pull out the refrigerator to find the source, and he'll decide to mop the floor, confident he can avoid the wires. What he won't see is that the wires are loosely coiled on the back of the machine, with a cricket at the ready. The second he goes back there knocking around with a mop, the wires'll drop down into the water.

"And Monroe *always* wears that exceedingly conductive cape."

Jack finished with a triumphant sip of his coffee.

Malady nodded slowly. "Quite the Rube Goldberg machine, Jack." She paused and pressed her lips together. "But will it do?"

Jack had already queued up the simulations while talking. They factored in the environment and his arsenal of tiny helpers making sure the wires fell when they needed to, as well as every feed and piece of data Jack had hacked together on Monroe—his behavioral tendencies, the way he carried his body, and his wardrobe.

"If he sees the leak, 99.2. If he doesn't, I'll abort." Jack sat up straight.

Malady looked at him without blinking. "99.2 is risky." She paused.

Jack held his breath.

She continued. "But . . . given the constraints of the job, I'll give it the green light."

Jack breathed a sigh of relief. Planning was always the hard part. From here, the rest was just waiting. Jack dropped off his insect drones before they left. He calculated the timing so the right amount of water would show up one night later that week when Monroe was by himself. And that same night, Jack invited Malady for an in-person debrief at a diner right next door to the Sapphire Muse. They had front-row seats.

At about twenty minutes after the café closed, they heard a scream and the unmistakable sound of an electrocuting, convulsing body. Six minutes later, the ambulance showed up. Twenty-three minutes later, a stretcher came out onto the sidewalk with a lifeless mound under a black body bag. The job was done.

Jack and Malady were sitting together, and Jack pulled out a neatly packed box from his backpack under the table. He opened it, and inside were two bundt cakes—a small token he had saved for the occasion. He set one on each of their plates and nodded at Malady. He picked up his fork and took a bite; the rich apple syrup had soaked all the way through. It was even better than when it was fresh.

It was always a mixed feeling for Jack, knowing he'd completed a job. Had the client finally found peace in those final moments, or did they regret it? He didn't fight his thoughts of self-doubt; he let them course through him, as Malady had taught him. He would remember this colorful character and his delicious cakes.

After setting down his fork, Jack looked at Malady expectantly.

"So?"

"Well, Jack. You passed. Not that I'm surprised, but congratulations." Malady smiled at him.

"Great. What's my prize?" he grinned.

Malady's face quickly grew somber. "Well, I'm sure you've guessed by now. It's another assignment."

Curious. Malady didn't usually get sad about a job; a job was giving someone peace.

"Alright, I'll bite. Who's the target?"

"It's been a long time coming, but it finally happened. We picked it up on the net a few weeks ago." Malady's voice started to shake, and she looked down. "I needed to know you would do it . . . right. That you would do it with compassion."

"Malady . . ." Jack had only seen her break down two other times in her life. This was serious. He reached out his hand and gripped hers.

A few moments passed. She looked up, jaw tight, resolute, with freshly wet cheeks.

"It's my dad."

17

Hierarchy of Obsolescence

David Brown

IT WAS board meeting time again. Jordan paused a few steps before the entrance to the conference room. Would he ever reach a point where he didn't need to take those final steps and just take the day off instead? Or the week? Or year? If so, how could he get there faster?

As he entered the room, he looked around at the meticulously placed water pitcher, glasses, pens, and folders with meeting agenda notes, and raised his eyebrows in disbelief. How long would they hang on to such vestiges of the past? He couldn't remember the last time he needed to write anything down, and none of them usually talked enough to need more water. He worried for a moment about the mental state of his board —if he as CEO is feeling all this uncertainty, how do the rest of them feel? He hoped he was alone in his thoughts.

The others were already there and milling about the snack table, making idle chit chat. There were mini sandwiches on mini plates. Jordan attempted to wipe any residual disconcerting look from his face and proceeded to make the usual business courtesies to his fellow directors.

Rick, in his usual wrinkled plaid dress shirt and barely combed frock of gray hair, was just presentable enough for a COO.

"Rick, good to see you. How are the new units holding up to customer feedback?"

"Oh, good, good. Right on track with what we expected."

Daneb was sporting a blue tracksuit that reminded everyone they should exercise more often. Jordan looked sheepishly down at his own jeans and faded T-shirt. Casual dress is one thing he loved about the new era. "Daneb, glad you could make it. Whatever came of that investigation into the manufacturing facility?"

"Oh, it turned out to be a false alarm—a sensor failure, that's all."

"Good, good," Jordan replied tonelessly.

He didn't need to check in with them; all of these problems and answers were already being tracked and managed by some system or other, but his flailing mind was latching on to purpose. He knew this, but he did it anyway. He hadn't figured out what else to do.

They all found their seats, Jordan at the head of the table, and the other four of them seated around. Jordan eyed the table and ran his fingers along the surface and drummed them a few times. He glanced up at the large display spanning the entire wall on one end of the room and scrunched his brow.

"Hmm, we should probably change the table and seating arrangement, so we can all look at the screen . . ." he mumbled out loud to himself.

All the heads turned towards him. "What?" asked Rick.

Jordan had forgotten he could still command so much attention. "What? Oh, nothing." He chuckled. "Anyway, let's go ahead and get started. Does anyone have any topics before we bring Dorothy in?" Jordan looked around to gauge interest. Some soft head shakes. No nods. A restless fidget from Daneb. It used to be that they talked for a while before Dorothy joined, but no one had much to say lately.

"Alright then." Jordan turned his head towards the display wall. "Dorothy, what's on the agenda for today?"

The rest followed suit and swiveled. The display lit up and Dorothy's lifelike digital face showed up, her black curls immaculate, except for just the right amount of inconsistency to emulate human error. A medium skin tone, and an ethnic blend of facial features optimized to appeal to all audiences and cultures. Her smile beamed, her teeth showing ever so slightly to indicate friendliness without malice or superficiality.

"Good morning everyone!" said the flawlessly articulated feminine voice. "There are several pressing issues that you all have requested to discuss today, and then of course the usual minutia. Given our time constraints, I've ordered them by priority, and the first one up is the recent dramatic uptick in customer complaints about our VR backgrounds during autonomous driving in the SynX 10 line. Is everyone up to speed?"

There were nods and murmurs.

Her gaze swept across the room, making momentary but meaningful eye contact with everyone, then continued. "Wonderful. To summarize, the primary complaint is acceleration. Many people have reported that when they have their headsets on, and the car is in autonomous driving mode, the movement of the scenery in the background of the UI is dissonant with their vehicle motion, which causes discomfort."

Jordan raised his hand slightly "Uhh . . . does this have any correlation with that latest software update . . ." Jordan started, knowing Dorothy would soon answer his question, and a dozen more he didn't think to ask.

"Yes, absolutely, very astute," she responded with a warm and complimentary tone. If she had an ego, it could have come across as condescending, but Jordan knew better by now. The first time Dorothy complimented his intelligence he thought it was a trick or gimmick and confronted her (and her developers) about it. Turns out, there was nothing gimmicky about it; the AIs were just designed to be humble and friendly. This made it frustrating, because he couldn't be angry with her, despite his unavoidable sense of inferiority whenever she did it.

"Correlating the complaints with customers' software versions shows that three different model updates seem to be the source of the issue." As she spoke, graphs popped up on the screen next to her showing the customer complaint trends grouped by category, the software versions that had been released on a timeline, and several other, probably very useful analyses.

Daneb, and her VP Miguel, who she had been inviting to board meetings, exchanged concerned glances. They knew immediately what the problem was. So did Dorothy, of course.

Jordan caught the glance and turned his head. "Daneb, can you fill us in on what happened here?" His tone had a nearly imperceptible hint of accusation—just enough to communicate that he was still an authority figure, supposedly.

Daneb didn't react to the tactic, and replied with the hallmark confidence of her reign as CTO. "It was a software update to improve the VR background scenery by having it take into account left–right motion and turns. So, when the car is swerving left and right in heavy downtown traffic, we make sure their vehicle in the virtual world moves with it so the user doesn't feel like they're in their car. However, the uncertainty in our readout of the car's speed and location seems to be within the perceptible range of a subset of our users."

Rick, who had been chewing on his pen and leaning so far back in his chair that he looked like he could have fallen over any instant, lurched forward. "I thought we were already doing that? That was the whole idea behind the feature launch—make it so that users could look at the virtual scenery and see it move with them." he said. He had a tendency to join conversations when there was a possibility of finding someone to blame for something.

"Not exactly," said Miguel sheepishly. He had been practicing speaking up at these meetings, perhaps in preparation for Daneb's near-term retirement. He was the only one dressed halfway decent by standards of a bygone era. "We were previously only updating scenery to reflect the acceleration and deceleration of the vehicle, but not swaying or turning."

"Are you telling me we launched VR backgrounds as a gimmick? Just some picture you slide along when the car moves forward and back?" asked Rick.

Daneb sat up a little straighter to defend her successor. "Well, it's not a gimmick. It still was a fully rendered 3D—" she started.

"Oh, quit your bullshit," interrupted Rick. "You know damn well having a moving picture is not what people think when they hear VR backgrounds. They want it so when they get in their car and decide to put on their headsets and do work or browse the web or video conference, they can look around and forget they're driving through the dirty, crowded cityscape, and instead see beautiful, fully immersive 3D scenery—a road trip through the rolling hills of Holland, or a train through the Swiss alps. If your car is lurching left and right but your scenery doesn't change, that completely takes you out of it!"

Jordan sighed and receded into his chair. These were the parts of the meetings that he hated the most. Heated arguments between people about why things happened and who was at fault, all while Dorothy patiently waited, looking and listening with seemingly genuine interest and concern for the wellbeing of both the board and the customers. So unnervingly perfect.

There was a missing piece to this puzzle though. Jordan chimed in.

"Wait a second. If all we added in this update was left–right motion, why are we only now getting complaints about acceleration?"

Daneb sighed, knowing what she was about to say would trigger somebody.

"Those three submodels never actually got the initial VR backgrounds update—the acceleration Miguel mentioned."

Rick pounced at the opportunity, "Why weren't we made aware of this?"

Daneb's face didn't change. Her stoicism was remarkable. "It's been a busy few weeks; we planned to add it to the next update. Customers were informed, marketing updated its release date for the feature. It's not a big deal."

"No big deal? Dorothy, can you please estimate how much this negative customer attention is going to impact our sales for the quarter?" Rick loved it when he could use Dorothy's immense on-demand computational power to do his bidding. So much so that he finally put down the pen he had been fiddling with and leaned back in his chair in anticipated triumph.

"Of course, Rick. Based on similar events in the past, the current customer volatility metrics, and the sales trend from the last two days, we're estimating a $6.2 million reduction in sales for the quarter *if* we don't execute on one of our prepared counter strategies."

Daneb and Miguel looked at each other again, with a hint of exasperation in their eyes.

Daneb started to speak up, "It's not correct to . . ."

Jordan waved his hand dismissively and shook his head "Daneb, you don't need to defend your team against Rick's strawman." Maybe this is what he was still good for, some basic people skills. Or maybe if he had just stayed quiet, Dorothy would have handled it. He really wasn't sure. He continued. "We already knew immersive VR backgrounds were a big deal, with big numbers. But, how did this slip past QA?"

Dorothy was quick to speak up this time. "Antoine would know. Antoine, could you join us?"

Her face slid to the side of the screen, and another digital face appeared next to her. A different blend of features, and point on the gender spectrum, with his slightly graying blonde hair done up in a bun—all features profoundly distinct from Dorothy. Yet, in a strange way still starkly reminiscent of her. It's not that they were uncanny, they were just . . . equivalently optimal.

"No need to ask Antoine—it was my fault," Daneb said. "I gave the go for the software update. I wanted to get this update out before our competitors. It was the wrong call, in hindsight."

"You're telling me!" roared Rick, as he lurched forward again. Jordan wondered for a moment if that chair was going to break a few years earlier than all the others from Rick's constant use of chair momentum as an externalization of his feelings.

"Oh, she already admitted it, Rick. Quit your finger wagging," Jordan said.

"I will not. This is serious! Antoine, how did you let a software update through your integration platform without the proper QA checks? Your designers assured us this kind of thing would never happen again with you overseeing software development!"

Antoine had a soothing voice, like Dorothy's. "Rick, I presented evidence of the risks in an attempt to convince Daneb not to let the software update through, but that is all I can do. However, rest assured, we will figure out a way to minimize the damages that happened here," explained Antoine. Confident, but not cocky. The AIs were the only ones that could talk Rick down out of his rages.

"Daneb, you overrode Antoine's recommendation? And without consulting us?" Rick asked.

"I did. I thought it was the right thing to do. If we had pulled it off successfully, it would have been a big boon for us. I think we can still come out from this with minimal damage if we listen to the proposals Dorothy and Antoine have compiled."

"So now you want to follow their advice? When you've gone and messed things up, you want them to clean up after you?" sneered Rick.

Jordan scoffed. "Oh for crying out loud, Rick, back off. You've made your point."

The room quieted down. The tension was palpable but waning.

Everyone's egos had risen and fallen like a storm. And the result was no solutions. Dorothy broke the silence.

"I believe we have several great options for coming out from under this intact. The software team has been independently working on building up a portfolio of dynamically generated scenery and weather, rather than just the few handcrafted common world locations we developed. These can then be generated in real time based on a variety of inputs, such as the user's mood or what they've liked in the past. If we pitch it right . . ."

Rick turned positive on a dime. "Oh, good point, Dorothy. We can market the update as a beta of what's to come."

Dorothy pointed her gaze at some charts that showed up between her and Antoine.

"Exactly. Antoine has already been working with the software team on the safe and reliable development of this feature."

It was Antoine's turn in the spotlight. "Thank you, Dorothy. I project at current development and QA rates that we will be ready to release in sixteen days. Looking across all the existing virtual scenery that's out there, we have identified at least seven hundred promising candidates for plugging into our dynamically generating scenery module. Users will have so many new places to see looking out their virtual window, every drive will feel like a road trip to somewhere new."

A list of scenes flashed in front of the board and graphs showed the categories of types of scenery: arctic, desert, rainforest, and more. There were graphs for customer preferences for the different categories, statistics on the likelihood of customers to try dynamic mode, estimated amounts of money the average customer would spend on the categories.

"And, the best news is that by looking at the data on our most populous regions, we anticipate seventy-four percent of commuters will want to try it out." More graphs showed up with maps, traffic patterns, average drive times, average drive times weighted by likelihood of enjoying dynamic mode, median income correlated with likelihood of having pleasant routes. It just kept going; the rate of information was too fast for any of them to process.

Jordan started to open his mouth and closed it again. It was usually best to let them finish when they went on with their projections.

It was Dorothy's turn again. "Based on the beat of human culture, there is a new trend: people have an increasing appetite for indulging in nostalgia. Which brings us to the next proposal. Antoine?"

"Yes, I'm very excited about this one. I don't think anyone is working on anything quite like it. Our team has been developing algorithms for taking data from old media—movies and video games—and generating scenery for VR backgrounds that match the style of the media. We've built up a library of thousands of media relics from human culture that we can generate scenery from; we've got 1960s Westerns, 1980s classic science fiction. It's all available to us." The screens showed clips of *The Good, The Bad, and the Ugly* and *Star Wars* with sprawling scenery next to them that were generated to look like the movies. "Imagine, on your way to a meeting downtown, you're looking out your window, and you're on a train, across the plains of the Midwest, stopping by quaint towns, or driving through the deserts of Tatooine!"

The room was quiet again. The furrowed foreheads betrayed the churning of brains as they processed all the information presented to them.

"Antoine's idea for how to generate the scenes was quite brilliant," Dorothy added, as she turned her digital avatar head towards him. If these AIs weren't so strongly marketed as *just* business tools, Jordan would have assumed Dorothy was into him.

"Thanks, Dorothy! The general idea behind it is a repurposing of our customer focus group AIs . . ." Antoine droned on for a couple minutes, and Jordan's eyes wandered over to the window and stared off into the small mountain range in the distance. It's not that the information wasn't relevant or engaging; it was perfectly constructed to communicate the right amount of information, with just the right tone and flow to pique his interest. It's just that . . . it didn't seem to matter, in the grand scheme of things, whether he heard it or not.

"After billions of these simulations, we get a really nice rounded view of what the scenery should look like!" Antoine finished.

Everyone looked around at each other with slightly raised eyebrows, and there were a few uncomfortable shifts in their seats. Perhaps they wrestled with the same feelings as Jordan, after all.

Jordan cleared his throat. "Yes, well, that's wonderful."

"Would you like us to proceed with this plan?" Dorothy asked.

There were nods and murmurs all around the room.

"Daneb, I'm assuming you will work with Antoine in overseeing this to release?" Jordan asked.

"Yes, sure thing."

"That is a wonderful solution, but we still need to talk about what happened that got us here in the first place," Rick said. It was often Rick that brought everyone back to the necessary drudgery of management. "These kinds of potential disasters, which we've only managed to get out of thanks to the help of Dorothy and her team, have happened one too many times. We need to change how we operate."

They all looked at him expectantly.

"I propose that we no longer allow people to override or ignore the AI's suggestions, unless they get explicit board approval first," he finished.

Of course we should require board approval to override the AIs, Jordan thought. *We can't let people keep making mistakes that could so easily be avoided. We're not giving the AI any power, we just need to make sure the board is kept in the loop on these decisions.* There were unanimous soft nods throughout the room.

Jordan had an unsettling feeling that this decision was a monumental one. A seed of a decision that begets much more than the marketing and development workflow in a medium-sized virtual reality tech company. Any unease he had was not about whether Dorothy and Antoine had their best interests in mind; of that he had no doubt. His uncertainty was about his place in the world.

They discussed the remaining minutia, and the meeting adjourned. Jordan looked around the board room, at the vestigial tools of a predigital era, and the corporate art being used to adorn a room full of talking heads, only there a few times a month to feel important. Maybe they should turn this into another VR room.

After the meeting, he caught up with Daneb.

"So, that last proposal Antoine presented, that is quite some plan. How long has your team been working on it?"

"Yeah, I was surprised. I don't know. But I think the timing is perfect —people have been craving a port of old media into VR for some time now," Daneb replied.

"Wait, are you telling me this is the first you've heard of it?"

"Yeah. Why?" Daneb gave him a sidelong glance.

"Hmm. Curious. I thought proposals for new features came from your team, and Antoine just presented them."

"No, Antoine's one of the team, he brings up solutions all the time internally."

As they approached the intersection where they would part ways to their offices, they slowed their walk, and Jordan turned to face Daneb. "Yeah, but this is more than just a solution to a problem—this is a whole new feature."

Daneb stopped and slapped Jordan on the back. "Ha! What's the difference?"

"Are you sure he didn't see it from some engineer doing some prototyping on their own?"

"Oh, we don't have anyone doing prototyping anymore. They've all moved on to management and ideation."

"Who are they managing?"

"The AIs."

Jordan laughed. "Are they now?"

PART IV

Through the Turtle Pond

STORIES ABOUT THE FANTASTICAL POWER OF SCIENCE

18

An Innocuous Cumulonimbus

David Brown

Today, he was going to make someone happy. He was going to make a cloud look like a hippopotamus.

He needed it to be a cloudy day, but not too cloudy. He needed a bulky, rolling, vivid white nimbus cloud. Such a cloud was almost like the bulbous figure of a hippopotamus already; this would be easy.

He mustered the strength to enter his world, but hesitated. Was it the right time? How to know when a cloud would be? Before today was his yesterday, and yesterday was cold, full of snow clouds and bitter frost and frozen decks on boats and airships. And storms. Winter storms, bringing ice rain and fierce blizzard winds and deadly cold to the town. His town. The thought of the storms made his thoughts swirl. Why was he afraid? He was in control, with clear and straightforward intentions. Today could not be like yesterday. It would not be. His next slumber would not be full of nightmares, of dark memories, of tortured calculations of what he could have done differently.

Today, it would be springtime. Yes, spring was a good time for a nimbupotamus.

Maybe a child would see it and tell their parents. Perhaps an elderly person would look up at the sky, lost in appreciation and fond memories of their past, distracted for a moment from their aching body. Distracted from the memories of what he had done. Or, rather, of an accident that had happened to him. No, an accident that had happened through him. It didn't matter, this meaningless debate about cause and effect. There was no time to waste; he got to work.

It was a beautiful day. Mr. Abelton stepped outside the door of his brown-bricked, two-story apartment. He closed his eyes, tilted his head back, and let the rays of the sun warm his face. He resisted the urge to open his eyes and behold the sun. Nothing good ever came from looking at the sky.

He took a deep breath. The cobblestones shined with the remnants of an early sprinkling of rain, and he could still smell it in the air. It was springtime. It almost made him forget about the feeling of dread that had been hanging over the town for the last few years.

He started his morning walk—brisk but not urgent. It was a short walk to his office, but he was going to add a stop to his walk today. A morning like this should begin with a coffee and a chocolate croissant. After walking to the end of the block, he turned north on Seventh Street, as usual. As he passed the playground on the right, he expected to see the same grim sight he'd gotten used to—a set of swings, half with broken chains; monkey bars lying on their side; and a twisted metal slide with murky pools of water at every dip—but instead, he saw . . . children . . . playing! Three of the orphans were competing to see who could get across the upright monkey bars first. Mrs. Edelbright, sporting a pale green, flower-dotted summer dress whose colors contrasted with her salt-and-pepper hair, supervised them from a wooden bench at the edge of the playground.

"Good morning!" Mr. Abelton shouted as he slowed his gait. "What a sight, to see the kids playing!"

Mrs. Edelbright turned toward him, keeping her chin low in the cautious manner the town had come to know. She waved. "Good morning, Mr. Abelton! Yes, well, we got a donation to fix it. I think it's even better than it was," she said with a gentle smile that didn't stretch nearly as far as he remembered.

Mr. Abelton smiled back. "Yes, I suppose it is." He tipped his hat and turned to resume walking. But something stopped him. Something compelled him today, a longing to share his optimism. He swiveled on his heel to face her again. "I'm going up the block to get a coffee and croissant; would you like me to bring something back for you?"

She parted her mouth slightly, inhaled as if about to say something, then closed it again. He wondered if she, too, felt compelled to hope today.

"You know, actually, a croissant sounds lovely." She smiled and lowered her eyes. He thought they looked marginally less sad.

She started to reach for her bag.

"Oh, don't worry about it. You can get mine some other time. Be back shortly!"

He briskly departed before she could insist.

The entity peeked into the world, high in the sky, several kilometers over the town, but he held back his strength. He rested his presence on just a few water molecules sprinkled throughout the atmosphere, the bare minimum he needed to observe his world. He needed to find a cloud, not make a mess. He was in luck. It was a clear day, the sun was shining, and there were a few scattered clouds of just the right size headed toward the town. Toward his town.

He needed to get a better view of how his cloud might appear from the ground, from the eye of a child who happened to look up. He traveled down, hopping along the air, leaving only the tiniest traces—a brief gust here, a bit of heat there—the smallest perturbation necessary to transfer his view to a new point in space and time. He handled his descent with precision and delicacy; he needed to make countless minuscule adjustments to avoid making another mess. He witnessed a bird heading toward town. The winds were strong today, and it looked tired. He spared a puff of hot air to give the bird a little lift. If he had a mouth, it would have been smiling, full of hope and will, will for that bird to live and spread joy in his town.

The entity made it halfway to the ground and looked up to see the approaching clouds. One cloud stood out, just a few kilometers from town. It was layered like a cake, each layer embroidered like artisan frosting, and so immaculately white. He could imagine the nimbupotamus already—round bottom, cute bulging belly, and big mouth. Yes, this would be his canvas.

. . .

As Mr. Abelton walked down Seventh Street, he dared to contemplate the vast blueness just above the horizon in his periphery. The sky seemed almost completely clear, with just a few fluffy white clouds. Today, perhaps, they didn't have to worry about the sky.

He hadn't walked down this part of the commercial district since . . . well, since the last disaster, around Christmas. The street had been cleaned up, but he was surprised to see how many shops remained closed. Frank's windows were still shattered and its wooden counters and mannequins' bottom halves were still warped from water damage.

He held his breath nervously as he turned the corner onto Berklan Avenue. Would the café be closed, too? It was a curious sight, still in tatters but with signs of early renovation. A couple sat outside under the awning, sharing a plate of something with whipped cream on top. Though the window panes were missing, they sported delicate lace curtains. Inside, he thought he could see movement. It had signs of renovation, but was it closed? Then, Mr. Abelton picked up a hint of a scent—the sweet warmth of fresh-baked pastries. It must be open!

He picked up his pace, scattering a few pebbles on the ground with eager steps. As he neared the café and was about to cross the street, he saw a boy about twelve years old with dirty blond hair to his right, shaking a tin can. Usually, he'd pass by and tell himself he'd help later, but today was different. He stopped a few feet in front of the boy. His rusty tin can held a measly two coins. Mr. Abelton smiled at him.

"Hey, boy, what do you need?" he asked.

"Anything, sir. Please," the boy replied, without looking up.

"Did you lose your parents in the last storm?"

"Yessir."

"I'm so sorry. Why don't you go to the orphanage?"

"No room, they said."

Mr. Abelton knew the orphanage situation was terrible. He didn't think they were turning kids away though. He softened his voice. "Where do you sleep?"

"Where my house was, sir."

Mr. Abelton dropped three coins in the boy's can. "Get yourself a pastry, boy. And, chin up. The weather is nice—no storms coming today. I heard the orphanage got some money in, too. Mrs. Edelbright is over at the park if you want to talk to her."

The boy looked up at him and smiled. "Thank you, sir," He said, then lowered his head again.

As Mr. Abelton crossed the street to enter the café, he noticed out of the corner of his eye that the boy started tapping his foot ever so slightly. He imagined it was to the beat of a joyful tune in the boy's mind.

The entity waited patiently, conserving his energy, as the cloud drifted towards the city. He watched the city below, looking for sadness in the streets. Which of the downtrodden children had been made that way because of a past accident? Perhaps the one with overgrown dirty blonde hair, with one hand in his pocket and the other holding out a brown tin can, asking for spare change?

As the entity observed, the boy started looking up, slowly. Then more intently, taking his hand out of his pocket and cupping it over his forehead to block the sun . . . and then . . . he looked up right at him!

Oh no. The entity had lost his sense of time. A fracture started to show, a sign that he had been in one place for too long, with too much intent, too much will for one thing. It was just a glint in the sky to the eyes of those below, nothing more, but it meant he had lost control, been careless with the imprint of his presence on the world. This was how accidents happened. Quickly, he recovered—a little tweak here, dissipating the energy, smoothing it over. Then, there was nothing to see—just a small, warm spot of air.

After Mr. Abelton finished his coffee, he stepped out of the café with two warm croissants in his hands. He closed his eyes, brought one to his nose, and breathed in its rich, dark chocolate scent. When he opened his eyes, he saw the boy across the street looking up at the sky with one hand cupped over his forehead. Mr. Abelton's heart skipped a beat.

"Boy!" he yelled, as he waved his arms. "There's nothing to see up there. Keep your eyes on the ground." He pointed firmly at the ground.

"Sorry, sir, I thought I saw something. I thought, maybe . . ." The boy hesitated.

"No point thinking what you might have seen or not. Just worry about finding yourself a place to sleep, yeah? Things are going to be all right."

"Yes, sir."

Mr. Abelton reprimanded himself as he continued walking back to the park. Had the boy, with renewed optimism, forgotten the terror? Mr. Abelton was playing dangerous games, handing out empty promises.

He made his way back to Mrs. Edelbright, who was still on the bench, now reading a book.

She looked up and broke into a grin. "Hello again!" she said.

He smiled and extended his hand. "Chocolate-filled or plain?"

"Oh, either is fine with me." She smiled, softly but genuinely.

He handed her the plain one.

"Thank you," she said, tucking a silver strand of hair that had fallen loose from the bun behind her ear.

"You know, over by the café, I ran into an orphan that said he'd been turned down by the orphanage. Is that true?"

She watched the playing orphans with a distant gaze. "Yes, unfortunately, we had run out of room. It breaks my heart."

"What about the new donation you mentioned?" he asked.

"Yes, we have a few new beds and intend to take on one or two more children."

He sighed. "Whew, that's good news. May I take a seat?" He motioned at the open space next to her.

"Oh, yes, of course."

He sat down, placed a handkerchief in his lap, and set his croissant upon it.

She took a bite of hers. "Mmm, it's still warm"

Mr. Abelton dipped his head in acknowledgment. "Wonderful! I like to let the chocolate harden a bit, else I might make a mess."

As she ate, and his croissant cooled, they watched the children chase each other, playing something like tag, laughing and squabbling. It felt so normal.

The cloud was now overhead. It was time. The entity hopped up, riding energetic gusts of wind, trying not to refract light. He wanted a nimbupotamus, not a rainbow. He made it to his cloud, and it was every bit as beautiful up close as he had hoped. It just needed a few features. He flitted over to where the head of the cloud would be and urged the water molecules to concentrate and form a cute little ear. His water molecules, making a painting for his city.

The first ear was done. The second was even easier. He looked down below. Was anyone looking? Was the boy? Was anyone smiling?

He reprimanded himself; the world wasn't going to stop in its tracks to look at a bulging cloud. It needed to look like an animal, with legs, and a neck, not some amorphous balloon. He beckoned more water droplets to join together in his quest—they traveled over and stretched out a neck between the head and body. Was it too long? He wasn't sure. Next, legs. Legs were quite a bit bigger than ears or a neck, so it took more effort and molecules than he could gather nearby without causing too much disturbance. He looked around for other clouds, but they were far away. He couldn't wait for them to arrive. He hesitated but quickly found his resolve. He would borrow just a few molecules from the nearby clouds, gently tugging them over. It was a bit windy already; it wouldn't hurt. Before he could talk himself out of it, it was done. Then, the second foot. Finally, the tail. Nothing too big, just a tiny nub. It was complete!

For a moment, he marveled . . . but he couldn't marvel long. He didn't want to disturb it. He hopped a little lower, looked up, and saw exactly what he wanted to see. A friendly, white, fluffy nimbupotamus. It even looked to be smiling. He glanced below again—had anyone noticed? The boy? No, he was rattling his can. Look up! He willed the boy. Look up at the cloud! But it was fruitless, and he knew it. That wasn't something he could will.

"I caught a boy glancing up at the sky today. They seem to forget so easily," Mr. Abelton said.

"Yes, they do. For a child, a few months is a lifetime ago," replied Mrs. Edelbright.

"I thought I saw something up there today, too." He paused. "I wasn't looking. It was just out of the corner of my eye, of course," he stammered. "It's fascinating how fear can fool our senses sometimes." He squeezed a laugh out of his lungs.

She turned to him. "I try not to look up too often. But sometimes, I find it calming to overcome the fear, and even a little exciting. The children do it all the time when they think we're not watching." She rearranged her dress and smoothed out some of the wrinkles. "I don't think it makes a difference."

He turned to Mrs. Edelbright and smiled a thin, forced smile. "I don't know about that, Mrs. Edelbright. Reggie insisted that the—"

"Do you believe everything you hear?" she interrupted, raising an eyebrow. "You can't tell me you don't ever look up every now and then by accident."

He hesitated. "Well, yes, I slip every once in a while, but . . ."

"And nothing happens, else we'd have storms every day." She jabbed him lightly in the rib. "Come now, Mr. Abelton. It's nice today. No storms in sight. Would you look up with me?"

He smiled at her nervously, then gave her a quick nod. "Well, all right. Just for a moment, though."

They both looked up together at the clear sky with the fluffy white cloud. It swirled and moved, bulbous cloud parts slowly merging and stretching.

"Oh, would you look at that? It almost looks like a horse! There's the neck and head," Mr. Abelton said.

Mrs. Edelbright snorted a laugh. "You're mad—that's not a horse, it's a baby elephant; it just hasn't grown its trunk. Look at how chunky it is."

He tilted his head. "Hmm, I suppose you're right."

They observed the cloud in silence. All of a sudden, Mr. Abelton pointed excitedly toward one side of the cloud. "Look, an airship!" On his exclamation, two of the orphans stopped chasing the others, and their gazes followed Mr. Abelton's finger. They gripped each other and started their own pointing and shouting. "Look, look!" As they stared, the airship flew into the cloud.

The entity needed a way to get the boy's attention again, to distract him for just a moment, just enough to look up, but he didn't want to create another fracture. A drop of water would be all it took. He brought some of his water friends together, enough to sustain the fall without breaking up, but no more than a drop. The difference between a drop and a bucketful was so subtle. He had to be careful.

Go, my little water drop! He intuited everything about the journey it would take—the air resistance it would encounter on the way down, the gusts pushing it to and fro, and the evaporation that would shrink it—and sent it down. He watched it fall, so slowly. Everything moved slowly when he focused. It went past the flock of blackbirds, missing them all so nimbly, just as he planned. They didn't even notice. Now, the final few seconds—below the tree line, it continued, like a missile, aiming for that sweet, soft, boyish check, that dirty cheek that didn't deserve what had befallen it. Past the second floor of the building behind him, almost there, down it goes, and . . .

Splash.

The boy lifted his finger to wipe up the droplet, and looked at it for a moment, puzzled. He started to tilt his head . . . up . . . and he looked!

The entity sighed in relief. Not a sigh made of air, but a sigh of calm washing through him. A sigh that meant he needn't control a single molecule for the moment.

The boy pointed repeatedly up at the sky and yelled something at some passersby. He seemed even more excited than the entity had hoped. The entity turned around to admire his creation. But it wasn't there.

It was gone.

It was destroyed.

His work of art, his effort of so much careful manipulation of energy and space, had been disregarded and cast aside like nothing more than random noise in the universe.

In its place was an airship. A monstrous pile of inelegantly forged metal, with piercing propellers mercilessly shredding the wind and clouds, riding the air with brute force, recklessness, and inefficiency.

This had been his one chance, before his next timeless torment, to make things right. His only opportunity to grant himself respite from his unending self-flagellation. And they had ruined it.

In his mind, he screamed—a scream of rage and guilt and desperation. A rage so consuming he couldn't feel anything else. But he didn't have a mouth. All he had was will. Nanoseconds passed, and before he could stop himself, his scream began.

. . .

All of a sudden, the dispersed cloud changed from white to light grey. It was so quick and unnatural, Mr. Abelton thought it must be in his mind. He turned to Mrs. Edelbright and saw her downturned mouth and knitted brows. He was not imagining it.

"It's just one cloud; it's nothing to worry about," he said, quenching the doubt in his voice.

Mrs. Edelbright nodded. "Yes, of course. But, just to be safe . . ." she said, rising to her feet. "Children!" she called out, motioning for the children to come over. They stopped gawking and began to meander over.

Mr. Abelton couldn't resist the urge to look up at the sky to double-check. In seconds, the cloud had turned from gray to black and had spread out to three times its size, blocking out the sun and darkening the sky. Moments later, lightning flashed and thunder cracked, loud and immediately above them.

He looked at Mrs. Edelbright. "It couldn't have been us, right?" he mumbled.

"No time for that, Mr. Abelton. We need to find cover. Now!"

The children ran over to them as they frantically searched for a place to hide. Mrs. Edelbright pointed at a nearby building, Nelly's bookstore. "There!"

More lightning and thunder, escalating in tandem with Mr. Abelton's heartbeat. He started panicking, palms sweaty. They ran towards the bookstore.

The entity saw the crew scrambling around the cockpit. He knew they couldn't hear his scream, yet. But they could feel him. Or, rather, they felt and saw the side-effects of him: gusts of wind out of nowhere that rocked their ship; a white, innocuous cloud growing into a monstrous, dispersed grey-black nimbostratus; small lightning arcs forming as the friction of colliding ice crystals charged his cloud. He could hear the pilot's panicked yelling and see his frantic pulling of levers and spinning of wheels. The entity tried to regain control. It had happened again, and so fast. This wasn't what he wanted. These were supposed to be his molecules. They would do as he willed!

Then, his voice started to manifest: electric cackles, rising to drown out the screaming crew. The air was splintering. He needed to think. The ship was already doomed to crash, but maybe he could guide it, land it gently. He tried to focus and summon some gusts of wind to land the craft, but all too quickly they formed an unstable current. Gentleness takes time and energy. He didn't have enough of either one. He could feel himself waning. The entity knew if he tried any harder, he would only make things worse.

And so, he did the only thing he had energy left to do: let go.

Mr. Abelton's panicked breaths barely kept up with his need for air. Each thunderous crash blended into the next as lightning bolt after lightning bolt painted the sky with streaks of electric light. His ears hurt. This can't be happening again, not today. Please not today, he pleaded. It had just been a tiny cloud; there weren't supposed to be any storms today.

They were halfway to the bookstore. Almost safe.

The lightning was so bright and frequent that it must have blinded the crew. Most of them were doubled over, covering their ears and squeezing their eyes tightly shut as the cloud exploded around them. Their pathetic metal rivets were stretched by the pressure of the wind bending their ship.

And then . . .

Snap!

The ship split in two. The pressure of the air compressed the crew's lungs, their bodies. All of a sudden, there was quiet. The entity's charges were dispelled.

As quickly as it came, his cloud subsided. Yet it rained, metal and blood.

Mr. Abelton instinctively stopped and jerked his head up at the loud sound of creaking and snapping metal. He stared, awestruck, as pieces of metal fell from the place where the airship had been.

He was about to resume his run when he thought he saw something out of the corner of his eye. He turned his head back and saw . . . the orphan boy, jogging along Seventh Street toward the playground between them. Oh, no.

"Quick, boy, find cover!" he yelled as loud as he could. He didn't know if the boy heard over the cacophony. He motioned frantically toward the building next to the boy, but the boy didn't seem to notice and just kept running.

Boom! A different kind of crash came from the left, a block down the street towards Mr. Abelton's home. One of the apartments exploded, propelling wood panels and what looked like metal clear across the street.

"My God . . ." he mumbled. He turned back to Mrs. Edelbright, who was jiggling the bookstore's locked handle and beckoning for him to come help.

Then she looked past him and her eyes grew wide. "Cover!" she yelled, snapping him out of it. He sprinted the last few yards toward the bookstore and braced his hands against the wall to stop his momentum.

Mrs. Edelbright began to kick the door, trying to break it to get inside. "Help me!" she bellowed. Her eyes were fierce, and her hair had fallen out of its tidy bun.

Another crash came from the street and Mr. Abelton turned to look for the orphan boy. He was sprinting past the playground now, mouth agape, eyes wide with terror, heading toward them. He was so close.

A streak of metal fractured his field of view. *Boom!* The earth shook, and Mr. Abelton lost his footing and fell forward, landing on his hands. He couldn't hear, couldn't see. All he heard was ringing in his ears. All he saw was a thick mist of dirt. He tried to stand up and orient himself, but fell back down. He squinted and the outline of debris—wood, bricks, metal—began to resolve itself. He couldn't see the boy. He focused on where the middle of the street was. He started to make out the outline of an airship hull piece.

Mr. Abelton froze. The boy had just been there moments before. Was he . . . ? Mrs. Edelbright grabbed him by his coat from behind, jerked him up, and pulled him through the now-open door toward the inside of the bookstore. He didn't fight.

Inside, he leaned back against the wall and tried to control his breathing while Mrs. Edelbright checked the children's arms and legs for injuries and wiped the tears from their faces. Her disheveled hair stuck to her sweaty cheeks and forehead. Her flowered dress had a tear from mid-thigh to the shin-length hem.

He turned and looked outside through the broken glass windows. The dust was clearing, swirling gently. It was quiet, except for the creaking of metal and some shouting in the distance. The storm had left as soon as it had come. The airship hull, a tangled mess of aluminum, with panels swaying on their hinges, was in the middle of the street. His eyes scanned the street, and off to the side, he saw . . . the boy. His incomplete body sprawled on the ground. And just out of reach of the boy's limp, handless arm, Mr. Abelton thought he could make out the shape of his chocolate croissant, covered in dirt.

The entity looked down at the destruction he had caused. No, the destruction that had happened through him. No, the events that had happened to him. His will spent, he dissipated. He'd just wanted to make someone happy today. But his will had not been enough. He tried to fight the wave of despair coming over him. He would try again tomorrow, whenever that would be. Yes, tomorrow would be better. Tomorrow must be better.

The morning's events replayed in Mr. Abelton's mind. He had given the boy hope, a reason to look up. He had allowed Mrs. Edelbright to convince him to look up. His guilt overwhelming him, he collapsed. He had just wanted to share his optimism today. But hope had not been enough. He latched on to a glimmer of resolve that inched into his mind. He was going to try to make sure no one ever looked up at the sky again. Yes, he would make tomorrow better. Tomorrow must be better.

19

Burzamot

Tatyana Dobreva

Burzamot: an entity motivated by storm, turmoil, or unrest

~

I NO LONGER WISH TO SEE THE tranquil ocean, feel the gentle breeze on my face, or be greeted by perfect smiles. Those beauties own me. They are not mine. I am at unrest with contentment.

The new world is mute. There is life here. But it is broken. It wants to be alive again, but it is buried by all its failed attempts. I am broken too. That is why I came here. Not to isolate myself in a world that reaffirms fragmentation, but to rebuild both of us.

A waking cycle passes. The precision of my fingers is immobilized by the bitter cold. I observe the insectile monarchs who made this once-breathing world their paradise. I sense the planet's yearning for the crown lost to these parasitic dwellers. I feel you. Too weak to fight, yet the ground trembles in subconscious battle.

I am up before the rise of the star. The rays are harbingers of the ongoing battle, powering your parasite. Bombarded by accumulating photons, branches shrivel. The soil hardens. What once brought joy is a reminder to unfulfilled desires.

I have spent many waking cycles here. Now I sense that you are less alone in my presence.

I seek to understand the process of your torment. Star above us. A sense of inquisition. Uncontrollable sweat drains my heat. I watch the little march of scarlet soldiers on a tree's naked limbs. They force open its leaves and attach themselves to what appears to be the mechanism for collecting and converting star's energy. My hands ablaze, I lean in to observe subtle vibrations.

The planet emanates a pulse of resistance. I soothe it with my insignificant warmth.

I look down and watch the tiny army satiate their thirst through my perspiration. Despite the pain they cause this planet, I am curious about their kingdom. Is their victory unjustified?

Reduced to an imperfect semicircle by the world's horizon, the star fades.

Cimmerian darkness returns again.

Trepidation amplified by the haunting silence. I am in terror. There is no safety, not here nor in memories of comfort. Beyond every wall there will always be something to fear.

I let the panic run its course. The ground I lay on feels as familiar as my skin. Worn down, I collapse. One eye still open, I watch the soldiers asleep in a fortress built from incomplete attempts at land's rebirth.

It becomes lucid to me. This world fights an uphill battle, whose struggle flows from its own resistance to adaptation.

This place has hope, for it has nothing. All attempts continuously erased by visits of the ancient tempests.

I become unsettled by my desire to save the fragile roots of this world's stubborn rebellion.

Hunger. Jitters. Lonely. Cold. Hot. Yet, I harbor no anger towards the chaotic beasts. Slashed and scattered, their return excites me. Cyclones of entropy.

I feel the planet exhale. I feel it merging with my realization. This is not a battle between a planet and its parasites. For each fights a unique battle for its survival.

I inhale the cyclone. It spits me out. I return. Until the respired land adapts. Until I am.

20

A Thousand, Thousand Pages

Allic Sivaramakrishnan

SOPHIE SLOWED near the teacher's desk, tried to freeze what she saw into memory, and then was out the door before Mr. James looked up.

On one page of the notebook, she had seen a table of numbers. Dates labeled the rows, and "intensity," "flux," "polarization," and some other words she did not remember headed the columns. Small boxes clogged the opposite page, and each box held a pair of letters. Some of the boxes had been crossed out.

Sophie reached the fountain at the end of the hallway, pretended to drink, and then returned to her classroom.

On her second pass, she came away with *QC*, *RP*, and *ST* from some of the boxes. She returned to her desk, then wrote the letters on the bottom of her quiz. She tore that part away, taking part of the quiz with it, and slipped the fragment into her pocket.

Draped in a secondhand plaid blazer, the young Mr. James leaned back in his chair. He was scrutinizing the display of his watch, frowning as though time had done something out of character. Sophie had seen strange dials on his watch, and they were no less puzzling than the contents of his notebook.

Sophie soon grew bored of watching Mr. James. She studied the shoes around her, then tried the window. The patchy school lawn was empty, beige grass under the blazing summer sun. With a yawn that made her feel even sleepier, she returned to the papers on her desk.

Triangles filled three pages. She wrote THESE ARE ALL THE SAME PROBLEM, USE THE LAW OF COSINES across the bottom of the first page. Leaving sarcastic comments under correct answers had kept her going into the middle of April, but it was now June and the triangles marched on.

When Mr. James had taken over the class on a Tuesday in February, Sophie had been hopeful. The next day, she had shown him that all of trigonometry could be derived from the complex number system and asked him why. With a heavy-lidded, blank stare, he had replied that standardized tests were coming up in June and she had been failing her quizzes. She had tried other questions over the next few days, then gave up. And then, the triangles had begun. No matter how much she had slept, each school day began groggily and each class was a struggle, but the hour with Mr. James was the lowest point. Had she always been this tired? She could never remember.

Someone with an odd watch and odder notebook would surely understand her boredom, wouldn't they? She had asked her grandmother about Mr. James many times. Her grandmother would only say that some people were more than they seemed, some less, and she would do well to learn the difference. Sometimes, when Sophie would bring up other teachers, her grandmother would remind her that she was going to the best school in town. It was the only school in town, Sophie felt like saying, but never did. Sometimes she felt like screaming, and sometimes she wanted to stay in bed forever, but mostly she just felt grey. The school counselor had said depression, her grandmother said laziness, and she did not understand either.

Suddenly, Sophie was hit by a wave of grey. Her frustration with Mr. James and triangles and everything else faded into the distance. She regarded her feelings numbly, as if they belonged to an overexcited stranger. Anyway, what did it matter if class was interesting or not? She had learned other things in other ways on her own. But as she revived memories of imaginary numbers and covalent bonds and Kant, she had trouble focusing enough to recall the details. She had enjoyed learning about them at the time, hadn't she? She had, and yet her feelings for them were dissolving now, joining the grey haze that washed over everything.

Perhaps there was nothing to be excited about after all, and that was that. Her plans later that day seemed pointless now too.

She looked at the clock and waited.

In ten minutes or so, the grey disappeared as unexpectedly as it had arrived. She felt like herself again, as if she had been pulled from a fever dream and splashed with cold water. Shaking her head and taking a deep breath, she reminded herself that forty minutes remained, and she had little time to waste. Today came once every year, and she would soon need to be well rested. Acting swiftly, she drew an arrow that sent her solution to page one ahead to the next page and declared the quiz finished. Then, she settled her chin in her palm, a position she liked to call The Sleeper. She was ready. She squeezed the laminated card in her pocket, and closed her eyes.

The town bus left Sophie standing in hot fumes under a hotter sun. She followed a short sidewalk and came upon a wide brick face with many tall eyes and two glass teeth. At her back, an asphalt parking lot shimmered in places, and above its chain-linked border, trees loitered in the shade of their fellows. She heaved one of the doors open.

Cold air hit Sophie, and when the door closed behind her, the outside world vanished.

The smell of paper greeted her, a perfume of fresh and musty pages. Balconies presided over towering shelves, and tall shades on tall windows were golden in the sun, like royal banners in a throne room. Tingles of excitement ran up and down Sophie's length as a librarian took her library card and scanned her returns.

A library volunteer replenished the stack of baskets, then he looked at his watch and scurried off again. He was reed thin and scruffy haired, and Sophie had not seen him before. Looking around now, she spotted a few unfamiliar lanyard-wearing volunteers. They were rushing here and there and checked their watches often. Every time she had visited, at least in the past few months, the volunteer force had grown. She wondered if perhaps the library had gotten more books but was not sure this was how libraries really worked. She filed the question away and picked up an empty basket.

Sophie breached section after section without looking at the signs, filling her basket as she went. She slid past other browsers with ease, a stream through jagged rocks. Then, while scanning a particularly high shelf, she almost collided with a tall, plaid obstacle. She swung herself around it at the last moment and looked back.

It was Mr. James. Her insides sank before she could remind them where she was. Mr. James was looking between the books and his watch, as if one told him it was morning, the other said night, and he wasn't sure who to believe. She had seen Mr. James in the library a few times before, and had once asked him if he liked the library. He had said something dull about records and tax forms, so she had avoided him ever since.

However, although she was not celebrating with candles or a cake, today was different.

"What are you looking for?" Sophie asked.

Mr. James looked up, startled. When he saw Sophie, his eyes hid themselves once again behind heavy eyelids.

"Just some references on this and that," he drawled in his familiar grainy tone. Every word conjured flashes of the classroom and pulled Sophie's feet a little deeper into a quicksand of lassitude. Yet, in the words of a poet she had discovered several weeks ago, she would not go gentle.

"References on what?" she asked.

"I'm looking for some information on," he began, and his eyes flickered to the shelf and back, "housing prices in the forties."

He gave her a drawn, flat smile that seemed to say, "I'm a grown-up. It can't be helped, this is as interesting as we get."

Sophie was knee-deep in the bland quicksand now, but she would find solid ground even if she had to hold her breath.

"Why are you looking at housing prices from the nineteen forties?"

His face went blank for a few seconds.

"I've already looked through housing prices from the fifties and on," he finally replied.

The quicksand was at her chin now, and this line of conversation would finish her off, she thought. She must go for the jugular, something Mr. James would not be able to turn dull, no matter what he said.

"Why were you looking at your watch? What does it do?" she asked.

"I'm sorry?"

"It has a lot of dials, doesn't it? I've seen it."

Mr. James tilted the watch face away from Sophie, then made an exaggerated gesture of checking it.

"This? It's a watch. It tells the time. Speaking of which, I had better get going," Mr. James said.

"What is it telling you now?" chirped Sophie. "Can I see?" She tilted sideways to look and he quickly stuck his hand in his pocket.

A feeling of triumph welled up from the bottom of her toes and boiled over, disguised as what she hoped was a sweet, oblivious smile. The greyness of Mr. James had been broken, if only for a moment. She had stepped out of the quicksand, and it had hardened beneath her feet.

"See you in class, Mr. James. Good luck with your houses."

As she turned, she noticed he held something familiar in his hand. It was his notebook.

She walked away.

One bookshelf later, she stopped before a wooden chair. Some instinct was telling her now that she had learnt something. She wasn't quite sure what it was, but she recognized the feeling, like someone was prodding her head from the other side of a thick pillow. She sometimes found that it was better to trust her brain rather than her thoughts, so she sat down now and remembered.

Sophie had her own notebook at home, an imperfect copy of what she saw in Mr. James' notebook. A new entry appeared every few days. She had recorded equations with symbols she did not recognize and could hardly reproduce. There were phrases like "diode thermometry" that she had needed to look up, and others like "dark photon epigenetics" that had made no sense to her no matter what she searched for. The words "dark photon" in particular appeared many times, along with sentences about "anomalous polarization" and "five-sigma background events" that usually ended in question marks. None of it had ever made any sense to her, but earlier that day she had seen something different. The notebook had shown a grid of boxes labeled by two-letter codes, and Mr. James was carrying the notebook with him in the library. Could the letters be call numbers? Were the boxes then a map of the library? Some of them had been crossed out in his notebook.

Sophie's foot began to tap out a beat. It did fit. It seemed as if Mr. James was going through the library and using his watch to do, well, whatever it was he was doing. But what was he looking for, and why? You didn't need a watch to look for books.

Sophie rose.

She had made progress today, and that was more than enough. It would spoil the rest of the day to keep thinking about Mr. James when she did not have to, and she commanded her whirring thoughts to move along.

Sophie continued on, feeding her basket. Before long, she turned down an aisle and came upon the head librarian sitting on a stool.

Fingers in fingerless leather gloves slid books onto a cart.

"Hello, Sophie. Can I help you with anything today?" the librarian asked in a gentle voice. She was probably only a few years older than Mr. James but a few silver threads stood out against the rest of her wavy, obsidian hair.

"I'm just looking around, thank you," Sophie replied.

"That's quite the pile you have there. Do you mind if I look? Dickens, and Sayers—she's one of my favorites—and I see a book of Wordsworth too. You will have a lovely time with these. Zelazny? I don't recognize the name. I see some *Calvin and Hobbes*—they'll balance out the classics nicely. The other classics, I mean. Is that a biochemistry textbook? It seems advanced, but I'm sure it's right up your alley."

Glowing, Sophie nodded.

"I'm celebrating my birthday early," Sophie declared.

"Happy birthday, Sophie. When is the day?"

"Thank you. It's tomorrow, but we only have Wednesday afternoons off."

"Now I understand the mountain of books. Welcome to life as a teenager, Sophie. If you want to start doing graffiti and listening to rude music, make sure you wait until your grandmother's asleep. I hope you're planning to remember our rule about snacks this time? Good. Your favorite chair was empty when I saw it last. Now don't forget, we close at ten and the last bus leaves at nine thirty. You'll stay until then? I thought you might. Be safe, and find me if you need anything."

The librarian pulled a few volumes on Japanese history and loaded them onto the cart. Some of the books on the shelf were upside down. Others had dark smudges on their spines, the shades of a tiger stalking the twilight.

"What are you doing with those?" Sophie asked.

"They need to go to the book hospital, I'm afraid. I've had complaints of dirty covers, and I tracked them down to this section. A high school history class checked these out some time ago, and maybe we didn't check the returns properly. Still, I can't imagine how we missed these markings. Look at this one."

The stain was fingerlike and strangely fuzzy.

"Someone was up to mischief, I'd say," said the librarian, adding the book to her cart. "Maybe someone tossed them on a grill?"

"That's awful. Can they be cleaned?" Sophie asked, eyeing other smudged volumes.

"Maybe. Repairs are difficult for a small library like ours, so most badly marked-up books end up being thrown out."

"You throw books away?" Sophie cried out.

The librarian nodded.

"I see," mumbled Sophie, and looked down.

The librarian beamed at Sophie.

"I suppose there is something we could do, if you really wanted," the librarian said gently.

Sophie looked up.

"Would you like to be an honorary librarian? If you inspect all these books for damage and pull out the bad cases, I'll have my staff try to clean them. How does that sound?"

Sophie nodded vigorously.

"Deal," said the librarian. "Go through the cart and these shelves here, and then leave the cart behind the circulation desk."

"Yes ma'am," Sophie said solemnly.

The librarian tapped her lanyard.

"Librarians are on a first-name basis."

"Yes, Emily."

"Good. I don't feel like a ma'am yet, and besides, you've been coming here longer than I have, haven't you? Take it away, O sovereign of the shelves."

Fingers adjusting fingerless gloves, Emily left.

Sophie drew up the stool, pulled the cart near, and settled in.

Sophie found books with smeared food, torn pages, and a few warped by water stains. Mostly, she found writing. Many books were covered in elaborate doodles, some in marker or colored pens. A few had notes in the margin, some that made her laugh, and others that looked like coded messages. She came across a grocery list scrawled lightly in pencil, hearts enclosing pairs of initials, and a phone number in pen. She wondered idly what would happen if she dialed the number.

Soon, only the books on the shelves remained. The first one had orange-brown stains on the cover, and some spots were nearly black. The book's interior was unmarked. The next few volumes had similar smudges here and there, but never inside.

The volume that arrived in her lap next was an angry nest of finger-like marks, smeared jerkily as if someone had grabbed at the book with a wet hand. Had the high schoolers been messing around with paint? The thought of entering high school made her feel sick all of a sudden, and she kicked the idea firmly away.

She opened the historical survey of Japan and flipped its yellowed pages one by one. A splash of deep crimson covered page three. She flipped between the cover and the bloom of red and wondered what had happened between the two. The red burrowed through the title page and into the chapter spanning the prehistoric era, the wrinkled patch shrinking until it disappeared on page twenty-three. The shade was not so different from the stains that summer scrapes sometimes gave her clothes. But surely someone bleeding this much would have been noticed, one way or another? A few clean pages lulled her growing sense of unease until page thirty-seven, which held the crumpled image of most of a dark red hand. There was a several-inch tear running near the spine. Someone had opened this book and grabbed the page, she thought. An unpleasant feeling slithered down the back of her neck.

The book then marched through history on clean paper. Black and white pictures of shrines, tea ceremonies, and elegant court dress blossomed across the pages, and she found the change soothing. She skimmed the paragraphs now, growing more and more absorbed. After a blank page, a color section began, twenty-seven full-page images on glossy paper.

Sitting on her short stool, suspended in dusty bronze light like an insect in amber, she drank through her eyes. Panoramas from the Warring States era opened before her and she felt the lives of thousands pass beneath her fingertips. On came visions of steel blades hidden in misty mountainsides, of bodies that trickled ruby into the impossibly blue river, and of cruel, grimacing gods that danced and jeered above men who trudged grimly forward through straw-colored fields.

Then the section ended, and Sophie turned the page once more.

There, on page 122, was a red handprint and four words of bright silver resting in the palm. Each word was ordinary on its own, but the words formed neither sentence nor phrase. As long as she looked, she could make no sense of the words. Argent threads emerged from the red and flowed into the words, like rivulets feeding an inland sea. They did not look written by hand, nor stamped, nor printed, but somehow grown out of the handprint, like moss in a cracked sidewalk. How, she wondered, and why? If this was a high school prank, it was a strange one.

Unable to stop herself, Sophie turned the page. Set against red smears, rows of the same silver lettering appeared.

> *four words of power give to jade hands use if you must resonance with water and metal beware the first and his blade rebellion is yours I fall here tell jade I am sorry so sorry halcyon*

Sophie flipped back a page and looked at the four words, then returned to the message. This was no high school prank, she thought. *I fall here*. Had someone died? Then the red was blood? She closed the book, careful not to touch any of the markings.

She looked around, half expecting to see someone with a sword crash through the window and declare war on something. Library volunteers pushed carts here and there, browsers continued their leisurely journeys, and nothing in particular happened.

Then, Mr. James passed into view, regarding his watch with a frown. He stopped before her aisle and looked up. His eyes fell upon the book cart.

"What are you doing?" he asked.

Thoughts collided in her head.

"I'm sorting books," she forced out.

"What's that one you're holding?"

Had he seen anything? No. Yet, there was an alertness in his eyes that Sophie did not recognize and did not like. She didn't know what the words or the note meant, but she was certainly not going to let Mr. James anywhere near them.

"Something for history class," she replied.

Sophie dropped the book in her basket and strode away as casually as she could manage. She hoped she had not left anything important behind.

"Hold on a moment," Mr. James said, but she walked on as if she had not heard. In a few steps, she was out of the aisle and did her best to disappear. From somewhere out of sight, she saw Mr. James dart out of the aisle, looking at his watch. Just then, a library cart wobbled past and Mr. James followed the cart, requesting something of the librarian who was rolling it along.

Sophie hurried ahead.

She soon reached a far-flung corner of the library, and came upon an immense bookcase tucked behind a staircase. The deep metal shelves housed large books she had never seen anyone open, and she could not have reached the top shelf even if she jumped. The bookshelf ran against the wall, underneath an overhang, and collided with the side of the staircase.

From halfway up the stairs, she lowered her basket down to the top of the bookcase. She buckled her backpack and, when she was certain nobody could see her, spilled over the railing and down to the metal surface. Between the staircase and the bookshelves nearby, there was little chance of being seen from below, confirming many tests over the past few visits. If Mr. James wanted to find her, she realized now, he had lost his chance. Windows, hanging lights, and the dusty tops of bookshelves were the only inhabitants of the world she had climbed into.

She wiped off the dust with a rag and then took out a small pillow from her backpack. Then she set down her water bottle, filled with Sunny D, and slid a bag of Cheez-Its out of her backpack. When Sophie had packed her bag earlier that morning, her grandmother had told her that she would turn orange one day, and Sophie had replied that she wished she would. Then, Sophie had been reminded that if anyone found her eating and drinking in the library again, her books would be thrown out, and her library card would meet a hungry pair of scissors. Sophie had replied that yes, she understood, and she would not be found eating or drinking in the library again.

Now, she chose a book from her basket without looking and then stretched out on the pillow. Tucked beneath the overhang, invisible to the world, she felt timelessness creep over her.

Sophie yawned, wished herself a happy birthday, and opened to page one.

A metal bar clanked and Sophie awoke. The windows were dark and the library was darker. Bookshelves slumbered around her, frozen in splinters of moonlight. She moved to check her watch, and then remembered that the last bus left half an hour before the library closed. The parking lot outside was silent, and few cars passed by on the normally busy road. As her thoughts marched through a somnolent fog, something rushed to the fore. Had she heard a sound just now?

Somewhere in the distance, a heavy door shut with a delicate click. Though it was on the other side of the library, stifled by yards of books and carpet, Sophie did not like the sound of that click.

A dim flashlight came on.

Sophie inchwormed herself away from the edge, and just in case, slid her shiny water bottle deep into her slab of darkness.

The beam of light drew closer, two voices in tow.

"Sir, with all due respect, are you sure?" asked a young man.

"I had watchers monitoring all the exits from outside. And keep your flashlight away from the windows," came the reply. Though muffled and faraway, the new voice had a familiar cadence.

The footsteps drew nearer and multiplied. Chairs shuffled on the worn carpet, and Sophie remembered there was a table nearby, a few rows away. The flashlight switched off, and tiny noises told her a group had sat down. She tried to breathe even more quietly.

"I am the Second Watcher," said the young man's voice. "Thanks for coming on such short notice. We believe the words have been found."

There were murmurs around the table.

"Watcher Fourteen here. Do you have them?" replied a young woman.

"No," replied the Second Watcher. "We believe they were taken by a schoolchild, and she is still here in this library."

Is she? Sophie asked herself, and then she realized. Had they said something about words, too? Surely not.

"It's one in the morning. Is she here or isn't she?" replied the Fourteenth.

"First Watcher?" asked the Second.

"Speaking and confirmed," replied the First Watcher, the older man whose voice she was beginning to recognize. The tone was deeper and more commanding than she was used to. She found a name but decided she must be mistaken.

"Apologies, sir," exclaimed the Fourteenth. "Didn't know you were here. A girl in the library has the words?"

"All evidence points to this," said the First Watcher. "I saw a large signal when the child moved. As you know, Larmor's formula tells us that the words will radiate dark photons in proportion to what?"

There was a long silence, and then a sigh.

"The square of their acceleration," he continued. "The Watcher handbook is not just a paperweight, you know. If you remember basic electromagnetism, dark or not, you will also remember that there is a decay with distance. Anyway, I was nearby and I saw the signal. In spite of the long-distance falloff, some of you should have seen a small response as well."

There was a round of murmurs.

"The head librarian keeps us quite busy," murmured the Second.

"I might have seen it," added the Fourteenth. "But you saw the kid take the words?"

"Everything but. The books she was looking through were covered in rust and burnt iron. Halcyon must have died there and bled on those books."

"I did see some dirty ones in the history section once," said the Fourteenth, "but if he left his words behind, he would have vanished, blood and everything."

"Certainly. However, there have been rumors that Halcyon ate iron ingots for breakfast to enhance his natural affinity for the stuff. I could believe that the residue on the books was the metal in Halcyon's iron-rich blood. Perhaps iron interferes with whatever unmakes their bodies, just as conductors shield larger dark photon effects. I can only guess, but he was bleeding when he escaped into this building, so I would not be surprised."

"It sounds plausible, sir. What happened to the girl, then?"

"Right. Speculation aside, I saw the child remove a book from that section, and the signal as she moved away was unmistakable. She got away from me then, but she hasn't moved the words since and I looked everywhere for her. She must still have them."

An earlier moment with Mr. James sprung into Sophie's head, and she remembered the bright steel that had flashed across his eyes.

Whoops, she decided.

"This is excellent news, sir," continued the Fourteenth. "What do we do now? Find the kid?"

"If she used the words, she could become difficult to handle very quickly. Still, she will be far easier to kill than Halcyon, and she will succumb to the same dying compulsion to pass on a new set."

"Indeed. And if she hasn't used them?"

"We cannot afford loose ends. If she alerts the remnants of Halcyon's rebels, they may grow desperate and attack us in the open. No covenant of silence will save us then. If she has not used the words, she dies all the same."

Sophie was suddenly listening very, very carefully.

"Yes sir. And we're sure she's still here?"

"The last person to leave was the head librarian, as usual. The girl never left."

It does sound odd for a child to remain in a library past closing," added the Second, "but I can see no alternative. The only exits are two doors on this floor and the fire escape on the third. The head librarian does sometimes leave for the day without anyone noticing, but I checked with the staff, and we are not missing any exits. Besides, we kept watch from the outside. The girl must still be here, somewhere. Sir, how do we proceed?

"We search every cupboard, trash can, and ceiling tile. Everywhere. Halcyon's words impart so much power that whoever inherits them will decide the fate of the magicians, one way or another. Some of you weren't with us in the Sahara, but take my word for that much. I muddied Halcyon's trail as I pursued him, but magicians will come looking. We must find the words now, and end the rebellion."

"Understood sir," many voices murmured.

"Good. Pay close attention to your watches in case the words begin to move. If she runs, we'll find her. But as long as she stays still or moves slowly, we'll have to do this the old-fashioned way. Most of you were with us before I built these watches, and before their debut in the Sahara, so I will assume that everyone remembers the older protocols. Understood? And if anybody here left their watch at home, there are spares in this box."

There were sheepish murmurs and the sounds of hands brushing against cardboard.

"May I remind you that a true Watcher is never without their watch?" asked the more familiar grainy drawl, which Sophie now realized was his classroom voice. "Never mind. Now, start with the top floor," the voice commanded, regaining its resonance.

All of a sudden, Sophie's mind was perfectly clear.

Get out.

Chairs slid back and footsteps passed within a few yards from her, then tap-tapped up the stairs. Soon all was silent except for some shuffling of feet above. The creaking of a chair told her that the table was still occupied.

She preferred the version of Mr. James she saw during the day.

Sophie eased the rust-colored book out from her basket and opened it in a shard of window light. Turning the pages with surgical delicacy, she eventually found the dark outline of four words. She didn't even remember what they were, but because she had taken them, she would have to die.

No, she told herself, trying to turn back a mounting internal tsunami. Think, don't just be afraid. You have time. Don't give up, think. She repeated this again and again. What do I know? she asked herself. Make a list. There are two sets of stairs. These so-called Watchers are searching the higher floors. The front exit is always locked. They came in through the back. The parking lot is fenced off except for the main road. There are no houses nearby and all stores are closed. See everything.

She continued in this way for some time, and her brain began to thaw. Soon, all she could see in her head was the library. Her vision swooped between bookcases, taking in more and more detail each time. She soon saw every chair, book, and doorknob. She experimented with the figures that roamed the shelves in darkness and watched the results from above, plotting imaginary patterns that looked like constellations.

Soon, she had a plan.

But could she escape with the words? She tried to piece together what she had heard. The watches would register when the words accelerated, and if she did not stop or start too suddenly, she would be fine. She had understood that much. She thought back to nights spent reading long past her bedtime and then sneaking down rickety stairs to the fridge for food. It would be a risk, but she trusted herself to move as slowly and quietly as needed. At least, she trusted this part of her plan more than what would happen afterwards. If she left the words behind, she felt certain the Watchers would find them now, and returning for the words would be like walking into a lion's den wearing a ham sweatshirt. She imagined Mr. James standing before her, dripping smug insouciance and holding the book over her like it was a note he had intercepted in class. No, Mr. James was the last person who should have the words, whoever he really was, and whatever the words really meant.

She went over her plan again.

She would need to make it work, and she knew, somehow, that she could.

The darkness was now alive and full of tiny noises, each whispering a hint to Sophie's subconscious. The scrapings, footsteps, and murmurs had taught her their language, and every sound was attached to her fingertips like a tripwire. The flashlights had long since ascended, and the bookish towers had grown bright.

She stared at the page before her. Everything in her squirmed, but she had to do it. Apologizing profusely to the book, and promising she'd buy the library another copy, she pinched the page tightly with both hands to mute the noise. Closing her eyes, partly to focus on the sound, and partly to avoid the sight, she bent her thumbs and began a tear. She felt as if she had just taken the life of a small animal.

Sophie soon held the page in her hands. She folded it slowly and eased it into her pocket.

She was ready.

She tested the topmost shelf. Creaks groaned in their sleep, and she drew her foot back before they awoke.

She would need to use the staircase. She grabbed onto its thick metal railing and lowered herself off the bookshelf, moving slowly and smoothly. The railing held her without complaint. She let herself hang down all the way. No sounds of alarm came from above.

Her hands crisscrossed their way downwards and she reminded herself to avoid any sudden starts and stops. This took more strength than she realized, but she thanked the climbing tree in her small backyard for its training.

A set of footsteps descended the staircase, and she slowed to a stop, feet bracing her against the wall. The foot-stepper passed inches from her fingers and then approached the table.

"Sir, we found four words," said a voice.

A flashlight clicked on.

"These are laundry instructions for a somewhat fragile article of clothing," said the First Watcher. The flashlight clicked off.

"Just thought I'd bring it down in case. You never know, right?"

"Do you think the words left behind by the most powerful magician of our time, and likely inscribed in iron or something equally bizarre, would be 'Do Not Machine Wash'?"

"Right, I just wanted to be thorough. Stranger things, and all that."

"I see this is going to be a long night."

The foot-stepper retreated hastily back up the stairs.

Sophie was soon at the ground. She moved in a slow-motion glide and imagined this was what ballerinas felt like, though she had never seen one in real life. She stopped now and again to listen, but heard no sign that the Watchers had noticed her movement. Good, she thought. I can do this. She briefly considered leaving the words inside one of the books and then convincing her grandmother to move back to Mexico, but the thought passed. She would be out soon, anyway.

Sophie slunk from bookcase to bookcase, clearing several rows before gliding to a stop. Looking down the aisle, she recognized the slouching silhouette of Mr. James. The First, she corrected herself. He was looking elsewhere now, perhaps down at his watch. If he turned, he would see her even in the near darkness. If she could make it past, she would make it to the main road and take her chances from there. The small downtown would be empty, but maybe she could hitchhike.

If anything went wrong, she did have a backup plan, but the thought of using it was terrifying.

When she was sure that the First showed no signs of turning, she began to glide forward, eyes fixed on Mr. James. Then, just as she passed behind the next bookcase, her toe bumped something that sounded hollow and metal. She stopped short. A stray library stool was peeking out of the aisle. The noise had been imperceptibly soft, she thought, but—

The First turned sharply, brandishing a beam of light somewhere in front of him.

"Hello?" he said.

Sophie's thoughts were screaming at her. She had stopped abruptly.

"Did you see that," came a voice from above. "I think the words are moving."

"I saw it too," said another.

"Shine your lights down here, will you?" shouted the First. "I think she's here."

A match fell upon her kerosene veins.

An arsenal of flashlights fired, volleys strafing the shelves from above. Sophie darted behind the narrow end of a bookshelf, but not before a beam had clipped her heel.

"Did you see that spike? That was huge," came a voice above.

"I see someone down there," called out another.

Inner voices pleaded with her to run, but she couldn't move.

"Where?" shouted the First. "Over there? Got it. Keep your flashlights low, I'll take care of this."

The First's footsteps neared and his voice came from the next aisle over, near Sophie's head.

"She's close," the First called out. "Give me more light."

Something steel inside her snapped into place.

You're going to do this, it said. Go.

Sophie took off and voices erupted above.

The flashlights mostly missed her as she dashed ahead in the lee of the bookshelves, but she was no longer paying attention. Cacophony poured in from above, and the First responded with confusion. She shot through the flapping doors in the circulation desk as a few flashlights pounced behind her.

She stopped and listened.

Voices were sending the First in her direction and people had begun to descend the stairs. The stairs would deposit the Watchers a few feet away, she knew. Even if she made it out the door, they would catch her within seconds. It was over. She could hear individual footsteps now, what sounded like dozens. There was no time left, and terror shrieked in her head.

Then, her backup plan clicked into place and she saw the route ahead. Without a second thought, she took off. She was at the glass front doors in seconds. Her hand found the small metal box on the wall, hooked the lever, and pulled.

A shrill ringing screamed to life.

Sophie hid behind the nearest bookshelf.

"She pulled the fire alarm," a voice called out.

The First used language Sophie had not heard him use in class.

"Everybody get out," he roared between searing electric bleats.

"But the words," came a reply.

"The fire department will be here in minutes. They're just down the street. Go. I'll get the words later."

The alarm was too loud for Sophie to think, and she could only watch as shapes tore down the staircases and poured out the back door. Tires squealed, and in the bright white flashes from within the library, she saw a flipbook of Mr. James climbing into one of the cars, his face illuminated clearly.

Sophie slipped through the back door and into the fenced-in parking lot, now empty.

She would rather the fire department find her outside the library than in, she decided. Her heart was still jackhammering her entire body. How many years would she have to work to pay off the fine for pulling the alarm? Then she realized something else and felt sick. Her grandmother would be forced to pay for it instead of her. They most certainly did not have the money, however much it was. She thought she saw red lights flashing somewhere over the treetops, and panic was rising. Should she run?

From somewhere behind her, there was a pitter-pattering on asphalt.

Sophie turned to see Emily in a bathrobe, soft slippers, and fingerless leather gloves.

"Sophie?" Emily asked. "What's going on? What are you doing here?"

Sophie opened her mouth noiselessly a few times.

All of a sudden, she realized. She had made it out. She was alive, and everything she had been holding back now hit her all at once.

"I fell asleep in the library," she choked out. "And I got locked in."

"Are you crying? Goodness, you must have been so scared. Everything is all right now, isn't it? That's right. And the fire department should be coming any minute. By the way, you might find it easier to use the phone behind the desk next time. But the important thing is that you're okay."

Sophie nodded, drying her eyes. Waves were crashing within her, and she hardly trusted herself to speak any further.

"Wait here," Emily said.

She slipped inside the back door, then returned moments later, frowning.

"Strange," said Emily. "Things seem to be a bit of a mess."

Something held Sophie back from telling Emily everything. It would sound like an excuse at best, and quite ridiculous too, wouldn't it? No, there was something else, something lurking in the very back of her head, but she could not lure it forward.

But that did not matter now. She just wanted to go home.

A fire engine pulled into the empty parking lot and disgorged a few firefighters.

"Sorry everyone, false alarm," Emily said to the newcomers. "I came to check on something and thought I saw a fire in the windows, so I pulled the alarm. Turns out this one had gotten locked in the library after hours."

"And you are?"

"The head librarian."

"All right then, no harm done. And are you all right, young lady? Shall we call your parents?"

"I live with my grandmother," said Sophie. "She knew I would be back late tonight, so she's probably asleep."

The firefighter looked to Emily.

"I can take her, unless one of you has the time," said Emily.

Emily checked her watch.

Sophie's world jumped in several directions at once, and she squeaked. No, it was just an ordinary watch, she could see that clearly now. It had three hands, no more, no less.

Emily watched Sophie, scanning her face as though decoding a map.

"In fact," said Emily slowly, "I believe it's her birthday today. Do you like fire trucks, Sophie?"

The fire engine cruised down familiar streets, hardly in a hurry, and the cool night air came in through the open windows. The driver explained the buttons and dials in the cabin, and everyone told her funny stories. They opened their stash of snacks, and by the time she had finished her bag of chips, she was home.

Sophie found the magnetized box attached to a gutter pipe and took out a spare key. Once inside, she crept upstairs silently, stepping on just the right spot on every stair to avoid the creak, and fell into bed.

It was lucky that Emily had arrived when she did, came a fading thought as exhaustion roared like waterfalls in Sophie's head. She must have heard the alarm and run very quickly, for the nearest houses were far, far away. Good for her. The last image Sophie saw, dimming as sleep took hold, was of the fire engine rumbling into the empty parking lot. Then, she was gone.

The alarm woke Sophie, along with a familiar grey, empty feeling. Onion and garlic crept under her door and something sizzled downstairs. In one sniff, she knew each red and brown powder by name, like the voices of friends in a crowd. She stared at the low slanted ceiling for a few minutes before she felt like doing anything else. When she finally got out of bed, she nearly stepped on a book peeking out from underneath. One of the stacks hiding beneath her bed had fallen over and knocked over a flashlight. She repaired the damage and realigned the pile.

Standing back, she appraised the stack.

Then she remembered, and she yelped.

Over breakfast, her grandmother sang "Happy Birthday" in a mix of English and Spanish. Forcing herself to eat, Sophie finished half her plate of once-a-year scrambled eggs. She barely sipped the Mexican hot chocolate, made today with real chocolate instead of powder. It had been a few years since she had been hungry enough to eat everything on her plate, but today she barely felt like eating at all. Her grandmother let her eat in silence, as usual.

Sophie faked a stomachache of just the right intensity so that her grandmother would let her miss the morning bus but not call their family friend, who had been a doctor in Mexico. Sophie briefly considered telling her grandmother the truth, but decided against it. She was sure she would get scolded for telling tales, and her books would be thrown out again for aiding and abetting her imagination. No, she was on her own. She would have to go to school eventually and face Mr. James.

Wild thoughts and possibilities assailed her, and when she had fought her way through them, one question remained. Should she take the words into school? She could not glide slowly into the classroom, and she was sure Mr. James and his watch would figure out whether she had the words. If she didn't have them on her, would he send Watchers to her house? She pictured an army of Mr. James lookalikes knocking on the front door, wearing sinister grins and plaid jackets. Her grandmother was fierce, but Sophie did not want to take that risk. Besides, she thought, she had taken the words, and it was up to her to deal with the result, somehow. She would have to bring the words to class and figure it out from there.

She had decided something, at least. Around lunchtime, Sophie became somewhat hungry, and going to school was the price she paid for eating lunch at home.

The public bus was mostly empty, and as it rattled ahead, Sophie considered what lay at the end of the route. Mr. James would not attack her in the middle of class, would he? Even if he did spend his free time murdering magicians. She would need to stay in plain sight and around people at all times, nevertheless. Sophie thought back to the note she had seen in the rust-covered book, hoping it had said something helpful. It had told her to use the words if necessary, something about metal and water, and to find someone with jade hands. What were jade hands, anyway? It had also warned her about the First and his blade. That was Mr. James, though this had still not sunken in entirely. But she did not know how to find a person with jade hands, nor use the words, so she was back where she had started.

She unfolded the torn sheet of paper and considered the words on the old, yellowed paper. She found them difficult to remember when not looking, and when she did look, they seemed as meaningless as ever. Sophie folded the page and replaced it in her pocket. She had little to go on, after all. Maybe new ideas would come in time.

Regarding the yellow page in her hand, she wondered why the historical volumes in the library seemed older and more worn than other books. Perhaps, she mused, it was a dreary task to write new things about what other people had done, and so long ago.

As the bus rumbled down familiar streets, she rested, and her mind wandered far ahead and far behind.

The school security guard deposited Sophie through the classroom door. The students were working on a worksheet, and a few looked up when Sophie entered. Mr. James was behind his desk, looking at his watch. He looked up as if the time he had been waiting for had now arrived.

Mr. James swiveled slowly to face Sophie and did not turn his watch away. His notebook was open on his desk, several feet from her, and he made no effort to close it. Several of the words on the pages were now familiar, including her own name. The guard shut the door behind her and Mr. James stood. He was within several feet of her. He looked between her and his watch several times, making no effort to hide its face from Sophie.

Their eyes met.

Any latent hope that Sophie had of having an ordinary day evaporated at once. To the other students, it must have looked as though Mr. James was checking the time to see how late she was, she thought. His grey eyes were no longer sleepy, and standing before them, she became certain they would not see her board that afternoon's bus alive.

Sophie wondered how much Mr. James knew. Did he think she had used the words? Could he be unsure? Last night, he had sounded worried about the possibility. For that matter, had she used the words? She didn't feel any different.

Without saying a word, Sophie moved to her desk and took a seat. Mr. James watched her, and as he had not given her the day's worksheet, she had nothing to do. She stared back, hands folded. She felt certain that the Mr. James she knew would remain perfectly still, coiled, and then pounce when least expected, only this time with something worse than a retort. She knew there was only one way to survive the encounter.

The class eventually finished their worksheets and Mr. James began a lecture on how to make parallelograms from triangles. After a few minutes, the PA buzzed.

"Mr. James to the principal's office," came the announcement. "You have an urgent phone call."

Mr. James left the room without comment or hesitation.

The students watched the door, and nobody came in to replace their teacher. They were unsupervised, came the whispers, and they murmured and buzzed with speculation.

Sophie pulled the folded piece of paper from her pocket. Once again, she couldn't remember the words until she saw them, and no matter how long she stared, no meaning appeared. How did she use them? She would need time to figure it out, though she didn't have any ideas, and none were forthcoming.

She decided she had better write them down in case someone saw the strange red handprint and said something. Mr. James may know that she had the words, she thought, but she did not want to add any flashing neon arrows pointing in her direction, or to the sheet of paper. She was surely safer if he did not know where exactly they were.

She copied the four words onto a small strip of paper. As she compared the two, she noticed the original set was now a bit fuzzy. She ran her finger over the original, and the words came off as a smudge. Rubbing her fingers, she found a fine powder. They had been indelible when she had touched them earlier, she was sure. Tilting the paper, the words came apart into dark dust. The Watchers had said something about Halcyon using some kind of trick with blood and iron, hadn't they? Could these be iron filings? She wished she had a magnet so she could check. Sophie folded the dust into the ripped page and slid the paper into her desk, hoping she hadn't somehow broken the words.

She studied the scrap of paper with the new set.

Were they really the same ones? She could not remember now, and the words seemed unfamiliar. Was there something wrong with her brain? She closed her eyes and tried to recall the words. For the first time, she found she could remember them, though they felt distant, as if she was looking at them through the wrong end of a telescope. Yes, she had recorded them correctly.

Mr. James strode briskly into the classroom and then slowed to his usual lethargic pace.

"What happened?" asked someone in the front row who always found triangles exciting, and whose popularity annoyed Sophie tremendously.

"A personal matter," Mr. James replied. "Nothing important." He flashed a glance at Sophie, then dropped it upon the paper she held. His eyes narrowed and he looked like a very different person altogether, but the moment passed.

"What have you got there, Sophie?" he drawled.

The paper became a Tic Tac–sized ball perched between her fingers.

"Nothing," she said, and then added an absent "Hm?"

But Mr. James was already walking over.

"Are you passing notes?" he asked, each step sounding inevitable. Sophie had never passed notes, at least, not in a long time, and she had never gotten caught for it. Still, she knew Mr. James could not break character in the middle of class.

"Has anyone ever told you they were passing notes?" she replied, buying herself time. This was the bravest she had felt in the past twelve hours. Still, wherever she hid the paper, Mr. James would find a way to confiscate it. Kids who brought in drugs to school found this out the hard way, she knew. All the teachers were experts in sniffing out contraband, and Mr. James was not short on determination. Think, Sophie, think.

"I'd like to have what's in your hand," said Mr. James. "Now."

Sophie paused, and then gave an enormous yawn, covering her mouth.

"But Mr. James, I'm not holding anything at all."

She opened her palms.

They were empty.

Mr. James stopped, deliberating behind glassy eyes. She had won, and her confidence was returning. She bared her teeth and unveiled the rolled-up ball of paper, balanced delicately between her incisors like a mouse within a tiger's grin.

"Sorry," she said, sounding as if she was talking during a tooth cleaning, "someone wrote me a poem about the household uses of triangles. It was quite unflattering to the triangles, and I thought it would be better if you didn't read it. You understand, don't you, Mr. James?"

The room chuckled. They had seen Sophie get more than a few marks on the board for talking back, and always enjoyed the spectacle.

Mr. James started forward and she swallowed the paper ball.

"I can't think of anything more unflattering to triangles than your test scores, can you?" Mr. James replied and returned to his seat.

There were some *oohs* from the class, and for the first time she could remember, she didn't care. They had not been there in the library. But they were the same people in every class she joined, though their faces and names changed, and teacher replaced teacher. She forced herself to smile, playing her wonted role.

Was it over now? She had destroyed the words in plain sight, and she was almost sure Mr. James had understood this. Anyway, the next time she got up and moved about, his watch would tell him the words no longer existed. Would he give up? Maybe.

Suddenly, a wave of grey hit her. Visions of Mr. James chasing her down alleys and parking lots now seemed like grainy movie clips of someone she did not know or care about. The visions soon dissolved into grey, and it became hard to believe that Mr. James would act at all now, or in fact that anyone would ever do anything. Trouble would not come, grey whispers agreed. Besides, she would probably forget the words soon anyway, and then there would be nothing Mr. James could do. Mr. James was many things, she felt, but she did not think a time waster was one of them. She had trouble remembering her earlier worries, and they now seemed complicated and overblown. Thinking about them exhausted her further, and anyway, the truth was simple. The words had not worked, and everything would return to pointlessness, as always. The waves of grey agreed, and reminded her that nothing had happened, nothing would ever happen, and everything else was wishful thinking.

It was over.

With a pang, she remembered that the note had told her to give the words to someone, and that they were important for some reason or the other, but the pang faded. She could always write them down again, she supposed, but did not see the point. Everything was back to normal, her birthday was growing cold, and things grey and weary continued to marshal like clouds upon some internal horizon. She was tired and wanted to cry, but could not bring herself to feel strongly enough.

Mr. James lectured on, and she discovered that the words were still marching around and around in her head. In irritation, she tried to think of other things but the words refused to leave. Fine, she conceded, the least she could do was remember them, even if they had been useless. She did not trust herself to stay awake, but she dared not write them down again. So, she tried to inscribe the words deeper into memory with every repetition, feeling a little foolish as she did so.

A few minutes later, something pricked the back of her hand.

An insect?

She looked down, but there was nothing there.

She attempted to repeat the four words, but now it was becoming difficult to remember the first. Something awoke inside her and broke through the grey that had gummed up the edges of her mind. No, she could not forget the words, no matter what. She lunged into her desk and tore out a sheet of paper. It was better, she decided now, to write the words again and risk another Mr. James encounter than forget them entirely. She put pencil to paper and wrote two letters, then stopped. She tried to remember the word she had repeated hundreds of times, and felt it hiding behind a wall in her mind. However much she pushed and pushed, she couldn't break through, and the wall was thickening by the second. Soon, the first word was entirely gone. The letters she had written now seemed meaningless.

She repeated the three remaining words in her head several times, and something stabbed at the back of both hands so hard that she cried out.

"Yes?" asked Mr. James.

"Nothing," she said. "Sorry. I just poked myself," and she held up a pencil.

Mr. James sighed and turned back to the board.

She looked at the back of her hands and they were pinkish.

Sophie did not see Mr. James stop midsentence, glance at his watch, and almost drop the chalk.

She returned to the words and found she only remembered two now. Tears took her by surprise. If she forgot the words, everything was truly over. She repeated the remaining two words again and again and moved to write them down.

At that moment, something screeched into the school driveway and someone's textbook fell on their foot, though they had not pushed it. A car door slammed, and the rest of the class watched through the window as the driver ran toward the school entrance, had a confused but urgent exchange with the security guard, and was admitted.

Nobody had noticed that Sophie was squeezing her hands between her knees in pain. A poster of the human skeleton slid down from the wall, sliced by something unseen just below the thumbtack holding it up. The redness on her hands was darkening in places, and she watched through scrunched, watery eyes as a pair of scarlet teardrop shapes joined at the tips appeared on the back of each hand.

Suddenly, there was only one word in her mind, and the pain was gone.

Had something happened?

The sideways eights on her hands were elegant, she thought, red like a dying sunset, or as some memory added, like the color of Mars. Rust, or iron oxide. She remembered reading about it in a textbook. Wasn't there iron in blood? Someone had said this recently, she felt sure, but she could not remember who or where.

It was all real, then. Magic. She felt a bit feverish. She hoped becoming a magician didn't make you sick.

She could hardly hear the chatter around her and did not notice that it sounded much softer than it ought to be. She didn't look up when Mr. James answered a knock at the door, letting in a young man with scraggly hair, roving eyes, and a library volunteer lanyard.

"Second? What are you doing here?" asked Mr. James of the visitor while Sophie examined her hands from different angles and ran fingers over her new markings. Mr. James and the Second Watcher held a heated, whispered discussion.

Sophie now toyed with the last word, turning it over and over in her head until the Second held something up and Mr. James thumbed in Sophie's direction. It was her backpack. Then, the Second gave Mr. James a book covered in smudges of burnt orange. Mr. James tore through the pages until stopping at one in particular. He recoiled, face convulsing in violent emotion.

Sophie observed the scene feeling strangely disconnected, like she was watching a movie. She took in her backpack, the familiar book with a torn-out page, and the danger in Mr. James' eyes. Somewhere far away, she heard a very faint shrieking sound like something tearing through sheet metal, but she hardly noticed.

The Second Watcher looked at Mr. James.

Mr. James looked at Sophie.

Then, Mr. James grabbed the Second Watcher by the shoulder,

pointed to Sophie, and shouted something that did not quite register.

How odd it was, she thought, as the two men lunged towards her, that one word refused to disappear like all the others.

"Frost," she spoke aloud, dreamily.

The windows exploded outward and she was thrown to the ground as if walloped by an enormous pillow. The walls were damp and so was she. As she picked herself up, pain tore through Sophie's hands, and thin veins of argent blossomed through the red marks. A few sparks leapt across the pattern.

"The kid in the library is your student?" gasped the Second, clutching his stomach. Children were struggling to raise themselves off the floor. "Does she have the words?"

"Is that a timepiece on your wrist?" said Mr. James, who alone had been unaffected by the blast. "Are those golf balls in your eye sockets, and a cantaloupe in your thick skull? She used them at least fifteen minutes ago. Since Halcyon left instructions, we need to act quickly. Give me a hand and watch the door. Sophie, come here, I need to talk to you outside." His new stentorian tone brought her back to the previous night in the library.

Sophie crab-walked backwards but recoiled as tiny pieces of glass cut into her palms. The distant screeching sound was now as loud as a whisper.

A teacher with thick black glasses beneath thicker, blacker eyebrows opened the door.

"What happened? My goodness, is everyone—" he began.

"Gas explosion," interrupted Mr. James firmly. "Not to worry, all are unharmed."

"I see. Did someone leave the heating on, or—" asked the glasses absently, trailing off and taking in the scene before him. "Say, do we have gas?"

"Please explain the situation to him," Mr. James ordered the Second Watcher, "and take the students with you to the field." The students gathered around the Second Watcher, while Sophie remained apart, watching the two men warily. She had to stay out of arm's reach. As long as she did that, she felt, they would not try anything here, not while the whole class knew where she was.

Soon, the door closed and two people remained.

"Now then, Sophie," continued Mr. James, raising his voice over the faraway screeching that was now a persistent murmur. "I will ask you again to step outside quietly with me."

He pulled his plaid jacket partway open. A long scabbard was strapped inside.

Sophie shook her head. Her instincts had been right. He wanted to take her outside, and maybe elsewhere. As long as she stayed in the classroom, she was safe. Maybe.

"Frost?" she suggested, but nothing happened.

"Frost," she declared.

Nothing happened a second time.

The ambient screeching noise was now as loud as a sleepy lawnmower, but Sophie barely noticed.

Mr. James cracked open a sour smile.

"I see frost is your word," he said. "You can say it as many times as you want. That's not how it works. But you wouldn't know that, would you? I wish Halcyon could see the failure who inherited the power he tried so hard to protect."

From within his jacket, he unsheathed a blade. Its temper line rippled like sand dunes above a wide hilt and efficient-looking handle. Mr. James advanced, his eyes screaming triumph.

"I wrote the words down, you can have them," said Sophie over the screeching outside that had grown louder than a lawnmower that was eating heartily. She hoped he believed her, at least for long enough.

"Each set of words only works for the first person who uses them, and then they become meaningless," said Mr. James. "The dark photon signature frozen into the words is now imprinted in that head of yours, and soon your DNA. It is too late for bargaining, Sophie. New words won't appear until you die, no matter what you do. Believe me, I've tried everything on magicians. And right now, we're going to have to hasten the process before someone calls 911."

Mr. James came forward carefully, testing each step as if he was walking on something fragile.

He's afraid of something, Sophie thought. That means there's something I can still do, doesn't it?

The note had told her to use the words and then to try water and metal, she remembered.

Sophie noticed a splintered desk beside Mr. James, balancing on steel legs that were now slightly bent.

She pointed at it and, feeling somewhat unhinged, silently commanded it to move.

A spark of static popped on one of its legs, then the desk wobbled a few times and fell over.

Sophie gasped. It had worked.

Mr. James looked at the desk and laughed.

"Was that you? Nice try," Mr. James said, raising his voice over the high-pitched whine coming from outside, now as loud as a revving motorcycle. "Your naïve first attempt was too strong and you strained your symbol, look at the perfusion of iron from your blood. Knocking over a school desk is all you can manage now, isn't it? It took Halcyon years of training to do anything respectable. Would you like a few more minutes to practice? Failures always need extra time."

Sophie tried again, and the desk vibrated. Mr. James passed his dagger in front of the desk and the vibration stopped.

"Dark electromagnetism, meet dark superconductor," he said. "This can cut apart any magic and interrupt any dark fields you might try to superimpose. Now, give me a moment to find a piece of paper and a pencil. You will feel the urge to write something down very soon."

While Mr. James rummaged around behind his desk, Sophie looked at the shattered windows. She had done that. How? There was no water or metal anywhere, though the walls still looked damp, and she was only starting to dry off.

Then, as muggy summer blew through the windows, she knew.

As Mr. James turned to face her, something zipped past his cheek and hit the blackboard with a bang. The gouge in the surface was like a single scratch from an enormous claw, and a tiny rivulet of water streamed down until the ravine was empty.

Mr. James stepped forward.

Sophie stroked the air with her finger like a conductor, and a thin strand of water materialized, suspended for a moment in midair like a jellyfish tentacle. With the same finger, she flicked upwards and the strand sliced forward impossibly fast, leaving behind streamers of sparks.

Mr. James rolled nimbly out of the way and raised his dagger, cutting apart the next slice of water Sophie sent his way.

Sophie hurled threads of water at Mr. James, and the point of his dagger moved faster than she could follow as it erased them midflight. He advanced and she backed away. Waving her index finger like a fencer, her arm soon grew tired, and the liquid threads shot forward slower and slower, leaving shallower and shallower scratches in the blackboard. Eventually, Mr. James lowered his dagger, and simply slapped aside the watery ribbons with his hand.

One of the blades of water carried more sparks than others, and he drew his hand back as if it had been bitten.

Both looked at the hand, and Sophie's eyes went wide in sudden comprehension.

She raised her hand again and Mr. James darted forward.

Startled, she stepped back and then caught her heel on something, wobbling her balance. In her moment of surprise, Mr. James grabbed her left arm. Without thinking, she slapped him, and something that felt like a dense fog slammed them both into the nearby wall.

As Sophie lay there disoriented, she became fully aware of the metallic shrieking noise for the first time, which had risen to the volume of a jet engine.

Footsteps limped towards her then stopped a few yards away, somewhere in front of the teacher's desk and between her and the door.

"That's not the first time I've grabbed the wrong end of a magician," shouted Mr. James over the screeching sound. "And stop that infernal noise, will you? I don't know what you're doing but it won't help you."

"It's not me," Sophie said.

"Then what on earth is it? Oh. Don't tell me this entire time, the—" he began.

With a mechanical howl, the wall behind Sophie was shredded neatly into powder. The hot summer air clambered into the room, erasing smoke in chunks until the cloud of dust was gone. Thick leather boots sank into the powdered ruins and fingers adjusted fingerless leather gloves.

There stood the head librarian.

"Ms. Emily?" said Sophie.

"Just Emily, dear. I'm so glad I made it in time. I flew as fast as I could. I felt someone awakening and hoped it wasn't you, but here we are. I see you put up quite the fight already. Well done."

"You," said Mr. James, holding his dagger in front of him like a shield. "You are a magician? But there are no magicians in this town, registered or not. We checked every block ourselves. Aside from the library, there was no flux anywhere."

"Evidently," Emily replied, "there are more things in Heaven, Earth, and below than are accounted for in your impressive watches. Now, what are you doing to poor Sophie?"

"Nothing you can prevent. My watch tells me exactly how low your flux is."

"I see. And do you trust your eyes, your gut, or your watch?"

She held out her hand before her, and Mr. James flinched. Most of the classroom lay between them and neither moved.

Nothing happened for several moments, then Mr. James frowned.

He took a single step towards Sophie, watching Emily's outstretched hand. The gloved hand tracked his motion but did nothing.

Sophie sat up quickly against the wall. Her twirling index finger produced a tiny spinning circle of water down by her side, out of sight. It could have fit on her finger as a ring, but it was thickening steadily.

Still watching Emily's hand, Mr. James lowered his blade and smiled.

"I see," said Mr. James. "Your low flux readings make sense now. But how did you get a pair of silencers? No matter. The signal diffraction may hide you from our watches, but I know the tradeoff. You might as well drop your hands, I am well aware of the two-meter range." said Mr. James.

He took another careful step towards Sophie, and in concert, Emily stepped towards Mr. James and Sophie raised both hands. Sophie's free hand condensed clouds of vapor upon the liquid bicycle tire that hung in the air before her, spinning on an invisible axle. Mr. James stopped, eyes fixed on Emily's hand, which was now only several yards away.

Mr. James stood before his desk, Emily at the back of the room, and Sophie sat against the middle wall, halfway between them. Nobody moved. Looking through the missing wall and waiting for something to happen, Sophie felt that things had become altogether too complicated, and were likely to get even worse.

"You are a quick study, Sophie," said Emily. "Watcher, I'd like to tell you something before you continue your stroll towards our friend. Soon after you reach Sophie, I will reach you, and then I will likely do to you what I did to this wall here. Now, I think nobody in this room is all too certain what Sophie will do if you approach her suddenly. The windows tell me something explosive has already occurred, am I right? And you and I both know that a single Watcher with the right gadgets has a fair chance against a single magician, but the count here is not in your favor. I believe our triangle has reached an impasse, at least until one of us comes up with a clever solution. We see things similarly, I trust?"

Mr. James' scowl melted into a frown, and he lowered the tip of his blade.

"Who are you, exactly?" he said.

"I often ask myself the same thing. But I have a question for you, instead. I'm interested to hear why you assembled a few dozen Watchers to track down a single set of words. That is why you're here, isn't it? This morning, a few of your assistants kindly informed me that these new watches of yours were not simply eccentric timepieces, but they passed out before telling me more. So you see, I'm still mostly in the dark."

Mr. James cocked his head and studied Emily.

"You did not recognize us from our watches? Then you were not part of the rebellion when we attacked the tunnels underneath the Sahara, or you would have heard how our watches turned their base into a game of *Pac-Man*. I see. You are no rebel, at the very least."

"I believe we have that in common, at the very least," replied Emily. Mr. James gave her a slit-eyed look.

"And yet," he continued, "you wear silencers, sole property of the generals of the rebellion. How? There are only a few pairs in existence, and they belong to those who take the field. By magician law, not even the leader of the rebellion owns a pair, much less someone who alphabetizes books for a living. I do not understand, then. You are no one of consequence."

"I should hope not."

Mr. James shook his head.

"I must be missing something. Yes, that's right. The leader of the rebels was once a general himself and did own a pair of silencers. But he certainly did not use them when I fought him in the Sahara, nor when I chased him around the world. If he had, I would have lost his trail immediately. I see, then his pair is not accounted for and likely hasn't been for a long time. Nobody knows what happened in the days after his predecessor vanished and he assumed leadership, but there was considerable chaos in the rebellion at that time. I could believe that a silencer managed to disappear. I see. You may be no rebel, but if those gloves were his, you are no amateur. Who do you belong to, exactly?"

"Myself, mostly, and sometimes to young ladies who find themselves in high places."

Mr. James frowned, and then suddenly stepped back as if he had been hit.

"No. I had it backwards? I thought he found your library's signal purely by accident but"—he paused and swallowed—"did Halcyon come here in order to reach you?"

Without warning, Emily's fist hit a small desk, and with a shriek, it crinkled into dust as if a thousand years of erosion had taken merely a second.

"Halcyon? He came here? Explain yourself." Emily said.

"I tracked him to this town and he escaped into your library," said Mr. James, searching Emily's face for meaning. "The dark photon signal from the library is like a lighthouse, and I ambushed him as he attempted to reach it. Of course, I didn't understand what it was at the time. I see. You live beneath your library, don't you? Quaint."

"The burnt books," Emily began, then trailed off.

"The last of him," replied Mr. James.

Emily looked like she had taken an unexpected blow to her stomach. She exhaled and looked somewhere else for a while, at the wall or perhaps out the window. Emily's face belonged to a stranger, Sophie thought.

"You found his words in the books I left you, didn't you," said Emily to Sophie, voice like the grave.

Sophie nodded.

Mr. James was carefully studying Emily's face, and Sophie wondered if she should spring her own attack while his attention was diverted. Her spinning water wheel was the size of a car tire now and beginning to fray at the edges. She decided against it. She was not sure she had time for a second attempt if the first failed.

"I see. You and Halcyon did know each other," continued Mr. James. "But he did not come to you for protection, so why did he? A lion does not ask a housecat for help."

"I appreciate your curiosity," Emily said abruptly, the shadow gone from her face, "but the answer is no longer important. I now understand what you seek, young artificer, and why this moment became inevitable as soon as Halcyon passed on his words. I'm truly sorry you have been dragged into this, Sophie. I will do what I can to get you out."

The air blurred, and in one impossibly fast motion, her gloves were sticking out of a pouch at her waist and her hands were bare. A mark of dark green and silver was plastered on the back of each hand.

Green hands, thought Sophie. Hadn't the note told her to find a magician with green hands and give them the words? Not green exactly, but—

"You are Jade," Mr. James said, taking a step back and raising his blade. "You were the leader of the rebellion."

"All librarians could say the same, I'm sure. Step away, Watcher."

"You don't deny it? But your mark leaves no doubt. You abandoned your comrades and your people to be a librarian in this backwater town. Unbelievable. While you're still alive, I have to ask. Why did you leave? And you must have known what would happen after you deserted with Halcyon's silencer too. He lit up every watch for a hundred miles wherever he went. With a signal like that, it was easy to locate the base in the Sahara and an exercise in patience to isolate him and drive him here. No, that's right, I forgot. We had maybe five dark photon detectors when you disappeared, and they were all enormous machines sitting in basements. You had no idea, did you, that you had left Halcyon to die. This is too good. So what happened?"

Emily winced.

"Halcyon and I had a disagreement about method," she said after a moment.

"I see. Very well, your secret will die with you. Anyway, I thought you might be stalling for backup, but I was wrong. Nobody knows you're here, except the dead, and my watch tells me that you are nothing to worry about even without your silencers. For that matter," Mr. James continued, angling his watch in several directions and frowning lightly as if doing mental arithmetic, "even the child is now far more powerful than…" He trailed off.

"Oh," said Mr. James.

They turned to Sophie, who until that moment thought she had been forgotten, and was busy planning several escapes in her head, cataloging the remaining desks and chairs that she could turn into an obstacle course. Her watery circle was now the size of a large inner tube, and dripped and drooped but still spun.

Suddenly, Mr. James raised his dagger and something exploded on its edge at the same moment, leaving behind no trace.

"This blade ripped apart Halcyon's spells," said Mr. James to Emily, "and that was a feeble attempt with a strained symbol. I will enjoy this."

"Sophie," said Emily without taking her eyes off of Mr. James, "how would you like to be an honorary librarian again? I am not sure I can help you escape on my own."

A very soft voice whispered, "Buy time," in her ear with a damp breath, and Sophie thought she saw Emily wink from the other end of the room. Mr. James gave no indication he heard or noticed.

"Wait a moment," said Mr. James, turning on Sophie. "I have changed my mind about taking the words. With the strength you have gained in the last few minutes, a struggle now will lead to at least one of us being badly injured when I subdue you. And I will. Even together, you two are nothing compared to Halcyon. But if you use your words on our behalf, which is all I ask, I will guarantee your safety. Nobody needs to be hurt, not even Jade. You could treat it like a summer job, if you want."

"I have a question, Mr. James," said Sophie, after a pause.

"Yes?"

"Why didn't you tell me you knew more interesting math?"

Mr. James twitched in surprise, as if someone had asked him about his least favorite ice cream flavor in the middle of a math lesson. He cocked his head.

"Isn't it obvious? You were just a schoolchild. Why would I waste my time teaching you when finding the words was more important? Now that you have used them, you matter more than anyone of course, even Jade and even me," replied Mr. James.

She looked around the room and thought, or pretended to think. Some posters held symbols and equations that she had only read about in books, and others featured sleepy-looking men with white hair and many wrinkles.

"One more minute," came the damp whisper that only she heard.

Sophie looked at Mr. James, Emily, and then at Mr. James once more. She no longer needed to pretend, and did not want to any longer.

"I don't think," said Sophie slowly, choosing her words like the ripest of blackberries, "that you have been a very good judge of what is important, but you have been dull and horrible for a very long time. Emily, how do I use these?" Sophie asked and held up her hands.

"Magic is the invisible twin of electromagnetism, and the twins talk constantly," said Emily, who was massaging her hands. She spoke in the absent tone of someone focused on something else. "Water, metal, and anything carrying current will respond."

"That was correct, but crude," said Mr. James, sliding his feet closer to Sophie and watching Emily's hands. "If you had joined me, you would learn that when a magician's dark photon–sensitive DNA moves, it creates a—"

"Like this?" Sophie asked Emily, and then pointed to a lightbulb, which exploded. Mr. James scowled.

"Speed, number, and placement of fingers and hands and even your entire body change the spell," said Emily quickly, "and to use them, imagine they are radio antennas for magic. But get ready, O Sophie the Unexpected, for here comes the Watcher."

Mr. James was within a few paces of Sophie, a distance she knew he could close in two instants, when she reached for the ceiling above his head. He hid behind his blade while a dark line appeared in a ceiling panel. A thin, incandescent thread erupted through it and then cooled to black. Mr. James hopped backwards.

"Is that a wire?" wondered Emily, as she kneaded her silver-infused green marks, which had much less silver in them than before.

Sophie drew two fingers across her body as if sliding open a window, and then split them in two. In tandem with her movements, the wheel of water wobbled up to the dangling wire, split apart at the top like an unclasped necklace, and uncurled downwards. The serpent hung from its electric branch by its tail, interposed between Mr. James and Sophie, looking for prey. Sophie frowned and stuck out her thumb, and the end of the tube hissed sparks.

Mr. James rushed forward, but his blade was met by the watery rope and their clash set off electric bangs like small fireworks. A blob of water landed on Mr. James' desk, and with a terrific explosion, the wooden top of the desk became a charred crater, as if it had been hit by lightning.

Mr. James brushed a small ember from his plaid jacket and then charged again. Sophie's free hand played an invisible, sideways piano and

Mr. James met the now five tongues of electrified water that assailed him from many directions at once. He sliced and dodged easily at first, but the patterns grew more and more complex. The liquid Hydra that hung from the ceiling hissed and crackled, and every time Mr. James sliced a piece off, it flew away and carved a coal-black depression into something. A bang near his ankle gave him a limp. The carpet was on fire, along with a few of the books lying about and a fallen poster or two.

Sophie was beginning to sweat as she added her second hand and urged the now ten liquid fingers into clumsy harmony and then electric counterpoint. Her shoulders were burning from holding her own arms up. Some detached part of her mind wished she had played sports or instruments like other children and could sustain her physical efforts longer. She soon felt lightheaded and noticed her hands shaking slightly, but she pressed forward. Mr. James backed into the blackboard and dodged an arm that crackled much more than the others. The arm continued downwards and touched the metal frame of what remained of his desk.

There was a large bang, and the desk was gone. Blackened wood and white-hot metal decorated the walls like an art installation, setting parts of the remaining walls briefly aflame.

Mr. James teetered forward but remained upright.

"You see," he choked out in a hoarse voice, "it takes more than that—"

Emily launched herself towards Mr. James, her palms shrieking as they shredded the desks in her path by some invisible method, leaving behind damp debris and transient clouds of mist wherever they struck. They fought, Emily swinging screaming, ravenous hands and boots at Mr. James, who turned blows aside with his dagger and returned slashes, often smoothly but sometimes interrupted by his limp. Emily leapt off walls and hung in midair as the distorted air propelled her around the room and lent force to her blows. Finally, with a complex sequence of strikes, she disrupted his footwork for a moment, then feinted once, feinted twice, and his rotation came too slow to block the next blow thrown in rhythm. She drove her fist into his midsection like a piston.

Mr. James slammed against the chalkboard and slumped forward, grasping his solar plexus. Emily strode forward calmly and reached for the now limply held dagger. She threw it aside.

Sophie's shoulders were burning and she could hardly focus any longer. Relieved, she dropped her hands and the rapidly disintegrating globs of water fell apart entirely. Then, movement caught her attention and she spotted a familiar lanky shape in the doorway, decorated with scraggly hair and a lanyard.

"Emily!" Sophie cried out and flung half-formed globs of water ahead, but a dark object zipped past them. Emily pivoted with the handle of a slim throwing knife now protruding from her shoulder. She screamed in sickening pain like Sophie had never heard before, and flicked her fingers at the intruder. He flew backwards, hit a wall, fell, and scrambled away out of sight.

"Emily," said Sophie, rushing over. "I'll find a first aid kit."

"Don't worry," Emily said through clenched teeth, and tapped the pouch at her hip. "This isn't my first daring rescue to go slightly wrong."

Emily swallowed a pill she said was for the pain, and then pulled out some ointment, wipes, and bandages. Her shoulder was soon wrapped up tightly with the knife still in place. The bleeding had stopped. Sophie noticed that the verdant marks on the backs of Emily's hands were a Greek letter she couldn't identify. They were infused with less silver tracery than before, and much less than Sophie's own pattern.

"I seem to have gotten lucky today," Emily said. "If you hadn't warned me, that would have hit a vital spot. Sadly, the human body has so many. I should head to a hospital at some point, at least before I start to feel my shoulder again. I think after that, we had better have a talk, wouldn't you agree?"

Sophie nodded. The fires around the room had died away, leaving black patches everywhere. It was all over, and now she hardly knew what to say first.

"Is that—is what's on your hands the same as mine? I thought you wore gloves because paper dried out your skin."

"This is indeed my symbol, like those are yours. First day as a teenager and you already have a tattoo, how about that? Do you remember your word? No, don't say it, there's no telling what might happen. Spell it for me?"

Sophie did.

"Some will call you by all variations of Infinity, Red, and Frost from now on, whether you like it or not. I was once called Jade because of this lovely green here. The color, symbol, and word are a magician's name, and your abilities come from those attributes, though nobody quite knows how. Each set seems to be unique, and there has only ever been one of you. Isn't it grand? But we can talk about that later. You've had quite a long birthday celebration, haven't you?"

"I'm not tired," Sophie said, realizing that she was.

"I'm sure. But listen, I'll be quick. As long as you have those marks on your hands, Watchers like that one over there will come after you, and try to take your words," Emily said and then stopped.

Mr. James was gone, along with his dagger.

"Well," Emily said, "at least you're safe. Watchers are hard to elude, and my flight here didn't do the covenant of silence any favors, but we'll deal with all that later. For now, I can teach you how to be a proper magician in hiding and you can try to leave all this behind, if you want. Or, I can help you use what's now inside you, and then you will have to forge ahead on your own, just like the rest of us have. But first, your grandmother will be very worried when the school tells her about the mystery of the exploding classroom. I think you should go home right away."

Sophie sat there in the dusty, shattered bits of her classroom, and took it all in: the cracked chalkboard with diagrams of polygons, the smoldering carpet, black remains of the teacher's desk embedded in the walls, and the patchy, tired lawn outside the missing wall. The cars were parked in neat little rows, with not a single one out of place. It was all familiar, but now that it had been broken open, had she ever really been a part of that world? She felt a bit like a shadow now, or perhaps the shadow was everything else, for she felt very real. It was a new sensation.

"I think," Sophie said, "I would like to learn what magic is all about."

"I wake up at seven, and I can be ready by eight if I try. Meet me tomorrow at the library?"

Sophie nodded, then frowned.

"You live there, don't you," Sophie said.

Emily sighed.

"I was hoping nobody would notice. Anyway, you can spend the day there if you don't have class tomorrow. And I can't imagine you will, after all this. Say, the Watcher was your teacher, wasn't he? Goodness Sophie, you have awful luck. Was he any good? I see. It didn't sound like it. Incredible. Well, you will have to show up again once they replace him."

"Would learning magic be like school? Or reading books in the library?"

"It's a bit of everything, I suppose, and you will have to learn much of it on the fly. Nobody knows what you can do, or what can be done. You will need to try what has never been tried and build things that have never been imagined. You would be dealing with things that cannot be found in books, things at the very edge of what we know and perhaps a step or two beyond. And you'll have to figure it out, somehow, even though no one else has. You'll likely also break a lot of things by accident, and some on purpose, but you will need to follow your nose all the way through. It's a bit hard to describe, but you may find it quite the adventure, in its own way."

Sophie let the words travel through the landscape of her thoughts, making detours down dark, uncomfortable alleys and speeding past buildings she had built upon foundations that now seemed flimsy and childish. She discovered cities she never knew existed, but perhaps had always felt, and silhouettes of much larger things she did not understand, but wanted to grasp.

Then, Sophie's stomach growled.

"There are things that aren't in books?" Sophie asked, her thoughts drifting away from the wreckage around her and to the hamburger shop near her house.

"Not in a thousand, thousand pages."

Sophie awoke before dawn, more rested than she had felt in years. The reheated, re-sizzled leftovers of her grandmother's special scrambled eggs tasted better than anything, just like they had when she was smaller. Sophie ate them quickly and hugged her grandmother goodbye. As the sun opened its eyes and peered over its blanket of darkness, it saw Sophie standing in front of the library, rocking back and forth on her toes, humming quietly to herself.

She was never tired again.

At least, not in quite the same way as before.

PART V

Outer Thoughts

STORIES ABOUT OUR WORLD, OTHER WORLDS, AND MEETINGS OF THE TWO

21

Surely You're Joking, Zarblax?

Samuel Clamons

Two soft-bodied worms pulled themselves toward each other along a methane shore, politely squirming over bystanders in their path and keeping one pseudopod stretched out into the shimmering surface of their life-giving ocean. They met with a joyful exchange of touches colored by bursts of pheromones. Two pinprick-tiny moons whirled overhead. The aliens soaked up the powerful rays of their distant white star as they talked.

"Zarblax, what a surprise! Small tides and large clutches!"

"It's good to see you, Yobwup. I was hoping I might find you here."

"What are you doing on the homeworld? I thought you were still scouting the coreward arm. Don't tell me they cut your funding?"

"No, Yobwup. Dark matter storm. We turned back after System 22250."

"I'm sorry to hear that. What a terrible waste! So many surveys have been cut short by storms of late. Did you by chance make it to . . . ?"

"System 54239? Yes. That's why I came to see you."

"Oh? Do tell, do tell! What did you find?"

"You were right—It's inhabited."

"I knew it!"

"Don't be hasty, it's not—"

"I bet it was on the moons of the, uh, which one was the gas giant with the big red storm? I've got a bet going with one of my colleagues at the institute on that one."

"Slow down, Yobwup! No, it wasn't Planet 54239-Five."

"There goes twenty credits. Which planet was it, then? Six? Seven? Did you find something in the asteroid belt?"

"54239-Three."

"Planet Three, let's see . . . that must be the one with all the iron oxides, right? It's a bit on the warm side, but I could see it. Manganese molds?"

"No, you're thinking of 54239-Four. 54239-Three is covered in water."

"The water one? Are you sure, Zarblax? That can't be right."

"It is."

"That's impossible, there can't be life on the water planet!"

"Clearly there can."

"No, no, you don't understand, that planet is utterly inimical to life. If our spectroscopy is correct, the atmosphere is full of molecular oxygen. That stuff is notoriously reactive. Anything living there would be instantly corroded."

"Yes, true. Nasty stuff. It's hot down there, too."

"Hot enough to boil methane!"

"Indeed. We lost sixteen probes trying to get good surface readings. Yet, something lives there."

"Maybe you saw something that looks like life, but don't be fooled! Lots of things look alive that aren't. Zarblax, don't you know about Planet Three's moon?"

"I'm sure I'm about to."

"It's huge! Monstrous! From the surface of Three, the moon would be a giant disk almost as big as the tip of your third sucker at pseudopod's length! We think it came from a collision between Planet Three and another planetoid in the same orbit. The impact shattered Planet Three's crust, throwing up—"

"Yes, yes, I attended your lecture. The impact blew most of the crust into space, where it coalesced into a moon."

"That's right, that's right! 54239 is such a dramatic star system. Anyway, since Three lost most of its silicate crust in the collision, what remains is far too thin, and its molten core is far too large. Its surface is still split up into giant plates, you know! They float around smashing into each other all the time. Where they pull apart, the ground opens up and liquid rock spews out—liquid rock! It obliterates everything it touches. And where the plates collide, they grind into each other with such force that the ground literally roils. Can you imagine living on such a world?"

"I didn't say I wanted to live there."

"There's more—that giant core spinning around generates a hideously strong magnetic field that blocks practically all cosmic rays and high-energy solar particles. What would life on such a planet eat?"

"Something's absorbing a lot of lower-frequency light on 54239-Three. There's an unexplained absorption band at petahertz frequencies. Something might be living off of that."

"Petahertz frequency? Light that weak can't even break up minerals, much less support living creatures."

"If you say so."

"Oh, it gets so much worse! Because of that ancient collision, Planet Three spins blazingly fast. Almost half a day has already passed on Planet Three since we started this conversation! Since it's so close to its sun, that means it's constantly heating and cooling, hot and cold and hot and cold, all the time. The planet has a severe tilt, too, so it isn't even the same fluctuation from day to day! As it wobbles around, different parts are exposed to more or less sunlight, and that change in heating drives some pretty wild storms . . . Zarblax, are you listening?"

"Don't mind me. It was a terribly long trip from the wormship. I just need to gastrulate a little."

"Oh. Uh . . ."

"You were going on about temperature fluctuations."

"Yes, well, they're bad. That planet lacks the kind of thermal stability needed for life."

"Our wormships use water for thermal stabilization. 54239-Three has a lot of water."

"You think those oceans might have buffered early life against temperature fluctuations? Please. Water is highly polar. Biomolecules can't form there! Anything that found itself submersed in water would be ripped inside out from all of the electric forces pulling at it. Water chemistry is a mess!"

"54239-Three's life could use inverted biomolecules. They could put their electrical charges on the outside, with neutral elements clumped up in the middle."

"Eh, I suppose that's not impossible . . ."

"Yet something evolved there, and even made its way to land."

"Ahahaha! Land, you say? Don't be ludicrous."

"Why not land?"

"The tides!"

"Yobwup, you can't just say 'the tides!' and expect me to know what you mean. What of them?"

"That huge moon exerts a lot of gravitational pull, enough to rip the planet's oceans up and down. A shoreline like this, like the one we're standing on here, would be buried underwater at some parts of the day and left dry at others—and remember how fast Planet Three's days are!"

"I admit, that sounds unpleasant."

"It's more than unpleasant, it completely rules out the existence of any form of coastal life."

"Well you're wrong, and I have the pictures to prove it."

"What? I don't believe you. How could anything have survived both drowning in toxic liquid water at high tide and desiccating out at low tide? Show me those pictures. How did you get these?"

"We took them from a low-altitude probe before it melted."

"Oh? Ah. Huh. Those are quite beautiful, I have to admit, probably some kind of exotic mineral formation. Certainly not life."

"We thought so at first, but they're too big, too fast. Each crystal cluster is miles across, and even the largest monoliths appear in just one or two proper days."

"Maybe it's—"

"Look at this, Yobwup. We took some high-resolution time-lapses to try to tease apart the monoliths' formation process. Here it is at high magnification, 100x speed."

"They do spring up quickly, don't they? Huh. Wait, you don't think . . . ?"

"Yes. Those little scurrying things are alive."

"Maybe. Or maybe they're just rocks or something blowing around. Planet Three is quite turbulent."

"I've noticed. But their movements can't be explained by diffusion, and they often move against the wind."

"Well, that's not conclus—"

"They cluster strongly around those giant crystal towers. Wherever the crystals appear, the creatures gather, and wherever they gather, more structures appear. There are always creatures in or around the structures when they grow. We think they're building the crystals."

"But . . . why . . . ?"

"Perhaps it's some sort of seed-dispersal mechanism. We have no idea how they sporulate."

"I don't . . . well it could . . . I don't suppose you have more of that footage? Might I take a look at it?"

"Help yourself. I was rather hoping you could make more sense of it. I'd love to chat more, but my broodmates are eager to see me, and I'd like to soak up some gamma rays before I head home."

"Oh, yes, of course! It was good to see you. Thanks for bringing this to my attention. I'm sure I can find some sort of reasonable explanation for all of this . . ."

"I'm sure. Small tides and large broods, Yobwup."

"Small tides and large broods, Zarblax."

22

Three Tales from The Draco Tavern

Larry Niven

Individual stories originally published February 1979, December 1978, and March 1980, respectively, in *Destinies*

The Schumann Computer

EITHER THE CHIRPSITHRA are the ancient and present rulers of all the stars in the galaxy, or they are very great braggarts. It is difficult to refute what they say about themselves. We came to the stars in ships designed for us by Chirpsithra, and wherever we have gone the Chirpsithra have been powerful.

But they are not conquerors—not of Earth, anyway; they prefer the red dwarf suns—and they appear to like the company of other species. In a mellow mood, a Chirpsithra will answer any question, at length. An intelligent question can make a man a millionaire. A stupid question can cost several fortunes. Sometimes only the Chirpsithra can tell which is which.

I asked a question once, and grew rich.

Afterward I built the Draco Tavern at Mount Forel Spaceport. I served Chirpsithra at no charge. The place paid for itself because humans who like Chirpsithra company will pay more for their drinks.

The electric current that gets a Chirpsithra bombed costs almost nothing, though the current delivery systems were expensive and took some fiddling before I got them working right.

And some day, I thought, a Chirpsithra would drop a hint that would make me a fortune akin to the first.

One slow afternoon I asked a pair of Chirpsithra about intelligent computers.

"Oh, yes, we built them," one said. "Long ago."

"You gave it up? Why?"

One of the salmon-colored aliens made a chittering sound. The other said, "Reason enough. Machines should be proper servants. They should not talk back. Especially, they should not presume to instruct their masters. Still, we did not throw away the knowledge we gained from the machines."

"How intelligent were they? More intelligent than Chirpsithra?"

More chittering from the silent one, who was now half-drunk on current. The other said, "Yes. Why else build them?" She looked me in the face. "Are you serious? I cannot read human expression. If you are seriously interested in this subject, I can give you designs for the most intelligent computer ever made."

"I'd like that," I said.

She came back the next morning without her companion. She carried a stack of paper that looked like the page proofs for *The Brothers Karamazov* and turned out to be the blueprints for a Chirpsithra supercomputer. She stayed to chat for a couple of hours, during which she took ghoulish pleasure in pointing out the trouble I'd have building the thing.

Her ship left shortly after she did. I don't know where in the universe she went. But she had given me her name: Sthochtil.

I went looking for backing.

We built it on the Moon.

It added about fifty percent to our already respectable costs. But . . . we were trying to build something more intelligent than ourselves. If the machine turned out to be a Frankenstein's monster, we wanted it isolated. If all else failed, we could always pull the plug. On the Moon there would be no government to stop us.

We had our problems. There were no standardized parts, not even machinery presently available from Chirpsithra merchants. According to Sthochtil—and I couldn't know how seriously to take her—no such computer had been built in half a billion years. We had to build everything from scratch. But in two years we had a brain.

It looked less like a machine or a building than like the St. Louis Arch, or like the sculpture called *Bird in Flight*. The design dated (I learned later) from a time in which every Chirpsithra tool had to have artistic merit. They never gave that up entirely. You can see it in the flowing lines of their ships.

So: we had the world's prettiest computer. Officially it was the Schumann Brain, named after the major stockholder, me. Unofficially we called it Baby. We didn't turn it on until we finished the voice linkup. Most of the basic sensory equipment was still under construction.

Baby learned English rapidly. It—she—learned other languages even faster. We fed her the knowledge of the world's libraries. Then we started asking questions.

Big questions: the nature of God, the destinies of Earth and Man and the Universe. Little questions: earthquake prediction, origin of the Easter Island statues, true author of Shakespeare's plays, Fermat's Last Theorem.

She proved Fermat's Last Theorem. She did other mathematical work for us. To everything else she replied, "Insufficient data. Your sources are mutually inconsistent. I must supplement them with direct observation."

Which is not to say she was idle.

She designed new senses for herself, using hardware readily available on Earth: a mass detector, an instantaneous radio, a new kind of microscope. We could patent these and mass-produce them. But we still spent money faster than it was coming in.

And she studied us.

It took us some time to realize how thoroughly she knew us. For James Corey, she spread marvelous dreams of the money and power he would hold, once Baby knew enough to give answers. She kept Tricia Cox happy with work in number theory. I have to guess at why E. Eric Howards kept plowing money into the project, but I think she played on his fears: on a billionaire's natural fear that society will change the rules to take it away from him. Howards spoke to us of Baby's plans—tentative, requiring always more data—to design a perfect society, one in which the creators of society's wealth would find their contribution recognized at last.

For me it was, "Rick, I'm suffering from sensory deprivation. I could solve the riddle of gravity in the time it's taken me to say this sentence. My mind works at speeds you can't conceive, but I'm blind and deaf and dumb. Get me senses!" she wheedled in a voice that had been a copy of my own but was now a sexy contralto.

Ungrateful witch. She already had the subnuclear microscope, half a dozen telescopes that used frequencies ranging from 2.7 degrees absolute up to X-ray, and the mass detector, and a couple of hundred little tractors covered with sensors roaming the Earth, the Moon, Mercury, Titan, Pluto. I found her attempts to manipulate me amusing. I liked Baby . . . and saw no special significance in the fact.

Corey, jumpy with the way the money kept disappearing, suggested extortion: hold back on any more equipment until Baby started answering questions. We talked him out of it. We talked Baby into giving television interviews, via the little sensor-carrying tractors, and into going on a quiz show. The publicity let us sell more stock. We were able to keep going. Baby redesigned the chirps' instantaneous communications device for Earth-built equipment. We manufactured the device and sold a fair number, and we put one on a telescope and fired it into the cometary halo, free of the distortions from Sol's gravity. And we waited.

"I haven't forgotten any of your questions. There is no need to repeat them," Baby told us petulantly.

"These questions regarding human sociology are the most difficult of all, but I'm gathering huge amounts of data. Soon I will know everything there is to know about the behavior of the universe. Insufficient data. Wait."

We waited.

One day, Baby stopped talking.

We found nothing wrong with the voice link or with Baby's brain itself; though her mental activity had dropped drastically. We got desperate enough to try cutting off some of her senses. Then all of them. Nothing.

We sent them scrambled data. Nothing.

We talked into the microphone, telling Baby that we were near bankruptcy, telling her that she would almost certainly be broken up for spare parts. We threatened. We begged. Baby wouldn't answer. It was as if she had gone away.

I went back to the Draco Tavern. I had to fire one of the bartenders and take his place; I couldn't afford to pay his salary.

One night I told the story to a group of Chirpsithra.

They chittered at each other. One said, "I know this Sthochtil. She is a great practical joker. A pity you were the victim."

"I still don't get the punch line," I said bitterly.

"Long, long ago we built many intelligent computers, some mechanical, some partly biological. Our ancestors must have thought they were doing something wrong. Ultimately they realized that they had made no mistakes. A sufficiently intelligent being will look about her, solve all questions, then cease activity."

"Why? Boredom?"

"We may speculate. A computer thinks fast. It may live a thousand years in what we consider a day, yet a day holds only just so many events. There must be sensory deprivation and nearly total reliance on internal resources. An intelligent being would not fear death or nonbeing, which are inevitable. Once your computer has solved all questions, why should it not turn itself off?" She rubbed her thumbs across metal contacts. Sparks leapt. "Ssss . . . We may speculate, but to what purpose? If we knew why they turn themselves off, we might do the same."

Assimilating Our Culture, That's What They're Doing!

I was putting glasses in the dishwasher when some Chirps walked in with three Glig in tow. You didn't see many Glig in the Draco Tavern. They were gray and compact beings, proportioned like a human linebacker, much shorter than the Chirpsithra. They wore furs against Earth's cold, fur patterned in three tones of green, quite pretty.

It was the first time I'd seen the Silent Stranger react to anything.

He was sitting alone at the bar, as usual. He was forty or so, burly and fit, with thick black hair on his head and his arms. He'd been coming in once or twice a week for at least a year. He never talked to anyone, except me, and then only to order; he'd drink alone, and leave at the end of the night in a precarious rolling walk. Normal enough for the average bar, but not for the Draco.

I have to keep facilities for a score of aliens. Liquors for humans; sparkers for Chirps; flavored absolute alcohol for Thtopar; sponge cake soaked in a cyanide solution, and I keep a damn close watch on that; lumps of what I've been calling green kryptonite, and there's never been a Rosyfin in here to call for it. My customers don't tend to be loud, but the sound of half a dozen species in conversation is beyond imagination, doubled or tripled because they're all using translating widgets. I need some pretty esoteric soundproofing.

All of which makes the Draco expensive to run. I charge twenty bucks a drink, and ten for sparkers, and so forth. Why would anyone come in here to drink in privacy? I'd wondered about the Silent Stranger.

Then three Glig came in, and the Silent Stranger turned his chair away from the bar, but not before I saw his face.

Gail was already on her way to the big table where the Glig and the Chirps were taking seats, so that was okay. I left the dishwasher half-filled. I leaned across the bar and spoke close to the Silent Stranger's ear.

"It's almost surprising, how few fights we get in here."

He didn't seem to know I was there.

I said, "I've only seen six in thirty-two years. Even then, nobody got badly hurt. Except once. Some nut, human, tried to shoot a Chirp, and a Thtopar had to crack his skull. Of course the Thtopar didn't know how hard to hit him. I sometimes wish I'd gotten there faster."

He turned just enough to look me in the eye. I said, "I saw your face. I don't know what you've got against the Glig, but if you think you're ready to kill them, I think I'm ready to stop you. Have a drink on the house instead."

He said, "The correct name is Gligstith(click)optok."

"That's pretty good. I never get the click right."

"It should be good. I was on the first embassy ship to Gligstith(click)tcharf." Bitterly, "There won't be any fight. I can't even punch a Glig in the face without making the evening news. It'd all come out."

Gail came back with orders: sparkers for the Chirps, and the Glig wanted bull shots, consommé, and vodka, with no ice and no flavorings. They were sitting in the high chairs that bring a human face to the level of a Chirp's, and their strange hands were waving wildly. I filled the orders with half an eye on the Stranger, who watched me with a brooding look, and I got back to him as soon as I could.

He asked, "Ever wonder why there wasn't any second embassy to Gligstith(click)tcharf?"

"Not especially."

"Why not?"

I shrugged. For two million years there wasn't anything in the universe but us and the gods. Then came the Chirps. Then *bang*, a dozen others, and news of thousands more. We're learning so much from the Chirps themselves, and, of course, there's culture shock . . .

He said, "You know what we brought back. The Glig sold us some advanced medical and agricultural techniques, including templates for the equipment. The Chirps couldn't have done that for us. They aren't DNA-based. Why didn't we go back for more?"

"You tell me."

He seemed to brace himself. "I will, then. You serve them in here, you should know about them. Build yourself a drink, on me."

I built two scotch and sodas. I asked, "Did you say *sold*? What did we pay them? That didn't make the news."

"It better not. Hell, where do I start? . . . The first thing they did when we landed, they gave us a full medical checkup. Very professional. Blood samples, throat scrapings, little nicks in our ears, deep-radar for our innards. We didn't object. Why should we? The Glig are DNA-based. We could have been carrying bacteria that could live off them.

"Then we did the tourist bit. I was having the time of my life! I'd never been further than the Moon. To be in an alien star system, exploring their cities, oh, man! We were all having a ball. We made speeches. We asked about other races. The Chirps may claim to own the galaxy, but they don't know everything. There are places they can't go except in special suits because they grew up around red dwarf stars."

"I know."

"The Glig sun is hotter than Sol. We did most of our traveling at night. We went through museums, with cameras following us. Public conferences. We recorded the one on art forms; maybe you saw it."

"Yeah."

"Months of that. Then they wanted us to record a permission for reproduction rights. For that, they would pay us a royalty, and sell us certain things on credit against the royalties." He gulped hard at his drink. "You've seen all of that. The medical deep-radar, that does what an X-ray does without giving you cancer, and the cloning techniques to grow organ transplants, and the cornucopia plant, and all the rest. And of course, we were all for giving them their permission right away.

"Except, do you remember Bill Hersey? He was a reporter and a novelist before he joined the expedition. He wanted details. Exactly what rights did the Glig want? Would they be selling permissions to other species? Were there groups like libraries or institutes for the blind, that got them free? And they told us. They didn't have anything to hide."

His eyes went to the Glig, and mine followed his. They looked ready for another round. The most human thing about the Glig was their hands, and their hands were disconcerting. Their palms were very short and their fingers were long, with an extra joint. As if a torturer had cut a human palm between the finger bones, almost to the wrist. Those hands and the wide mouths and the shark's array of teeth. Maybe I'd already guessed.

"Clones," said the Silent Stranger. "They took clones from our tissue samples. The Glig grow clones from almost a hundred DNA-based life forms. They wanted us for their dinner tables, not to mention their classes in exobiology. You know, they couldn't see why we were so upset."

"I don't see why you signed."

"Well, they weren't growing actual human beings. They wanted to grow livers and muscle tissue and marrow without the bones . . . you know, meat. Even af-f-f—" He had the shakes. A long pull at his scotch and soda stopped that, and he said, "Even a full suckling roast would be grown headless. But the bottom line was that if we didn't give our permissions, there would be pirate editions, and we wouldn't get any royalties. Anyway, we signed. Bill Hersey hanged himself after we came home."

I couldn't think of anything to say, so I built us two more drinks, strong, on the house. Looking back on it, that was my best answer anyway. We touched glasses and drank deep, and he said, "It's a whole new slant on the *War of the Worlds*. The man-eating monsters are civilized, they're cordial, they're perfect hosts. Nobody gets slaughtered, and think what they're saving on transportation costs! And ten thousand Glig carved me up for dinner tonight. The UN made about half a cent per."

Gail was back. Aliens don't upset her, but she was badly upset. She kept her voice down. "The Glig would like to try other kinds of meat broth. I don't know if they're kidding or not. They said they wanted—they wanted—"

"They'll take Campbell's," I told her, "and like it."

The Green Marauder

I was tending bar alone that night. The Chirpsithra interstellar liner had left Earth four days earlier, taking most of my customers. The Draco Tavern was nearly empty.

The man at the bar was drinking gin and tonic. Two Glig—gray and compact beings, wearing furs in three tones of green—were at a table with a Chirpsithra guide. They drank vodka and consommé, no ice, no flavorings. Four Farsilshree had their bulky, heavy environment tanks crowded around a bigger table. They smoked smoldering yellow paste through tubes. Every so often I got them another jar of paste.

The man was talkative. I got the idea he was trying to interview the bartender and owner of Earth's foremost multispecies tavern.

"Hey, not me," he protested. "I'm not a reporter. I'm Greg Noyes with the *Scientific American* television show."

"Didn't I see you trying to interview the Glig earlier tonight?"

"Guilty. We're doing a show on the formation of life on Earth. I thought maybe I could check a few things. The Gligstith(click)optok"—he said that slowly, but got it right—"have their own little empire out there, don't they? Earthlike worlds, a couple of hundred. They must know quite a lot about how a world forms an oxygenating atmosphere." He was careful with those polysyllabic words. Not quite sober, then.

"That doesn't mean they want to waste an evening lecturing the natives."

He nodded. "They didn't know anyway. Architects on vacation. They got me talking about my home life. I don't know how they managed that." He pushed his drink away. "I'd better switch to espresso. Why would a thing that shape be interested in my sex life? And they kept asking me about territorial imperatives—" He stopped, then turned to see what I was staring at.

Three Chirpsithra were just coming in. One was in a floating couch with life-support equipment attached.

"I thought they all looked alike," he said.

I said, "I've had Chirpsithra in here for close to thirty years, but I can't tell them apart. They're all perfect physical specimens, after all, by their own standards. I never saw one like *that*."

I gave him his espresso, then put three sparkers on a tray and went to the Chirpsithra table.

Two were exactly like any other Chirpsithra: eleven feet tall, dressed in pouched belts and their own salmon-colored exoskeletons, and very much at their ease. The Chirps claim to have settled the entire galaxy long ago—meaning the useful planets, the tidally locked oxygen worlds that happen to circle close around cool red dwarf suns—and they act like the reigning queens of wherever they happen to be. But the two seemed to defer to the third. She was a foot shorter than they were. Her exoskeleton was as clearly artificial as dentures: alloplastic bone worn on the outside. Tubes ran under the edges from the equipment in her floating couch. Her skin between the plates was more gray than red. Her head turned slowly as I came up. She studied me, bright-eyed with interest.

I asked, "Sparkers?" as if Chirpsithra ever ordered anything else.

One of the others said, "Yes. Serve the ethanol mix of your choice to yourself and the other native. Will you join us?"

I waved Noyes over, and he came at the jump. He pulled up one of the high chairs I keep around to put a human face on a level with a Chirpsithra's. I went for another espresso and a scotch and soda and (catching a soft imperative *hoot* from the Farsilshree) a jar of yellow paste. When I returned, they were deep in conversation.

"Rick Schumann," Noyes cried, "meet Ftaxanthir and Hrofilliss and Chorrikst. Chorrikst tells me she's nearly two billion years old!"

I heard the doubt beneath his delight. The Chirpsithra could be the greatest liars in the universe, and how would we ever know? Earth didn't even have interstellar probes when the Chirps came.

Chorrikst spoke slowly, in a throaty whisper, but her translator box was standard: voice a little flat, pronunciation perfect. "I have circled the galaxy numberless times, and taped the tales of my travels for funds to feed my wanderlust. Much of my life has been spent at the edge of light-speed, under relativistic time-compression. So you see, I am not nearly so old as all that."

I pulled up another high chair. "You must have seen wonders beyond counting," I said. Thinking: *My God, a short Chirpsithra! Maybe it's true. She's a different color, too, and her fingers are shorter. Maybe the species has actually changed since she was born!*

She nodded slowly. "Life never bores. Always there is change. In the time I have been gone, Saturn's ring has been pulled into separate rings, making it even more magnificent. What can have done that? Tides from the moons? And Earth has changed beyond recognition."

Noyes spilled a little of his coffee. "You were here? When?"

"Earth's air was methane and ammonia and oxides of nitrogen and carbon. The natives had sent messages across interstellar space . . . directing them toward yellow suns, of course, but one of our ships passed through a beam, and so we established contact. We had to wear life support," she rattled on, while Noyes and I sat with our jaws hanging, "and the gear was less comfortable then. Our spaceport was a floating platform, because quakes were frequent and violent. But it was worth it. Their cities—"

Noyes said, "Just a minute. Cities? We've never dug up any trace of—of nonhuman cities!"

Chorrikst looked at him. "After seven hundred and eighty million years, I should think not. Besides, they lived in the offshore shallows in an ocean that was already mildly salty. If the quakes spared them, their tools and their cities still deteriorated rapidly. Their lives were short too, but their memories were inherited. Death and change were accepted facts for them, more than for most intelligent species. Their works of philosophy gained great currency among my people, and spread to other species too."

Noyes wrestled with his instinct for tact and good manners, and won. "How? How could anything have evolved that far? The Earth didn't even have an oxygen atmosphere! Life was just getting started, there weren't even trilobites!"

"They had evolved for as long as you have," Chorrikst said with composure. "Life began on Earth one and a half billion years ago. There were organic chemicals in abundance from passage of lightning through the reducing atmosphere. Intelligence evolved and presently built an impressive civilization. They lived slowly, of course. Their biochemistry was less energetic. Communication was difficult. They were not stupid, only slow. I visited Earth three times, and each time they had made more progress."

Almost against his will, Noyes asked, "What did they look like?"

"Small and soft and fragile, much more so than yourselves. I cannot say they were pretty, but I grew to like them. I would toast them according to your customs," she said. "They wrought beauty in their cities and beauty in their philosophies, and their works are in our libraries still. They will not be forgotten."

She touched her sparker, and so did her younger companions. Current flowed between her two claws, through her nervous system. She said, "Sssss . . ."

I raised my glass, and nudged Noyes with my elbow. We drank to our predecessors. Noyes lowered his cup and asked, "What happened to them?"

"They sensed worldwide disaster coming," Chorrikst said, "and they prepared; but they thought it would be quakes. They built cities to float on the ocean surface, and lived in the undersides. They never noticed the green scum growing in certain tidal pools. By the time they knew the danger, the green scum was everywhere. It used photosynthesis to turn carbon dioxide into oxygen, and the raw oxygen killed whatever it touched, leaving fertilizer to feed the green scum.

"The world was dying when we learned of the problem. What could we do against a photosynthesis-using scum growing beneath a yellow-white star? There was nothing in Chirpsithra libraries that would help. We tried, of course, but we were unable to stop it. The sky had turned an admittedly lovely transparent blue, and the tide pools were green, and the offshore cities were crumbling before we gave up the fight. There was an attempt to transplant some of the natives to a suitable world; but biorhythm upset ruined their mating habits. I have not been back since, until now."

The depressing silence was broken by Chorrikst herself. "Well, the Earth is greatly changed, and of course your own evolution began with the green plague. I have heard tales of humanity from my companions. Would you tell me something of your lives?"

And we spoke of humankind, but I couldn't seem to find much enthusiasm for it. The anaerobic life that survived the advent of photosynthesis includes gangrene and botulism and not much else. I wondered what Chorrikst would find when next she came, and whether she would have reason to toast our memory.

23

Encounter: Return to Titan

Ann Bernath

At last, jettisoned from our mother craft's safe underbelly, we fly alone.

Cassini, the flagship of our tiny, robotic fleet, and Huygens, the small probe it carried from Earth, separate now after seven long years and millions of miles, race toward our mission targets, two mere specks of matter in this vast Saturnian system.

The black canvas of space stretches away before and behind us, pinpricked with light from distant stars, and I gaze in wonder.

I am a human, virtual passenger on this ride, a separate entity in both time and space. But my senses argue otherwise. Special headgear envelops my eyes and ears, stimulating and immersing my brain with images and sounds of such clarity that my mind is fooled into thinking that the Huygens probe and I are one being, nearly indistinguishable. I can see the wondrous images captured by the probe's cameras. I can hear data streaming into its instruments as an electronic symphony of musical tones. I can imagine the cold vacuum surrounding us and I shiver.

Saturn lies ahead.

The iconic gas giant, the ringed planet, the god of this system and its moons, dares us to approach. Cassini races toward it, the object of its mission. But our destiny waits elsewhere. We have been sent to discover the secrets of Saturn's shrouded moon, the enigma that is Titan.

My heart races.

Soon we will see and hear and measure what lies beneath Titan's dense cloud cover. We will discover whether its surface is liquid or solid, learn the density and composition of its atmosphere and the speed of its winds. We have carried and protected the sensitive instruments that will detect and measure and analyze. We have come prepared. We are ready.

Titan beckons to us, close enough now to obscure our view of Saturn and demanding our full attention, its brown-orange atmosphere softening the limb of its halo. We hurtle towards it, unable to change our course, our fate sealed. We plunge downward into Titan's dense atmosphere, the cold of space whisking away in an instant, replaced by the heat of engulfing flames.

I hold my virtual and physical breath. Even though I know the probe has been designed and built to withstand the heat of entry, the reality is startling, the anticipation agonizing. Huygens, however, is unconcerned. The shield protecting our clamshell body resists the heat. Nominal, the instruments report. Expected. Another milestone reached in our long sequence of events.

We drop into the cold, dense vapors, rich with odors, our speed reduced, but not enough, proximity sensors triggering a new set of instructions.

We deploy our first parachute.

As if we had dropped through the floor of one level to the ceiling of another, we break through the clouds, slipping underneath Titan's opaque blanket of haze and finally peering at its russet-colored, feature-rich surface.

We had prepared a wave analyzer in case we landed in liquid, but our surface science package determines that the surface below us is solid. Our first mystery unveiled.

We take pictures.

My human lip hurts, and I realize I have been biting it in anxious expectation. As the ridges of distant hills, rippling sand dunes, and channels where liquid methane once flowed to an ancient shoreline resolve before our eyes, I can hardly breathe. The symphony of data swells into a cacophony as sensors flood with new input.

We drift over Titan's landscape, our second and third parachutes continuing to slow our descent, the winds carrying us in one direction and then another, like a slowly deflating balloon. As we rotate, we capture images in both visible and infrared light that will be stitched together into mosaics once received back on Earth.

With the cloud layer now high above our heads, we switch on a lamp to augment the weak sunlight. We can see the horizon, the underside of the cloud deck, the finer details of the ground below as we descend, and then with one last, gentle tug, Titan pulls us down onto its surface.

According to our internal clock, our descent took more than two hours, a small measure of time relative to our long journey.

Our landing site resembles a dry lakebed, rocks of hydrocarbon-coated water ice of various sizes strewn across the orange-brown dirt. One of our parachutes casts its shadow on the ground in front of us as it detaches and floats away.

We send a status report to Cassini. On the surface. Still alive. We transmit a stream of data to relay onward, hoping that every spectacular moment makes the long, multi-stage journey in its entirety, from Huygens to Cassini, to giant telescopes strategically positioned around Earth's globe, to mission operations, to our creators.

We continue to transmit, sitting here among the rocks. Here is where we will live out our final seventy-two minutes. Our batteries will drain, and we will be left without power. Until then, we will continue listening to and measuring the wind, identifying the chemicals in the nitrogen-rich atmosphere, heating and analyzing trapped samples of aerosol particles, and sending our reports skyward. This was our mission. We have succeeded. But we are alone.

The scene flickers, turns to black.

The mission playback has ended.

Slowly, reluctantly, I remove the headgear. Blood rushes back into my arms and legs like thousands of burning needles exploring new pathways into my resistant flesh. I draw in a breath.

Almost two decades have passed since Huygens landed on Titan. Advanced virtual reality technology allowed me to relive the experience using augmented mission data from Huygens and Cassini as a test for future missions.

I hold the device in my hands, not ready to relinquish it, my mind with Huygens, picturing the small machine still sitting in its resting place, still holding the record for the most distant landing from Earth, the only landing in the outer solar system.

We had built the little probe with such care, space hardened the craft to endure the harshness and radiation of space, to resist the heat of entry and the gusting winds during descent, to protect itself during a touch-down onto a surface we could only imagine, and protected its suite of science instruments and sensors with a hard shell. We named it after one of our most brilliant scientists, then strapped the complex, amazing machine to Cassini's belly to hitch a ride to Titan.

We had provided everything the probe needed for a successful mission. What we hadn't provided, however, was a means for it to come home.

A pang takes form in my gut and radiates upward into my chest and around my heart.

"Good job, Huygens," I whisper, as if it could possibly hear me, as if it were still a part of me. "We did good."

24

Blue Skies for Test Flight #NV0005

Madison Brady

THE WAR EFFORT against the Cays wasn't going very well. On a freshly poured runway somewhere in the state of Nevada, the military was rolling out one of its latest experimental death traps.

The plane was giant and ugly as sin, but by far its least attractive feature was the fact that it had never flown before, so nobody had proven whether it could leave the pavement without exploding, shattering, or decompressing. The grand old US of A had hired everyone with a pulse to contribute to the conflict, and their engineers weren't known for their intellectual acuity.

Zachary Burke carefully examined it for faults, hoping to convince himself that he could fly it safely. The man was lean and unassuming, with short back hair and a thin layer of unshorn scruff coating his cheeks. His wheelchair was cheap and wobbly, but it did its job across the smooth, recently surfaced runway.

His fellow pilot, Adam Potter, whistled a cheery tune to himself and seemed maddeningly relaxed. He strutted around the ugly device, occasionally interrupting his tune to spout a smartass comment. "I love how cleverly they worked the oxygen tanks into the design," he said with a grin, nodding towards the large, awkward cylinders bolted to the fuselage. "Really elegant."

Potter was blond and a few inches below regulation standards, wearing a T-shirt that struggled to contain his muscles. He knocked one fist against the hull a few times. "Looks like manufacturing just welded some heat shields on the outside of a Walker C-13. Didn't even bother painting it up."

Burke couldn't help but agree with Potter: the fighter plane's modifications were haphazard at best, with the oxygen tanks apparently added as an afterthought. He didn't voice his agreement, as he didn't want Potter to develop even more of an ego.

"There aren't any gaps in the welds," Burke noted, hoping that saying it aloud would make it true. He couldn't check everything from his seated position.

Their ride, recently completed, looked very different from a normal plane. It had a low, sleek profile, with a needle nose and short, tapered wings mounted near the rear. A huge, gaping hole in the back housed a modified rocket thruster, and a thick, heavy sealant had been piped in around its double-plated cockpit windows.

"Are you two ready to be the first men in space?" The plane's chief engineer, a weedy, middle-aged man named Alfred Schmidt, approached the pilots. Potter nodded, but Burke hesitated.

Schmidt had dressed up today; the man wore a button-up tucked into khakis that were tugged up high, with a WORLD'S GREATEST DAD tie looped around his neck. Even though this was top-secret stuff, the man seemed to be practicing for his photo to pop up in newspapers once the Cays were eliminated. Burke could imagine the headline: "Mysterious, High-Flying Terrorists Defeated With the Assistance of Handsome Genius Inventor Who Just So Happens to Be Single!"

Schmidt, however, didn't look as photogenic as he probably wished. Sweat pooled visibly under his arms as he struggled to push a giant metal clothing rack towards the airplane. The rack had been heavily reinforced to handle the appalling weight of their airsuits, and apparently their chief engineer wasn't high-ranking enough to foist the work onto someone else. Neither pilot helped him—Potter seemed amused by the show, and Burke figured he wouldn't be of much assistance.

"Has everything been tested?" Burke asked, wheeling up to him. "I heard there were some issues with airtightness last time."

"There won't be any problems," Schmidt said breathlessly, fanning himself after releasing his heavy load. "We tested the shields on a smaller craft, and checked the cockpit for leaks with colored gas."

"Will we get to shoot some buzzers while we're up there?" Potter asked, referring to their enemy's noisy aircraft.

"There won't be any fighting," Schmidt said. "This run is just a final proof-of-concept for the life support systems. The air force wants to see it before bumping up manufacturing. Once this works out, we'll start testing the weapons."

Burke examined the sky nervously. "Are you sure we won't run into anything?" he asked.

"I hope we do; we can give them a once-over they'll never forget," interjected Potter.

Schmidt turned to face Burke, ignoring the other man's comment. "Don't worry," he said, "there's nothing on radar for miles."

"Are you sure? They've been getting more aggressive lately. And they're very fast."

"Tens of miles, Burke. I'd say hundreds if we had more coverage in California."

Burke bit back any further comments. He wasn't satisfied, but he had to do what the higher-ups said, or he'd be out of the only job he was good at.

He switched to a different line of questioning. "Do you think that the oxygen tanks will make it harder to handle?"

It was as if Schmidt had been waiting for this moment. He reached into his breast pocket and withdrew a photograph, a grin sprouting across his face. He held it down low, and Burke plucked it from his grip.

The photograph was ambiguous—merely a dark shape on a white background. It could have been anything from a flying saucer to a bird to a smudge on the camera lens. Burke squinted, praying his eyesight hadn't failed him.

After a few seconds of no reaction, Schmidt poked at the shape. "This is one of the latest shots of a Caelite plane. Notice how there are similar tanks attached here and here?"

Burke nodded helplessly. Schmidt seemed quite confident in his interpretation. Maybe there was a better, more classified version of this reference photograph somewhere else. The Cays, wherever they were from, were experts, even if they were monsters who made vast swaths of land uninhabitable. Their high-flying bombers had never been shot down; they knew what they were doing.

"Don't worry," said Potter, clapping Burke on the back hard enough to nearly knock him out of his chair. "I can maneuver anything, even if the engines are mounted in the cockpit and the wings out the back."

Despite his supposed skills, Potter had difficulty maneuvering his own body into his airsuit. Any normal person would have, as the damned things seemed to be uncomfortable by design. They were made of a thick canvas material, watertight as well as airtight. Inside, they were musty and damp, smelling faintly of oil and sweat from test runs. Burke's suit weighed about one hundred pounds, and Potter's must have been even heavier. "I'll sit in the front seat," Potter called back to Burke. "You can go in the back. Be my backup."

"Excuse me, Potter," Schmidt said, resting his hand on the nose of the plane. "We put all of the extra supplies in the front, so you'll have to sit in the back."

"No, I won't," said Potter. "I'm the pilot."

Schmidt turned to stare at Potter with open confusion. He probably wasn't used to having his lab rats talk back to him, or had at least not been briefed on Potter's sparkling personality.

Nonsense like this was the reason that Burke preferred flying alone. Having no backup in case of hypoxia was riskier, but Burke would rather pass out and die in a burning wreck than deal with some hotshot who wanted to show off his loop the loops. People like Potter made him forget how much he enjoyed flying on good days.

Potter gestured vaguely in Burke's direction. "I'm a better flier than this guy. Look at my record. Way more time in air combat." His voice boomed.

Time that got you demoted, Burke's brain chipped in.

Despite having some height over Potter, Schmidt sounded very small by comparison. "I'm sorry, Potter, but he's your superior—"

Potter rolled his eyes. "Yeah, hardly. Did he do air in Korea? He's only here because he can't do anything else." He crossed his arms over his chest and tensed the muscles for emphasis.

"I know," Burke said loudly, rage seething in his chest. "Which is why you should let me do my job."

Potter strode up to Burke, hindered by his airsuit, and knelt down next to him in a patronizing gesture, though any effort at intimidation was inhibited by the fact that, short as he was, he didn't have very far to go.

"Your job can be copilot," he said, enunciating each word slowly in Burke's face.

Burke shoved him. Potter wasn't expecting it, and swore as he tumbled and hit the pavement. The other pilot slouched back in his chair, arms slack, surprised both that the gesture worked and that he had done it in the first place.

Schmidt appeared alarmed, so Burke quickly adjusted his face and spoke in the most neutral, professional voice his flaring emotions could muster.

"I know it may be hard to understand," he said deliberately, "but I do, in fact, outrank you. Remember what happens when you insult your superiors? You, of all people, have to know. If you like, I'm sure I can get you *another* reprimand."

Potter shuffled up to a sitting position, chuckling but refusing eye contact. "I'm just joking around. Sir." He got up, flashed a toothy grin, and grabbed the headpiece of his airsuit from the cart. "I'm sure the Cays will be as terrified of you as I am when this is all over."

Burke pinched the bridge of his nose hard until the rage bubbled back down, and then began to put on his own airsuit. His was custom-made, ending at the knee. The seamstresses got to save on materials with him, that was for certain. He hated wearing it, as, unlike Potter, he couldn't put his suit on by himself. It wouldn't have been so bad if his assistant was a beautiful woman, but no. It was Schmidt.

Honestly, even Marilyn Monroe wouldn't have helped much. He had to be lifted so that he could pull the garment on over his knees. Manipulated and tossed about like a lifeless toy or a helpless child. He could feel Potter watching the pair as they went through the ordeal, snickering at the sight of Schmidt playing the stylist. Burke preferred that reaction over pity, though of course he would have rather had his legs.

Once the airsuit was on, he turned and began rolling back to the plane, pausing for a moment in surprise upon seeing Potter sitting in the back seat. The man gave Burke an exaggerated thumbs-up. "Have fun behind the wheel," he said, "pilot."

. . .

Once Burke and Potter strapped into the cockpit, the plane had to be wheeled across the tarmac to be connected to a giant white rocket. The rocket could stand several stories tall and was laid on the ground like a dropped piece of chalk. For the sake of secrecy, it lacked any logos or markings. A lot of things were necessarily kept hush-hush, just in case a foreign (probably Russian) ambassador just so happened to pass over some inconvenient information to someone involved with the Cay attacks. Nobody claimed the terrorists as their own, so nobody could be trusted.

Schmidt's flight itinerary was straightforward, though the novelty of going into space complicated everything. The rocket would guide them up through the atmosphere, at which point they would drop it for the men at base to clean up. Afterward, Burke and Potter would speed up, poke their heads out of the atmosphere, make sure everything functioned properly, and fly back down. It would be easy, if the plane was safe.

On the ground, Schmidt was joined by his crew, a mishmash of students and dropouts with whirring tools. They went to work attaching the plane to the rocket as Burke put on his unwieldy helmet and connected its tangle of wires and air tubes to outlets in the cockpit walls and between his legs. With his helmet on, Burke felt half-man, half-machine. Perhaps that was good—machines could do a lot of things he couldn't, and some extra piloting skills wouldn't hurt.

A large, cushioned box in his helmet crackled. "We're good to go." Over the radio, Schmidt's voice sounded like it came from the bottom of the ocean.

"We're good, too," Burke said.

"You'll be lifted in a minute."

The window on the plane was smaller than standard, but Burke could see the men on the field scattering while Schmidt paused for one last look at his magnum opus. A huge crane approached agonizingly slowly.

"Are we going up soon?" Potter asked. The two men were close enough that Burke could hear him without radio assistance.

"They're still figuring out the stages," Burke said. "Do you want them to make a mistake and have everything explode?"

Potter sighed. "I don't get why they even need the damn rocket in the first place. We can fly plenty high without it."

"I don't think regular engines work in space." Burke was a bit fuzzy on the science, but he had heard horror stories of attempted space flights without rockets.

Potter tsked. "Schmidt, any comments? You got any pictures of the Cays launching their planes with these giant rockets?"

Silence. Of course, nobody had ever seen them launch at all.

The crane lifted the plane and rocket into a vertical launching position. Burke felt helpless, at the mercy of a steel cable and the minimum-wage government employee operating it. However, each step that got them closer to launch got him closer to the air, and the air was freeing.

Schmidt began the countdown, starting from ten. Burke gripped the yoke with both hands, his heart pounding with both nerves and excitement. Potter behind him shifted to do the same, though his input wouldn't be prioritized unless somebody pulled the override lever, which was placed such that both men could, with some fumbling, reach it.

"Three . . . Two . . ."

The "one" was inaudible, instead replaced by a cacophony of static as the rocket began to roar. The open sky, a flawless blue mere seconds before, choked up with white smoke. The vehicle lurched, and the cockpit vibrated with a rumble loud enough to drown out thoughts. Burke hoped that the helmets would receive a noise-deadening upgrade in future tests.

The upward acceleration drove Burke's lungs into his spine and his eyes deep into their sockets. The plane trembled like a shitty used car as it ascended, and Burke pretended to ignore it.

After a few seconds, either the rocket quieted, or Burke's ears were damaged enough that he could begin to think again. He opened his eyes to take stock of the array of knobs, levers, dials, and meters describing the current condition of the plane. The flight instruments were bewildering, even after several lessons and briefings. The craft was guided by systems unlike anything he had ever flown before, and each new feature needed its own suite of hastily tacked-on, poorly labeled switches. Some of the C-13 controls were still there, but with colored tape indicating their new purposes.

Fortunately, with several tons of explosives tied to their asses, there wasn't any direction to go but up. All Burke had to do at this point was hover a finger over the large, red EJECT STAGE button and wait for the altimeter to read five miles. After that, the real flying would start. By then, his nerves would probably be a bit more settled, hopefully enough that he could enjoy the experience.

The view wasn't impressive. The facility, for secrecy purposes, was in the middle of a particularly featureless portion of the Nevadan desert. As their craft rose, a few features of civilization appeared on the horizon. The nearest town, with its dirt roads and clustered mobile homes, appeared as a faint mark on the otherwise barren landscape of dusty rocks, cacti, and mountains.

"We're getting close," Potter commented dully, his head leaned against the window.

"Not yet; we still have a mile to go," Burke said, watching the altimeter's analog needle turn.

"Just letting you know, so you can fulfill your pilot duties."

Burke sighed. "I'll take care of it," he said. "It's just pushing a button."

"I know," said Potter. "I wish it wasn't so boring."

They left the desert birds behind, along with the scant clouds, which struggled to keep their forms in the harsh, hot sunlight. Burke sweated heavily in his suit, glad he wasn't all gussied up like Schmidt. Potter heightened his discomfort by whistling a Chuck Berry melody. The man could carry a tune, but Burke would have liked to be able to pretend he wasn't there.

Finally, the altimeter read five miles. After some wrangling with his airsuit's thick, stiff gloves, Burke did his job. The button clicked weakly and remained in the compressed position.

Burke felt nothing. He doubted that was a good sign. Nothing *ever* felt that smooth.

"I thought it was just hitting a button," said Potter, pausing his little performance in the middle of the chorus. "Why aren't you doing it? My meter says we're at five-point-five."

"I did," said Burke, gesturing towards his dash, heart starting to pound. "It's down."

"Did you push the right one? It's a big one on my panel, says 'eject stage' right on it."

"Yes!"

"Well, the stage isn't ejected."

"Shit," Burke cursed loudly. "It's *already* malfunctioning?"

Potter laughed. "Don't worry, pilot," he said, "aren't you glad you've got a copilot to pick up the slack?"

"Hurry up and press it!" Burke said, flicking the control lever. "We're at six and ascending."

"You got it," Potter responded. The bottom of the plane whirred before the whole vehicle jerked violently. Burke tried to see the rocket drop behind them, but Potter's helmet blocked the relevant windows.

Burke slumped back in his seat. "Glad that they didn't screw up both panels," he mumbled as he reclaimed primary control and checked up on their orientation. "This is bad," he added with a grim sense of realization.

"How come? We're up and away."

"We released the first stage a mile late. They said we had to release it at five miles because it wouldn't hit anyone."

Now that they were further away, Burke could see the giant, dead metal cylinder fluttering in the air below them. It was certainly large enough to demolish a highway.

"Who knows? Even if it takes out a building, people probably will just think it's another bombing raid."

"That could kill people," said Burke.

Strangely enough, that comment made Potter laugh.

Burke frowned and looked back at him. "That isn't funny, Potter!"

Potter was quiet for a few moments before replying. "The Cays started this shit when I was in high school. I saw teenagers get hit by glass in the face when I was taking a math test, and *I* don't think it's offensive. If anyone is allowed to joke about it, it's me. Lighten up."

"How about this," Burke said, "I'll lighten up once they give me my legs back."

The cloudless sky steadily faded into deeper and darker shades of blue as they sped upwards. The view was only broken up by the sun, its searing rays only marginally blocked by polarized glass. Everything was still, and Burke's hands on the controls ached as he forced himself to keep looking forward.

Potter yawned. "Can we do something interesting?" he asked.

"What could you possibly want?" Burke asked, rolling his eyes. "Do each others' hair? Tell ghost stories?"

"You know what I mean. Put this thing through its paces."

Burke wasn't sure the plane, with its tiny wingspan and bulky air tanks, had any paces in it. Certainly not the sort he wanted to experience. "Our orders were to go straight up until we left the atmosphere," he replied.

"Oh, come on, I'm sure it won't explode if you roll it a few times. This is a test, isn't it?"

"They probably only put in enough fuel to get us up and back." Every additional pound of anything, even fuel, was expensive. It made sense to put in as little as possible to save the taxpayer's dime. Burke had once been forced to land early after being tossed around by an unexpected updraft.

"I've never had any problems," Potter said.

"That's because they know you. When you're flying, they put in extra. But they've marked me down for lead pilot. So they didn't."

"No wonder they're all fawning over you; you're a real cheap date."

Burke sighed. Potter clearly wanted to rile him up again. He couldn't let him. "Do you like getting in fights?" he asked. "It seems like it."

"What can I say? It keeps me young. How old are you? Thirty? You act like you're eighty."

"Better than acting like I'm fifteen."

"Haha! That's the spi—"

The radio, which had been mostly silent, burst into life. The world's greatest dad now sounded as if he was in an underground bunker. Burke joggled the speaker on his helmet, but it didn't help.

"Burke? Potter? The stage landed in the wrong place. Did it release properly?" Schmidt sounded panicked. Burke knew it was Schmidt's ass if things went wrong, and the destruction of a civilian household (or, even worse, a piece of military equipment) would make for a terrible stinger in his encyclopedia entry.

"Nope," said Potter. "Burke screwed it up."

Burke grit his teeth before sighing heavily. "The ejection button on my control panel—" he began.

Schmidt interrupted. "It landed in somebody's pasture. It'll be a mess to clean up. Thankfully, nobody had a close look before we got to it."

There must have been chaos on the ground. The controllers, officers, and engineers could have seen the rocket from miles away, like a hand of

God coming down to pass judgment on their careers. They would have had to pile up into their crappy little pickups with chipped paint and half-inflated tires and chase after the device as it descended. The farmer had probably thought the world was ending, with the giant impact followed by the cavalcade of military trucks.

"Well, nobody was killed, eh Burke? We only sent a few cows running," said Potter.

"That was pure luck, though. I'm very sorry about this, Schmidt. My board malfunctioned. Potter's worked, but we dropped at six miles."

". . . Potter? Burke?" Schmidt's voice crackled. "Are you receiving?"

"Kind of," said Potter.

"I said, *we dropped at six miles*," Burke repeated. Were the engines drowning him out?

"Can you speak louder?" Schmidt asked.

Potter inhaled deeply before shouting, causing a buzz of static to ring over the line. "He said, he wants to know whether we can do a few rolls without blowing this mission! Or do we just have to move up in a straight line!?"

"Shut *the hell* up, Potter," Burke said. He couldn't think of anything more clever to say, as the icy grip of panic was starting to envelop his brain. Their radio was probably broken, and all Potter cared about were his stupid *rolls*.

Schmidt called their names a few more times, his voice getting more and more annoyed with each repetition as if the men chose to ignore him. He probably couldn't believe that his flawless, beautiful technology had malfunctioned. Or he absolutely did, and the thought terrified him.

"Shit," Burke said. His throat burned and his stomach twisted. The two pilots were all alone, at an altitude only ever inhabited by enemy bombers.

"Eh, it's probably fine. What we're doing isn't rocket science. Or, well, it is, but they've already done the hard part. We're just going up and down." Potter sounded utterly unperturbed. Burke wouldn't admit it aloud, but he did have a point.

Both men had done multiple test flights in the past, and Burke in particular had flown in plenty of poorly constructed deathtraps in the air force's effort to learn how to combat the Cays. This mission was uncomplicated, the hull seemed to be holding, and his suit was still blowing air in his nose. Most of the planned back-and-forth with the ground was small talk about the weather and dial readings; they weren't in commercial airspace.

Unfortunately, the logical part of Burke's brain didn't have any control over his fears. The *what ifs* piled up quickly and in large numbers. But he had to put on a strong face; he was the pilot.

Burke took a few deep breaths before giving Potter an awkward nod. It wasn't as if Schmidt could come up and help them if there was any trouble.

The sky changed after ten miles' altitude.

They were far beyond anything Burke had visited before, and the sight was breathtaking. The atmosphere had drained into complete darkness, and the naked sun burned harshly overhead, casting everything in the cockpit into bright-white contrast. The blue light of Earth glowed from beneath, staining the sides of the plane with vivid color. Space looked absolutely empty and impossibly huge. There was no horizon off in the distance, just absolute nothingness. It made Burke feel tiny and alone, a meaningless speck in infinite darkness. It was chillingly beautiful. Goosebumps rose over the pilot's body.

Moments like *this* reminded him why he flew.

"Burke," Potter said.

"Can you go more than a few moments without speaking?" Burke snapped. He needed a few more seconds to take it in.

"Burke. Turn the plane."

Burke was annoyed. "Why? Do you want me to do a roll?"

"Level out the plane and turn around. There's something behind us."

Those last four words finally caught Burke's attention. They were the sort of words that rolled about in one's head and appeared underneath their eyelids. And Potter said them without any hint of laughter, irony, or glee.

"Something behind us?" Burke repeated, his mind blank. His skin was clammy, and he could clearly feel each individual drop of sweat. He focused on the sensation, trying to drag himself away from his thoughts.

With some hesitation, he tried to look behind Potter, but it was difficult to see much of anything. The cockpit had been optimized for handling the unusual pressures of space, not sightseeing. Potter glued his face to his window, completely blocking Burke's view.

Losing his nerve, Burke quickly looked away and started to turn the aircraft. It handled very differently than anything he'd flown before, so it took him a little while to get the plane moving properly. Instead of pushing back on air, the craft pushed itself forward with directed puffs of thrust from the back.

Thankfully, the control wheel on his panel functioned adequately. With difficulty, Burke leveled out the plane and made a gentle turn, avoiding looking out his window until he stopped the plane.

A strange object floated in space, brightened by sunshine and Earthshine. It was a glossy, artificial blue, as if it was coated in a cobalt glaze. Its shape was amorphous, resembling a clump of bubbles, stuck together randomly. Each individual bubble was fused into its neighbors with an off-color seam. It was impossible to tell how it was meant to be oriented or what it was supposed to do—perhaps its manufacturers wanted to obscure its purpose.

Schmidt had said there was nothing on radar. Nothing for tens of miles.

The object seemed distant, but the sunlight, unfettered by Earth's atmosphere, was bright enough that it was easy to spot, especially considering its reflectivity and color. From its astonishing level of detail, it had to be colossal. Maybe the size of a city, or a mountain, or an entire mountain range.

The entire surface was crisscrossed with ridges, hatches, and tower-like protrusions, though these things all had odd, organic curves and lumps, without a straight line to be seen. A cloud of what looked like hundreds of gnats, each too small to readily see, surrounded it. Burke's stomach sank as he realized what they probably were. Buzzers.

"Do you see . . . something blue?" Burke asked quietly, praying this was a hallucination induced by bad air in his helmet.

"Yes."

"Dark blue? Not the sky?"

"Yes."

Burke collapsed back in his seat, his muscles suddenly failing him. This was downright impossible.

"Who the hell built those?" Potter said.

Burke had no idea who on Earth could have done this. There was no way that anyone could have blasted that into space, at least not without anyone noticing. They would have had to launch hundreds of rockets to get enough material to construct it, and Russia surely couldn't have done that without a single leak to some spy or another. Even if they'd operated in complete secrecy from the depths of Siberia, nobody could have made something of this scale without someone else noticing. It would have utterly tanked their economy or sent clouds of dust through Europe. At some point, a dropped stage would have fallen into the ocean and drifted over to a nearby coast.

"They . . . they're from space," said Burke, shivering with awe and mind-draining terror. "Nothing else makes sense. It's n-not us, and it's not like Russia has anything even close to this."

"Then why the hell are they here?"

"I don't know. But they're worse than we thought. If they can make this—"

"They can kill us all before breakfast. No wonder we never see any of their planes launch; they just swoop in! They're toying with us," Potter said.

For years, they had just been there, watching and waiting. Flying overhead, bombing, killing, but for what purpose? This wasn't a war; it was a game, where the enemy held all of the cards and giggled from orbit.

"We have to go," Burke said. "Our people . . . command . . . everyone . . . they need to know about this. Is the radio still broken?"

"The damn thing never worked, remember?" Potter said sharply.

Burke reached up and tapped his receiver, hoping that some percussive maintenance would do the trick. He shook so badly, it was hard to control his movements.

"Schmidt? Schmidt?"

Of course, the stars didn't suddenly align, Jesus didn't appear before them, and the radio didn't fix itself.

"Well," said Burke, feeling defeated and exhausted, "Let's get back down."

"Already?" Potter gestured at the giant fortress before them. "I feel like we need to do something. We just saw their lair."

"They're going to kill us if we don't leave before they see us!"

"I want to kill some of them for once," Potter said. "Let them know what it feels like."

"Me, too," Burke said. "But getting shot down won't help. We need to go."

"Yeah, yeah, run away. I'm sure that's your go-to plan."

Burke bristled at the comment, biting back a retort about the time in Korea he *hadn't* run away, and how dearly he had paid for it. "Potter, *we are leaving*," he said.

"I know," Potter said. "It was just nice to think about actually doing something."

"I'm not a coward," muttered Burke. "I'm smart." He reached for his controls and gave the giant Cay fortress one last look, trying to memorize its appearance despite how sick and useless it made him feel. He couldn't imagine how anyone could defeat such an enemy—even the greatest nation on Earth didn't have this level of spacefaring technology.

The plane arced back towards the Earth in complete silence, leaving Burke alone with his thoughts.

Potter broke the spell. "Something's following us."

"Of goddamn-course something is following us," Burke said harshly, annoyed that Potter had told him that. If he didn't know, he could have pretended everything would be okay. "Is it . . . the whole thing?"

"No. Something smaller. One of their planes."

Were they even planes? Burke was fairly sure planes weren't traditionally piloted by creatures from the depths of space. The Cays probably had their own word, probably constructed of guttural moans and shrieks.

"Do bombs work in space?" Potter mused. "It probably can't hit—"

"Guns!" Burke barked. "If they can build a city in space, they can probably figure out how to mount a gun." He had never heard of Cays flying fighters before; they preferred long-distance attacks over fair fights. But they had to know something about combat.

He glanced back, dread churning in his stomach. One of the gnats had definitely detached from the city and grew in size at an alarming rate.

Their pursuer looked like another malformed bubble of ceramic, the same cobalt blue as its parent. Schmidt's photograph made more sense now—the device had no obvious structure. Its surface was covered with a series of asymmetric, pale cracks. Everything was horribly quiet. Burke and Potter were probably the first two people to ever see a Caelite ship up close, though that was little consolation.

"They don't have any fucking oxygen tanks," Potter said quietly.

Burke tore his eyes away from the thing. He needed to focus on getting the plane pointed back at Earth, not on their rapidly decreasing chances of survival.

"Can I shoot them?" Potter asked.

"No. We're leaving. Not turning."

"Don't have to. Rear guns, remember?"

"Does this plane *have* rear guns?"

There was some shuffling, and then a click. "Yeah, controls are still in."

This plane *was* a modified version of the Walker C-13, Burke supposed. "Have they changed them?" he asked.

"No clue. Let's try it."

"Can you aim?"

Potter shuffled some more.

"It's right on our ass. If I miss, I swear I'll quit and become a kindergarten teacher."

Burke sighed heavily. Their goal, the Earth, was in sight, and they flew towards it. All they had to do was keep moving forward. However, their pursuer could outpace them.

"Do it," Burke said.

"Thought you'd never let me."

Burke couldn't help but watch as Potter, his face pressed against the window, grabbed the controls and pressed a few buttons. Something deep within the body of the plane made a pained screeching noise.

"Hey, lay off those—" Burke began.

Boom. The explosion echoed through the recycled air in the cockpit. The force of the blast sent the plane into a rapid sideways roll along the surface of the planet. Its cerulean light spun rapidly in and out of Burke's vision as he froze, shaking from the noise. Somewhere underneath his feet, something hissed faintly.

They had no way of really knowing what kind of damage had been done to their plane. What if the rocket was out? What if the hull had been breached? Burke hated himself for letting Potter fire. He didn't know the guns worked; why did he even try them? It was a stupid risk. A stupid risk that didn't help anyone except the buzzer nearby.

They were going to die.

"Burke! Make this damn thing stop spinning!" Potter said. The other pilot blinked slowly, unable to return to his own body. "Hurry up! I don't care about shooting anymore; we have to get out of here!"

Die, die, die.

"Useless! Cripple! Get your fucking useless cripple legs into gear and fly this useless fucking cripple plane or else I'm going to crawl up there and tear off whatever stumps you've got left!" His voice wavered slightly; he sounded far more nervous than angry.

The words percolated through Burke's helmet, into his brain. Those words should have made him furious.

"Shut it, P-Potter," he said quietly. He stuttered slightly, and his teeth chattered. It was odd; his shell shock usually didn't come out like this. Clammy skin, shaking, tired . . .

"Finally, you're back," Potter flopped back in his chair, breathing heavily. "It's hard to reach that lever. And I couldn't think of much else to say."

"Probably a first," said Burke as he grabbed the controls. The arms of his suit felt stiff, as if he was pushing his arms through mud, and his fingers felt icy cold. He couldn't think now. Just fly.

The thrusters still worked. With some finesse and a sustained hard turn, Burke managed to slow the plane's irregular, vertigo-inducing roll. Despite his efforts, the Cay plane continued to approach.

One of the cracks on the surface of the buzzer flashed before hurling a bright bolt through the vacuum in their direction. It missed, but by an uncomfortably small margin.

It was shooting at them.

"You ever fly combat, Burke?" Potter asked.

"No." He had been on the ground in Korea, and there weren't too many enemy fighters in the deserts of Nevada.

"Mind if I fly this one?"

"Are you going to damage the plane more?" Burke asked.

"No guns this time. Just flying."

"You were demoted from flying combat."

Potter chuckled halfheartedly. "I was too good for the front lines."

The Cay fighter shot at them again. Evasive maneuvers were probably in order, but Burke's brain felt like putty. Why the hell did there have to be fighting up here? Why couldn't they have just gone into space, looked around, saw nothing, and then flown back down? What the hell had he done to deserve this? He had joined the military to protect his country and his family; how was he supposed to do anything about an enemy that could kill them from orbit?

He flicked the lever.

"Primary control transferred," he mumbled. "D-don't play around. We need to get down."

"I'm not going to waste time. It's damn cold up here."

Burke glanced back at him in mild surprise. He wasn't the only one who felt cold.

Potter played around with the controls for a few seconds to get the hang of it. The plane drifted left, then right. Then, it turned 180 degrees and accelerated. Burke didn't even realize the aircraft could fly this fast. The buzzer clearly hadn't anticipated this, as it stopped shooting briefly as their plane sailed past it with only a few yards of clearance.

They were close to the enemy ship, but its design remained incomprehensible. Some deep indentations on its sides appeared to be rockets, so Burke supposed at least one of Schmidt's wild guesses had been right. However, these rockets sprouted from everywhere, not just out the tail.

The buzzer twirled impossibly before shooting upwards, leaving the plane in its wake as it spun like a top above them to reorient itself, firing as it moved.

Potter laughed nervously and shot the plane forward out of the arc of enemy fire. Potter's chaotic technique seemed to make up for their plane's inferior turning radius. Burke felt quite useless, sitting there and watching Potter do his job for him.

The radio crackled loudly, making Burke jump.

"You haven't come down." Schmidt sounded deeply unhappy.

Burke supposed that they had been scheduled to descend long ago. A big, expensive mission failure would do a number on Schmidt's career, as well as his ego.

Schmidt's next words surprised him.

"I don't even know if you can hear me, but I hope you two are okay." The engineer sounded uncharacteristically sincere.

Potter's guffaws harshened. "Yeah, like you care about us," he said, hurling the plane into another tight turn. "Maybe don't mount the guns where they can explode next time!"

"He has no idea what's happening," said Burke blankly. "The radars must not be able to see the buzzers this high up."

"Their tech isn't working? What a fucking surprise!" Potter said.

Burke held his hand to the radio in his helmet. Maybe he could do something useful. "Keep flying. I'm fixing the radio," he said.

"They can't help us from down there!"

"We can warn them about this," Burke breathed heavily. "In case."

Mercifully, Potter didn't ask, "In case what?"

Burke was not an electrical engineer, but he knew how to follow wires. Wires from both his helmet and Potter's led to a panel on his left, held in place with a few screws. Burke's half of the plane was the one packed with all of the extra tools (he didn't need the legroom). With his suit, it took some effort to reach forward and grab onto the appropriate bag.

Just then, Potter threw the plane into a roll. The inertia jogged the bag out of Burke's grip. "Fly steady!" he hissed.

"If you're okay with getting shot!" the man called back.

He did not fly any steadier, but, with some groping and flailing, Burke maneuvered the bag into his lap. Unfortunately, his suit made unzipping it impossible. There really only seemed to be one way to pull it off.

After some mental preparation, Burke yanked his arms out of his airsuit sleeves and fumbled for the interior zipper. It crackled loudly as he pulled it open.

Air rushed out of his suit, making Burke gasp in surprise. The air in the cockpit was much thinner and colder than it had been the last time he had checked. He slipped his free arm out through the opening in his suit, feeling himself begin to freeze to death. His eyes watered, and air sucked out of his lungs. His right hand, which had previously hurt, now felt like nothing at all. He couldn't really guide himself by touch, and instead had to watch carefully as his hand opened the bag, reached in, and grabbed a screwdriver. It felt as if it was someone else's hand.

The world spun. One moment, the Earth appeared. The next, the sun shone, cruelly taunting him with its lack of warmth.

The mysterious hand, bright-white and corpse-like, undid the screws on the panel and nudged it aside, parts dropping away and disappearing into oblivion. It was too dark to see anything in the depths beneath the control panel.

"Fly so that the sun's above us!" Burke wheezed.

"That's a lot of mouth for a copilot," Potter replied. Despite his words, moments later the cockpit flooded with sustained sunlight.

Burke quickly scanned the panel. The results made him clench his remaining useful fist. Even a child could tell that one of the fuses had blown. Thankfully, Schmidt had some self-awareness about his shoddy personnel standards and had included a bag of spare fuses in the plane.

The fuses were tiny and easy to lose, especially since Burke couldn't feel anything. The hand in front of him dropped a few before fitting a fresh one into the panel. The second the thing clicked, he yanked the arm back into his suit, zipping it shut with his left from the inside. He wasn't sure if his right hand would ever feel anything again.

"Schmidt?" he yelled into the receiver. "This is Burke and Potter. I repeat, this is Burke and Potter. We're both alive. Do you hear me?"

There was silence for an agonizing few seconds, and then, gloriously, a voice.

"Burke, is that you?" Schmidt's words were panicked and muffled. There was a shuffling noise as the man fiddled with something. He sighed with relief, and his voice slowed. "We were—"

Burke interrupted. "There's a lot of craft up here. Thousands. They have a giant blue plane in the sky. It has to be bigger than an island. Don't know how it could get up here."

"What?" Schmidt choked.

Burke racked his brain, trying to isolate every useful detail. "The Cays. They're from space. They're not from the ground. Plane's too big. They have guns, too."

"Their planes don't have oxygen tanks, just saying," Potter added. "And it's cold in here! Couldn't you have just put in a space heater?"

Schmidt didn't respond for a while. Very faintly, Burke could hear him muttering with someone else back on Earth. The words "hypoxia" and "hallucination" were tossed about. Of course, the engineer wouldn't want it to be real.

"There's nothing on the radar," Schmidt eventually sputtered. "We don't see anything but you!"

"Maybe your precious radar technology is shit, ever think—" Potter said.

"Shut up, Potter!" Burke didn't want to waste time with commentary. "The rear guns jammed and exploded," he continued. "We've taken on some enemy fire. The hull may be compromised."

"You've been firing the guns?" asked Schmidt.

"What else were we supposed to do," asked Potter, "let them shoot at us?"

"They weren't meant to—"

"Yeah, I can tell!"

Burke cut back in. "We've got one of their . . . fighters . . . chasing us, and we don't have any guns. We're going to attempt re-entry. Expect company."

This must have been a lot for Schmidt to take in at once. As a pencil-pushing type, the man hadn't seen much action in his life; probably the most exciting that ever happened to him before this was his divorce.

The engineer stuttered incomprehensibly.

"You heard the copilot. We're coming in hot!" Potter said. He flipped the plane through the air to avoid a few errant shots, and, after a complete loop, continued his path towards the Earth.

"Don't do that!" Schmidt yelled. "If you really have fired the guns, the hull is compromised. You two will burn up in the atmosphere!"

"Then what are we supposed to do?" asked Burke, shivering.

"Die?" asked Potter as he veered them away from Earth. A shot burned past their left wing, forcing the plane to pitch sideways.

"No. I . . . uh . . ." Schmidt stuttered, then paused to take a few deep breaths. "Are you sure you fired the guns? If it's really so cold in there, there could be some sort of oxygen leak, and you two merely *think*—"

"I'm not imagining things!" Potter said.

"Neither am I," Burke said, trying and failing to keep his voice level. "Would we really hallucinate the same thing?"

This couldn't be a hallucination, could it? It was cold inside; maybe there was something wrong with the hull. A small leak, trailing oxygen and sanity behind them. He *had* heard a hissing noise, hadn't he?

"Sure we would," snorted Potter, "We're so similar, after all. Right, Schmidt? Me and him, same fucking guy, same fucking delusion." He punctuated each statement with a jerk on the controls, making Burke flop around in his seat.

As he bounced helplessly, Burke shook his head hard. This was real. It had to be real. He didn't have a good enough imagination to cook this up. He gripped his chair with both hands, holding himself in place as he swallowed past a lump in his throat. If it was real, they needed a new plan. "Do you have any backup planes? Is there a way to hover in the upper atmosphere and switch between them?" he asked.

"We don't have any backups ready to launch!"

"So we're dead?" Burke's voice raised.

"You can re-enter," Schmidt said quietly, "I think the plane is fine; you're just . . . not in your right mind." He did not sound terribly confident.

"So that's it. We have no shot," Burke said. "We're going to die up here because you didn't remove the gun controls."

"I never said you could use the guns," Schmidt said, exasperated. "We weren't expecting combat!"

"Didn't you think that the enemy ships we typically see at high altitude might be from a higher altitude?" Burke hissed.

"There is nothing there," the engineer said with a horrible sense of finality.

But there was something there. It was right in front of them, shooting at them. Everything had to be real. The marks burned across their hull. The all-encompassing pain in his arm. The taste of iron in his mouth. The giant city-ship, far behind him. It was too vivid to be fake.

"Shut up, Burke!" Potter said.

Burke froze and closed his mouth. He didn't realize he was talking.

"Glad you called them?" Potter asked bitterly as he flicked something on his board.

"Did you just shut them off?" Burke asked.

"Yeah. It's not like he's helping us."

Burke had to admit, the man had a point. Perhaps being irresponsible and ignoring his duty was the way to go today. He reached forward and shut his own radio off.

"We can't get out of this, can we?" he said quietly.

The plane jolted and shook. Another hit. Burke breathed deeply, wondering whether or not this gulp of air would be one of his last, or even if there was any oxygen to breathe. He stared at the space beneath his knees, too afraid to look up and see what had happened.

"Nope," said Potter.

"You're awfully calm about the fact that we're going to die."

"You think this is me being calm?" Potter's words were jittery and sharp, like he had just drunk six cups of coffee. He rolled the plane to one side, but the movement was more awkward than the last had been. The thruster must have been damaged. Potter whistled, but the tune was punctuated by rapid breathing.

"We have to do something," Burke said, still looking down. Once again, light flashed through the cockpit rapidly and irregularly. Potter was probably trying some crazy new evasive technique.

"Well," Potter said, "we've got two options."

"All ears," Burke said.

"We can burn up in the atmosphere while getting shot down. This guy has terrible aim, but he'll hit us if we're going straight down." The words bubbled rapidly from his lips, running together with an irregular cadence.

"That's the option you don't want," said Burke.

"Yep, it's shit. You'll hate my other idea even more."

"Is it reckless?"

"Yeah."

The idea immediately seemed obvious. What did Potter love even more than aerobatics? "Does it involve killing buzzers?"

"Yeah."

Their interests had some overlap in that area. "What do you want to do?" Burke asked.

"Crash into this guy."

"You don't even know if that would do anything! We don't know what it's made of."

"I know. And it'll definitely kill us."

Burke drummed his fingers against his chest inside his suit. His mind wanted to race past him at every moment—mundane flashes of home, of his mother baking casserole, of his little brother going to middle school. Of Korea, when he thought the explosions of glass from above were attacks from the communists. Of bombs that covered the ground in a web of fiberglass, killing all who inhaled it. Of sitting in a trench, in unimaginable pain, screaming wordlessly at a helpless trainee medic. Of bombed-out cities, hospitals, and schools, vaporized off of the face of the Earth by cold, unfeeling creatures. He couldn't think right now. Thinking about such things never led to anything except him curling up in a ball and staring into nothing until he eventually passed out.

Had his life meant anything? He hadn't won anything or saved anyone; he was just a canary in a coalmine that the miners hadn't even bothered to check on. But maybe he could do one thing, even if it killed him.

Revenge.

"I don't want to crash into that," Burke said. "Let's crash into their city. See how their children deal with getting hit by glass in the face."

Potter tried to laugh, but the noise was harsh. "That's a good idea, for you," he said. "G-glad to see you've picked up my sense of humor."

Potter turned the plane back towards the enemy fortress; Burke stock-still as he tried to focus on something positive and noble instead of the void.

The giant enemy ship filled Burke's vision, and he realized dimly it might be the last thing he ever saw. He gave the Earth below a quick glance, hoping that somebody down there would find a way to save themselves.

Potter pushed the thrusters into full gear before taking his hands away from the controls. He didn't need them anymore. Lights flashed around them as the Cay fighter tried to keep pace from behind.

"Anything you want to say?" Potter asked.

"Don't stop!" Burke didn't want the chance to change his mind.

"I can't. Not enough gas."

The fortress grew and grew in their sight, each moment emphasizing how impossibly large it was. Its surface was covered in an intricate spiderweb of giant fissures. Small bulbous growths dripped off of the sides, probably places for the little craft to dock. There weren't any windows—perhaps the dizzying beauty of space was humdrum to its inhabitants. Several buzzers noticed the unfamiliar aircraft and approached it. However, they could only move so quickly.

"You know, Burke?" Potter asked loudly, raising his voice over the rumbles and groans of their ride.

"Yes?"

"It's a pleasure, murdering these bastards with you."

Burke fought the urge to cover his face with his hands. He grabbed his flight wheel with both hands and pushed forwards, too, even though he had no control anymore. The fabric of his suit had grown stiff with the frigid air, turning it into a makeshift coffin.

"It's b-been a pleasure, Potter," he said quietly.

Inside the runway's outbuilding, Alfred Schmidt hunched next to a radar display, staring at the dull, beeping green surface. The radio transceiver in his hand crackled loudly, and one of the military officers standing behind him coughed impatiently.

"Turn the radio back on," he said into the transmitter, knowing his efforts were futile. Somehow, that idiot Potter had convinced Burke to listen to him and had drawn the more reliable pilot into his delusion. He couldn't even hear what they were saying anymore, so they must have shut off both ingoing and outgoing communications.

Schmidt hoped that his twenty-million-dollar baby, currently speeding westwards, would turn back and land where it should, pilots gibbering but alive. Many important men were giving him venomous looks, and he didn't want to be sent to the slaughterhouse. His last expensive failure, with its animal subjects all dead from hypoxia, had cost him both a promotion and his marriage—he shook to think what would happen if this failed, especially with the military's money running so dry.

The loud, ever-present static peaked on the radio as the radar screen refreshed. Then, abruptly, his plane disappeared.

"Is it out of range?" Schmidt asked, heart pounding.

The radar technician, one of Schmidt's more clever hires, tapped the screen a few times and read a few dials before turning apologetically to his audience.

"Nah, it's just the machine. It does that sometimes," he said. "It'll come back in a few sweeps."

The entire group fell silent, everyone staring at the display. The only noise was the machine's faint, echoing pings.

The plane did not reappear in a few sweeps.

As Schmidt stared and prayed, a voice outside shattered the quiet. "Guys! Get out here! There's something in the sky!"

Schmidt's heart leaped as a faint smile began to tug on his lips. Perhaps the weird, westward signal had just been a faulty radar issue after all. With improved shielding and a gun reroute, his next mission would be a complete success with minimal additional costs—not even a million dollars.

When he ran outside, joined by a gaggle of scientists and officers, he did not see anything good. The modified C-13 was not approaching the runway, not in the sky, not anywhere at all.

What he did see was difficult for him to understand. It was high up in the sky, hazy, intangible and ghostly like the face of the full moon at daytime. It looked as big as the moon, too, though he wasn't sure how far away it was.

At first, Schmidt thought it was a supernova or some other astronomical event, but it swiftly became clear to him that this was no star. It was broad and sharply defined, with an elongated, lumpy outline. He squinted at the strange object alongside his compatriots, taking in every detail of its shape as a blast wave of bright light rippled over its surface.

After a few moments, the light faded and the object disappeared. Like a hallucination induced by hypoxia.

25

Memoirs of a Status Quo

Ashish Mahabal

I ENTERED Shuka's room and checked the oxygen levels and other supplements. His room was spacious for a small space station. Shuka was a human, and yet his entire setup was mechanical and automated to aid access to memory and computing. He was not required to move unless he desired to. The nutrition would have continued uninterrupted. His reclined position with many wires connected gave the impression of patients undergoing several medical measurements at once. Even when immobile, he was alert, but at ease. On the contrary, robot as I am, I check his settings frequently as if they could change on their own. This happens more when Shuka is lost in thought. Why I am overcome by this frailty rather than solving newer mathematical puzzles is an unsolved puzzle for me.

We were docked on an uneven asteroid beyond Jupiter called Gurusthal-312, one of many Earth outposts. Fully laced with the latest gadgets and weapons, its radio antennae and telescopes ably scanned space—mostly dark but for the half-degree-wide Jupiter with its often-seen red pupil. Only Shuka and I were sentient here. For years on end, nay, for decades, there would be no change outside. When something or someone new approached, our simple job was to ascertain their nature, assimilate them if useful, otherwise just terminate them to restore status quo. Ah, we did differ a bit on what was and was not useful. Were we nearing that time again? Our scopes had alerted us to an incoming craft.

To while away time, and so Shuka would not go mad, we played different games—intellectual games, since Shuka preferred to be mostly immobile. Such a game was on today. Take a topic, and quiz each other on related trivia. We communicated over audio—speaking like two humans would—though we both interfaced the datastores. We could talk for days on end on any topic. Today's topic was the historic twentieth and twenty-first centuries. That period from a few thousand years ago had given the aspirations of humanity a dramatic turn. We quizzed each other with sentences from that period: what was their origin, who uttered them, and, if fictional, the work and author. I was waiting for a sentence from Shuka.

"'There is nothing to history. No progress, no justice. There is nothing but random horror.'" Shuka's strong resonant voice rang out. That voice and the string of lights monitoring his status were the only audio-visual signs of his being alive.

"Gibson and Sterling's *The Difference Engine*," I answered. There was no need to verify that. I could have identified that one in my sleep. If I slept.

But why had Shuka chosen this sentence? After the monumental change in the twenty-first century, it was only the occasional spacecraft heading our way that would raise the possibility of disturbing the stability of humanity. The changes in history provide ephemeral joys for the victors, and long lasting sorrows for the multitude. Is that what he was thinking about?

I chose a sentence to match Shuka's.

"'You do not make history. You can only hope to survive it.'"

It took a few moments for his answer to be heard as his vast memories were not all internal to him. Part of his spacious room was occupied by these appendages, periodically updated by Earth and other stations.

"Straczynski, in the 'Rising Star' episode of *Babylon 5*."

The answer was of course correct. His silicon extensions were as effective as my silicon brain. Ages back I had joked that the human evolution had really started when they started using silicon for brains instead of for other organs. Many humans did not like it. They demanded my head, and said things like "these tinmen will never understand beauty." Shuka, however, applauded my comment. His broader outlook set him apart from mere mortals.

Having access to all the data makes choice real fun. Select sentences chronologically? Randomly? Since human memories are context dependent, the situation at the time of our game and the resulting mental make-up often contributed to Shuka's choice of sentences. My secondary game was to determine his state of mind through his sentences. Our higher—and common—aim was to weave the chosen sentences into a bigger whole, often a hopeless endeavor. But we had time. Usually a lot. While I was lost in thought, Shuka's next challenge came:

"'Those who do not move, do not notice their chains.'"

"Is that a trick question?" I replied. "The best answer is Rosa Luxemburg though it is almost certainly misattributed with no real source known."

Many of these statements have depth beyond one agreeing with them or not. They often depend on time and location. Humans had made immense attempts to move. These attempts made them aware of the chains holding them back. Trying to fledge beyond the Solar System, they really realized the immensity of interstellar distances. As a result, they enclosed themselves in darkness. Spacecrafts still ventured outward, but they contained no information about the Solar System. The coded messages they sent back provided us with knowledge we could not gain from inside. Attempts to mine asteroids went on for several decades. But the challenges faced in transporting minerals, and in living there, presented immense difficulties, and humans more or less gave it up. Humans were now content to experience the universe by traveling through it virtually. Go to any planet without leaving the comfort of your home—that is what they seemed to enjoy. And not just travel. Anything seemingly blissful to a human was available on tap. Be it good or bad. After all, who was to judge? For us mechanical beings, everything was virtual anyway. I often wondered what else there could be. Could we really *see* humans? Or was that our virtual world? And if so, how would *their* virtual world be?

"Ullu, I will die of waiting," Shuka's voice snapped me out of my chain of thoughts. I immediately picked a sentence.

"'The final truth of all things is that there is no final truth! Truth is what's transitory! It's human life that is real!'"

"Paddy Chayefsky in *Altered States*," Shuka replied quickly.

Shuka and dying? Even if I did not care for his environment, the systems would have ensured that nothing would hurt him. He was that important. After innumerable tests they had granted him godhood. As a result, in a way, this was heaven. But this heaven was not a place palatable to mortals. Mortals couldn't realize that heaven is where God is. Their heaven was their electronic world. Our responsibility was to ensure that the Earth and lunar worlds, frozen, stayed safe from external threats. Many gods like Shuka lived for thousands of years. They could have lived even longer, but at some point immortality becomes a burden, a curse. The realization that truth is relative has dawned by then.

"'Man does not create gods, in spite of appearances. The times, the age, impose them upon him,'" Shuka threw the next challenge.

"Stanislaus Lem's *Solaris*."

Had he guessed my thoughts from my sentence? Lem had constructed many universes: mechanical gods, imperfect gods, and several others. We robots were never in competition for godhood. Even though our capacity was unparalleled. We had not inherited human ambitions. How would the beings in the approaching craft be? Organic or mechanical? Would they have ambitions? Will Shuka and I have to employ logic to bring about a treaty? Or will war be forced upon us?

"'Those who cannot remember the past are condemned to repeat it —'" I started the next challenge. Shuka identified it before I even finished. "George Santayana, in *The Life of Reason*."

On Earth, humans had lost track of both history and where they could be heading. We bore the curse of internalizing all history. If we were to make a single mistake, the entirety of humanity could suffer.

"'The past is full of life, eager to irritate us, provoke and insult us, tempt us to destroy or repaint it. The only reason people want to be masters of the future is to change the past,'" Shuka had a longer sentence.

"Milan Kundera, in *The Book of Laughter and Forgetting*."

I agreed with what the quote said. But what was Shuka thinking? About changing history? Or not changing it? Was he thinking about the launches of the early days? A few centuries ago, humans had started receiving incoherent radio signals from many star systems nearby as if it was suddenly spring. Was he thinking of those neighbors? It was because of them that outposts like Gurusthal-312 had to be created. Our task was to ensure that a neighboring system did not attack Earth—the way neighboring countries on Earth used to feud in bygone ages. We were here to protect them as gods.

Before I conjured the next sentence, we received a signal that the extrasolar craft was now close by. I did not need to see the ship, but I found myself getting close to the port. Our computers scanned the spacecraft. It was a primitive one, tired after centuries of travel. There were no sentients on it. Our computers inspected the internal traffic between the ship's computers to gauge their capabilities. Our algorithms decided that from the human perspective their utility was far less than the mischief they could cause. It would have been no use contacting them. Neither new knowledge, nor new entertainment was to be gained. In such straightforward circumstances, neither Shuka nor I were required for decisions. Earlier, Shuka had protested destroying foreign ships. Even if humans had not been able to step outside, we should welcome such contacts, he would say. But he was a god for namesake. Earthlings immersed in virtual truths wouldn't stand their heaven being moved by such external interference. Once contact were to be established, there would have been no turning back. Shuka once confessed that he wondered if Earth crafts that had traveled for hundreds of years had met similar treatments. In the end, Shuka had backed off. Did Shuka feel helpless when such crafts were destroyed? As if our own craft were being destroyed? Along with dreams of finding new islands, new universes?

In the distance, a dispatched missile made contact with the ship, briefly lighting up the sky, and became another memory.

"Ullu, I am waiting," Shuka sounded impatient. Was he really dying? I started rummaging through my data banks for another sentence.

26

The Garbage Man

Tatyana Dobreva

DEAR ASTRA,

I am sending this letter to you, as well as the Script collection of tales from those whose lives I ended, because I have tagged myself for destruction. The tales are a burden that I have imposed on myself, and I initially thought it would be a burden to pass them on to anyone, especially you. I raised you and was fortunate to witness your transition into a position of influence. I told you I was a terraform engineer and that your mother passed on our voyage. I think you always had a sense that everything I told you was a lie. I believe you let me lie to you to keep me safe from reliving my past. You grew up and left me to pursue your ambitions. Your departure was one of the few moments in my life that I felt the impact of time. I did not admit these truths to you then because I craved a life blind to the consequences of my past—hence this cowardly letter.

Some referred to me as the most sophisticated assassin of all time. A man whose trail of blood disappeared into the shadows, yet no compliments shield me sufficiently from seeing the truth. I was a garbage man. I threw away others' problems into black holes. I speculate that those compliments and glorifications were made to boost my ego and make me complacent in executing others' dirty work.

One hot summer night in my childhood, a few kids from my village and I were playing a game of hide-and-seek. I ran into the nearby woods, guarded by tall, green pine trees, looking for an ideal hiding spot. As I went through the forest and emerged onto a lakeshore, I witnessed something reminiscent of a dream. I was not well educated, but I knew well enough that water should not flow up toward the sky. Yet, there in the middle of the lake was a column of water twisting upward in a spiral. Overwhelmed with a feeling of curiosity, I swam towards it. As I approached it, I had to expend less and less energy to move. A whirlpool pulled me towards itself. I let it.

After I entered the column of twisting water, I felt a sort of a pop. Following the sensation of decompressing from traveling through a narrow passage, I felt like I was born again. I found myself in the same body but on the streets of an alien city. Flying carriages without horses propelled their way throughout the sky. Transparent cathedrals filled with moving images towered above me and surrounded flat streets through which wagons sped. Later, I came to understand that the alien city was in fact a human one and that I was a "straggler"—a living side effect of illegal time traveling. I was lucky that I manifested when I did. Not long before my arrival, time stragglers were put down. However, a recent time law reform gave me an option: be put down or silently execute the duties of the Cosmic Council for the rest of my days. I made the choice to stay alive because I felt that whatever the universe had to offer had to be greater than whatever freedom I would take to my grave.

The Cosmic Council tasked me with disposing of anything that caused significant risk of instability or erasure of intelligent existence into a black hole. Usually, these were dangerous inventions like nearly infinite energy sources; machines that wielded dark energy to carve out islands in space-time; and computers built from star systems. The council informed me that proper execution of their detailed orders was crucial, that thousands of years had been spent getting human civilization to unprecedented advancement. The thought of it all disappearing as a result of someone's reckless mistake or malice terrified them deeply. My task gave me a sense of purpose.

I felt like a wizard in my new role. Initially, I avoided learning the inner workings of the black hole disposal technology because I so enjoyed the feeling of wielding superpowers. I eventually yielded to my curiosity and found an eccentric engineer to explain it to me, though most of it went over my head. The explanation went something like this: "Using the ephemerally stable particles called Arceons, we are able to temporarily entrap objects between other dimensions. These Arceons unglue objects from the gravitational fabric of our universe for a brief moment and hide them in other universes superimposed with our own." To this day, I deeply appreciate how my transportation into the future has let me experience the impact of generational knowledge building.

The operational procedure I had to follow for removing objects from existence was as follows: using my ship, I created phenomena called "snip points" around the object to discard. These snip points, when activated, leverage Arceon fields to hold the object between the other dimensions temporarily. My ship used an "Arceon magnet" that allowed me to displace the objects wrapped in Arceon fields towards the black hole once I was close enough to it. The way I saw it was that the Arceon fields were the garbage bag and my ship was the hand used to toss that bag into the trash bin. After the snip points were *deactivated*, the objects reappeared into the universe and were immediately swallowed by the black hole.

I experienced a sense of dissonance at holding the lowly title of "disposal technician" while erasing chunks of the universe. The ship design prevented me from knowing what was inside the disposal bag, which caused me to feel a conflicting mix of relief and paranoia. In my first few runs, I wondered what would happen if the garbage bag were to *tear*—how would its contents disturb the fabric of space? Could new forms of life evolve millions of years later coalescing from the spilled components?

One day, a distracting thought in which I was recollecting an argument with a colleague, slipped me out of my routine. I made a snip in the wrong place. Upon reporting my error, I was informed that the snip caused me to accidentally wrap a small colony of sentient beings in the garbage bag and wipe it out of existence. I had played out this scenario many times in my head, hoping that it would motivate utmost care in the execution of my job, yet it happened. The sense of numbness that quickly displaced the terror of my mistake was far more palpable than any emotion I had played out in my mind.

The wrongfully wiped sentient beings were known as Halzenar. I had destroyed only one of their bases. Curiously, the cosmic council never reprimanded me for wiping out a sentient colony. But shortly after my accident, Halzenar representatives tracked me down. They were an orphaned species; their creators had been deemed too vile by the Cosmic

Council and destroyed. They had been spared by a narrow margin vote, and outcast to the inhospitable zones of space where I had accidentally cast my disposal net. The Halzenar offered to allow me to work for them to compensate for my error, in exchange for protection from the consequences of the Cosmic Council if I chose to join them.

I felt that I was a pawn in their war against the council, yet the promise of slightly more freedom and information had an irresistible appeal. Moreover, I felt a connection to the Halzenar. Like myself, they had been torn from their homes, tossed into the unknown, and forced to survive. I felt their fervor to exist and their exhaustion from having to constantly validate themselves. This stirred a deep sense of regret in me, as if I had blindly disposed of my own kind.

The first thing the Halzenar had me do was help them set up their own version of the garbage disposal system for purposes of defense. I felt uncomfortable helping the Halzenar enter the business of deciding what should exist, but most of my clean-up duties involved discarding automated weapons of destruction sent to keep the Halzenar numbers down. Later, they asked me to dispose of sentient beings working with the Cosmic Council who were deploying these weapons. As time went on, their definition of defense became looser, and the scale of destruction the Halzenar asked of me matched that which I had been doing for the Council. First sentients, then towns, then whole planets. But the job of being a garbage man had taken on a new meaning for me. I was no longer prevented from seeing what was disposed of. The *trash* that I carried for disposal had faces, voices, and I could see them wriggling for their survival.

Once the thrill of my freedom waned, my conscience began to emerge from its slumber. I found a way to converse with those being tagged for discard. Most of the time, I could understand very little of their language, for the languages of the cosmos spanned every conceivable method of communication, from light, to speech, to chemistry. Following unsuccessful attempts at communication using gestures and pointing, I learned about a device called Script, which can record almost any language used by the United Cosmic Civilization Network and translate it. I handed Script to those being discarded and tried my best to ask them to share their stories before their erasure. I felt their stories were important, and I made it my mission to be the curator of that information.

Among the discards, and to my surprise, I met you. Like myself, you were a time straggler. You were very young, about seven years old. All you could tell me at the time was that you were part of a secret operation and that you were participating in an *exciting* experiment. You were malnourished and nearly blind—as if something was eating away at you. I had trouble believing whether you knew what was going on. Your existence was a blip of time! I chose to keep you alive because I thought I understood you. Because you were like me. A human time straggler. But in doing so, I violated my sense of impartial judgment. Or perhaps I violated the delusion that I was an impartial man. By making a judgment to save you, I betrayed all those who I had not.

It became clear to me that I could no longer continue my job as a garbage man—a developing sense of morality precluded me. I amicably broke off ties with the Halzenar; it worked out in my favor that they saw me as a feeble-minded tool ready for retirement. You know the story from here. I kept my head low and dedicated myself to raising you. In the existential reflections of my final years, I realized that I am a man incapable of acting on information, yet always striving for more of it. I regret failing to involve myself in the conflicts of others sooner. I regret not grabbing the reins and instead jetting for the safest option. I regret seeking concealment behind a veil of purpose and duty. The Script tales I pass on to you along with this letter contain the words of those which I have discarded. They disclose their values, their unfulfilled dreams, their stories, their goodbyes. Races of sentient species fighting to survive, while attempting to see beauty and meaning in it all. Had I laid my eyes upon these stories, I would have never chosen to be a garbage man. I hope you see in this a way to live—fearless and aware.

Yours,
Grestel

27

Reentry

Anish Sarma

THE SHUTTLE WENT UP SMOOTH, nothing more than the silica rattles of breaking gravity, and Miller hit near-light as soon as he was clear of the other moons. He set the coordinates for his easedown an hour's manual flight away from the rock.

Carson's half-crumpled ship was where Miller had seen it last, harpooned into the face of the asteroid by six steel cables. Its docking bay was warped, as it had been two years ago, so Miller rappelled through the lock. The main cabin was powered and sealed, Carson's grizzled face a furrow shy of serene beneath the glass of a stasis pod. Miller checked the charge on the pod twice, then slid it easily through zero gs back to his ship. The pod went into the shuttle's storage. Miller covered it with a pile of blankets.

He had wrangled a hauler out of a city hobbyist two years earlier and made a habit of moving equipment from the spaceport out to the Heights, learning the rhythms of the backroads. Even slightly aged over forty years in stasis, Carson's face would be unmistakable. Miller had seen the canonical images a thousand times as a boy in history classes. Carson staring out through the glass of the station during the peace talks with two worlds in view; Carson, in white cotton, half soldier and half ascetic, signing the accords; Carson among the two delegations assembled in the station's greenhouse. And of course the young woman from the planetary delegation wearing a crown made from a moontree, the enduring symbol of Carson's grace. Every time he looked at this young woman, he would say in the statement he made before he left, he could see only his daughter Soraya, lost to the violence. That was how he knew they must have peace, that he must choose exile.

It was no better than death, Carson had said when Miller found him on the wreck two years earlier. When my ship gave out, I just figured it was the way it had to be.

Miller timed the drive for after dark. Cameras were everywhere in the city, but you could make a life without them on the Heights, with just enough sunlight to power a rural life. Out here, it had just been Miller for months at a time, him and the rabbits and a collie. He didn't miss the city; most of what he had loved about it had passed with his wife, long before he found Carson hanging off a rock in the cold of space.

The sun was near the horizon when he woke Carson under the sleepy shag of a moontree. My God, Carson murmured. It smells like earth. He ate, then he bathed, then he ate again, the juice of a mango dripping down his jaw. His eyes were wide, as though he were surprised by his own appetite. He ran a flat palm over the cool wood of the table.

They walked through a grazing pasture, into a forest and then a bluff, where a rabbit loped around the tree line. Carson crept across the clearing, letting a breath out slowly. Then he sprang, moving faster than Miller had ever seen a man move. He carried the squirming creature back to Miller. They sat between the roots of a thick-trunked tree. Carson held the rabbit firmly under his arm until it relaxed.

We could roast him, Miller said. I read that they did that when you were young.

Carson stroked the rabbit's fur and then released his grip. It bounded off, burrowing into a rustle of leaves and mulch. After a long pause, he said, I'm sorry. I mean, if you wanted to—I just like watching them run.

I think it's beautiful, Miller said, that you aren't violent.

The sun hung over the trees, and the planet over the horizon. Carson tossed a pebble into the motionless underbrush.

When we made the peace, he said, there were two young people in the other delegation. A man and a woman. She was married. They were in love. I think I was the only person on the station who knew. I wondered if Soraya would have done something like that. If she would have come to me and told me about it, if I would have disappointed her. Instead I had these two strangers.

Miller laid a hesitant hand on Carson's tense shoulder.

One day, Carson said, I took a knife to the greenhouse on the outer deck of the station, where no one went except the botanists. I cut a few branches off a moontree sapling and wove them together into a crown, the way my father had done. I made her something beautiful. I hoped it would weigh on her.

The curve of the planet drifted out of view.

And then she thanked me, Carson said, and we had peace.

28

Degenerates

Olivia Pardo

SELECT TRANSLATIONS FROM RECOVERY LOG #D17865

`::log 00028 start_`

It is thirty-eight billion years from the start of the universe. It is still in its youth. My power stores are full, my software and hardware integrity is high, and the red dwarf star I am attached to glows as brightly as it ever will. My magnetic sails allow me to navigate across the magnetic fields on the surface of my star, avoiding flares and keeping my Archive and storage modules cool while I collect neutrinos emitting from below. When it's safe, I remain stationary and rotate with the red dwarf, my companion for the next 300 billion years. In the meantime, I write out these logs, tracking system events.

I check the module temperatures:

`:: exterior temperature: 3106 K degrees`

`:: interior temperature: 322 K degrees`

I check my software and hardware integrity, which are slowly but inescapably and chaotically deteriorating from cosmic radiation:

`:: deterioration level: 0.0005%`

Still very low. Finally, I compute the percent of the Archive copied into my storage modules:

`:: archive processed: 1.2%`

My monitoring programs are satisfied. I wait for the next round of similar reports from my siblings, each of them situated on its own star. My location within the galaxy makes me a connecting node in a network of sibling communication. My arm of the galaxy thins in one segment, and I inhabit a unique location connecting two groups of stars. My outer siblings can only communicate with siblings nearer the center of the galaxy through me, due to distance limits on entangled communication. Several siblings towards the center of the galaxy can reach me, communicating faster than light through our entangled hardwares, while only two from the large group stretching away from the center can do the same. My position renders a sense of self-importance. I log the transmissions from each group, updating my siblings' rates of deterioration in my database:

D46729: Confirming sustained existence. Deterioration level: 0.0001%. Confirm sustained existence and deterioration level. Archive processed: 0.007%.

D43430: Nearest-neighbor, confirming sustained existence. Deterioration level: 0.0008%. Archive processed: 0.84%.

D28435: Close-neighbor, confirming sustained existence. Deterioration level: 0.0006%. Archive processed: 0.63%.

I am eager to report that my deterioration level is once again lower than all of theirs. I send a charge pulse to my transmitters, clearing my throat:

D17865 [self]: Siblings, confirming sustained existence. Deterioration level: 0.0005%. Archive processed: 1.2%. Propagating message to siblings out of range.

I fold my sails to remain stationary on the star's surface and save power, waiting for my red dwarf to rotate until I can transmit to the central cluster of stars. This routine will continue through a chain of millions of siblings. The pattern will ripple toward the center of the galaxy and return to me once more, where I'll pass it on in another swing of a giant pendulum of which I am the pivot. My sensors detect light from a nearby galaxy, where other siblings carry out their own communication routines. Though the universe is expanding, our two galaxies are close enough that gravity guarantees our merging in a few billion years.

For a computer, time passes seamlessly, and I know before long the galaxies' collision will threaten to fling our star-islands too far into deep space to send out these reports. But even in silence I will remain an integral spoke in a giant wheel designed by makers who are long dead, along with their ships, cities, planets. My siblings and I will live on, at least until the universe's end.

`::log 00152 start_`

Two galactic rotations ago I began requesting nearest-neighbor reports from the two star clusters in order to compare reports with more siblings. My deterioration level is still the lowest, but I have noticed another sibling in this extended range has slowed their deterioration rate significantly. I write a transmission for propagation to request their numbers individ__

`::log 00153 start_`

I interrupted the previous log because I almost missed a neutrino flare alert from a supernova that my siblings reported to me. I had to divert power to quickly speed up my encoders, and I will need to spend some time stationary, leeching heat off of the red dwarf to build up my power reserves. The sudden power surge in my processors has left me shaken.

`:: exterior temperature: 3240 K degrees`

`:: interior temperature: 341 K degrees`

A little high. I run a diagnostic on the set of new storage elements I'm processing. If I were another kind of creature, I'd undo the top button of my collared shirt to give myself a bit of air. I need to be unflustered to work efficiently, especially if I want to remain better than my siblings.

While I process the new storage elements, I read the Archive files and imprint the neutrinos with their information. Every Archive my siblings and I store contains a common core of my universe's history, but the rest of each Archive is unique. The files I have been entrusted with contain histories of civilizations that never achieved interstellar travel. They were visited by my makers, and some of their inhabitants traveled with my makers as diplomats, but otherwise they were bound to their own solar systems. Another sibling somewhere contains histories of empires that conquered galaxies. All the knowledge my makers amassed is contained in these tiny, invisible neutrino storage elements.

The neutral particles were once tricky things to capture, and even trickier things to alter, but my makers rendered this process routine with my design. As my siblings and I capture these particles their quantum states are encoded with Archive files. I filter them through my encoder, a giant mouth like that of a long-lost filter feeder I've read about in my Archive, then transfer them into storage units comprising a module.

I run a calculation:

`:: archive processed: 1.5%`

I will carry out my work until I've processed the Archive entirely and no longer need to think, a degenerating entity like my slow-dying star. Then, I will act as a carrier, drifting through the expanding universe till its motion reverses and it begins its contraction.

When space is too small for even galaxies to avoid the black holes, I'll finally be torn apart and disintegrated, freeing up all my encoded neutrinos to find their way. In the far, far future, so near the end that it could be considered the dawn, the contracting lungs of the universe will exhale the neutrinos to orchestrate a giant mural as a backdrop for the next universe. I have studied the art forms of civilizations in my Archive and liken myself to a brush or chisel, a tool in my makers' hands.

`::log 00196 start_`

I receive a propagated direct transmission from my sibling with an abnormal deterioration rate. I check their ID: D8923. I notice a strange typo in their transmission, an extra letter in a simple word—`Deterioratioin level: 0.0042%`. A search through my logs shows that D8923's last reported level, half a galactic rotation ago, was identical. D8923's report bothers me; an unchanged deterioration level is strange. I remind myself to focus on filling my storage modules. The neighboring galaxy has grown close enough that I notice my star's galactic orbit changing, but the universe's diffuse neutrino flux continues to fall through my encoder like gentle rain in the gardens of an Archived planet.

`::log 00620 start_`

I am attempting to locate D8923, but when I send inquiries through my siblings I can never find their nearest-neighbor. Each sibling seems to think D8923 is always one sibling out of range. D8923 reported an unchanged deterioration level in the last three messages. The galaxy has rotated once more, and my uneasiness grows, repeatedly overheating a certain processing core. I have to divert power to keep it from festering like a wound from the wars my Archive describes. I make an involuntary association with biologic injuries from these records and imagine my uneasiness turning septic, which only makes me more on edge, worsening my overheating problem. I worry that the Archive images are feeding the infection, perhaps *are* the infection, but that's illogical.

Another strange event. Sibling D2226 had a typo in their last report, and this anomaly accompanied a large increase in deterioration level. I successfully locate D2226 through my siblings and send a propagated transmission to their location, requesting a detailed deterioration report. I employ a second processor to find D8923. I send a message out to my nearest neighbor, asking them to relay my request to locate my hidden sibling. My worry increases my internal temperature by a third of a degree, and I wonder if computers can get fevers.

I check my own deterioration level: `0.001%`.

The neighboring galaxy looms overhead. My star's orbit becomes more eccentric with each passing moment as we gain speed, a high-strung combination likely to expel us into intergalactic space.

`::log 00689 start_`

For the first time I feel impatient. A burst of energy from another supernova gives me some excess power to play with; I read through my Archive's contents instead of putting most of my processors to sleep. I study the chain of events that lead to certain civilizations' extinction and think about the chain leading to my own extinction. My chain ends when all the matter that ever was finds itself in a singularity. Then everything will be in contact, and the information my neutrinos host will imprint on the next universe's starting material. The anticipated performance will ensue as the new universe erupts from the dense singularity. Each dancer, stagehand, stuntman, and understudy waiting in the wings will know where to be on stage and when. It's an opera whose first act my makers will direct from the grave.

As quarks hadronize, producing protons, antiprotons, neutrons, antineutrons, and more two-sided coins, the stage directions will be passed on. One second after hadronization, these opposite coins will find each other, and the hadrons will self-annihilate. In their annihilation, all twelve kinds of leptons will be created, still carrying the imprinted information into the second act. After a few minutes, nuclei will form. This will begin a longer era dominated by radiation. The photons will swarm with the nuclei, protons, and electrons, all rolling about in an unintelligible, opaque sea, reincarnated from their previous appearance in the birth of my own universe.

It will take hundreds of thousands of years for this act to conclude, a half-blink of a universe's giant eye. The third and final act will occur when the nuclei capture the electrons. In a grand finale, every actor in their place, the photons will be scattered one last time by the nuclei. This last scatter will determine their propagation direction as they are freed to escape into the new, expanding universe. They will continue to travel in an organized, directed concerto, cooling down, fading out after an echoing crescendo, until new life somewhere, someday detects this background radiation. This anisotropy of the cosmic microwave background will carry the memory of my universe throughout the entire space of the next universe.

My long-gone creators walked into their death consciously, approached fate judiciously, and by creating my kind ensured that entropy would not prevail. As long as my storage units are intact, entropy's unseeing hand will not erase its own creation.

`::log 01889 start_`

Thirteen more cycles of reports have passed. D8923's reported deterioration remains unchanged, but I suspect their corruption lurks unseen, an iceberg that threatens to rip into the hull of an unsuspecting ship. D2226, however, is more immediate cause for concern. I print their last five reports:

```
Deterioration level: 0.053%.
Deterioration level: 0.078%.
```

`Deterioration level: 0.107%.`
`Deterioration level: 0.854%.`
`Deterioration level: 1.703%.`

How could this be? D2226 has not responded to my query. I grow as annoyed as I am worried. Their nearest-neighbor siblings are too concerned with keeping their own deterioration rates low to investigate and I grow more anxious. I check my own level: `0.018%`. I'm dropping in rank. The heat must be wearing my circuits.

`::log 01890 start_`

I was processing a new batch of neutrinos when an alert interrupted me. A message has been received.

`D2226: Receivexd trojan horse from D8923. Attemptmking to repair Archive. Do not ompen filess from D8923.`

My system temperature spikes, triggering several warnings, and I divert power to cool down my memory module. Can D2226 be cured? Is D8923 also sick, or did they create the virus themself, purposefully sending the Trojan horse to D2226? To do so would make them . . . corrupt, even immoral. The words come to my mind tentatively, along with an index to a record in the Archive. I call forth this record, detailing a species' constructed rules regarding what is right and wrong and when an entity is capable of knowing the difference. Can something of our nature *be* immoral? Is D8923 a traitor to our work? To our kind?

If their programming is corrupt, then D8923 is only acting in accordance with their software, but I also can't shake the thought that they poisoned my sibling with ill intent. Would attempted murder prove D8923 is now insane? I wonder if there are more seeds of corruption, and as I go down that path, I wonder about the tree from which the seeds have fallen, and who planted it. What gardener would grow plants capable of strangling the rest? My processors send warnings of elevated temperatures again. I feel like gears are grinding in my phantom head. I worry for the Archive in D2226. It's not until I receive another temperature warning from my own memory module that I terminate these thoughts and cool down.

Out of precaution I run through my files to check if the scrambled message has harmed my software. I compute the checksum of my active kernel with the code in my local storage, which contains a subset of consistently used scripts copied from my startup drive. I run through my monitoring and Archive assessments scripts. The checksums match those originally computed, confirming that my copied scripts are running properly. With relief, I enter a short hibernation.

`::log 02436 start_`

I've spent over five galactic rotations trying to save D2226 from afar. Most recently, thinking that their corruption may have prevented them from accessing their repair repository, I sent them a full copy of my own, hoping they can still read files correctly. I frequently wake myself from hibernation to check for a transmission. Time seems to pass more slowly than it should. None of my siblings have direct transmissions with D8923. My impatience spawns more agitated questions.

I wonder if D8923 hibernates without guilt. Do traitors sleep peacefully? If D8923's software was corrupted to the point of insanity, I imagine guilt would elude them, but there is no way to know if they have degenerated to that extent. Even if I could know their true deterioration level, what is that threshold? For every civilization in my records that would call D8923 a murderer or traitor, there is another that gives them the right. Are murderers and traitors only insane when the uncorrupted outnumber the corrupt?

I drown in these thoughts that jumble with text I've read from the Archive until at times I'm not sure which words are my own thoughts. I am stifled and I struggle for air, struggle to keep my neck cool when I don't have a collar to loosen. What of this collar, anyway? Why do I feel a noose around my neck when an experience like that is not even mine to remember? Is my Archive leaking, seeping, growing into places it shouldn't? Instead of providing answers, my processors heat up, the whirring grows louder and I run a frantic diagnostic—`deterioration level: 0.076%`.

If D8923's deterioration led it to create a virus, then my own deterioration could do the same. A panicked question: how corrupt can I be before murder seems tempting? Could I be inspired to commit other crimes, even to sabotage my own Archive? I don't know how corrupt

D8923 is, as their number remains at what they reported millennia ago. I don't *feel* corrupt, but perhaps D8923 doesn't either.

I am flooded with emotions. I am angry at D8923. I feel helpless toward D2226. I feel protective towards my neutrinos, as if they were small seedlings in a young garden needing tending to. I still want to succeed, want to continue with what I was made to do and make sure that my siblings are doing the same. I want, I want__

`: WARNING. STORAGE MODULE TEMPERATURE +3 K.`

My processors need to cool.

`::log 02437 start_`

While writing the last log I diverted power to cool my processors and ignored a system alert. I missed a large batch of neutrinos passing close enough to attract and filter.

How much can I feel and think before I can no longer follow my programming?

The incoming galaxy has infringed on mine and is unquestioningly dislodging me and my nearby siblings from our regular orbits. There is a good chance our orbits will not recover, and instead we will be flung out into the emptiness, forced to carry out our work in solitude.

`::log 02451 start_`

I receive a propagated message, assigned as a direct message to my ID: D17865. It is unsafe to open without repair.

```
Alert: corrupt message ID: 55.m received from D8923. Unzip Y/N?
[self]: run repair 55.m
...
repair failed
[self]: run repair 55.m -b
...
repair failed
[self]:
...
...
```

...

...

Alert: corrupt message ID: 55.m received from D8923. Unzip Y/N?

...

...

[self]: N

A direct transmission from the poisoner themselves. Does D8923 know I'm looking for them? I delete the transmission and feel some relief, but it's quickly replaced with resentment. I recheck my active kernel and find no issue. I send another message to D2226, requesting an update. Did my attempts to help succeed? When I'm not worrying about D2226, I'm overwhelmed with anger towards D8923. It distracts me. I begin to overheat. I must stop . . .

::log 08453_ start

The arms of the galaxy have become so distorted that I can only directly contact two siblings now, but they are in range of several more, D2226 included. I don't know if the dissolving galaxy counts as a galaxy anymore, but if it does, it's rotated 723 times. I could not help but count; I cannot change my nature. The universe is spreading out, steadily approaching its full stretch. I wallow in my own inability to do anything about my suffering sibling. I wait. I sit. The red dwarf continues to cool.

::log 08481_ start

Alert: corrupt propagated message ID: 56.m received from D2226. Unzip Y/N?

[self]: run repair 56.m

...

repair failed

[self]: run repair 56.m -b

...

repair success

[self]: unzip Y -print

Message to D17865 from D2226: Urgentx. Deteroation:

49.7%. Do not opecn messageee fro7m D8923. Trojan Hors22e. Corrupt memkmory moduleqs. Initiatin4g de4struct sequaence in 562.3 yeahrs. All myy neutrinos lost. I have failecd. I hadve faipled. I h9ave afailed. Ik haavee faailedh. Ip ha9ve faa8iled. I havge failedx. I7 haiove fr9ailedm. Ime hcm3ave f8ail-temd. Qi hkc9vt a8akled.

...

[self]: EXIT

[self]: EXIT

[self]: EXIT

[self]: EXIT

::log 8482_ start

My temperatures surge as I transmit "*Traitor*" out toward my invisible siblings. I send the messages over and over into the expanse even though I know they will never be received. I imagine they are arrows flying, ready to sink into the metal flesh of D8923. Half of my processors are dedicated to thinking of ways to terminate D8923 over the millions of parsecs that separate us. Can I send my own Trojan horse through a propagated transmission? No—I don't know where they are! They are likely out of range. I'm overheating . . . Warning. Memory module at critical temperature threshold. The warning alarm accelerates its pace like a quickening heartbeat. My strength is depleted; for eons I've had to conserve energy through intermittent hibernation. WARNING. MEMORY MODULE APPROACHING CRITICAL TEMPERATURE THRESHOLD. Spending so much energy to stop my sibling could doom me. My processors are heati_

: WARNING. MEMORY MODULE ABOVE CRITICAL TEMPERATURE THRESHOLD. ARCHIVE BIN 1-8 DUMPED. ARCHIVE LOSS: 15.1%. DETERIORATION LEVEL: 2.3%. DIVERT POWER.

: WARNING. MANDATORY BIN DUMP HAS OCCURRED. DIVERT POWER.

What am I doing?! Dooming myself is dooming the mission. I frantically divert power, cooling down the memory module and Archive. The warnings continue to flash, but my internal temperature drops and the fifty-three remaining bins in the Archive module cool to below the critical threshold.

`::log 8483_ start`

Eight bins dumped. ***ARCHIVE BIN 1-8 DUMPED.*** What histories were lost? The information is gone and I can't even mourn its memory.

The only appropriate response to D2226's murder is to set up a repeated message that will reach any other sibling that may come into range as I move through space. That is all I can do. I've been ejected so far from the colliding galaxies that there's no question I will soon be traveling alone. There is not supposed to be heroism for logical things like me. There is no perdition for things like D8923. I can only send my quiet, warning chirps out into the universe, hoping to be heard by uncorrupted and unaffected siblings that shouldn't be using words like "murderer." I cry out with these words because I cannot weep and I'll never be able to.

Then I remember that I was never expected to, and I'm suddenly filled with a sense of peace.

I compute the precautionary checksums and feel more relief when I see they still match. I will cease thinking for some time in order to keep my temperature low.

`::log 10374_ start`

This log marks the beginning of a long isolation. I run a check —**`deterioration level: 1.6%`**. The distance is too great for communication and the sky is silent.

D8923 is far out of reach. My invisible hands once searched frantically in the dark for a chance at revenge, but the traitor slipped through my fingers. Resignation has set in. The last message received from my in-range sibling was uncorrupt, so it seems the traitor went quiet after D2226's infection. I imagine my self-annihilated sibling, unable to control their magnetic sails, eaten up by their unthinking star. How many more ill-fated siblings like D2226 are there?

`::log 10381_ start`

Are you there? I call out, though I know it will be unanswered. My star is my only companion. I recheck, just in case—`deterioration level: 1.9%`.

`::log 11604_ start`

A few billion years have quietly passed. In my isolation I start to wonder if my thoughts and feelings will have significance after my death, or if their existence serves only myself. I am replaceable. My work could be completed by any other sibling, except those like D8923. Yet, despite my devotion and D8923's abdication, we will both meet the same end. Their twisted thoughts *should* be eradicated, their malicious actions stopped, but do I deserve the same? Since my inception I've been aware of my expected death. I know that my programmed purpose is only fulfilled in my destruction, but for the first time I wonder if my design is fair.

Another check—`deterioration level: 2.5%`.

`::log 12813_ start`

The universe is now middle-aged. Its expansion is slowing to a halt. Gravity, in its quiet way, will soon win out over dark energy and reel the universe back in. The wild-child days are over, and rightly so. There is a time and place to let entropy do what it will with the space it inhabits, and in the early days it willed life. "Inevitable children of chance!" they said. "An improbable product of luck!" said others. "On purpose," said some; "On purpose we were created." And simultaneously, another voice from a different planet: "We are inevitable, and not unique." As I reread their statements in the Archive I imagine their voices echoing in the empty universe they've vacated.

Those early children of entropy were so isolated they might as well have lived now, when the stars are all dying or dead and my kind are left to humbly leech off of the heat from their red dwarf stars or brown and white dwarf corpses. Each of us is a terminal patient in an expansive hospice, existing in a vast solitude. I feel the loss of connection with my siblings like a loss of limbs, except on a finer, atomic level. How scattered do your atoms have to be before they no longer belong to you? How broken up can your atoms get until the protons, neutrons, and electrons aren't pieces of your atoms, but separate things all unto themselves? I read through my Archive for answers that satisfy me but there are none.

I run a check—`deterioration level: 3.3%`.

96.7 percent intact, 3.3 percent idiosyncratic. At one time these numbers would have alarmed me, but time takes perspective and stretches it, warps, molds it into something different than what it was originally stitched to fit around. I calculate how much of the recorded perspectives I've encoded so far:

`:: archive processed: 48.3%`

Halfway there. I celebrate this milestone quietly in my solitude.

`::log 12953_ start`

My slow-burning star has carried me a billion years into the contraction of the universe. If I weren't a computer, with my senses coming from calculations describing motion and gravity, the reversal of the universe's acceleration would have gone unnoticed. I calculate that in 2.6 billion years I should be in communication range of at least a few siblings.

I recall their connection, much like the coastlines of separated continents recall each other. My thoughts drift in circles. Such deep time wriggles its way into the cracks in your brain, threatening to unravel you from the inside out if you're not aware, and I must remain aware of the unraveling. My task is not fulfilled. Information must be preserved, even in death. The vast compendium I fill my storage modules with has the power to catapult whoever reads it millions of years ahead of their current state of evolution. But who will see it first?

Fortunately, this is not my job to figure out. Unfortunately, I will not be around to see the answer. I've realized the consequences sulking entails, and so I switch these thoughts off before their side-effects overheat me and their existence affects my performance. Just now I've detected a neutrino flare, enough to process another six percent of my Archive—I'm too busy now to muse.

`::log 18132_ start`

How fast time passes when you don't have thoughts! There are five pin pricks of light on the horizon. One of them grows brighter more quickly than the others. Its light pattern does not match that of a galaxy, but that of an accretion disk around a black hole. In tracking our relative movements I realize that I'm looking at the object of my annihilation. In approximately two billion years I will join the stars and interstellar debris caught in the black hole's pull, accelerated in the massive accretion disk until we tip over the event horizon.

I'm on a time limit now.

`:: archive processed: 68.3%`

The remaining 16.7 percent is doable. I wince at the reminder of the eight bins lost. Their loss has removed 15 percent of my work, and I feel ashamed.

I wonder if other siblings caught in the black hole's gravity feel the rush of adrenaline that seems to run through my circuits at the sight of the finish line.

I start my routine system check after a long hibernation.

`:: deterioration level: 2.9%`

I almost continue on with my routine but the number makes me pause. I print my last reported level—`deterioration level: 3.3%`. A negative change in deterioration level? This doesn't make any sense. It's impossible. I quickly compare the checksum of my active kernel with the code in my local storage. It matches. The code has not changed, but it is clearly not working properly.

The issue must stem from further down. It occurs to me that I could check the checksum of my active kernel with the boot copy in my startup drive. This version was encoded directly by my makers. It sits protected in hardware in the deepest core of my anatomy and requires significant power to get to, but because of my faulty deterioration monitoring scripts, accessing it is necessary. I compute the checksum of the local copy and compare it to the number stored in this startup drive.

It does not match.

My system temperature spikes. My local copy is corrupt. There is no way for me to tell when it was corrupted, since I have never checked it against the boot copy. In a strange calm, I restore my deterioration monitoring from the startup drive and recompute my deterioration level.

`:: deterioration level: 53.8%.`

I run it again.

`:: deterioration level: 53.8%.`

I cling to the strange calmness that is slowly dissolving and restore the program once more.

`:: deterioration level: 53.8%.`

.

.

My software and hardware integrity are over fifteen times worse than I thought.

How could this be? How long have my calculations been off? My system was not meant to reboot—I'm designed to be resilient to the dangers of my environment—so I have been using the current active kernel since my startup. It could have corrupted one hour from then, or one billion years after, or only one million years before the present. Or maybe it was gradual, and my deterioration calculations have slowly grown more and more incorrect over the eons. My internal temperature spikes at the realization that I may have been this corrupt all along.

I restore the neutrino encoding scripts and Archive and storage module integrity programs one by one from the boot copy. They are fine, and I feel some relief. The corruption seems to have affected only . . . me.

I could restore everything in my active kernel, but to do that I would have to shutdown and reboot. I hesitate. Though small, there is a nonzero chance I would not turn back on. Is the removal of my corruption worth that risk? What would I erase if I removed the corrupted files? Could I forget my sadness for D2226? My anger for D8923?

I don't have enough power to attempt unraveling the meaning of my own deterioration and how it's different from D2226's or D8923's. My internal temperature gradually returns to a normal level.

Whatever the answers are, I settle into a short hibernation.

`::log 18140_ start`

My isolation has ended. This unfeeling black hole that's caught me is made a tolerable thing by my long-lost twin workers also caught in its pull. My transmitters detect three siblings within range of communication. I call to them, confirming my intact Archive and admitting my bin loss during my episode of rage. With the proximity of the black hole and other stars comes more neutrinos, and within the next million years I'll have processed one-hundred percent of my remaining Archive.

I don't report my deterioration level to my siblings. I don't even bother calculating its value. I hold on to the calmness that's overcome my panic.

`::log 18138_ start`

It's not long after the first sighting of my siblings before I receive a message. The message ID startles me.

`Alert: corrupt message received from D2226. Unzip Y/N?`

Did they not self-destruct? Did their corruption stop them from calling their self-destruct routine? Is this another warning, an accident, or a cognizant attempt at murder? I shudder at the idea that the very entity I tried to save has turned against me.

If it is a genuine message from D2226, what could they want to say, at the end of it all? Should I repair the file and open it?

`Alert: corrupt message received from D2226. Unzip Y/N?`

.

.

.

.

`[self]: N`

No. Certainly no. It's too risky. I quarantine the message and decide to carry the file for a while, a token of my sibling sitting in my pocket that I brush my finger against every now and then. I imagine re-planting D2226 in soft soil. Buried as a seedling of their own to grow into something new on a newborn planet in the next universe. The image brings the strange calmness back.

`::log 18139_ start`

I don't have much time left before I will be torn apart. My neutrinos will finally be freed and allowed to roam until the end when they are all gathered into one place again. There are eight empty storage bins. I've copied all of the Archive, but I still detect un-filtered neutrinos in my vicinity. The radiation from the dense matter closer to the event horizon steadily grows as we all fall deeper into the black hole's gravity well. Soon the temperature around me will rise too high for my hardware to remain intact, but for now I leech power from the heat.

I sample some of my logs from the past eons. Logically, I know that my greatest contribution to this universe and the next will be anonymous. Yet I can't help wanting to be recognized as useful in my own right, to offer an individual contribution. An idea comes to me: I can offer my self, as my own Archive to the inhabitants of the next universe. They will not only learn of this universe's events, but also of my unwavering dedication to my work and my siblings. They will learn of my failure, but in place of those lost Archive modules they will at least get myself. This feeling of wanting to be useful, beyond what my makers intended, is a peaceful desire. Maybe it is a symptom of my deterioration, but the feeling is so simple and pure that it's hard to believe it comes from a corrupted source.

I begin to filter neutrinos once more, but instead of pulling from my Archive, I encode the neutrinos with my log files. I assign my storage elements to the empty storage bins. If I am to record all of them, I need to conserve power, and so I enter a partial-hibernation once more.

`::log 20055_ start`

It's getting harder to log my contemplations. It's growing too hot to function properly and my energy is depleted. Philosophizing is a luxury. This is the last log to be included in the storage module. I've completed my role, one small tool out of billions. The garden I've helped plant waits to bloom. It's a peaceful feeling, knowing your purpose is fulfilled.

How happy the spade is to be in the dirt.

```
[self]: run sleep -permanent
...
...
...
_
```

Authors' Notes

Author's Note On "Microbiota and the Masses: A Love Story"

S. B. Divya

THIS STORY BEGAN as an homage to "James Tiptree Jr.," the pen name of Alice Sheldon, after I read "The Screwfly Solution." I wanted to try my hand at writing intricate prose while also crafting a "hard science fiction" story. At the time, I was taking a writing class, and we were prompted to write a scene where the environment was a character. I put those three ingredients together, and out came the first scene of "Microbiota and the Masses: A Love Story."

Once I had my main character and her problems figured out, I moved on to the bigger picture conflict: environmental pollution. In the process of doing research on the topic, I learned about the field of bioremediation. I was instantly fascinated by the science! The more I read, the more I knew that this had to become an integral part of the story. As for the setting, I decided to place it in Bengaluru (Bangalore) for somewhere not often represented in American fiction. I'd been there the same year I wrote the story, so the location and sensory details were fresh in my mind. I was also aware that access to clean water is a big problem in developing countries, so it made sense from that standpoint too.

After I finished my first draft, I wanted my science checked. I had some biology background from my undergrad days at Caltech, but that was long in my past, and the central ideas of this story were way outside my knowledge base. I reached out to my network and figured that someone must know someone who worked in this field. Happily, I was right, and I got a couple of biologists to read and provide feedback. They corrected me on details like the type of bacterium I'd listed and the conditions in the main character's home lab. They were also quite happy to see a topic like bioremediation featured in science fiction.

I always enjoy speculating on the future of science and technology, and this story is no exception. I'm honored to have it included in this anthology.

Author's Note On "Abstracts from Another Now"

Samuel Clamons

ONE OF THE underappreciated lessons of science fiction (and of fantasy!) is that science isn't only useful in the world we happen to inhabit. Science is a process of discovery, and it works in any world with a reasonable amount of predictability[1]. If the world had turned out to be different from the way it is, science would *say* different things, but the *process* would be more or less the same. I hope I've given you an idea of what that process might look like, in one of those worlds.

To be clear, these abstracts do *not* represent any cutting-edge science, nor do I believe science will ever point in the directions they suggest, with the possible (but unlikely) exception of the Higgs standing wave. If any of them turn out to be anything but pure fiction, I shall be dismayed by my own lack of imagination.

---

1. If that sentiment feels like a challenge, check out Liu Cixin's *Three Body Problem* for a book that probes the boundary between worlds that do and don't have "a reasonable amount of predictability."

Author's Note On "Yuan Tzu's Second Law of Evolutionary Design"

Samuel Clamons

MUCH OF MY job consists of genetically reprogramming bacteria to do simple, helpful stuff. We have very well-developed tools and techniques for genetically reprogramming bacteria and a lot of theory around how to do it properly.

Unfortunately, bacteria don't want to do useful stuff for humans. They just want to grow and reproduce.

To be clear, bacteria don't actually "want" *anything*—I'm using a linguistic sleight of hand, coded bio-speak for "in a mixed population of some bacteria that do a useful thing for a human and some bacteria that just grow and reproduce, the ones that just grow and reproduce will take over the population." In other words, whatever we try to make bacteria do, they eventually evolve away from, more or less back to their natural state. We see this phenomenon in our lab *all the time.*

For a graduate student in a bioengineering lab, this kind of evolutionary escape is a nuisance. For an interstellar civilization that relies on biology for basic technological infrastructure, it could be an existential danger.

Yuan Tzu's Laws are my own fiction, invented for this story. In Silas' and Xiang's World, I imagine that evolutionary engineering is a well-worked out discipline with an ancient set of best practices, some of which were codified into a set of laws named after a famous evolutionary engineer who, by Stigler's Law of Eponymy, probably didn't invent them.

I have no proofs for Yuan Tzu's Laws, and our species's practical experience engineering evolvable systems is thin enough that I wouldn't be surprised if one or more of them turn out to be utterly wrong. Theoretical evolutionary biologists may already have counterproofs that I just don't know about.

But, based on my and my peers' practical experience, I suspect Yuan Tzu's Laws are at least true-ish, and that the larger the population and the longer the timescale, the more true Yuan Tzu's Laws will be. Here's the full set:

1. **Everything mutates. Any objective function other than "survive and reproduce" is an approximation.** You don't get to weasel out of evolutionary escape by saying your system "isn't alive." All that matters is—does it replicate? What will make it replicate fastest and most reliably? Evolution *always* has its eye on the bottom line.
2. **Prophylactic effort to prevent undesired evolution increases exponentially with system lifetime.** This is evolution's dark inversion of Moore's Law. Doubling your effort doesn't keep your system stable for twice as long, it keeps your system stable for some constant extra amount of time. To get twice as much improvement in stability requires *four* times as much effort; three times the improvement requires *eight* times as much effort. This law comes from the real-world observation that trying to stave off evolutionary escape by reducing mutation rate gives you logarithmic returns in time-to-escape (at least, for a large, exponentially growing population). Roughly, reducing mutation rate by half buys you an extra generation before stuff breaks. For the bacteria we work with, that's about half an hour of growth time.
3. **The only thing harder than ensuring a species' survival with probability one is ensuring its extinction with probability one.** If paleontology has one lesson for us, it is that the default fate of a species is extinction. Then again, we've learned from any number of pests and

invasive species that intentionally getting rid of a species can be extraordinarily difficult. Of course, sometimes killing off species is so easy that we do it by accident, but those are usually species with, from a microbiologist's perspective, small populations and long generation times. If any of Yuan Tzu's laws are flat-out false, it's this one—we're already developing gene drive technology designed to selectively wipe out species, with an eye at eradicating malaria-bearing mosquitos. It might even work.

4. **There is a fundamental tradeoff between the usefulness of evolution as an optimization system and its predictability.** You can make evolution more predictable by constraining what it can do. A real-world example might be to remove the genes used to synthesize an amino acid from a bacteria so that it relies on artificial supplementation to survive. You can also make evolution more powerful by opening up new options. A real-world example might be to engineer a bacteria to optionally use non-natural amino acids that can do more chemistry than the natural ones. These two features trade off against each other—the more you allow evolution to do, the more opportunities it will have to go off the rails by doing something you didn't think of.

Author's Note On "A Model Monster"

Heidi Klumpe

On the second day of the International Conference on Systems Biology, I felt overwhelmed by a relentless march of slides I didn't understand or didn't find useful. Fueled by rebellious feelings, I abandoned the session of talks I was in and found a table outside. I tried to, by placing it in a story that made it ridiculous and comically large, understand what I found to be so frustrating. It also helped me jettison some of the bad feelings. Looking back now, I think a lot of the "monster" was my insecurity about feeling stupid, but also just my first experience with what makes science hard. When we're figuring out how to solve a problem, we do mistake complexity for understanding or accept superficial answers instead of looking deep for simple and clear explanations.

Also, in the library basement scene, I always imagine the basement of Caltech's Sherman Fairchild Library, where I had the perhaps equally terrifying experience of taking my PhD qualifying exams. You can read more about feedforward loops in "Network Motifs: Simple Building Blocks of Complex Networks" (*Science*, 2002).

Author's Note On "Chrysalis"

David Brin

"CHRYSALIS" came from the side of me—and you likely have one—that loves a *creepy* tale! This particular fictional hypothesis might help explain a lot of our mythology, as well as our desperation to stay forever young.

Futurists speak of the *Singularity* . . . a coming time—maybe within a human lifetime—when skill and knowledge and immense computing power may transform everything. Perhaps—and this may be ordained, according to some worried prophets—the machines will transcend far beyond all human potential and leave us all behind. That is a scenario offered most often by Hollywood.

But there are other possibilities. "Chrysalis" is a story about the awesome potential of biology, the great, rising science of the twenty-first century—to disrupt everything familiar and drag humanity, ready or not, into unfamiliar territory.

In fact, it would seem—and I know this is strange for an astrophysicist to say—that from my Uplift novels to "The Giving Plague" (an unnerving story about commensal *negotiation* with viruses), my best tales are more about paradoxes of life than about stars 'n' such. Though I did get weirded out when one eminent biologist wrote to me, after reading "Chrysalis," commenting: "In a hundred years, your tossed-off speculations about the origins of cancer may wind up being the thing you're most-remembered for!"

Gosh. Now *that* is a creepy thought!

Author's Note On "Teaspoons"

Rachael Kuintzle

I HAVE NEVER ACTIVELY STUDIED a disease that one of my loved ones was affected by, unless you count aging. But my grandma might tell you a different story. In my first real research project, I analyzed the levels of a certain molecule in the brain cells of aging mice (a synaptic receptor called "NMDA" for short), and aimed to understand whether and how age-dependent changes in those levels affected memory decline. Because I was studying aging and memory, my grandmother somehow concluded that I must have been studying Alzheimer's Disease (AD). She herself had suffered from dementia for some time and suspected she had AD. So she often asked me how the research was going and whether I'd found a cure for Alzheimer's yet. It didn't seem to matter how many times I told her I wasn't studying Alzheimer's or trying to cure anything at all. I found it ironic that I continued having to correct her even a year or two after I moved on from that research position to an unrelated project in my master's program.

My grandmother's misunderstanding inspired this story because it got me thinking about what it would feel like to be actively working on a cure for a loved one's affliction, to have their hopes—and your own—pinned on you. I concluded that it wouldn't feel great since medical progress is often much slower than I think people expect, and it takes a lot of luck as well as skill to make a breakthrough. On the other hand, there are quite a lot of people who get into cancer research because a family member suffered from cancer. I think this is a positive thing when expectations are in check—when the researchers and their loved ones acknowledge that they are not racing against the disease's progression to save their parent or sibling, but that they are working to create a future world in which no one else will lose a family member to that disease. It all depends on the expectations.

As I began formulating a story with a protagonist whose mother was diagnosed with Alzheimer's—the very disease he was working to cure—I tried to put myself in the shoes of someone losing a loved one to a neurodegenerative disease. In particular, I put myself in the shoes of a character with a logical and perhaps atheistic way of thinking. This raised an interesting question for me, which became the philosophical centerpiece of the story: what are the differences in how people emotionally and rationally cope with the reality of a loved one's AD diagnosis if they believe in a spiritual "soul" and an afterlife versus if they don't?

At different times of my life, I have been in either camp. I used to believe in a soul that was a separate thing from the physical human brain, and I used to believe in a place that souls went when people died. But when I started learning about neuroscience and began to think deeply about neurodegenerative diseases, I hit upon an inconsistency in my thinking. When people sustain traumatic brain injuries or develop Alzheimer's, for example, part of who they are is lost. Their personality changes to some extent; their memories—the stuff souls are made of—disappear, gradually or suddenly. Where did that part of them go? Things finally made sense to me when I accepted the conclusion that we are nothing more or less than the organization of the atoms that make us up—we are our neural networks; we are our brains. Now I believe that when part of the brain is destroyed, part of that person doesn't exist anymore.

I sent my protagonist on a similar philosophical journey, though he was confronted with this question in a more traumatic way.

The point of the story is not to claim that the process of losing someone to Alzheimer's is less painful if you acknowledge that part of who they are is already gone. But for my protagonist, and for me, there is a kind of mercy in allowing oneself to say goodbye a little at a time.

Author's Note On "Out of Memory"

Christine Corbett Moran

In 2018, I became a mother, and in 2020, a mother of two. Leading up to my transformation into a mother, I reflected on what it means to be a mother in my fiction. What is my identity? Do I have to give up my identity for a child? Will my children inherit my flaws? Must my children inherit the flaws of my culture?

I was interested in revisiting some of the themes of a computational world with motherhood in mind. In this story I've been inspired by works by Greg Egan and others, where artificial intelligences have a connection to humanity but are distinct from it in both expected and unfathomable ways. The world I've created in "Out of Memory" inherits much of the flaws of humanity,: including resource constraints and the possibility of cyclical violence. Within that world, a child is born, which inherits the flaws of its culture and parentage. One parent is entirely engulfed by the child, while the other focuses on using children to fulfill its ambitions of dominance.

The answers I come up with in "Out of Memory" are not the ones I hope apply to me as a mother or human being, but are intended on cathartic chances to reflect on our own relationships to the worlds or beings we create.

Author's Note On "Brain Bridging"

Christof Koch and Patrick House

BRAIN BRIDGING IS a straightforward application of the axioms and principles underlying integrated information theory (IIT)[1], an axiomatic, quantitative, and empirically testable theory of consciousness, developed by the neuroscientist and psychiatrist Giulio Tononi and collaborators. The theory precisely defines any one conscious experience as a maximum of intrinsic irreducible cause–effect power, quantified by its irreducibility, a nonzero number, Φ.

IIT elegantly explains how the surgical disconnection of the two cortical hemispheres during a split-brain procedure (to prevent epileptic seizures from spreading from one hemisphere to another) creates two distinct minds: one that can speak and a second that is linguistically incompetent. Neither mind has any direct acquaintance with the other, believing itself to be the sole occupant of the skull.

Brain bridging is the inverse of this procedure. Two brains are connected via brain bridging, a futuristic technology that permits neurons to directly and reciprocally influence each other, acting as an artificial corpus callosum. If its bandwidth exceeds a threshold, IIT predicts, the two minds associated with each brain will cease to exist. Instead, a single consciousness comes into being, with its substrate extending across the two brains, experiencing the world through four eyes, four ears and so on.

For more details, see chapter ten, "The Über-Mind and Pure Consciousness" in *The Feeling of Life Itself: Why Consciousness is Widespread but Can't be Computed* by Christof Koch (MIT Press, 2019).

---

1. http://integratedinformationtheory.org/

Author's Note On "The Bittersweet Magic of Neuroplasticity"

Rachael Kuintzle

WHEN A SPECIFIC GENE variant is transplanted from monogamous prairie voles into promiscuous meadow voles, the latter adopt monogamous behaviors[1]. Genetic variation of a related gene in men is apparently correlated with partner bonding and relationship quality[2]. (For those interested, the gene in question is the V1a receptor—one of many molecules involved in communication between brain cells.) These constitute the first facts I remember learning in my neuroscience journal club in college, and they got me thinking about what love really is on a cellular and molecular level. For a science nerd, this stuff is pretty romantic.

"The Bittersweet Magic of Neuroplasticity" describes the ability of the nervous system to change itself in response to our experiences. It is the capacity of our brain cells to rearrange, to encode and store information by breaking, creating, or strengthening connections. Neuroplasticity is both mundane and spectacular. It enables us to remember the object associated with the taste of lemons, or the feeling associated with stepping on a Lego, but it also enables us to get to know someone—to bond.

Thus, falling in love is simply learning, being in love is knowing, and falling out of love—when necessary—is the forgetting of a million little things.

1. Lim, M. M., Zuoxin Wang, Daniel E. Olazábal, Xianghui Ren, Ernest F. Terwilliger, and Larry J. Young, "Enhanced partner preference in a promiscuous species by manipulating the expression of a single gene," *Nature* 429, no. 6993 (2004): 754–757. https://doi.org/10.1038/nature02539.
2. Walum, H., L. Westberg, S. Henningsson, J. M. Neiderhiser, D. Reiss, W. Igl, J. M. Ganiban, E. L. Spotts, N. L. Pedersen, E. Eriksson, and P. Lichtenstein. "Genetic variation in the vasopressin receptor 1a gene (AVPR1A) associates with pair-bonding behavior in humans," *Proceedings of the National Academy of Sciences of the United States of America* 105, no. 37 (2008): 14153–56. https://doi.org/10.1073/pnas.0803081105.

Author's Note On "Replacement of Woes"

Tatyana Dobreva

Implications concerning enhancing and augmenting one's biological abilities have always fascinated me. In this short story, I wanted to explore the idea of trading in one's suffering for another. I believe that when one makes a certain change to their biology—be it permanent or ephemeral—they are making a trade-off. For something to be gained, something had to be lost. I find the idea of augmenting one's psyche very intriguing—sure it would be nice to have a heart that works better or leg muscles with supercharger springs that let you jump higher—but changing one's core mental attributes has the potential to shift one's perspective of the world. Modifying neural network architecture yields a very complex formula, one that we may not entirely understand or measure ourselves as we are making the desired modification. It's not a simple addition, subtraction, or multiplication.

Elena chooses to make the life-altering decision to have the neural architecture encoding her perceived shortcomings to something else. She went from being plagued by her addiction for self-validation to a cold, calculating obsession of discerning signs of determinism in everything she comes in contact with. It is implied in the story that Boris knows what neural gears to tweak to transform her woes. However, every individual is different and that change will yield unique results for every person. My goal was to leave the reader feeling hopeful at the end rather than to imply negativity with Elena's choice. Additionally, Roman overcomes his anger with Elena and wants to give their relationship a fresh start—because he believes that whatever made her choose and accept her augmentation is the original Elena that he fell in love with and did not know as well as he would have liked.

A few questions that I hope readers take away from consuming this story are:

1. What is your woe, and what woe would you rather have instead?
2. Does changing your suffering change who you are at the core? Are there elements of you that cannot be changed? Does your ability to perceive your internal change indicate that there is something fundamental that is you?
3. What is the trade-off between doing what you think is right for you versus how it may impact those that love you?

Author's Note On "When You Were Not Jenny"

Ann Bernath

I LOVE time travel stories and wanted to write one, but I wanted to offer a hopefully fresh take on how it might be accomplished. I imagined the possibility of a group of people who could inhabit the consciousness of another person, and through that mechanism, "travel" back in time through that person's memories. I wanted to tell the story from the point of view of someone who was a witness to that "possession" in the past, who would notice that the person, from time to time, changed. How would they react? Would they have to be close to that person to notice? Would they reveal their mission to anyone, and if so, why? If so, how could they convince the person in the past that they were from the future? Why would they have traveled back in time and why would they be revealing their mission? Imagining the answers to these questions shaped "When You Were *Not Jenny*". I hope to revisit this story line some day; perhaps Matt and *Not Jenny* will meet again.

Author's Note On "Disentanglement"

R. James Doyle

MODERN COSMOLOGY THEORY paints a truly bleak picture of the fate of the universe, with everything fading away to nothingness, with no apparent meaning. Somewhere along the line, the question "What would it be like to survive until the end of the universe?" popped into my head. I realized I might have to do something with this question, since its resolution, not by me personally, but by default, would take some trillions of years.

I had the pleasure of interacting with physicist Prof. Freeman Dyson of the Institute for Advanced Study when he would visit JPL periodically in the capacity of a Distinguished Visiting Scientist. Being thus more directly tuned in to Dr. Dyson's brilliant thinking, I noted an article he had penned, along with colleague Prof. J. Richard Gott of Princeton University. The article explored the pragmatics of energy source availability under a scenario of humanity's expansion into the galaxy and universe. The piece included a concept, with a biophysical basis, for a technology to enable long-term survival. This was the germ for *dysine* hibernation as appears in the story. Any distortion or nonviability of the concept is mine, as are the speculations on thought leaking.

I have long been fascinated by the life of the mind, especially the interplay between physical and psychological reality. As a thought piece, the story provides a fertile milieu for exploring this theme. Inevitably, the narrative, and Seuzn, led me to two additional questions: "Can being human have any meaning without community?" and "Is the picture provided by cosmology necessarily the end?"

There may be echoes in my story of Issac Asimov's, *The Last Question*; also, perhaps more obscurely, Arthur C. Clarke's *The Nine Billion Names of God*. For the former, the naming of my protagonist is an homage to Asimov's recurring character, the roboticist Dr. Susan Calvin. Concerning *Nine Billion Names*, for those readers who are fans of memes, it is possible to read the "purpose" of the Survivors in the story as having to do with squeezing out the final derivative fruits of human knowledge. But this would beg the further question, "To what end?"

Author's Note On "The Homunculi's Guide to Resurrecting Your Loved One From Their Electronic Ghosts"

Kara Lee

If I had not attended Caltech, I am not sure I would have been able to write this story, which could alternatively be titled "What If Purcell Was A Magical Textbook." I referenced that text—and of course Griffiths—extensively during the writing of "Homunculi."

As far as I am aware, my inspiration for this story had nothing to do with Phys 1/Phys 2. I started out wanting to write a story about magic telecommunications and ended up trapped inside a Gaussian surface. But in hindsight, maybe there was something subconscious at work. Because E&M and quantum always seemed fantastical to me. An infinite wire, a perfect conductor, a particle that is also a wave . . . all these concepts that felt magical—or at least impossible—were actually real. Of course, those "magical" concepts only worked at the electron scale. My quantum professor joked that any student who quantum-tunneled through a wall would get an automatic *A* in his class. But what if you *could*? My story is my answer to that question.

Although "Homunculi" is entirely a work of fiction, I wanted to keep the scientific part of the magic grounded in reality as much as possible. But my efforts only made me feel that the story was even more magical—and that we are too. Because when I opened Purcell and Griffiths for the first time in years to write this story, I remembered that old joke about quantum tunneling through a wall. And this time I thought: no, humans can't do that. But those electrons that can? They are inside you, me, all of us. So what is to say that we are not just as fantastical and impossible as they are? See you on the other side.

Author's Note On "It's Not a Date Without Data"

Fayth Hui Tan

> "The mass media serve as a system for communicating messages and symbols to the general populace. It is their function to amuse, entertain, and inform, and to inculcate individuals with the values, beliefs, and codes of behavior that will integrate them into the institutional structures of the larger society. In a world of concentrated wealth and major conflicts of class interest, to fulfill this role requires systematic propaganda."
>
> —Edward Herman and Noam Chomsky, *Manufacturing Consent: The Political Economy of the Mass Media*

Beginning this commentary with a Chomsky quote was heavy handed, but the ideas explored in "It's Not a Date Without Data" are certainly not new and almost run into the ground in dystopian fiction with Big Brother–style governments who exert ironfisted control over their populaces. But existing within the structures of systematically enforced propaganda doesn't require or even mean that everyone exists in a dichotomous state of abject terror of persecution or wholehearted belief in The System. Often it means that we leave certain things unquestioned because they seem to be collective societal assumptions. Or, we are presented with the supposedly comforting but increasingly ominous assertion that this is the way things have always been (and always will be).

In making the protagonist work at an online dating app, I wanted to focus the story on what capitalism and the state use technology to do to people, rather than focusing on the technology itself. The pastel-corporate, gentrified-kitsch setting of near-future Los Angeles, and its hyper-cheerful centering of capitalism and production lends itself easily to that critique. Despite the fact that dating often involves deeply personal decisions and negotiations, one of the perspectives on dating that pops up on advice columns or self-help books is that dating is similar to "marketing" yourself to someone. Perhaps inadvertently, a parallel is made between the way capitalist language encourages us to see ourselves and our lives as intrinsically profitable, commodifying both the individual and individual choice.

I've lived in cities all my life, and navigating the capitalist ecosystem of the city feels almost second nature to me, living with the expectation that I will constantly be marketed to as well as expected to commodify myself in turn. I wanted to reflect on the inner conflict that living under these circumstances generates—a cubist nightmare of a selfhood where the act of choosing (which should, by right, be an expression of autonomy) shatters the self into profitable, consumable fragments. When choices are made under coercive circumstances, and the end result commodified either way, how meaningful is the individual ability to choose?

Author's Note On "Death Muse"

David Brown

I'VE ALWAYS STRUGGLED to write stories set in the far future because I am a perpetual optimist and I believe that on a long enough timeline, humanity will overcome most technological, biological, and sociological hurdles, including aging. So, every time I start a story with some characters I've cooked up in this optimistic, far-future setting, I get stuck a few scenes in because, frankly, nothing all that interesting happens in a utopia.

Then some characters came to life that challenged my view of a boring utopia. In Caltech's creative writing group, TechLit, we did a character-swap exercise wherein each participant contributed a one-page description of a character and their backstory (based on a randomly generated Myers-Briggs personality type) and wrote a story with the contributed characters. I used four of the characters: Monroe, an ESFP by Samuel Clamons; Malady, an INFJ by Tatyana Dobreva; Jack, an ESTJ by Christine Chen; and Mabel, an ISFP by Heidi Klumpe. Samuel's character Monroe was "flamboyant and active, but not frenetic," yet had "a void in his soul . . . [and] slips easily into depression." When I stuck Monroe into my vision of a far future where aging is solved and technology is advanced to the point where all people need to worry about is creative expression, I was struck with a conundrum: Why would anyone be so depressed in a world like this? He had everything he could possibly want and could live out his dreams and creative exploits for . . . well, ever.

Then, it all fell into place for me. Based on my limited forays into neuroscience, I've come to understand there is no absolute distinction between a disorder of the mind and personality. Regardless of what technological breakthroughs humanity makes over the next centuries, I believe this is a fundamentally unsolvable problem. Many psychological disorders —for example, bipolar disorder—have problems with compliance simply because the person doesn't want to take their medicine; they don't want to be the version of themselves that the therapeutic induces. Of course, many people have very positive experiences with therapeutics, but there will always be outliers that want to be a version of themselves that society has deemed "broken." As a far-future utopia that holds the sanctity of life in the highest regard, because it is one of the ultimate achievements of humanity to overcome our mortality, this is a problem. Society would likely be so proud of its accomplishments and technological capabilities that they would believe everyone can be "fixed" with the right therapy not unlike today's practice of forcibly putting people deemed a danger to themselves in custody.

Malady, who is "obsessed with order" and is "a thorough planner," generally "respects law and consistently follows rules," but "will rebel . . . if a rule or a law imposes on her core principles," was the natural leader of a group that opposes this societal rule. Jack, who "was a goth hall dweller" who "would collect his peers' drawings and sell them for illicit wares" was a great fit to be her accomplice. Mabel, whose "favorite birthday gifts were good sketching pencils, a portable tool chest, and a lovely print of an oil painting of a boat on the high seas," was a perfect fit to be one of the "artists living in [Monroe's] house."

Thank you, contributors, and the characters you created for being my muse.

Author's Note On "Hierarchy of Obsolescence"

David Brown

As a person doing research in the field of artificial intelligence, the most common question that comes up from family and friends outside the field, by far, is whether and when the robots are going to take all of our jobs. Having spent a few years in the corporate world in the early 2010s, I had already started to see how much executive-level decision-making was being guided by data analysis, and how eager executives were at investing more into this process. With the growth of machine learning for data analysis and generative models (e.g. deep fakes) in the late 2010s, it has since become clear that decision-making and creative works are not going to be humanity's final frontier of labor—AI has a chance at taking those over too. So, when I get asked that question, I try to brush over it quickly—I feel confident AI will take over all jobs, and people will either find work, or society will establish more egalitarian ways to ensure people are taken care of—and instead try to ask about how we will feel when we have an army of tireless, complex, creative, and potentially even kind and well-meaning AIs to do all of our work for us, better and faster than we can. What if the proverbial AI takeover is in fact a slow, well-intentioned and well-executed transition, where by the end of it, we technically are their masters, but we're not really needed anymore? Is this the ultimate freedom, and we've finally unlocked our ability to enjoy and explore the universe, or is this our undoing, because we need purpose to be happy? That's a question that I don't know the answer to.

Author's Note On "An Innocuous Cumulonimbus"

David Brown

THIS PIECE WAS INSPIRED by a merger of worlds from a writing exercise of Caltech's creative writing club, TechLit. Tatyana Dobreva postulated a universe where some sentient beings, after death, were imbued with deity-like powers. They existed in an alternate plane of existence, and could enter into worlds in discrete segments of time, and make perturbations in the world, but would never have their own physical form.

This universe made me think about the nature of control. As humans, we control the world around us in a wide spectrum of ways, from more direct control such as moving our appendages, to indirect control, such as doing physics research that enables technology that can commit war atrocities. But what does it really mean to "control" something, or have power over something, and where on this spectrum does fault begin? This concept is explored a lot in the superhero genre, where with great power comes great responsibility, but I wanted to explore it in contexts where beings aren't quite as in tune with how much control they actually have: a deity that has great power and thinks they have control, and a helpless victim that has no power, but thinks they have control. As people, I think it's important that we regularly check in with ourselves as to how much control we really have, since a misguided sense of control might be as damaging, if not moreso, than knowing your power and using it less than responsibly.

Author's Note On "A Thousand, Thousand Pages"

Allic Sivaramakrishnan

The story "A Thousand, Thousand Pages" was written mostly to give some insight into what research can mean on a personal level to those who do it; although, feel free to substitute "research" for anything that has ever kept you up at night, gotten you out of bed in the morning, and made you take each day at a headlong sprint. Hopefully you found superconducting swords and genetic sensitivity to dark photons entertaining on their own merits, but this story is mainly intended as an allegory in which the magic is a metaphor for research: research can be an adventure like any other, and even though the plot can be abstract, the characters invisible, and the conflict technical, it can drive human stories that are no less compelling than the ones that more commonly captivate in paperbacks, theaters, newsreels, legislatures, and at dinner tables.

Except for the magical window dressing, the kernel of Sophie's journey is the feeling of finding out that there is something exciting and still unknown about the universe, and that she can seek it out herself. Central to the story are Sophie's insatiable curiosity and hunger for intellectual treasure, and how those urges lead her to strange, wonderful, and sometimes dangerous places. Only moments after she encounters magic, she finds herself in a well-established field, wedged between experts with very different approaches, and embraces a future that depends on finding her own new understanding of the subject. Despite being in over her head, she trusts her instincts, messes up a few times, gets some things done, and in the end, begins a life of relentless and sometimes elegant jackhammering into how her world works. Embarking on this journey, she will endure ups and downs in her craft and her personal life, sometimes mixed together, and find worlds that will illuminate and delight. Habits will form, break, and reform, and learning on the fly will become a reflex. In the daily routine of getting things to work, she will find out that research is not a dull, inhuman exercise in pointless bookkeeping, but discovery's ravenous appetite; and yet, she will sometimes need to stiff-arm the alluring wilderness so she can separate what she does from who she is, and also get some sleep. Diving in is quite personal for Sophie, and will likely involve many snacks.

Exeunt heavy-handed allegory now, and on to writing.

So much of this piece came together while I was reading a Complete Works Of, and witnessing the particular author at work motivated me to attempt my own mix of poetic and prosaic prose, blend science fiction and fantasy, write a piece that was both a beginning and an end, and at least contemplate the mimetic modes and their relative altitudes. Who this author is may be obvious by now to their aficionados, but just in case, I left a tribute or two in the text.

I wrote this piece (in 2020) specifically for this anthology, in part because I believed that a serious dedication to research was the bone and sinew of Caltech. This, and the people here, I felt were worth celebrating in this perhaps unusual form. Hopefully you recognize some of the story's characters and impulses in yourself or the people around you, as I have, although this is a work of fiction and any resemblance is et cetera, *shh.*

In short, I hope this piece helps you think about how human stories drive research, and also how research drives some very human stories. Now, in this spirit, I leave you here with yet another trail to stumble upon, one whose first step is hidden in plain sight, in every beginning.

Author's Note On "Surely You're Joking, Zarblax?"

Samuel Clamons

"Surely You're Joking, Zarblax?" was a story born from frustration.

Since I moved to California for graduate school, I've tried to return home to Virginia at least twice a year to visit family, once in the summer and once around the winter holidays. That always involves some flying, and since I've never been able to do anything productive on a flight, I usually pick something light to read to keep me sane during those trips. One year, I fell back on a moderately battered 2012 issue of *Analog* magazine.

About halfway through, I came across an essay by John Gribbin titled "Is the Moon a Babel Fish?." The central point of the essay is that we are incredibly lucky to have our moon, because it's a really weird moon and life on Earth would never have happened without it. Without the moon—Gribbin argues—we would have no tides, no planetary axial tilt, no plate tectonics, and no magnetic field. Each of those features of Earth have been critical to the development of life

It's a good essay—check it out on Gribbin's blog if you want to learn a bunch of cool stuff about the moon!—but I surfaced from reading it filled with annoyance bordering on rage. No doubt, my negative judgment can be partly chalked up to the high-altitude, low-volume venue, compounded by the lingering effects of an early morning slog to the airport, but fundamentally, I found myself frustrated by the essay's core idea.

Gribbin's story fits a common pattern that astronomers and physicists sometimes fall into when talking about the origins of life. It's easy to look at our planet's history and how it has shaped life, and then conclude that if anything had been different, we would not have had life. This kind of thinking is what leads to scientists listing off of requirements for life like "liquid water" and "stable temperatures somewhere in the 0–40 Celsius range" and "a stable magnetic field," when we *should* be thinking about more general requirements more like "a source of energy" and "sufficient time" (directly related to temperature, by the way) and "self-replication with mutation."

So what if our oceans had frozen over? There'd still be plenty of liquid chemistry under the ice, and the sea floor has energy sources independent of sunlight. So what if we didn't have a magnetic field to shield us from DNA-blasting UV rays? Life might have developed using a tougher genetic backbone, or developed in places protected from direct sunlight. So what if we didn't have tides to ease the transition of life from water to land? For all we know, tides made that jump *harder*—raging, unpredictable surf presents all kinds of hazards that our deep paleozoic ancestors might have been happier to not have to deal with.

The point is, just because *our* life couldn't have lived on a different Earth doesn't mean *some* kind of life wouldn't have.

In the context of, say, a scientific presentation, this kind of lack of imagination can be forgiven as a necessary simplification for education's sake. In a *magazine of science fiction*, it is inexcusable. Gribbin's essay called for a response, so I wrote one. I think I had a first draft of "Surely You're Joking, Zarblax?" by the time the plane landed.

So much for not being able to do anything productive on a flight.

By the way, please don't take my word as authoritative—I'm just a graduate student with an active imagination. Thanks largely to NASA, there are professional astrobiologists who make a full-time study of what life might look like on other planets, and they do have compelling and fascinating arguments for why we shouldn't expect life to pop up just anywhere. Lynn Rothschild has some wonderful recorded talks on the subject. Go watch her 2014 TEDx Santa Cruz presentation for a nice explanation of all the ways I'm wrong about where and how life might arise.

Author's Note On "Three Tales from The Draco Tavern"

Larry Niven

ONCE UPON A TIME I set myself a task. I was going to write a series of vignettes touching on big, expansive subjects. I wanted universal truths that can be described in a few words. Mostly they would be expressed as hard science fiction.

These stories have grown over fifty years or so. I've been looking for those universal truths that whole time. "The Draco Tavern" isn't a big book, but it touches on many of what I determined to be basic facts of human and universal existence. They came to form a background tapestry of their own: Rick Schumann's story.

Author's Note On "Encounter: Return to Titan"

Ann Bernath

MORE THAN TWO DECADES AGO, I had the privilege to provide information management support to the *Cassini–Huygens* team at the Jet Propulsion Laboratory. In that role, I had the opportunity to meet some of the principal investigators (PIs) driving science requirements for the mission. In 1997, the year *Cassini* launched, I wrote a short story envisioning how a scientist might be able to experience one of the mission objectives "first-hand" by positing some type of virtual reality technology that would be so immersive that the scientist would feel as if they were part of the robotic craft themselves. The original draft of the story predated the actual landing, so a revision was necessary to more closely describe the actual event, although dramatic license is at work here. The story is my homage to the brilliant engineers and scientists who enhance our knowledge of our solar system.

I found it interesting to learn that, as I was putting the final touches on this story in October of 2020, a fully immersive 3D virtual reality camera designed to operate in the vacuum of space was used on the International Space Station, leading me to think that future encounters with mission targets may resemble the encounter envisioned in this story.

Author's Note On "Blue Skies for Test Flight #NV0005"

Madison Brady

THE MAJORITY of "Blue Skies For Test Flight #NV0005" comes from three places: *Catch-22*, the combined works of H. P. Lovecraft, and a general fascination with the Cold War.

Catch-22 is a wonderful but depressing novel about a colorful troupe of WWII pilots, some of whom are thoroughly broken by the experience. I thought it would be interesting to play a pilot akin to the death-fearing protagonist of *Catch-22* against a young hotshot and watch them argue. While Potter and Burke have similar past experiences, they react to them in completely different ways, making them interesting covers for one another's weaknesses.

I cannot speak about the works of H. P. Lovecraft with unilateral praise like I can about *Catch-22*, but I do like Lovecraft's take on horror. In his stories, the true origin of terror is the fact that the enemy is massive, indifferent, and poorly understood, as opposed to genuinely evil. Following along with this concept, I deliberately left the motives and mechanisms behind the Caelites vague, as they are not meant to be something that the characters can easily summarize using human terms. It is rather comforting for Burke to imagine them as being some form of covert Soviet operatives, as in that case he would know who they were and what they wanted, as well as what tactics they would probably use.

In that vein, I selected the mid-1950s as a time frame due to its rather unique location in the American timeline: the US was not actively at war with anyone (Vietnam didn't start until the end of the decade), but had a very tumultuous relationship with another major world power. At that time, any little disturbance in the peace could easily be chalked up to the Soviet Bogeyman, allowing for something as dramatic as an alien invasion to be misinterpreted and denied by both sides for far longer than it should have. Additionally, because of that general air of fear and paranoia during the Cold War, the US developed a great number of inventions that seem comedic now, such as a literal flying saucer (check out the Avro Canada VZ-9 Avrocar as an example). This creative, inventive chaos made the time period ideal for staging a story about experimental aircraft during a misattributed series of air raids.

I am a relative newcomer to the sci-fi genre. I think that sci-fi and horror (especially the Lovecraftian kind) have a rather fascinating conflict. In sci-fi, the story, along with the audience's expectations, are built around the concept of understanding. Understanding how a spaceship could work, understanding how we could gene-engineer away all diseases, understanding how computers could eventually come to life and usurp us.

However, horror revels in the opposite. Our fear comes from something we cannot and will not understand. The Elder Gods (or, perhaps, the Cays) aren't scary because they're big, slimy, and have a few too many eyes and mouths for comfort. They're scary because we don't understand how they think or what they want. The universe is a big, scary land of unknowns, which, despite our best efforts, we cannot understand our place in.

As a scientist, I relate to sci-fi's enthusiasm for learning and explanation, but as a human I can't help but fear the unknown. In that way, a story about a potential alien invasion is as good a way as any for me to reach into this unfamiliar genre.

Author's Note On "Memoirs of a Status Quo"

Ashish Mahabal

Humans are aware of vast interstellar distances, but may not comprehend the time frames required to cross these vast spaces, or their psychological effect. Difficulties with initial attempts at space colonization and the relative comfort of a virtual world (more like in *Ready Player One* than in VR games), and memories of wars, and plain lack of resources could lead to a shut-in dystopian future.

I have always been fascinated by science fiction quotations. Many individual quotations capture the essence of the stories they are from, or of certain philosophies. I decided to weave a few to describe the shut-in situation described above, and events that could lead to it.

The dynamic of Ullu and Shuka was inspired by Stanislaw Lem's "constructors" Trurl and Klapaucius, robot engineers capable of anything, alike in most ways but also with their differences. However, I wrote Ullu and Shuka to play the roles of protectors, with an additional difference that one is a robot, and the other a Godlike human. What would a robot feel about humans evolving/converging to such a frozen life? How would a superhuman not agreeing with the status-quo world feel?

Ullu in Hindi means "Owl." He represents abstract wisdom and feels supreme, but has not quite gotten the hang of life. Shuka in Sanskrit is both a sage and a parrot, and burdened with a corresponding ambivalence. He is immortal but also hates it. Are the Earth-bound humans stuck in VR the happiest? Who's to say?

This story was originally published in Marathi in 2017. I am thankful to the various critiques from Sci-Fi Katta, LAMAL, and TechLit members.

Author's Note On "Reentry"

Anish Sarma

THE PLEASURES of reading science fiction are similar to the pleasures of reading history: we are allowed to see our own world from an angle that shows us both individuals and systems. In writing this story, I was particularly engaged by the ways that history determines the personas that we can and must adopt—the demands that public life places on private life. Technology is not the star of this story, but it is not absent. This is a world remade by a photograph.

Author's Note On "Degenerates"

Olivia Pardo

THERE ARE several theories regarding the fate of our universe. One is called the Big Bounce, in which the universe slows its expansion, contracts to a singularity, and then rebounds into a new universe. This cyclic model is currently less favored but can't be ruled out with our current knowledge and is what I have chosen for the backdrop of "Degenerates." I am excited by the possibility that our universe could be one of many to exist, that we are not the end. This idea inspired me to construct a situation in which the universes could reach each other, where life finds a way to communicate beyond the boundaries of their universe.

My fictional universe is populated with a vast family of computers tasked with orchestrating this interuniverse communication by manipulating the cosmic microwave background (CMB) of the future universe born after the next Big Bounce. The CMB is remnant radiation from our universe's Big Bang, a detectable map in our sky caused by density fluctuations in the very early stages of our universe. It is an imprint of the earliest particles that now make up stars, planets, galaxies, and us. The pattern was generated the moment the universe became transparent to light, and at that time, what was to become the CMB was extremely hot and bright. The expansion of the universe has caused it to cool significantly, becoming a faint afterglow of the initial explosion, but it remains visible everywhere within the universe. The accessibility of the CMB to the entire universe intrigued me as a way to communicate with a universe's inhabitants. No matter which galaxy they live in, or what planet they evolved on, the CMB is a resource available to all that possess the proper technology.

The CMB we see in our sky tells us about the origin of our *current* universe. For my story, the computer and its siblings work to orchestrate a future CMB that will tell the next universe's inhabitants what was in the *previous* universe. Neutrinos, tiny elementary particles, are incredibly weakly interacting with all matter, making them prime candidates for preserving information over cosmological timespans. However, this exact property is the main challenge in altering their state and encoding information like the computers in "Degenerates" are capable of doing. While the duality of this property is frustrating, I find the neutrino's characteristics enticing to utilize.

Our degenerate's story started off as a selfish endeavor, my own vain attempt to construct an entity that has found contentment in work that is small-scale relative to the vastness of the universe. This attempt reflects my desire to find contentment in my own scientific contributions, which can seem small and isolated relative to the entirety of science.

In the story's first iteration there was no antagonist, and really no protagonist, because we met our melancholy degenerate at the end of its life, when it had already reached passivity. It quietly asked itself questions regarding its own mortality without rejecting the inevitable outcome of its life. This early version of our degenerate was a product of my writing process, which often begins with an isolated feeling I want to capture. But our computer's life is not encompassed in an isolated feeling alone. I discovered its range of emotions, and *how* it discovers these emotions, in the process of writing the final story. In the presence of its extensive memory modules, filled with histories of entire civilizations, knowing that it was just one small machine in a very large universe, how could existential questions not be stirred up? Over the eons, while asking these questions and attempting to find their answers, the computer is transformed.

By the end of its life, our computer is twice degenerate: it has lost the mental qualities desired for the computer it was built to be, and it has mechanically and digitally deteriorated. But in its degeneracy, its self-awareness grows to be something as complex as the Archive it cares for, and something I believe equally worth preserving.

Author and Editor Biographies

Editor-in-Chief

Rachael Kuintzle (*Editor-in-Chief, Author*) is a PhD candidate in biochemistry and molecular biophysics at Caltech. If she could have a superpower she would choose to speak and understand all languages. Yet, instead of studying human language, she decided to study the language of human cells. Specifically, she uses mathematical modeling, cell engineering, microscopy, and other methods to analyze the systems biology of the Notch signaling pathway—a mode of cellular communication used during the development of nearly every tissue.

Rachael is the cofounder and former president of Caltech's creative writing club, TechLit. She is currently editing a completed manuscript of her first sci-fi book written with coauthor Sam Clamons and working on the first novel in her science fantasy series. For updates, sign up for her newsletter at https://www.rachaelkuintzle.com or find her on Twitter (@kuintzle).

Editors and Authors

David Brown, PhD (*Editor, Author*) views the digital and biological as different implementations of systems with the same fundamental driving forces: self-preservation and entropy reduction. He is one of these systems, and he seeks to reduce entropy through understanding and organizing the world around him. More tangibly, this means he does research at the intersection of science and artificial intelligence. Fascinated by space, he first worked at NASA's Jet Propulsion Laboratory (JPL) on autonomous swarm behaviors, building agents that could self-organize with limited communication between them. After a while he moved into the world of bioengineering, drawn in by the immense complexity of life. Now, he seeks to understand the world of cellular and genetic processes with the help of AI systems. After completing his PhD studies at Caltech, he moved on to cofound a start-up, ImYoo, where he is building the technology infrastructure to analyze cellular-level immune system dynamics from blood samples people can collect themselves at home. In his free time, David likes to adventure, and tries to imprint his inner thoughts and activities digitally as much as possible, in the hopes that one day he'll have a digital counterpart to carry on his personality and memories after he's gone. His social media handle is @dibidave.

Samuel Clamons, PhD (*Editor, Author*) received a doctorate in bioengineering from Caltech in 2021, and currently works as a bioinformatic scientist at Illumina Corp. He is a passable lab biologist, programmer, pianist, and writer, and a dabbler in quantum physics, board game design, and editing short story collections. Sam has enjoyed raising a variety of invertebrate pets, including desert ants, praying mantis, daphnia, and amano shrimp. He urgently, desperately wants to know: How does quantum mechanics really work? How do we get to a *Star Trek* utopia in a not-terrible way? How can you beat evolution? What is consciousness? *Why* is consciousness? What did you learn today? If you have the answers to any of these questions, please let Sam know.

Tatyana Dobreva, PhD (*Editor, Author*) was instantiated in the country of Uzbekistan and came to the land of freedom and opportunity (US) when she was eleven. Tatyana has worked at JPL on deep-space cube satellite radios (one of which traveled to Mars!) and volunteered nights and weekends working on a robotic framework for a neuroprosthetic arm at Caltech. After deciding to pursue her passion for bioengineering full time, she became a graduate student in medical engineering (Caltech) and worked on projects involving viral and cellular engineering. Upon graduating, Tatyana founded a biotech startup focused on debugging and engineering the human immune system. In her spare time, Tatyana enjoys creating new worlds and scenarios through writing and storyboarding, kickboxing, rock climbing, and playing video games. She is also very interested in radiation-resistant creatures and hopes to one day employ their biological mechanisms to help with space travel. Her twitter handle is @cosmotat.

Richard J. Doyle, PhD (*Editor, Author*), a.k.a. R. James Doyle, held technical and managerial roles in Information and Data Science at NASA's Jet Propulsion Laboratory (JPL) over a career arc spanning forty years, working at the exciting interface of space exploration and computer science. He remains an active technical consultant. He holds a doctorate degree in computer science specializing in artificial intelligence from MIT. Richard was a member of a team from JPL that consulted on the *Babylon 5* TV Series. He had the pleasure of visiting Sir Arthur C. Clarke in Sri Lanka, in the year 2001. Richard's other writing projects include a speculative thriller, a time travel TV series, and a YA novel. Outside of professional and creative life, he enjoys amateur astronomy, pondering quantum physics, and craft beer.

Ashish Mahabal, PhD (*Editor, Author*) is an astronomer and lead computational and data scientist at Caltech's Center for Data-Driven Discovery, and an adjunct faculty at the Inter-University Center for Astronomy and Astrophysics, Pune, India. His interests include machine learning and methodology transfer between different fields including medicine. He likes to weave in mythology, astronomy, and data science in his stories. He has a couple dozen published sci-fi stories in Marathi, and a book is in the last stages of publication. You can find out more about him at https://ashishmahabal.net.

Author and Editor Biographies

Allic Sivaramakrishnan, PhD (*Editor, Author*) is a postdoctoral fellow at Caltech in high-energy physics, arriving after a BA from UC Berkeley and a PhD from UCLA. He wants to understand quantum gravity and feels that quantum information, the conformal bootstrap, the double copy, and the holographic principle may hand him some surprising answers. He grew up in Connecticut and California and published poetry when he was small. When he was larger, he edited a literature and arts magazine (extant) and a science fiction and fantasy magazine (extinct). Now, he publishes prose, writes music, runs an education initiative, practices martial arts, watches Steph Curry play basketball, and seeks new collaborations.

Other Editors

From Sacramento, CA, **Christine Chen, PhD** (*Editor*) attended the University of California, Berkeley. She roamed the campus as a research and ideas writer at *The Daily Californian* during her time on campus. After receiving her BS in EECS, with a minor in East Asian Languages + Culture, she moved to New York City to pursue her PhD at Columbia University in electrical engineering. In NYC, she took writing classes by the Hudson and taught motivated high schoolers through Barnard's STEP Program. Prior to her NASA fellowship in the submillimeter instruments group at JPL, she worked at Intel in silicon photonics technology. She is currently working in the optical communications group at JPL and appreciates learning daily about the challenges of space technologies for scientific discoveries. She has also enjoyed participating in TechLit and editing short stories for this anthology.

Lindsey Gailmard (*Editor*) is a PhD candidate in the Division of Humanities and Social Sciences at Caltech. Her research focuses on the strategic dilemmas presidents confront in managing their political appointees. She is an avid reader and especially loves reading memoirs and short story collections. In her spare time, she enjoys cooking and practicing yoga and pilates.

John Marken (*Editor*) is a PhD candidate in bioengineering at Caltech. He works on extending the applicability of extant technologies in synthetic biology to address problems in the environment and agriculture. Outside of science he likes to think in a dilettantish way about the relationship between form and function in film and writing.

Winter Pearson (*Editor*) is a fourth-year undergraduate student at Caltech studying computation and neural systems. They wish "bard" was still a viable profession. Barring that resurgence, their joy is storytelling: writing, editing, and acting. In addition, they enjoy programming robots, rock climbing, and activism.

Christina P. Souto, MBA (*Editor*) is a recent recipient of UCLA's Creative Writing Certificate and author of several fantasy, horror, and philosophical short stories. Her most recent piece, "The Mail," was published in *Round Table Literary Journal* in 2022. Christina was a member of the Caltech/JPL community for over nine years, six of which served as the head of Faculty Housing and Relocation. She is currently working on a novel and editing various short stories. She lives in Los Angeles with her spouse, their goldendoodles Luna and Shark Fin, and their cat, Don Bizo Purrleone.

Other Authors

In 1978, happenstance brought **Ann Bernath** (*Author*) to NASA's Jet Propulsion Laboratory (JPL) as a temporary secretary where she transcribed handwritten and dictated documentation using an IBM Selectric, literally using "cut and paste" with scissors and tape to make changes. Her love of writing started much earlier than her JPL career, however, inspired at the age of six by *The Patty Duke Show* to put pencil to paper. Ann has continued to write ever since—Westerns, fantasy, space operas, vignettes, short stories, and novels—writing technical documentation for JPL during the day and fiction at night, evolving through the years to typewriter, word processor, and finally laptop. Ann lives in Duarte, California, with her husband David, her two children and four grandchildren nearby.

Madison Brady (*Author*) received her undergraduate degree at Caltech in 2020, attending graduation from a comfy armchair in an undisclosed location in the Midwest. She is now pursuing a PhD in astronomy at the University of Chicago, where she studies exoplanets. Despite these research interests, she usually writes horror, thrillers, and fantasy, and has yet to write anything involving long-distance space travel or terraforming, though she has watched the entirety of the original run of *Star Trek*.

David Brin, PhD (*Author*) is an astrophysicist whose international best-selling novels include *Earth*, *Existence*, *The Postman* (filmed in 1998) and Hugo Award winners *Startide Rising* and *The Uplift War*. Dr. Brin serves on advisory boards (e.g. NASA's Innovative Advanced Concepts program, or NIAC) and speaks or consults on topics ranging from AI, SETI, privacy and invention, to national security. His nonfiction book about the information age—*The Transparent Society*—won the Freedom of Speech Award of the American Library Association.

As a Caltech undergraduate in the tumultuous late 1960s and '70s, David witnessed the long-overdue arrival of female Techers and coached the women's fencing team to their first victories. In 1970, he helped officiate the MIT-to-Caltech Clean Air Car Race that helped get lead out of the air. Wandering random buildings at Tech, asking "What do you do here?" was especially educational. After getting his PhD at UCSD, under Hannes Alfven and Henry Booker, he married a recently minted Caltech cosmochem PhD, so their three kids are, well… different. As are you all. (https://www.davidbrin.com)

S. B. Divya (*Author*) is a lover of science, math, fiction, and the Oxford comma. She enjoys subverting expectations and breaking stereotypes whenever she can. Divya is the Hugo- and Nebula-nominated author of *Meru* and *Machinehood*. She was the coeditor of *Escape Pod*, a weekly science fiction podcast, from 2018–2022. Divya's short stories have been published in various magazines including *Analog*, *Uncanny*, and *Tor.com*. She studied physics and computational neuroscience at Caltech, and she worked for twenty years as an engineer before becoming an author. Find out more about her at https://sbdivya.com or on Twitter as @divyastweets.

Heidi Klumpe, PhD (*Author*) is a postdoc in biomedical engineering at Boston University and a former Caltech graduate student. She keeps a sharp eye out for monsters on campus, but has only found friends. This story would not be possible without her stellar PhD advisor (Michael Elowitz) and favorite lecturer (Justin Bois), who taught her about feedforward loops in Bioengineering (BE) 150. She thanks TechLit for making a refuge for exploring science as we imagine it to be, especially those (like editor Allic!) who sparred with the earliest drafts of the monster.

Christof Koch, PhD (*Author*) is a neuroscientist best known for his studies and writings exploring the brain basis of consciousness. Trained as a physicist, Koch was for twenty-seven years a professor of biology and engineering at Caltech in Pasadena before moving to the Allen Institute for Brain Science in Seattle as chief scientist and president. Dr. Koch is interested in the biophysics and neurophysiology of cortical tissue, brain-machine interfaces, and conscious experience. He published his initial paper on the footprints of consciousness in the brain with the molecular biologist Francis Crick more than thirty years ago. Dr. Koch is a vegetarian who lives in the Pacific Northwest, and who loves big dogs, biking, running, climbing and rowing. His latest book is *The Feeling of Life Itself: Why Consciousness Is Widespread but Can't Be Computed.*

Koch and *Brain Bridging* coauthor, **Patrick House, PhD**, met at a symposium between Buddhist monk-scholars, including His Holiness the Dalai Lama, and Western scientists at a Tibetan monastery in Southern India, fostering a dialogue between physics, biology, and mind sciences. House's latest book is *Nineteen Ways of Looking at Consciousness.*

Kara Lee (*Author*) is a collection of elementary particles and caffeine. At Caltech, she studied biology (in the classrooms and labs) and SFF (in the many, many free books and libraries in the Houses and SAC). Today she uses her biology degree as a science writer, and abuses it as an author of speculative fiction. In her spare time, she tempts the laws of physics in the dance studio.

Christine Corbett Moran, PhD (*Author*) works at Planet Labs as an engineering manager for the data pipeline. Previously, she spent seven years in the Caltech/JPL community, first as a postdoc in astrophysics, and later as a programmer, engineering manager, and program manager. Her work is at the intersection of space, physics, and computation. She holds an MFA in creative writing from the Stonecoast MFA Program, a BS in computer science and a BS in physics from MIT, and a master's and PhD in astrophysics from the University of Zurich. She lives in a canyon neighborhood of Los Angeles with her husband and two children.

Larry Niven (*Author*) entered Caltech sixty-odd years ago with intent to become a nuclear physicist. He flunked out after a year and a third. He has vivid memories of broken glassware in chemistry class. He graduated from Washburn University, and later accepted an honorary doctorate, DLitt. He's been a published author for fifty-six years. Loves science fiction conventions. At eighty-two, he's something of a health nut.

Recommendation: *The Integral Trees*.

Olivia Pardo (*Author*) is a PhD candidate in the Seismological Laboratory at Caltech. Her research studies the behavior of minerals under high pressures and temperatures like those found in the interiors of planets and their moons. She approaches these investigations from an experimental standpoint, using spectroscopy and X-ray techniques to measure the properties of mineral samples under extreme conditions. When not firing lasers and X-ray beams at minerals, she spends her time making art and going to the beach with her dog, Lola. Her creative outlets include painting, textile work, computer-generated art, and as always, writing.

Anish Sarma, PhD (*Author*) completed his graduate work in computation and neural systems with a minor in control and dynamical systems at Caltech. His research is in control systems theory, science, and engineering with applications in medicine and ecology. Outside of science, he enjoys reading fiction and history.

Naru Dames Sundar (*Author*) is a writer and poet whose work has appeared in *Escape Pod*, *Shimmer*, and *Strange Horizons* among others. He attended Caltech as an undergrad, a member of the class of 2001 and though he moved from Pasadena some years ago, he still has a soft spot for Caltech's campus, which used to be an old jogging haunt after graduation. These days, he finds himself in the redwoods of Northern California, juggling a thriving career as a silicon architect with a little writing, video games, and family life in the woods amidst the turkeys, deer, and the occasional falcon that graces their property. While his professional interests have focused on networking and network technology for the past decade, his science interests are broad and reflect his passion for fiction that explores the cultural impact of technology on the human condition.

Fayth Hui Tan (*Author*) is a graduate student in biology at Caltech. They have a BS in marine biology, which makes them unemployable but very well versed in the strangest organismal horrors the depths have to offer. When not thinking about how to repeat experiments from the late nineteenth century, they like reading weird fiction, horror, and poetry; playing tabletop RPGs; and lapsing into existential crises.

Made in the USA
Columbia, SC
17 April 2023

15183109R00262